Midnight Waltz

Maria Giakoumatos

Blysster Press

Email the author at maria_giakoumatos95@hotmail.com

Website: https://mariarantsaboutstuff.wordpress.com/
Facebook: https://www.facebook.com/mariagiakoumatosauthor/

"MIDNIGHT WALTZ" Printing History
Blysster Press paperback edition March 2018

Blysster Press

A new kind of publisher for a new kind of world.

ISBN 978-1-940247-36-6

Printed in the United States of America
www.blysster.com

DEDICATION

~~

To my grandma Mary and grandpa Louis, who always encouraged me to use my creativity to make something. Here it is!

~~

To my parents Mary Ann and Kostas. As crazy as the family may be, you always want what's best for me and put me before yourselves.

THANK YOU

~~

First and foremost, I'd like to thank the sea of test readers (aka friends) who've read my drafts in their various forms over the years. Even if you just read a snippet, listened to me ramble about plots, or just "liked" one of my Facebook statuses ranting about my book, your overwhelming support has kept me going. To Sarah, Colin, Nick, Jackie, and Denisse, your interest and support in my writing has carried me from my wacky elementary school stories all the way to my first published novel. Your encouragement gave me the confidence to share my stories with all who wish to read them. Special thanks to my cousin Anna, who listened to my crazy ideas since we were little kids.

This beautiful cover art is brought to you by my talented buddy Kayge Abendroth. You were the perfect photographer for this project. Shout out to Eric and Amalea for letting me smear fake blood all over your hands. You all were tons of fun to work with and seemed to know what to do better than me, so thank you so, so, so much for dealing with my last minute plans to get this done!

A gigantic thank you to my editor Charity Becker. Her patience and dedication to helping me—and writers, in general—to bring out my best work is amazing, and I am incredibly grateful to have her by my side. To my fellow Blysster Press author T.J. Tranchell, thank you so much for all the marketing advice! As a new author, I super appreciate your guidance! I'd also like to thank all my teachers back in school who not only taught excellent writing lessons, but tolerated my spooky stories every time we had a creative writing assignment. Thank you to my third and fourth grade teacher Karen Helander, for allowing me to stay in from recess to write stories, some of which actually evolved into the *Infernal Symphony*.

Last, but certainly not least, I'd like to thank my mama and baba Mary Ann and Kostas for supporting my dream to become a writer since I was three years old. Even if it meant trying to decipher my scribble books that even I couldn't tell what they were about after a day or two. Or if it meant taking the train with me to Seattle and sitting around for almost two hours when I was sick and needed to get my cover art started. (Thanks, Baba!)

Just kidding, one last thank you! To all my readers, I cannot thank you enough for taking interest in my book. It's a dream come true to finally share my characters and their adventures with the world, and would love to continue doing so! I hope you enjoy *Midnight Waltz*!

More from Maria!

While *Midnight Waltz* is my debut novel, I'm not new to writing. I thought it might be fun to show my readers some of my earliest work to see how far I've come.

I wrote a really morbid short story when I was in 8th grade that almost got me sent to the school counselor's office. So there's that. And a lot of other creepy short stories from school assignments or just for fun. Check them out on my blog! https://mariarantsaboutstuff.wordpress.com/

I also have some emo poetry from when I was in 9th grade, but you don't want to read that. Trust me.

Midnight Waltz is my first published work. I hope to bring you its sequels (and some unrelated works, too) very soon!

PRELUDE

~~

"We need you to drive over here as quickly as possible. We have a situation."

Olivia Mavro tossed her phone onto her bed and groaned, burying her face in her pillow. If there were any other teenage girls up at one thirty a.m. on a Tuesday, they were either bingeing on Netflix, cramming their homework, or getting drunk at a house party. Any of that sounded more appealing than a late night paranormal investigation at an old Victorian mansion. She changed into jeans and a blouse, tied her black hair in a messy ponytail, hurried to her car, and drove away from her peaceful neighborhood.

She parked along the gravel road and ran up the large, grassy hill leading to the mansion. A young man in a suit leaned against the spiral staircase, awaiting her arrival. Despite the dim lighting, he wore sunglasses.

"Thanks for answering my call, Miss Mavro. I'm sorry to trouble you at this hour."

"It's fine," Olivia said, setting her purse on the marble floor. Following the man up the stairs, she asked, "So, what happened here?"

"We caught three middle school boys breaking in on our radar. By the time we arrived, they were in Mistress Emily's room, all trembling in fear."

Olivia rolled her eyes. "It's like they've never seen a dead body before."

"They probably haven't. Not everyone is as privileged as we are."

He led her to the end of a hallway, to a girl's bedroom filled with teddy bears and dolls in black dresses. Two boys were slouched in the corner of the room, both unconscious. Another man in a suit knelt beside a third boy who sat on the floor, his face colorless.

"I've already taken care of the other two," the man beside the boy told Olivia. "This one has some interesting information to share."

Olivia crouched in front of the boy. She stroked his arm and smiled. "Can you tell me what happened?"

"T-the girl," the boy stammered. "Sh-she spoke to me." He pointed a shaky finger at the black lacy bed placed in the center of the room. A teenage girl lay sleeping upon the sheets.

"That's impossible," Olivia said. "She's dead."

"She did!" the boy cried. "She told me she needs my soul to survive! She tried to bite me and—"

The smile disappeared from Olivia's face. She peered up at the first man she met. "Wipe his memory." She rose and let the man take her place. He placed his palm on the boy's forehead.

"H-hold on!" the boy stuttered. "What are you doing? Who are you people?"

"That doesn't matter," Olivia said, walking toward the bed. "You won't remember." She narrowed her eyes, gazing at the sleeping girl. Her black dress and hair were too intact around her frail body. She couldn't have just moved, let alone at all in the past hour. Olivia looked back at the boy. "It'll be like this night never happened."

But the boy lay unconscious in the man's arms, as silent and still as the dead girl he claimed could speak.

CHAPTER 1

~~

The silence was killing him. It spared no mercy as Anthony Olsen stood behind his high school, awaiting the answer to what he believed to be the world's most important question. With every passing second, he was becoming more uncomfortable in his skin. Across from him stood a girl of the same age, her black ponytail swaying in the gentle spring wind. She brushed the loose strands of hair away from her rosy cheeks. If his mind wasn't preoccupied by anxiety, he would have been admiring Olivia's beauty, as he did every day in class.

"I'm sorry, Anthony," Olivia said after what seemed like hours to him, her green eyes keeping a firm gaze on the grass around her boots, "but I can't return your feelings for me. I'm not interested in dating you."

"Oh," was all Anthony could manage to say in response. He ran a hand through his messy brown hair, hoping that straightening it would, by some miracle, change Olivia's feelings.

"I don't really know you," Olivia said.

"We've had math together for the past two years," Anthony offered. "I sat behind you last quarter, and then we worked on that group assignment together that one time. . . You know what I'm talking about, right? The geometry one?"

"Right," Olivia said, her narrowing eyes meeting his. "We never really talked, though."

"We can start now."

Olivia wrinkled her nose. "Maybe when you don't reek of weed and cigarettes."

Anthony blushed and tugged at his rugged gray sweatshirt. "Oh, I don't smoke. Not cigarettes. It's my aunt—"

"You hang around those stoner guys, right?" Olivia asked. "The ones that are in my English class but never show up?"

"No, of course not."

"Then why are they waving to you?"

Anthony turned around and spotted two boys in baggy jeans and sweatshirts, waving at him from across the schoolyard. One wore an Elmo baseball cap, the other a Cookie Monster cap. *Their timing couldn't be any worse,* Anthony thought.

"I gotta go," Olivia said, smoothing her black cardigan. "Let's pretend this never happened. See you in class tomorrow?"

"Y-yeah." Anthony stared after her as she walked away. Only the ghost of her floral perfume remained, lingering just for a moment before it, too, disappeared.

"You got some nerve, asking out the most popular girl in our school," the boy in the Elmo cap said, shaking his head in disapproval.

"Shut up, Cory," Anthony grumbled. "It was going okay until you and Tyson showed up."

"We could tell from a mile away that it wasn't going okay," Tyson said. "She turns down every guy that asks her out. She thinks she's too good for them or something because she comes from a rich family."

"I don't think that's the case," Anthony said, walking home with the boys along the street. "She doesn't seem like a snob."

"Have you seen her family's mansion?" Cory asked. He reached into his sweatshirt pocket and withdrew a lighter and joint. "If there's one thing her family's got, it's *money*."

"And spooky stuff," Tyson said with a shiver, lighting his own joint.

"Oh God, not the Mavro Manor stories again," Anthony groaned, covering his ears with his hands. "I swear, you're the only guys over the age of ten that still care about that dumb abandoned mansion. Everyone knows that ghosts aren't real."

"But it isn't ghosts, remember?" Tyson said. "It's—"

"A dead chick," Anthony interrupted. "At midnight on the night of the full moon, Emily Mavro rises undead from her slumber and seeks the soul of an unfortunate human to avenge her mysterious death. I know our local lore. Only a town as boring as Kent would have such a ridiculous story."

"It's not just a story though," Tyson said. "Her undead body still rests in that house. People have seen it."

"I'm sure Olivia can tell you all about it," Cory said. "She's the one that cleans up that place."

"If she cared to talk to me," Anthony said. "The only reason why I bother showing up to math is so I can see her. Do you know how hard it is to keep up with senior level math when you're only a junior?"

"I dunno how *you* of all people are in a nerd class," Cory said with a sneer.

"I used to be a nerd in middle school. That's why." Anthony sighed and looked up at the sky. "I used to actually care about school back when I lived with my parents. I used to care about a lot of stuff." *Maybe if I still did, Olivia would like me.*

"Have you heard anything about when your parents will be back?" Tyson asked.

Anthony shook his head. "It's not like my aunt and uncle tell me anything. They already told me they're kicking me out when I'm eighteen, so hopefully they'll be back before then or I'm screwed." He stopped in front of the brown lawn surrounding his house. "I'm *already* screwed." He waved goodbye to his friends before walking up the concrete steps to the faded "bless this mess" welcome mat.

Anthony threw his backpack on the floor by the front door. Unzipping the top, he pulled out his textbook and notebook. Though he tried to sneak to his room before his uncle could notice him, the creaky floorboards gave him away.

"Tony!" his Uncle Mark bellowed from the kitchen. "I hear you, boy! Getchyer ass over here!"

Anthony groaned and set his book on floor. He stomped over to the kitchen where his uncle slouched in a wooden chair, drinking a can of beer, his food-stained t-shirt slightly rolled up over his fat belly.

"What's up?" Anthony asked.

"What, you come into the house without sayin' hello to yer uncle?"

"I have homework to do."

Uncle Mark let out a loud belch. He stroked his brown stubble and shook his empty beer can. "Tony, can you get me s'more beer?"

Anthony glared at him. After living with his aunt and uncle for two years, he learned that he never had a choice. He opened the fridge, grabbed the first can he could find, then set it down on the table in front of his uncle.

A pale woman strutted into the kitchen from the garage. Her pointy face was wrinkled in disgust, her brown eyes sharp and stern. She held her cell phone out in front of her like a weapon. "Tony, do you know who called me today?"

"No," Anthony said.

"Your school's office, that's who." The woman placed her hands on her thin hips. "They said you and your little friends were cutting class and smoking behind the school."

"Sorry, Aunt Lisa."

"Don't be sorry, you jackass. Unless you didn't bring your auntie some." She pinched his cheek. "Stay outta trouble, you hear? I don't like having to deal with your school. It ain't my job." She leaned down to give her husband a kiss.

"Tony's always causin' trouble," Uncle Mark said. "Just like his father."

"I dunno what my sister saw in that dirty pig," Aunt Lisa huffed. "He's the whole damn reason those two got messed up on drugs. God bless the day they come and take their sorry son back home."

Anthony stormed out of the kitchen. He slammed his bedroom door and flopped down on his bed—the only escape from his aunt and uncle until night, when he could sleep and dream of living with a loving family whom he'd be proud to introduce to Olivia.

~~

Later that night, Anthony lay on his bed, watching an old horror movie on his laptop. The glow of his phone screen caught his eye. Picking it up off his nightstand, he squinted at the bright "one new message" notification on the screen. When Anthony read the message, he let out an exasperated sigh, shut his laptop, and pulled on a sweatshirt before sneaking out of his house. Cory and Tyson waited for him at the bottom of his driveway.

"What are you guys doing here?" Anthony asked them.

"We're here to cheer you up," Tyson said.

"We felt bad about interrupting your little thing with Olivia today," Cory said, "so we're going to take you somewhere to get your mind off things."

"Thanks, but I'm doing just fine," Anthony said.

"Oh, c'mon, dude," Tyson said, seizing Anthony's

shoulder before he could leave. "We came all this way, just for you. The least you can do is tag along."

Anthony looked from one boy's eager face to the other. "Where are we going?"

"If you come with us, you'll find out," Cory said. "It's not like your family cares if you go out."

"I know. They're asleep, anyway." Anthony glanced at his phone. It was eleven forty five and he had just begun to watch his movie. "I'll go, but only for an hour."

He followed after his friends, attempting to predict where their destination would be. Leading him through a nearby forest, Anthony hoped that whatever was past the broken branches and leaf-paved path was more exciting than a new spot for smoking.

When they made it out of the forest, Anthony's heart sank into his stomach. A wooden bridge lie ahead, arching over a small creek, leading up a grassy hill toward a black pointed fence, surrounding an enormous mansion.

"Mavro Manor? Really?"

"Yeah," Cory said. "We figured since you like Olivia—"

"That I'd want to go to her mansion?" Anthony interrupted. "Right, because going to her family's mansion will take my mind off her. What if she's in there?"

"She's gotta be gone by now."

"We're not going in," Anthony said, turning to leave. "I'm not trespassing on Olivia's family's property."

Tyson and Cory each grabbed his arms and steered him toward the mansion.

"No, dude, we've come too far to back out," Tyson said.

"C'mon, we know you like that cheesy horror junk," Cory said. "Don't think of it as trespassing. Think of it as being part of one of those movies you like."

I could be watching one of those movies if I didn't agree to this, Anthony thought as his friends dragged him to the mansion.

"Just because I like watching horror movies doesn't mean I want to break into haunted mansions."

"But what if we find something cool?" Tyson said. "Like the dead chick or a ghost?"

"We're not, because ghosts aren't real," Anthony said, his heart pounding harder. "If Olivia catches us—"

Cory interrupted him with a groan and rolled his eyes, picking the front door's lock. "What ever happened to you not caring about anything?"

"I care about *Olivia*."

"Why do you care about someone who doesn't even give half a crap about you?"

Anthony fell silent and remained quiet, following his friends inside. A massive chandelier hung above their heads in the entrance. Their footsteps echoed on the checkered marble floor. While the house's décor was drab, gloomy, and drowning in black lace, the furniture was polished and free of dust. Not a single cobweb hid in the corners.

Looks like Olivia does a pretty good job with the place, Anthony thought with a smile. The thought of Olivia spending her evenings at the manor was oddly comforting to Anthony. Comforting enough to allow him to stray from his friends and explore on his own, to admire Olivia's work. Somehow, being in Mavro Manor made him feel closer to her. A closeness that, due to the day's earlier events, he may never achieve in person. He walked up the spiraling staircase, using the light of his phone to navigate through the dark hallway lined with wooden doors. The walls, while covered in gray floral wallpaper, were bare, though tiny holes and scratches were indicative of photographs that were once displayed. Wandering to a door at the end of the hallway, he opened it and closed it behind him after entering the room.

Like the rest of the house, the curtains were black and lacy, reeking of old wood. The shelves were lined with dolls in black dresses, along with teddy bears with black bows around their necks. In the corner was a small tea table with a satin black tablecloth, dolls sitting in chairs around it, and miniature tea cups were placed on the table with a small teapot.

Anthony's eyes widened when his gaze fell upon the bed. A figure lay beneath the black canopy upon fluffy sheets and pillows. At first, it appeared to be a large doll, but when he looked closer, he noticed that it was a human. A girl, not too much younger than him.

It was *her*.

Emily Mavro lay on her back, her eyes shut, her hands folded over her chest. Her frilly dress lay neatly against her dainty body, her black hair draped over her shoulders, as though she had not budged an inch in her slumber. The chain of her silver cross ran over the white bandage taped to her neck, just barely visible under her dress collar. Taking a cautious glance at her face, Anthony touched her hand. It was cold. Freezing cold. *Deathly* cold. She looked as if she was sleeping peacefully.

Or dead, Anthony thought.

Yet she was cute and alluring, though in an unsettling manner. Her perfection was doll-like, manufactured, unrealistic, inhuman. She wore a pleasant expression on her white face, almost too pleasant for someone who died a mysterious death. Her pale lips were curled into a smile, as if she knew a secret and was proud to let it die with her. Anthony couldn't take his eyes off her, and when she opened her eyes, she was looking at him, too.

Anthony took a step back from the bed and froze. *Did she just open her eyes?*

Emily's smile grew wider, her eyes—those glowing green eyes—threatening. Hungry. She reached for his neck with icy hands.

CHAPTER 2

~~

Anthony awoke to the sound of crows cawing outside. He couldn't remember falling asleep, but the morning sun on his face told him he had.

"What? Where. . .?" Rubbing his eyes, his vision cleared to reveal a room filled with black lace and dolls. No posters of rock bands or superhero action figures were anywhere in sight.

Oh, yeah, Anthony thought, patting the black bed sheets he lay upon. *This is Emily's room. I came here last night. But why am I still here?* Anthony's hand flew to his neck, over his bruised flesh. *She bit me. . . but what happened after that?*

"Did you have a nice rest?"

The sudden voice brought Anthony's attention to his side. Emily sat beside him, greeting him with a warm smile. "I was not very tired since I have been asleep for so long, so I let you have my bed for the night."

Anthony sprang off the bed, backing away to the corner of the room. "H-how are you doing that?"

"Doing what?"

"Talking! And moving! Y-you're *dead*!"

"*Undead*," Emily said with an annoyed huff. "There is a difference."

"When I got here, you were dead—I mean, sleeping."

Anthony took a deep breath, trying to remain calm. "I—I think I get it now. You're just some kid my friends hired to give me a scare."

Emily wrinkled her brow. "What are you talking about? This is my house. No one hired me to be here."

"Y-you can drop the act now," Anthony stammered. "There's no way a person can be undead. You can't prove it."

"You saw me unconscious earlier. Now I am awake."

"That doesn't prove anything."

Emily bit her lip in thought, then held out her palms. "My hands are really cold. Do you want to feel them?"

Anthony pressed himself flat against the wall. "N-no. Do you at least have an explanation for how you're awake?"

"I took part of your soul when I bit you," Emily said, adjusting herself on the bed for comfort. "If I sense a potential servant nearby, I wake up to take part of their soul." She cocked her head. "By the way, what is your name, servant?"

"Anthony." His eyes widened in shock, his hand flying back to his bruised neck. "Wait, you *took my soul?*"

She held her thumb and index finger just a smidge apart. "Just a little."

"That's both creepy and physically impossible."

"No, it is not, because it is the only way an undead body like mine can survive."

Narrowing his eyes, Anthony stared at Emily's calm face. *This girl is loaded with crap. She didn't even bite me hard enough to draw blood.* "I don't remember agreeing to any of this."

"It is part of our bond," Emily said with a shrug. "I take part of your soul, and in return, you let me live off your energy."

Anthony raised his brow. "I don't see how I benefit from this."

"Do you have to benefit from everything you do? Think of it as helping out someone in need." She slid off her bed and walked toward the tea table, her steps dainty and graceful. Smoothing the back of her black dress, she took a seat between two large teddy bears.

Anthony scratched his head, hoping this was all a twisted dream and he'd soon awaken in his own bedroom. "Look, I think we had some sort of misunderstanding. Whether or not you really are undead, I didn't come here to be your servant. My dumb friends just wanted to—hold on, where are my friends? What did you do to them?"

"I did not do anything," Emily said, pouring invisible tea into her dolls' teacups from a white teapot. "The Mavro family patrols the area. Your friends were probably chased away. You are the only person I saw last night, and I made sure to keep you safe."

"Thanks, I guess," Anthony muttered. He reached into his pocket to check his phone, but the battery was dead. "Do you know what time it is?"

"I do not, sorry."

"Don't you have a clock to tell you when midnight is?"

Emily chuckled and set down the teapot. "Why would I care when it is midnight?"

Anthony could hear Tyson ranting about the local tale in his mind. Even just imagining it was enough to annoy him. "Well, you know, on those full moon nights, you awaken at midnight. . ." His voice trailed off as Emily's expression turned blank. "It's what the stories say about you."

"They are wrong. I do not need a full moon to be awake. The moon is not out right now, and I am up. But I do feel the most energy on the night of the full moon. I usually just do not have the energy without the moon, but since you are my servant, I can just use your soul to keep me energized."

"Right, sure." Anthony peeked out the window at the bright sky. It had to be almost noon by now. The novelty of meeting an undead girl was already wearing off and becoming underwhelming. "Look, it's been great talking to you, Emily, but I gotta get going. I need to go to school, and my aunt and uncle are probably wondering where I am. Actually, I doubt that." He backed toward the door, giving her a wave. "Anyway, I hope whatever part of my soul you took gives you a happy and healthy life."

"Wait!" Emily cried, jumping from the table and rushing to his side. "You must not leave!" She seized his arm in her cold, thin fingers. "You are supposed to stay here with me, or else I will fall back asleep!"

"I thought my soul will keep you alive."

"It only lasts so long. Unless you keep giving me more, I have to stay by your side. Your spiritual presence will give me energy."

Anthony wrinkled his nose. "I still don't get how this works."

"You do not have to. Just. . ." She pouted and trailed off in search of an excuse. "Please stay a bit longer? I get really bored being all alone."

Anthony sighed. *I'm already late for school, so I might as well ditch.* "Fine."

"Wonderful!" She skipped back to the tea table and tapped an empty seat beside her. "Let us play tea party."

Anthony failed to hide his scowl. "You're fourteen or something, right?"

"Yes," Emily said. She drummed her fingers on the wooden chair. "Come on. Sit down."

"Aren't you a little old for dolls?"

Emily flushed with anger. Rising, she marched over to Anthony, growling in frustration, her hands balled into fists. Anthony flinched, afraid she might punch him, but instead she wrapped her arms around his neck and stood on her toes.

"Wha-what do you want now?" Anthony stammered, scrunching his shoulders to hide his neck.

"Bend over!" Emily shouted. "I need to take more of

your soul! Maybe you will *behave* after that!"

"Oh, hell no!" Anthony pushed away from her. "Sorry, but I'm not gonna let you bite me so I can play with your stupid dolls."

"Then can you at least do something else for me?"

Anthony hesitated. "Maybe."

A distant gaze washed over Emily's eyes. "I have not left here since I died. I cannot leave on my own. Not only do I lack the energy, but I would have no place to go. So please, *please* take me with you."

Anthony backed farther away. "If you're implying that you want to live with me, I can't let you. I hardly even know you, and even if I did, it's not like I have my own house."

"Please?" Emily's voice rose in desperation. "I hate it here! There are so many painful memories in this house. You do not understand what it is like to be stuck in the place you *died*."

Anthony slumped his shoulders and sighed. Emily's words struck through his chest like an arrow poisoned with guilt. *I'd give anything to be away from my house. I can't deny her the very thing I want. I'd be devastated if someone took that chance from me.* With a sigh, he said, "I can't believe I'm saying this, but you can come with me."

Emily clapped her hands together, her face brightening with joy. "Really? Thank you so much—"

"*But,*" Anthony interrupted, lifting a finger to silence her, "you can't stay with me forever. I'll let you stay the night, but after that, we gotta find somewhere else for you. I'll help you find a place and a new servant or whatever if need be."

Emily's excitement fell with her brow. "This does not sound like that great of a plan."

"That's fine." Anthony wrapped his fingers around the doorknob. "Good luck with the next guy that stumbles across your room."

"Wait!" Emily cried, rushing to his side. "I will follow

your plan. Just take me away from here."

~~

On the other side of town, an elderly woman rose from her rocking chair at the sound of a knock on her front door. Bringing her shawls closer to her body, she made her way to the entrance. She let out a gasp and straightened her circular glasses when she opened the door and saw the two individuals on the other side of the threshold.

A short, teenage girl in a black Hello Kitty t-shirt stood on the porch, her fiery red hair tied into pigtails. Towering over her was a man in his twenties, dressed in leather pants and a black hooded jacket beneath his trench coat. Pointed ears sprouted through his white hair, red eyes glowing at the elderly woman from beneath his bangs. He removed the cigarette from between his pierced lips and grinned.

"Good afternoon!" the man said. "You must be Miss Greyword. Matilda Greyword?"

"Yes," the old woman replied, squinting in confusion. "And who might you be?"

"I'm Simon," the man said, reaching into his pocket and withdrawing an ID card. A gold cross was printed in the right corner. He nodded to the girl. "This is my assistant Karin. We're paranormal investigators from Eden."

"Pleased to meet you," Karin said, beaming as she waved hello.

"I've already had numerous investigators search my house for spirits," Matilda said, pulling the tattered brown shawl closer, "and I don't remember calling any more for further assistance."

"I am fully aware of all this," Simon said. "Please let us in and I'll happily explain."

Matilda backed away, allowing the two investigators to enter. Simon scraped the cigarette against the bottom of his boot, then tossed the butt into the nearby bushes.

"Beautiful home," he said, wiping his feet on the red welcome mat. He surveyed the various shelves of books and china dishes, the orange furniture, and the walls covered in floral paper and family photographs. "It's a shame this place is haunted."

"How did you know about me and my house?" Matilda asked.

"That's a secret," Karin said, following Simon into the kitchen. "Everything Eden does is secret. Consider it your lucky day to have us as your visitors."

"I wouldn't go as far as calling her *lucky*," Simon said with a chuckle. "Eden investigators rarely do house visits. House hauntings are normally pretty easy for most paranormal investigators to take care of. Ghosts are too harmless to waste our time on and too unbelievable for the public to accept. Even if a person's house was haunted by a ghost, no one would actually believe them. We're willing to let a few ghost witnesses slide at the cost of society labeling them as psychos."

"But the other investigators told me I had a demon in my house," Matilda said, keeping a careful distance from him, "not a ghost."

"And I definitely sense a demonic presence."

"Is there a difference?"

"Big difference. See, there are three main types of entities." Simon leaned against the granite kitchen counter and raised his index finger. "Ghosts are the spirits of deceased humans. They are harmless and rarely make their presence known. If they do, it's because they are the spirit of a loved one trying to get your attention, usually to console you in grief." He smiled. "Opposite of a problem, right?"

Matilda shrugged. "I suppose."

He held up two fingers. "Poltergeists. Same as ghosts, just obnoxious assholes. They cause a ruckus because they get a thrill out of scaring people. Lights flickering, rearranging furniture, slamming doors—again, nothing too harmful usually. Just really annoying. But then there's the third kind." He raised a third finger. "*Demons*. The rarest of the bunch and the nastiest. They are evil spirits from hell that were never human, but they will do anything to get into a human's body. While ghosts can roam freely between Earth and spirit realms, demons can't. God holds too much power over Earth. If a demon tries to live on its own on Earth, it will burn."

"Then how is a demon here?" Matilda asked, sitting at the kitchen table.

"If a human summons a demon into a vessel, like a household object, animal, or even their own body," Karin said, taking a seat beside Matilda, "the demon has a chance at survival. It won't be as powerful, but it's still dangerous."

"And that's in my house?"

"That's right," Karin replied. She glanced at Simon, who nodded in response.

"How did it get in here?" Matilda asked.

Simon looked up to the ceiling and shouted, "Is Johnny home?"

"My grandson Johnny is upstairs in his room," Matilda whispered, rising from the table. "He doesn't like to be bothered."

"That's too bad," Simon said, leaving the kitchen.

"Hold on, young man!" Matilda cried. "I just told you he doesn't like to be bothered." She hurried after Simon and Karin, her frail, aging legs struggling to support her speed.

Simon pushed Johnny's bedroom door open. A preteen boy in a black t-shirt and skinny jeans sat on his bed, listening to the screaming vocalist of a rock band blare from his stereo.

"Who the hell are you?" he shouted at Simon and Karin, glaring at them through a curtain of black hair.

"It's gotta be around here somewhere," Simon

muttered, ignoring Johnny. He dug around through Johnny's dresser, then under his bed.

"Grandma, who the hell is this guy?" Johnny said. "Make him stop touching my stuff!"

"Found it!" Simon withdrew a small board from under the bed. The alphabet and numbers were inscribed in the wood, along with a few simple commands. "Your little grandson here managed to summon a demon through this Ouija board."

"Ugh, I'm so sick of all these stupid ghost hunter people invading our house!" Johnny grumbled. "That's just a dumb toy, you idiot! My friends and I were just screwing around with it one night for fun!"

"*You're* the idiot for using it," Karin mumbled, rolling her eyes. "I thought people only messed around with them in cheesy horror movies."

"This is a device for communicating with spirits," Simon said, holding out the Ouija board. "Demons can use them as portals into our world, and that's exactly what happened when you and your friends screwed around with it. Now it's living in your house—in your *room*—and is only three steps away from taking over your body." He wrinkled his nose. "Though from your attitude, I'd assume you're already possessed."

"Johnny, how dare you play with such a thing?" Matilda scolded.

"Because it's just a dumb toy!" Johnny yelled.

Simon swung his backpack onto the floor, unzipped it, pulled on a pair of black leather gloves, and withdrew a small vial of water. "Just a toy, you say?" He unscrewed the vial's lid and poured a tiny drop of water on the Ouija board. Black smoke rose from the wood, causing it to reek of decaying flesh. Suddenly, the stereo and lights shut off, and the bedroom door slammed shut. Simon unzipped his jacket and handed it to Karin, then pulled a wooden cross from his bag.

"Wh-what's going on?" Johnny whimpered.

A low, throaty growl emitted from the Ouija board, as if in response.

"Think it's just a toy now?" Karin asked with a smirk.

A long shadow extended from the board, stretching to the ceiling, forming the silhouette of a horned figure, its menacing claws raised above its head. Despite the sunny weather outside, the bedroom became dark.

"It's the demon!" Matilda cried, backing onto the bed.

"What do we do?" Johnny screamed.

"Leave everything to us," Karin said, taking a seat between Johnny and Matilda. She slipped on Simon's jacket and giggled, hugging herself with the oversized sleeves. "Simon is a badass exorcist."

CHAPTER 3

~~

Emily breathed in the morning's fresh air with a dreamy look on her face. "It has been so long since I have been outside! The yard does not look too different than it used to. I imagined it would have dried out, but it is still beautiful."

"I know the girl who takes care of your house," Anthony said. "She's part of your family. Speaking of which, won't your family freak out when they realize you're gone?"

"They will be fine. Will your family mind me staying?"

"My aunt and uncle are at work for most of the day and are usually too drunk to give a damn about anything when they're home."

Anthony helped Emily over the fence and led her to the main road. Emily clung to Anthony's arm with wide eyes, watching the cars whiz by. Anthony realized that this was probably the first time she was exposed to anything invented after 1910. *I guess she really is undead,* Anthony thought. *No one can be that spooked by a car.*

When they reached a crosswalk, Emily pointed to the cars at the stoplight. "What are those?"

"Cars," Anthony said. "We use them for transportation."

"Like automobiles?"

"Exactly, but newer."

Emily shook her head, watching the cars pass. "No. You are wrong. These are far different."

"I'm one hundred percent right this time. You can't argue that."

"Are these all houses?" Emily asked Anthony as they entered his neighborhood.

"Yup. See that one with the purple door? That one's mine."

"How many people live in it?"

"Me, my uncle, and my aunt."

"Do you have any servants?"

Anthony refrained from laughing. "No. No one does around here." He unlocked the door and led Emily down the hall to his bedroom.

"This is your room?" she said, examining the super hero figurines on his dresser. "It's awfully small."

"Most people don't live in a mansion like you."

"You have so many pictures on your wall," Emily said. "Lots of girls and those car things."

Anthony looked around, too, but to find something to change the subject with. "Why don't I get you something to eat? Once my family gets home, you'll have to stay in my room, but I can sneak stuff to you."

"I am undead. I do not eat."

"Makes sense."

"Are you going to school?" Emily asked, plopping down on the bed.

Anthony glanced at the clock on his nightstand. "I should probably get going. Will you be okay on your own for a bit? Here." He turned on the TV that sat on his dresser across from the bed and handed her the remote.

Emily's eyes lit up in awe. "Wow! There are people in a box! How did you get the people in the box?"

"I didn't." He tried to think of an explanation she

could understand. "You know what photographs are?"

She nodded, though her attention remained on the screen.

"It's kind of like a moving photograph," Anthony said.

"That is amazing!"

"Yeah, pretty crazy. Push that button to change channels."

"Channels?" Emily repeated, inspecting the remote in confusion.

"Yeah," Anthony said, swinging his backpack onto his shoulder. "You sure you're gonna be okay?"

Emily was too engaged in channel surfing to answer.

By the time Anthony made it to school, lunch had just ended and his fourth period class had just begun. Instead of going straight to class, Anthony snuck to the backside of the school, where he found Tyson and Cory sitting against the wall, smoking joints.

"Yo, Anthony!" Tyson called, waving to him.

Anthony sat beside him. "I figured I'd find you guys here."

"Where've you been, man?" Tyson asked.

"Home," Anthony replied, debating whether to tell his friends about Emily. "Wasn't sure if I wanted to come today or not."

"I know what you mean," Cory said. "We must have gotten really wasted in the woods last night. My head's been throbbing since I got up this morning."

Anthony cocked his head. "What are you talking about?"

"Last night in the woods. We took you out to get your mind off Olivia."

"I don't remember any of that."

"Then we must have done our job," Tyson said with a proud thumbs-up.

"Right." Anthony narrowed his eyes as he studied

them. *Do they not remember going to Mavro Manor?* "Is that all we did?"

"Yup," Tyson said. "You okay, man? You don't look too hot."

"I gotta go," Anthony said, dropping the joint and jumping to his feet.

"But you just got here," Cory said.

Anthony ignored him. Something wasn't right. He knew they went to Mavro Manor the night before. How else would Emily be in his room?

Hurrying inside the school, Anthony recalled Emily's words from the morning, taking a shortcut to his car. *The Mavros—they must have done something to them.*

He froze when he spotted Olivia at her locker. He turned to head the opposite direction, hoping to avoid her, but he was too late.

"Anthony?" he heard her call.

Anthony spun to face her. "Oh, hey, Olivia. Didn't see you there."

Olivia slammed her locker shut and knelt on the floor to stuff her backpack with textbooks. "Why aren't you in class?"

Anthony's eyes darted to the wall. "Why aren't *you*?"

"Leaving early. It's. . ." She trailed off, zipping her backpack. "It's a family emergency."

Anthony's heart beat faster. *Did they find out Emily left?*

Olivia stood up and slung her backpack over her shoulders. "Anyway, about yesterday—"

"Sorry, I gotta go," Anthony cut her off, racing down the hall before she could question him. Between the "family emergency" and his friends' lack of memory, Anthony knew he had to return home to Emily before someone else did. He wasn't sure what the Mavro family would do to Emily if they caught her, let alone him, and he didn't want to find out.

~~

"That went well," Simon said, flopping onto the orange couch near the entrance of Matilda's house. He rested his cross on the floor beside him, letting out a sigh of relief. "It's been a while since I had that much fun at a house mission."

Though his pale skin was free of wounds, the entire house was a mess. Picture frames fallen to the floor, furniture tossed aside, curtains ripped. Matilda and Johnny cowered behind the railing of the staircase.

"Is it over?" Johnny whimpered.

"Yeah," Simon said. "It was a feisty one, but fairly weak. Sometimes you just gotta let them run their course."

"That was super cool!" Karin rushed to Simon and flung herself onto his torso. "*You* were super cool!"

"You!" Matilda shouted, pointing a trembling finger at Simon. "You're just as monstrous as that demon from the board! Get out of my house!"

"Is that really how you treat someone who saved your life?" Simon said. He nudged Karin off as he rose from the couch and walked over to the stairs.

"G-get away from us!" Matilda cried, spreading her arms in front of her grandson, backing away from Simon.

"I will soon, don't worry. I'll even call my friends to come over to help clean your house and confiscate that Ouija board. See, I'm not that bad. But I guess you're pretty freaked out about all that demon business. I'll tell you what." He smirked, leaning against the railing. "I'll just erase your memories of everything that happened. All of this will be nothing more than a bad dream that you won't even be able to remember when you awaken in the morning."

CHAPTER 4

~~

Anthony let out a sigh of relief when he found Emily sitting on his bed, watching TV. "Thank God you're alone!" he said.

"Were you expecting someone?" Emily asked, her attention fixed to the flickering screen.

"No," Anthony said, not wanting to alarm her. "My uncle is home and my aunt will be back from work soon, but they'll be too drunk to notice if we chill in here. So, what are you watching?"

"*The Wizard of Oz.* I remember reading the book. It was one of my favorites. What is your favorite book?"

"I don't read."

"You do not read and you do not play tea party. You are quite the boring servant."

Anthony rolled his eyes. "Sorry. If I knew I didn't meet the requirements, I wouldn't have signed up for the job. *Oh wait,* I never did in the first place."

"Were you not going to find me a new servant today?"

"Oh, right." Anthony scratched his head and sat behind her. *I can't risk taking her out of the house. If her family catches us, they'll probably send her back home.* "I have a lot of homework to do today. I don't think I'll have time. You'll just have to make do with my place for now."

"That is fine with me, as long as I stay awake."

Anthony's eyes fell upon Emily's bandage. The white square covered the entire left side of her neck. "Is that how you died?"

"Do you not know it is rude to ask a lady how she died?"

"I don't think it's usually possible to ask. I didn't mean to be rude. I'm just kind of curious to know more about my new roommate."

"I cannot speak of my past."

He cocked his head in interest. "Why not?"

Emily didn't answer. Her back remained facing him.

Anthony drummed his fingers on his knee. "Can you at least tell me why you want to be alive?"

Emily hesitated before speaking. "I have my reasons. Just as you have your reasons for letting me stay with you. You act as if you do not like me, but if you truly did not, you would not have brought me here. I never had a servant stay with me as long as you have. They would get scared when I would wake up, but you are not afraid of me anymore." Her eyes met his. "Why are you letting me stay?"

Anthony looked away, thinking for a moment. "You claimed to hate your house," he mumbled. "I hate my house, too. I'd take any opportunity to move in with someone else. I'd feel guilty if I denied you that chance."

Emily smiled in satisfaction. "Fair enough." The TV regained her attention as an advertisement for dolls appeared on screen.

"By the way, I don't necessarily *dislike* you," Anthony mumbled, resting against the wall. "I can't say I like someone who won't even tell me one thing about herself, but it's kind of nice having company." He awaited her response, though her silence made him question if she was listening.

After some time, she said, "It hurt." She ran her fingers over the bandage. "Only for a second, but I still remember the pain. When I remember it, I can feel it. And when I feel it, I remember how horrible it felt to die. Dying helps you escape pain, but you cannot escape pain when you are already dead." Her voice and shoulders trembled. "Now you know one thing about me. Does it make you happy?"

No, Anthony thought, slouching with guilt. He hadn't made a girl cry since he refused to share his toys with his cousin as a child, yet here he was now, ten years later, leading a girl to cry over her own death. He heard a door slam within the house, the shouting voices of his aunt and uncle announcing their arrival. Anthony shut off the TV and moved his laptop from his desk to the bed, logging onto his Netflix account. "I got a ton of movies on here," he told Emily, who looked at the laptop with watery eyes. "I'm going to let you pick one, and we'll watch it together."

"Any of them?"

"Yup."

She scrolled through the array of movies. "But there are so many choices."

"That's the beauty of it."

"What about your homework?"

Anthony stared at her for a second or two, then said, "This is more important."

~~

Outside the elderly woman's home, a man in his early thirties sat in the driver's seat of his black SUV, his eyes scanning over the documents resting against the steering wheel. He squinted in the inadequate light of the sunset. A sudden rapping on the window drew his attention. He unlocked the doors and opened the window.

"Yo, Jason!" Simon said. "Didn't expect to see my supervisor tonight. Where's the wifey?"

"She's back at headquarters," Jason replied. He cocked

his head to the back seat. "Hop in. I've got somewhere to take you."

"An escort? How fancy," Simon said. He got in and scooted to the far left of the car, Karin taking her seat beside him.

"You brought Karin with you?" Jason asked, fastening his seatbelt over his black suit.

"My mission today was pretty low-key," Simon said with a shrug. "You said you wanted her to gain more field experience."

"It was so fun!" Karin said. "I got to help Simon get rid of the demon. He was super badass!"

"Did you tell Sakura about this?" Jason glanced at Simon from the rear view mirror as he began to drive.

Simon rested his head against the window and peered outside. "No. Why would I?"

"She *is* your girlfriend."

"Way to rub it in," Karin grumbled, slouching in her seat.

"She's busy on her own mission," Simon replied. "Besides, I think she trusts me enough to go on a one-day mission with a teenager." He narrowed his eyes. "Wait, you didn't come here because of that, did you?"

"No," Jason said. "I didn't even know you brought Karin with you. I came because there's an emergency at Mavro Manor."

"The place where that Emily girl lives?" Karin asked, perking up.

"Where she *did*. Someone kidnapped her."

~~

When night fell, Anthony returned to his room after his shower and found Emily curled up on his bed. She was fast asleep, wearing one of his gray t-shirts—which fit her like a dress, her bare white legs poking out from beneath. *She's gonna get cold sleeping like that,* he thought, pulling the covers over her body. She didn't seem to notice, sleeping still as a corpse. *Can she even feel warmth or is she always cold?* White bandages were wrapped from her wrists to above her elbows. He never saw them before, since they'd been covered by her dress sleeves. After seeing her cry earlier, he didn't dare to think of asking about her arms. He placed his backpack at the foot of the bed and rested his head against it, lying down on the floor.

~~

Simon stormed through the front door of Mavro Manor, Karin trailing close behind. He headed straight to the parlor, where a young woman sat in one of the elegant armchairs. She held her phone above her face, giggling at photos, her legs dangling over one of the arms. When she noticed Simon and Karin, she turned around to sit up and smoothed her fitted dress.

"Hello, Simon. Have a seat." She gestured at the sofa beside her and beamed.

Karin flopped onto the sofa, engaging herself in cellphone games, but Simon remained standing. "What the hell is this about, Erika?" he said. "Is this some sick joke?"

"What do you mean?" Erika asked, raising her drawn-on eyebrows. "I thought the message I told Jason to tell you was pretty clear."

"Yeah, that's real classy, having our boss run your errands," Simon groaned.

"I'm busy watching the house."

"If you're so busy watching the house, then how did someone steal the kid? Do your freaking job for once!"

She averted her gaze from his glare. "It's not like I'm watching it *all* the time. I have a life." Her expression hardened, and she tucked a strand from her black bob behind her ear. "I may be below Jason, but as investigations manager, I'm still *your* boss, so show some respect."

Simon rolled his eyes. "Anyway, what's the deal with this situation? I didn't think anyone even cared about Mavro Manor anymore. Eden gave up on Emily's case years ago."

"*I* still care," Erika said, pointing a finger at her chest. "This house is my family's property. I'd take on the mission myself if I wasn't so busy."

"Right," Simon muttered. "So you want me to go hunt down whoever took the Mavro kid?"

"That's it."

Simon sat beside Karin and scratched his head. "I dunno, sounds pretty lame."

"Can I go with Simon?" Karin asked, sitting up. "Everyone says I need more experience."

"I honestly feel more comfortable with you tagging along to hunt demons over kidnappers," Simon said. Then he looked back to Erika. "Sakura will be back from her mission in a few days, and I already told you that we wanted some time away from work before Easter."

"This really won't take that long," Erika said. "I know you're good at getting jobs done quickly, and I already got Drea on board to join you—"

"*Drea*? She hates me. You know that."

Erika rested her elbow on the arm of the chair, holding her chin. "You need to work with people other than your girlfriend."

"You can work with me," Karin said, nudging Simon's arm.

"And to make things better, I have a secret weapon for your mission," Erika said.

As if on cue, another person entered the parlor. Olivia Mavro dropped her leather purse to the floor and straightened her cardigan. "Sorry I'm late. I had to deal with drama at headquarters. What can I do to help?"

"I want you to guard the house with me tonight," Erika said. "In the morning, I want you to join Simon and Drea to find the little thief and bring him back here to me. I'd like to interrogate him before taking him to headquarters."

"If you already have Simon and Drea on the case, then why do you need me?"

"Drea and Simon are in charge of getting him and Emily, but you're the one who'll take them to him and keep him under control. We already got a lead on who the kidnapper is, and we believe he is a schoolmate of yours." Erika folded her hands. "You're familiar with Anthony Olsen, right?"

"He's just some loser who has a crush on me," Olivia said, wrinkling her nose in disgust.

"Maybe if you gave him some attention, he wouldn't be kidnapping dead girls," Simon said.

Erika burst out laughing, but Olivia flushed and curled her fist.

"Shut up!" Olivia shouted. "I have nothing to do with the guy. He's no threat to Emily or Eden."

"He technically is," Erika said. "Even though Emily's mystery is a cold case, she's still Eden's property. Stealing from Eden is a serious offense."

"But it's not like he knew what he was doing," Olivia said, concern washing over her face. "He's an idiot, but he's not a criminal. Don't you think that's a bit overboard, taking him to Eden headquarters? We don't even know why he took her."

"Rules are rules," Simon said. "He messed with Eden, now we mess with him."

"B-but that's not fair!" Olivia stammered.

"You said you don't care about the guy, so why are you freaking out?" Erika snapped.

Olivia fell silent.

Erika took a deep breath. "That settles it. Simon, I want you and Drea to stop by to pick up Olivia tomorrow morning around seven, then head straight to Anthony's house. I want him back to me alive, but you're free to use any force necessary. Clear?"

"Yeah," Simon grumbled.

She smiled. "Great. You and Karin are dismissed."

~~

Anthony was awakened the next morning by the doorbell. It rang multiple times in a row, followed by a series of harsh knocks on the door.

"Open up!" a woman's voice shouted. "We know you're in there!"

"You have got to be kidding me," Emily grumbled, rolling onto her side. "It is *them*."

CHAPTER 5

~~

Panicked by the abrupt awakening, Anthony ignored Emily and hurried to the door. When he opened the front door, a woman in her mid-twenties shouted, "Don't move!" pointing a gun at his chest. Behind her stood a man of the same age, leaning against the house and smoking a cigarette. The end of his trench coat grazed against the cement.

The woman said, "We are on the search for a young girl by the name of Emily Mavro and suspect you for kidnapping her. Please step aside and let us search your house."

"H-hold on one minute," Anthony stammered, staring at the gun. "You can't barge into my house."

"Oh, sorry." The woman pulled out an ID card from the pocket of her leather coat. On the right hand corner was a tiny golden cross. "Now, if you'll excuse me." Tossing her black dreadlocks over her shoulder, she pushed past him and stomped into the house.

"Whoa, hold on a second!" Anthony shouted, though he was reluctant to chase after the armed woman.

"Calm down, Drea. We aren't even sure if he's hiding her or not." The man glanced at Anthony from behind his white bangs. "Don't mind Drea. She won't hurt you. She's just really bossy and thinks—"

"I hear you, Simon!" Drea yelled from down the hall. "I

found Emily!"

"Eden filth!" Emily screamed from the bedroom. "Get away from me!"

Anthony flinched at the sound of things hitting the wall, followed by more screaming.

"Simon!" Drea shouted. "A little help, please! She's going to ruin my hair!"

"Oh, my God, this woman," Simon groaned, scraping his cigarette against the bottom of his boot. He shook his head and sighed. "Told you she's harmless. She walks in all high and mighty with a gun, yet she can't even deal with a kid. You mind if I come in?"

"Uh, sure," Anthony muttered, stepping aside to let Simon through. Though Simon seemed friendlier than Drea, his red eyes and pointed ears were off-putting.

Anthony followed Simon into the bedroom, where he found his figurines, video game controllers, and comics scattered about the floor. Drea sat on the floor against the door, avoiding Simon's gaze.

"You were throwing my stuff?" Anthony asked, scrambling to gather his belongings, checking for damage.

Simon marched up to Emily and lifted her over his shoulder, unfazed by her thrashing.

"No! Let me go!" Emily screamed as he carried her to the door. "Where are you taking me?"

"We're taking you to headquarters before our boss throws a fit," Simon said.

"You cannot take me anywhere! I will never go with you Eden filth!"

"What are you gonna do with her?" Anthony asked. "You can't force her to do anything she doesn't want to do."

"Sorry, dude, but if you have any objections"—Simon withdrew his own gun from his coat—"I'd be happy to hear them."

Anthony backed away from the gun, his hands raised

over his head, too afraid to speak. Despite Drea's aggressive entrance, he found Simon's calm composure far more intimidating.

"Wait! Stop!"

Anthony jumped at the sound of a familiar voice.

"Olivia?" Anthony said. "What are you doing here?"

Standing in the doorway, Olivia ignored Anthony's question and looked from Drea to Simon. "Drop your weapons. He's no threat."

"Get back in the car," Drea ordered. "We're just about done here."

Olivia placed her hands on her hips and let out an annoyed huff. "Are you giving *me* orders? Put the guns away *now*."

"Right, sorry," Drea mumbled, she and Simon holstering their guns.

Dang, what's her deal? Anthony thought, raising his brow.

"So fierce," Simon chuckled. He held up his empty hands. "Better?"

Olivia rolled her eyes. "Anyway, the boss called. We're changing the meetup location. She doesn't want outsiders coming into headquarters."

"Fine with me," Drea said, rising to her feet. "We better get going. I'm sure we're already behind schedule for the boss' standards."

"No!" Emily shouted. Breaking free from Simon's grasp, she scurried to Anthony's side. "You will never make me go with you!"

"Emily, it's gonna be okay," Anthony muttered, squeezing her shoulder. He nodded to Olivia. "I know this girl. She won't let anyone hurt you." He hoped she believed him, because he struggled to believe his own words as he gazed at Olivia. Something about her seemed different as she stood there, dressed in the same leather clothing as her comrades.

Emily looked from Anthony to Olivia, then back at him. "I do not trust her, but I trust you."

After being ushered into the SUV, Anthony and Emily took their seats in the back beside Olivia, who kept a straight face. Simon drove while Drea polished her gun in the passenger seat.

"So," Anthony whispered to Olivia, "you're with them?"

Olivia nodded, staring at the road ahead of them.

"Don't tell him anything," Drea said the second Olivia opened her mouth to speak.

"You guys just barged into his house with guns. I think he deserves some sort of explanation."

Neither Simon nor Drea responded. Olivia took their silence as permission to speak and turned to Anthony. "We're paranormal investigators from an organization called Eden."

"You mean you guys study ghosts and haunted things?" Anthony asked, raising his brow. Though he knew Olivia cleaned Mavro Manor, he never saw her as superstitious. "But ghosts aren't real."

"If you knew what's really out there, you'd piss yourself," Simon said with a laugh.

Anthony took a deep breath in an attempt to remain calm. "Then why haven't I seen anything before?"

"Is the undead girl next to you not enough evidence?" Drea asked.

He glanced at Emily. She hid her scowl, gazing at her feet. The fact that he could see her made her far more believable than a ghost.

"I understand if this is hard for you to believe," Olivia said. "Eden uses a scientific process to find a rational explanation for any sort of phenomena before labeling it as supernatural, so we are also a bit skeptical when someone mentions ghosts."

"And if you can't find an explanation?" Anthony asked.

Olivia paused. She stared at the back of Simon's seat, as if she were waiting for him to give her further permission to speak. "If we can't use science to explain a phenomena," she said after a moment, "we treat it as paranormal and handle it accordingly to keep it hidden from public eye."

"Though Emily may be pretty well known to the locals, very few people actually believe in the Mavro Manor stories," Simon said. "It's not enough to cause some sort of societal panic. It's not much of a threat if it all just remains a local legend, but we keep watch on the house to make sure no one messes with her. Outsiders interacting with Emily is already risky, but for someone to take her crosses the line." He peered back at Anthony, stopping at a red light. "If you hadn't taken her to your house, we probably wouldn't be having this conversation."

"It wasn't my idea to go to Mavro Manor in the first place," Anthony grumbled. "Way fewer people would care about it if Emily wasn't there."

"We try to keep most paranormal phenomena a secret," Olivia said. "Emily just happens to be a special case since her parents left orders to leave her in her room. Eden is technically a secret organization, as hard as it may be to believe, given that *these* two just invaded your house."

Drea turned in her seat to face Olivia. "What did you expect us to do? Just ask him to hand over Emily and come with us? We were given permission to do whatever we wanted, so we weren't breaking any rules."

Olivia pursed her lips and crossed her arms.

Anthony peered out the window. They drove through a thick forest, one that Anthony recognized all too well. His heart sank into his stomach when Simon parked outside Mavro Manor's familiar black gates. Even in broad daylight, it appeared as daunting as it had the night he visited.

Olivia gave Anthony a lopsided smile. "Welcome back."

CHAPTER 6

~~

Anthony followed the Eden members into Mavro Manor, dreading whatever was yet to come. Walking into the parlor, he glanced at Emily, whose face was scrunched with anger rather than fear.

A girl around Emily's age was laying on one of the couches, playing a game on her phone. She sat up when Simon entered the room, her eyes brightening.

"Welcome back," she said, tossing her phone aside to give him a hug.

"Great to see you, Karin," Simon said, patting her head. "Don't you have school today?"

"I really wanted to see you, so Erika said I could take the day off and join her."

"Sounds like something Erika would do," Olivia grumbled.

A young woman entered the parlor, her floral skirt rippling with every step. "Is someone talking about me?" She grinned when her gaze met Olivia's. "Good to see you, Sis."

"Yeah, real good," Olivia muttered, slumping onto the couch.

"I didn't know you have a sister," Anthony said, though he realized there was very little that he did know about Olivia.

"It doesn't come as a surprise that she never mentioned

me," Erika said. She beamed at Anthony and held out a hand. "Pleasure to meet you, Anthony. Thanks for your cooperation."

"Thanks." Anthony shook her hand while keeping a careful watch on Erika. "I didn't have much of a choice."

Erika laughed and sat in the armchair at the back of the room beside the fireplace. She gestured to the couches and chairs placed around a wooden coffee table. "Have a seat. We have plenty of fun things to discuss."

Anthony took a seat on the couch beside Olivia, keeping a comfortable distance between them, while the others took their seats across from them. "So, you're the boss?"

"Of investigations, yes," Erika answered.

"Cool." Anthony waited for her to say more, but she simply kept on smiling at him.

After a moment, Erika asked, "So, why did you steal our precious Emily?"

"I didn't. It was her idea to leave. I wouldn't have agreed to anything if I knew you'd invade my house."

"But we did, just like how you invaded *my* family's home." She folded her hands in her lap and leaned forward. "I'm sure you already know from the local ghost stories that Emily doesn't have a soul. A body without a soul cannot awaken, so what did you do to wake her up?"

"Nothing," Anthony said with a shrug. "I just stood next to her and she got up."

Erika narrowed her eyes. "I'm not buying that. My family has been keeping close watch on Emily for years and we've never seen her awaken. Not for this long, at least."

"Why don't you just keep her with you if you care about her so much?" Anthony asked. "If you just leave her in an abandoned house, people will come looking for her."

"We have to leave her at Mavro Manor," Olivia said, holding her chin in her palm, resting her elbow on the arm of the couch. "Emily's parents ordered Eden to leave her body in her room. The Mavro family always held a position of power in Eden, so no one ever questioned their request. They set up a barrier to protect her from any evil spirits and left it at that."

"But you bring up a good point," Erika said to Anthony. "Now that Emily's awake, we can get a better understanding of how she is able to survive without a soul. Keeping her at Mavro Manor will only hamper our studies." She pointed to Drea. "Bring her back to headquarters with us. I'm sure both the science and spirituality departments will have a blast with her."

Drea nodded and marched over to Emily. Seizing Emily's wrists, Drea yanked her to her feet.

"You will never take me to that horrible place!" Emily shouted, struggling to break free.

"Simon, erase *Anthony's* memory," Erika said, saying Anthony's name as if it were a curse. "I have no use for him anymore."

"Whoa! Hold up!" Anthony scooted away from Simon and closer to Olivia, cowering behind his raised arms. "Can't we talk about this a bit longer before doing anything crazy?"

"I have to be at headquarters in an hour for a meeting, so no," Erika said, rising from her chair.

"You cannot separate me from my servant!" Emily cried, Drea dragging her toward the door. "I drank part of his soul! He is connected to me!"

Drea cocked her head and froze. "How can you *drink* his soul? You may be undead, but you're still human."

"Drea's right," Karin said, peeking up from her phone screen. "Drinking a soul is impossible, even for monsters." She looked to Simon. "Souls can only be taken through magic, right?"

"Right," Simon said. "Even if she did happen to use magic, I don't sense any spiritual presence in Emily nor a diminished one in Anthony, so whatever she's doing to stay alive has nothing to do with taking any part of anyone's soul."

Erika stopped in the doorway of the parlor. She pointed to Anthony. "Do you feel any different than how you did before Emily supposedly took your soul?"

"Not at all," Anthony replied.

Erika held her chin in thought. "You see, we never actually talked to Emily, as she'd always been asleep, and those who did encounter her while awake were not too helpful. None of them stuck with her nearly as long as you have, and she would never be awake for more than a few minutes at a time. Eden never issued a formal investigation on her condition either. We just know she doesn't have a soul."

"But she still has her mind since she's able to speak and think," Simon said. "While we never had a full investigation on her condition, we at least know that much. A spell must have been placed on her to keep her young and undead. As to why the spell was placed on her, no one knows."

"I have not the faintest idea myself," Emily said, all eyes falling on her.

"If you guys know that something weird has been going on with Emily for the past hundred years, why haven't you investigated?" Anthony asked, wrinkling his brow.

Erika leaned against the doorway and sighed. "It's complicated. Even if we did investigate, we'd have very few leads. But if she's been staying awake with you, then there might be something you can do to lead an investigation in the right direction."

Anthony's eyes darted from Simon to Erika. "Like what?"

"Just keep her with you for now. I'd like to see if the bond you two share has anything to do with her spell."

"So we're not taking her to headquarters?" Drea asked,

loosening her grip on Emily.

Erika shook her head. "We'll spare her and Anthony for now." Her icy gaze met Anthony's. "Just don't try anything funny. Eden has you under close surveillance."

~~

The car ride back to Anthony's house was silent. As much as he wanted to speak to Olivia about Eden, Anthony kept his gaze fixed on the wooden cross dangling from the rearview mirror. He couldn't stop worrying about what she must think of the entire situation. She was paying even less attention to him now than she did in class. However, when Simon parked outside of Anthony's house, Olivia followed Anthony and Emily out of the car.

"Can I talk to you for a second?" Olivia asked him.

"Yeah, okay," he said, pausing at his doorstep.

Olivia rocked on her feet and took a deep breath. "I'm sorry I got you tangled up in all this. I'm kinda the one that brought them here."

"It's chill," Anthony said, still struggling to make eye contact with her. "They let me and Emily come back home, so. . ." He shrugged. "I'm sure things will be fine."

"Eden's not that easy to get rid of," Olivia said. "They'll still be around. *I'll* still be around. So since we'll probably be working together a lot, do you think we could. . ." She looked down at the ground and blushed. "I mean, don't take this the wrong way, because I really don't care about you or anything, but um. . . do you think we could be friends?"

Anthony raised his brow, unsure whether to be insulted or honored by her request. "Uh, yeah, sure. We can be friends."

She smiled, her attention turning to Emily. "It's nice to finally see you awake. I've been taking care of you for a very long time. I look forward to getting to know you."

Emily responded with an empty stare.

"I gotta go, but I'll see you two around." Olivia rushed back to the car, leaving Anthony alone with Emily at his front door.

"That was odd," Emily whispered. "You know her?"

Anthony let out a long sigh, making his way to his bedroom "Kinda. I like her."

"She is really pretty," Emily said, following behind him. "Way too pretty for you."

"Yeah, I know, thanks," Anthony grumbled, flopping onto his bed. "That's why she turned me down when I asked her out. Now she's acting weird and saying she wants to be friends."

Emily sat on the floor and peered up at Anthony with curiosity-filled eyes. "So you asked her out because she is pretty? Not because you were friends before?"

"Yeah, pretty much."

"That is not very smart."

"I don't need dating advice from a fourteen-year-old."

"I am technically much older than you are," Emily said, crossing her arms over her stomach. "I had an older brother around your age, too."

"You did?"

"Yes, and he had a girlfriend, unlike you."

Anthony buried his face in his hands. "You really suck at cheering me up."

"I never said I was going to make you happy. I am just trying to understand the situation."

"Well, so am I, because now I got those freaky Eden people on my back."

"*Them.*" Emily wrinkled her nose.

Anthony sat up. "Why do you hate them?"

"I just. . ." Emily trailed off and pouted. "I just *do*. My parents always told me to stay away from them, even though they were members of Eden. Eden does not care about its people. Just about the information they can gain." She dug her nails into the carpet. "They are nothing but power-hungry monsters. Now that they know about us, they will keep harassing us until they get what they want. Even that Olivia girl told you so."

"But what they want is to figure out how you're alive. Don't you want know?"

"I do not need them to tell me. Even if they find out, what will they do with that information? It will not benefit me to know. It will just be another fact they can add to their understanding of magic to increase their power."

"Eden may be power-hungry, but I don't think Olivia is. She'll keep them in line."

From Emily's firm gaze, Anthony knew she was not convinced. He forced a smile and said, "I'm sure things will be okay. After all, what exactly can they do when we're in the safety of my own house?"

CHAPTER 7

~~

It wasn't until he scrambled to dress himself for school that Anthony realized Emily wasn't fast asleep on his bed. Only a bundle of sheets remained in her place. *What's she got to do so early in the morning?* he thought, zipping his hoodie. He swung his backpack onto his shoulders and hurried to the kitchen to grab a toaster pastry, but was in for a shock when he saw who was at the table.

"Good morning," Karin said, beaming. "About time you woke up."

"What are you doing here?" Anthony cried. "And *them?*"

"Who, us?" Drea asked. She and Simon sat beside Karin and Emily, each with a plate of pancakes in front of them, their leather coats and backpacks hanging on the backs of their chairs.

"Yes, *you!*"

"Erika told you we'd be keeping you under close surveillance," Simon said, pouring syrup on his meal.

"I didn't think it'd be *this* close," Anthony grumbled.

"I told you they will keep harassing us," Emily said, leaning back in her chair, watching the others eat.

"Hey, I'm not all that thrilled about this either," Simon said. "I'm supposed to be on break with my girlfriend, not babysitting."

Drea rolled her eyes. "Your whining just makes it a whole lot worse." She gestured to Anthony with her fork. "We just need to watch over you and Emily for a bit, figure out how she's staying awake. Once we do, we'll leave you alone."

"I'm not buying that," Anthony said. Dodging Drea and Simon's glares, he reached into the cupboard for the pastry box. "I don't even know who you are, but you're in my house."

"We're paranormal investigators," Simon said. "We already told you that."

"I know your jobs, but I don't know *you*. Besides, I thought paranormal investigators carried around funky gadgets that see like heatwaves and stuff, not *guns*."

"We're special," Simon said with a shrug. "We do things a bit differently."

"Yeah, just a bit," Anthony muttered.

"I don't know why you're so hostile. I'd be pretty happy if someone surprised me with breakfast," Karin said. "We're trying to at least be somewhat nice after all that happened yesterday."

"I cannot be charmed by pancakes," Emily said, lifting her nose. "Undead girls have no use for food."

"So if I buy you a doll, will you like us?" Simon asked.

The corner of Emily's lips twitched, suppressing a smile.

"She doesn't need any more dolls," Anthony said. He stuffed a pastry into his backpack and closed the cupboard door. "I appreciate the gesture, but I don't have time to sit around and eat. I missed an entire day of school yesterday, and don't really want to listen to another lecture from my aunt about why I shouldn't skip."

"I already called in sick for you," Drea said. "You're staying home with us. No need to rush your breakfast."

Simon nudged an available chair with his foot. "Join the feast."

Anthony dropped his backpack to the floor and groaned. *There really is no escape from these people.* "Awesome."

"Beats going to school," Karin said. "All the investigations Simon's taken me on were totally fun."

"That's because I only take you on the ones that I think will be fun and not too dangerous," Simon said. "If Erika didn't excuse you from school on her own, I wouldn't have let you tag along for this one. All we're really doing is observing Anthony and Emily, reading over documents. Nothing that exciting."

Karin shrugged. "I still get school credit for it."

"Your school gives you credit for working with Eden?" Anthony asked, taking a seat at the table.

She nodded. "It's an Eden school, so yeah. They encourage us to get field experience in whatever job we might be interested in once we start high school."

"I didn't know Eden had schools, let alone different jobs."

"Eden has everything," Emily said. "They may have even more now, but I remember they had their own school, housing, and hospital, all at headquarters. Most of the members like to keep their identities secret from outsiders."

"But Olivia still goes to public school."

"She's a bit different than most of us," Simon said. Before he could explain further, his phone rang. He withdrew his cell out of his pants pocket. "Hi, honey! What's up? Wait, what? Right now?"

Anthony raised his brow. Watching Simon rummage through the contents of his backpack, he caught a glimpse of Simon's scarred palms before he pulled on a pair of leather gloves.

Simon pushed his plate aside, making room for a wooden cross, bag of incense, lighter, censer, and a vial of holy water. "Okay, talk to you later. Love you, too. What? Uh-huh. I'll tell him that. Alright, bye, honey!" He hung up and passed the incense to Karin. "Have fun." With the cross in one hand and the holy water in the other, he made his way to the front door.

"Yes!" Reaching for the censer and lighter, she hummed with excitement. She burned the incense, filling the kitchen with the scent of rosemary.

"What's going on?" Anthony asked, his eyes darting from Karin to Drea.

"Let me guess, a demon spotted us?" Emily asked, toying with her cross necklace.

"Probably," Drea said, withdrawing her gun from her jacket pocket.

Anthony's eyes widened. "A *demon* is on its way here?"

"I wouldn't worry," Karin said. "Between the incense and the barrier Simon's creating, we should be fine."

Just as Simon was returning from the entrance, the floorboards burst upward, sending nails and splinters showering all over the living room. Ducking his head beneath his arms, Anthony peered over them to see a massive, gray creature pull itself up from the new hole in his floor.

"What the hell is that thing?" Anthony cried, springing away from the table. Emily backed away with him toward the kitchen sink, her grip tightening on her cross.

That thing looked like a winged snake. Its head brushed the ceiling as it rose, its black scales shining ominously, flicking its razor sharp tongue.

"You guys stay back!" Simon shouted, swiping a hand over his cross. With a puff of white smoke, a long blade extended from the top.

"H-how did he do that?" Anthony asked Karin, who carried her plate of pancakes with her. "That thing with the cross?"

"It's white magic," she replied, hopping onto the

kitchen counter. "He's an exorcist. Fighting demons like this one is his specialty."

"And that freaky snake thing is a *demon?*" He gaped at the demon, watching Simon and Drea dodging its flailing tail, smashing the wall around it.

The demon let out a menacing hiss and lunged toward Simon, baring its fangs. He ducked beneath its head before it could strike, slashing the side of its neck with his sword. Green goo splattered out of the monster's wound, gushing onto the floor. Springing upon the table, Drea withdrew her gun and fired at the demon. It howled and thrashed in pain, smoke rising from the holes in its body.

With an ear-splitting crack, a second snakelike monster broke through the kitchen floorboards. Tossing her plate aside, Karin dove to the ground with Anthony and Emily to avoid Drea's gunshots, but the bullets slid off the demon's slippery scales. Letting out an angry hiss, the demon smashed its tail against the wall and cabinets, debris raining from the ceiling. Anthony covered his head with his arms to protect against the falling plates.

"I got the first one," Drea shouted to Simon. "You take this one."

Simon took one last swing at the first demon before ripping off his shirt, revealing numerous scars scattered about his torso. Cringing, a pair of bat wings ripped through the skin of his shoulder blades, smoke and blood seeping from his torn flesh.

"H-he can do that?" Anthony stammered, scampering after Emily and Karin toward the entrance.

Simon swooped down upon the slithering demon before it could attack. The blade of his cross glowed white, slicing through the demon's neck.

"That's freaking nasty!" Anthony exclaimed, the demon's head tumbling to the floor before him. He pinched his wrinkled nose shut to block the stench of the beheaded demon, green blood and smoke spewing from its wound.

"Nasty? I just saved your life!" Simon huffed, tossing his hair. "It didn't hurt any of you guys, did it?"

Before anyone could answer, the first demon lunged from behind. Just as Simon spun around to face it, the demon punctured his shoulder with its sharp tongue. He dropped to his knees, clutching his wound. "Dammit, Drea! I thought you had this one!"

"I was reloading!" Drea shouted, rushing into the entrance.

Suddenly, the front door flung open. With her bat wings outstretched, a young woman dove onto the demon snake, slicing off its head with one swift swing of her glowing cross sword. Blood rained from the demon's severed neck. The woman landed on her feet, her face veiled by the longer side of her asymmetrical hair. She swiped a gloved hand over the blade of the cross, and it retracted into the wood.

While Anthony was thankful for the woman's sudden appearance, he couldn't help but cringe and keep his nose pinched shut. Smoke reeking of decayed flesh emitted from her wings as they folded, shrinking and sinking back into her shoulder blades. Her scarred skin sealed over them without a single drop of blood escaping her body.

Kneeling beside Simon, she asked, "Are you okay?"

"Yeah," Simon said. Tucking a strand of purple highlights behind her pointed ear, he kissed her and squeezed her hand. "It hardly even scratched me." He smiled and ran a hand down the side of her neck, over her leather collar, their red eyes meeting. "Thanks for the backup, Sakura."

Sakura did not return the smile. "Why are you bleeding beneath your wings?"

"They're fine," Simon said, flinching. Buckling over in pain, his wings sank back into his body, more blood dripping from his torn flesh until it sealed. "I just haven't used them in a while and my skin got weak. That's all."

Sakura rose, crossing her arms beneath her black crop top. She peered down at the demon corpses, their blood pooling around her boots. "Well, looks like I got here at just the right time. I take it you're Anthony?"

Anthony nodded, his words lost in his trembling jaw. He placed a hand over his racing heart, still shaken by the ambush.

"Erika was telling me about you in the car." She looked to Emily and smiled. "And you must be Emily. Pleasure to finally meet you."

Emily narrowed her eyes and mouthed, "Eden filth."

"Well done!" Erika said. "You guys kick ass!" Stepping over the dead monsters with caution in her stilettos, she waved her hand in front of her wrinkled nose. "Ugh, but could you find a less gross way to kill them?"

"These two were oddly resistant to bullets," Drea said, scratching her temple. She shook her head and sighed, heading back to the kitchen. "I gotta grab my backpack and bandage Simon."

"I don't need your help," Simon spat. "They're just scratches."

"Let her do her job," Sakura said, ruffling Simon's hair.

"Wh-what the hell was all that?" Anthony stammered. He dropped to the floor, his shaky knees giving out. "Those monsters, my house—"

"Relax," Erika said. "It's all over now. I already called my people to clean up the mess and repair any damage before your people see it. It'll be like nothing ever happened."

I'll still remember *what happened,* Anthony thought, struggling to control his breathing "Those demon things—"

"Chimeras, to be precise," Sakura said. "Bits and pieces of animals fused together to house a demon soul. Making freak creations with magic is what Lucifer's Disciples does best."

Anthony furrowed his brow. "Who?"

"They are the cult of black mages that are usually responsible for any demonic occurrence," Emily said. "They happen to be the ones who took my soul for whatever purpose they have." She stared down at her shoes. "They also placed a silencing spell to prevent me from telling Eden any personal secrets, including information about my family's history and my death."

"That's annoyingly convenient for them," Drea said, bandaging Simon's wounds.

Karin narrowed her eyes. "I don't get how they could make such a specific spell. I didn't think it was even possible."

"And I don't get how they made it through the barrier I made," Simon said.

"It must have not been strong enough," Sakura said, holding her chin. "Those monsters get tougher and tougher with each one they send."

"So, there's stronger ones out there?" Anthony asked, his eyes widening.

It disturbed him when the Eden members all exchanged dark laughs.

"Just because I said *tougher*," Sakura said, "doesn't mean these ones were exactly what we call *tough*. Chimeras are the lowest ranking monsters, used for the dirty work."

"And more of these monsters will be attacking to get Emily away from us?" Anthony asked, hoping this wasn't true.

"A *lot* more," Erika said. "The chimeras attacking is a sign that Lucifer's Disciples knows that Emily is awake and is in your house, meaning your home is no longer safe. And now that she's away from Mavro Manor's spiritual barriers, they'll do anything they can to steal her away from us. They want her undead and asleep for a reason, so her being awake is a major threat to them."

"Then why can't we just go to Mavro Manor to

continue our investigation?" Karin asked.

"Mavro Manor is off-limits for investigations," Erika said, shaking her head, "and I can't let you guys stay at headquarters since non-members like Anthony aren't allowed in, but I can move you into a safe house owned by Eden. I want you all to continue the investigation there and I want a report every night on any findings about how Emily is able to stay awake around Anthony, anything about her past that might be of interest to Lucifer's Disciples—got it?"

"Got it," Sakura answered, giving her a thumbs-up.

"Great. You guys are awesome." Erika turned to leave, but stopped in the doorway, directing a sweet smile at Emily. "Most importantly, don't let any demons get their hands on our little princess."

CHAPTER 8

~~

"I know I told you the other day that we'd be working together," Olivia said, resting her elbow on the door of the SUV, "but I didn't expect us to be housemates."

"Neither did I," Anthony muttered, peering out the window at his house from the back of the car. Emily sat between them, playing Anthony's handheld video game console. "They told us they'd meet us in the car a half hour ago. What's taking so long?"

"Simon's probably changing your aunt and uncle's memories to make up some excuse for your absence," Olivia said.

Anthony looked to her with narrowed eyes. "What do you mean by changing their memories?"

"It's a white magic skill some exorcists use. Implanting memories, erasing them—how else do you think Eden manages to keep any sort of major paranormal occurrence secret from the public?"

Anthony stared back outside. "Like those freaky snake chimera things?"

"I heard about that," Olivia said. "It's pretty rare for Lucifer's Disciples to send demons that big to someone's house, especially to an outsider like you. It's no wonder why Erika's moving us off their radar."

"I guess the fact that you guys are hanging around Emily is pissing them off, because I didn't have any issues with them until today."

Emily tapped Anthony's shoulder with the console. "What is wrong with it? The screen turned black."

Anthony took the console from her and flipped the power switch. "Batteries are dead."

"The what?"

"It has no power in it. You need to plug it into the wall when you're done playing with it so it can have more power in it when you want to play. Get it?"

Emily pursed her lips. "So I cannot play with it now?"

"Nope."

Emily groaned and tossed her head back. "But I was so close to unlocking the next level."

"You can unlock it later." He watched Simon exit the house and sit on the doorway steps, lighting a cigarette. "So what's the deal with Simon and his girlfriend?"

"What do you mean?" Olivia asked. She glanced out the window and waved to Simon.

He responded by holding up a hand and saying, "Five minutes," his voice muffled by the car windows.

Anthony cringed, recalling the battle scene in his house. "Earlier today, when they were fighting the chimeras, these big bat wings grew out of their backs. And their eyes are red and their ears are pointy."

"Oh, right, sorry," Olivia said with a chuckle. "I forget they aren't completely normal to outsiders."

Anthony raised his brow. *If she thinks they're normal, then what does she consider weird?*

"They're Phobia," Olivia said. "Demons in human bodies, kind of like the chimeras. Lucifer's Disciples makes them to fight against Eden, since demons can't survive on Earth very long without a vessel, like a chimera or human."

"So they're evil?" Anthony asked, his heart beating

faster.

Olivia shook her head. "They used to work for Lucifer's Disciples, but left them for us. I guess you can say they're among the few demons with a moral compass and wanted to repent for all the horrible things they did. Granted, it took a lot of effort for them to learn white magic since it's powered by heavenly entities, and even more effort to convince Eden that they aren't double agents, but now they're among the strongest exorcists Eden has."

"That's some dedication," Anthony said. "Are they kind of like possessed?"

"Not quite. A possessed person has a demon in their body while still holding onto their original human soul— more of a parasitic relationship. To become a Phobia, a human loses its soul through a black magic ritual to create room for the demon. Because a Phobia only has a demon inside the human vessel, the demon can freely manipulate the body to use its powers. They're not nearly as strong as if they were in hell since no demon can truly be at full capacity on Earth, but they're still pretty powerful." When she noticed Sakura, Drea, and Karin approaching the car, Olivia sat up straighter and unlocked the doors.

Sakura opened the door to the driver's seat. "Thanks for waiting. You all doing okay?"

"The game machine does not work," Emily grumbled.

"You can borrow mine if you want," Karin said, she and Drea taking the middle seats. She unzipped her backpack, pulled out her pink gaming console, and handed it to Emily.

Emily's jaw dropped. "Can I play the same game as I was earlier?"

"I'll hook you up," Anthony said, taking the console from her to switch the games.

Once Simon was settled in the passenger's seat, Sakura drove to an isolated house nestled upon a hill. It appeared to be like any other house with fresh green grass and blooming flowers bordering the exterior. Nothing indicative of Eden nor paranormal phenomena.

"Here we are," Sakura said, parking the car in the driveway. "Our new home for the time being."

However long that will be, Anthony thought, following the others inside. Despite being annoyed about being dragged away from home, this house was far cleaner than his own, more welcoming, and attractive. It was refreshing to see a kitchen free of empty beer bottles and crusty pizza boxes. *As long as no creepy monsters attack us, this might not be that bad.*

"I didn't know Eden had such nice houses for investigations," Olivia said, surveying the kitchen and family room. "I always heard they're pretty dinky and cramped."

"Erika hooked us up with a good one this time," Drea said, setting her suitcase on the wood floor of the kitchen. "I'd like to say it's because we're a larger group, but it's probably to honor Emily."

"Mavro Manor is still better," Emily muttered.

"Can't we make the best of things?" Anthony asked. "It sure beats staying at my place."

"You mean that tiny excuse for a room?" She curled her lip and shivered. "Anything beats that."

"Alright, so there's enough rooms upstairs for everyone to share with one other person," Simon said, leaning against the granite counter. "Sakura and I will share the master bedroom, the rest is free game."

Karin glared at Sakura, then smiled at Emily. "Then I'll take her." She snatched Emily's wrist with one hand and lugged her suitcase in the other.

"Meet back here when you're done unpacking," Simon said. "I'm taking us all out to dinner."

"W-wait!" Emily stammered, struggling to keep up with Karin. "I do not know if I—"

"We're gonna have so much fun rooming together," Karin interrupted, dragging Emily up the stairs and into one of the bedrooms. "I've never been on an investigation where I had to stay overnight somewhere. I'm glad I get to room with someone my age."

"I see." Emily smoothed her skirt and sat on the edge of her bed. "You are quite young to be working for Eden."

"I don't really work for them yet," Karin said, tossing her luggage onto her bed. "I'm not able to officially work until I'm an adult, but I already know I want to become an investigator and exorcist. Simon told me he'd teach me white magic a while ago, but he hardly teaches me anything or lets me help him on investigations. All I ever get to do is burn incense or sprinkle holy water." She unzipped her bag. A wooden cross sat upon her folded clothes. Gazing at it, she sighed. "He always says stuff like I'm too young and that I'm not ready to fight demons."

"He probably says that because he is worried you will get hurt."

Karin's eyes lit up. "You think he worries about me?"

"I would assume so," Emily said. "I cannot speak for him, but it seems likely."

Karin grinned in satisfaction and continued unpacking her suitcase, organizing her clothes into her dresser. "I hope you're right. I really like him. But he likes *Sakura*." She glanced back at Emily, who remained seated on the bed. "Don't you have a luggage?"

"This is all I have," Emily said, running her hands over her skirt. "I was not planning on joining this investigation, so I am a bit unprepared."

"We're about the same size. You can totally borrow my clothes."

Emily peered over at the collection of graphic t-shirts and miniskirts Karin folded into her dresser. "I am not sure if they will suit me."

Karin gasped and clapped her hands together. "Oh my God, we should totally go shopping! I bet you haven't been to a mall before."

Emily didn't say anything, hoping her silence would change the subject.

"So, were you part of Eden?" Karin asked, returning to her unpacking.

"My parents were. They tried to keep me away from it, though."

"That's so weird. I can't imagine anyone not wanting to be part of Eden. It's seriously the best thing ever." She sat on her own bed across from Emily.

"Do your parents work for Eden?" Emily asked.

"They don't. I never met my parents. They gave me up for adoption when I was really young. I don't know much about them, just that they weren't able to take care of me."

"I am sorry."

"Don't be," Karin said with a shrug, "because I'm actually really happy they gave me away. Eden sometimes recruits new members by picking up orphaned kids to join their school. Drea started the same way. Not having a family makes it a lot easier to hide your identity." She beamed. "I'm so thankful they chose me. I get to meet so many cool people, including you!"

A nervous smile spread across Emily's face.

Meanwhile, Anthony lay on his bed underneath the open window. Despite the large number of people staying in the house, it was much quieter than his ever was. He hoped that by rooming alone, he would have time to relax while the Eden investigators did whatever it was that they were planning to do.

He sat up at the sound of a knock on his closed door. "Come in."

The door opened and Olivia entered the room, avoiding his gaze. "Hey, um, just wanted to see if you were settled in and stuff."

"Uh, yeah," Anthony said. He wasn't sure who he was

expecting at the door, but Olivia was not it. "I'm settled."

"That's good. Drea is still working on her side of the room. I figured I'd give her some space." She clutched the bottom of her striped cardigan. "You're not mad at me, are you? For letting them drag you here?"

"This is kind of the opposite of a problem," Anthony said with a chuckle. "I'm excused from school and I'm away from my family. It's like vacation."

Her lips smiled, but her eyes were dull. "I'm glad you feel that way." She glanced at the ceiling, then to Anthony. "It's warm in here. There's a balcony outside Simon and Sakura's room. Do you mind if we talk there? They're both downstairs."

"Uh, yeah, sure." He followed her down the hall to Simon and Sakura's room, and through the glass door leading to the balcony.

Olivia leaned against the railing. "We're safer talking out here. The house is bugged."

"Oh," Anthony said, taking a seat in one of the plastic chairs. "I didn't realize paranormal investigators had such tight security."

"Eden is different," Olivia said. "While we are secret to most, we technically work for the government. They know we're here, but they usually try to stay away from our business. As long as we keep the paranormal out of the public eye, they let us do whatever we want."

"It's pretty cool that you get to be part of something so important."

Olivia laughed. "Being the cleaning girl of my family's mansion is of no importance. I'm worth nothing to Eden or the Mavro family. The only reason I'm on this mission is because Erika's too busy to stick around."

"I don't think that's true," Anthony said. "I'm sure your family cares about you." Though the words felt like a lie as he thought of his own family.

Olivia shook her head. "My father used to be lead exorcist and is now the chairman of Eden's west coast branch. I think I've only spoken to him in person about three times in my life because he's too busy for me. My older brother Spencer is heir to my father's position, and Erika is investigations manager. Another family monopolizes the other departments. My parents have no use for a third child, so they just make me take care of Mavro Manor. That's why I live in Kent, so I can be close. My mother lives with me, but now that I'm older, she spends most of her time at headquarters in Seattle."

Anthony was speechless.

Olivia rested her arms on the railing, holding her chin in her palm. "Being rich is the only good thing this family ever gave me, and my popularity at school is all I have to keep me going." She tucked her hair behind her ear, keeping it out of the cool spring breeze. "It's sad, though. None of my school friends can know the real me, and I'm not that close with anyone at Eden since I don't hang out at headquarters much. I only handle issues specifically related to Mavro Manor, but I don't even know much about it or Emily."

"To be fair, it doesn't seem like anyone from Eden knows much about this case," Anthony said. "Not to defend your family or anything, but if they need a whole investigation on Emily's death, then I doubt even your sister or dad know."

"I guess you're right. My family is so weirdly secretive, all the answers probably got lost over time." She sighed. "But I don't really care. Once I turn eighteen, I'm ditching them and Eden so I can live a normal life in the normal world."

Anthony raised his eyebrows. "Are you sure? You think Eden sucks, but things aren't much better anywhere else."

Olivia paused for a moment before she spoke again. "I don't know. People in the normal world are too nice. Too naïve. Once you know what's in the shadows, it's hard to forget."

Anthony rose from his seat and stood beside her, peering out at the nearby forest. "Maybe you should stop comparing yourself to your family. So what if they're all powerful and you're not? That doesn't mean you're worthless."

Olivia peered at him from the corner of her eye.

"I know what it's like to feel like you have no spot in the world," Anthony said. "My parents are in jail, my aunt and uncle treat me like crap, and I only hang around those losers at school because they're people to get high with so I can forget all my problems. You actually have the potential to have an awesome life if you just change your mentality."

For a while, she just stared at him in silence, her lips slightly parted. She appeared as if she had something to say, and Anthony was eager to hear her response, but they were called to leave for dinner before she could speak.

CHAPTER 9

~~

Inside the restaurant, Anthony took a seat between Emily and Olivia at the first available table to accommodate their large group. Chandeliers and fancy white columns created an exotic feel when paired with the framed photos of Greek islands and ethnic background music. While the others looked over their menus, Anthony was distracted by the other customers sitting around them. Though he wished to feel safe in the company of his new companions, the demon attack from the morning left him with persistent anxiety. At the sight of something sliding toward him, he flinched, then blushed when he saw it was just a glass of water.

"Good evening," the waitress said, passing the rest of the glasses around the table. "Welcome to Yianni's. Would you like anything else to drink?" Brushing brown hair behind her ear, she grinned at Simon.

"Bring a bottle of your finest wine to the table, sweetheart," Simon said.

The waitress giggled and blushed. "Anything else?"

"We're good, thanks," Sakura said, glaring at Simon.

"I'll be right back then," the waitress said. She winked at Simon before walking back to the kitchen.

"You can't call the waitress *sweetheart*!" Sakura whispered, punching his arm.

"She started it," Simon said. "I was just playing off of her vibes to get quicker table service."

"Right." Sakura rolled her eyes.

Simon squeezed Sakura's knee and smirked. "Are you mad at me?"

Sakura buried her face in her menu. "Shut up. I'm trying to pick something."

"You *are* mad." He kissed the tip of her ear. "I love you."

"Simon," Karin said, scowling at Sakura over her menu, "she says she's trying to pick something. Just leave her alone."

Simon shrugged and picked up his menu.

But at the jingling of the bell on the front door, his attention was drawn to the entrance.

"Shoot!" Simon murmured, averting his gaze from the customers entering the restaurant.

"What is it?" Anthony asked.

"Don't look at them," Simon whispered. "Everyone, act natural and don't bring up anything *weird*."

Anthony couldn't help but peek at the customers. Two teenage girls in fluffy black dresses walked to a nearby table, their pigtails bouncing with each step. He noticed Simon was sneaking glances at them, too.

"Simon," Anthony whispered, leaning over the table to talk to him, "who are those girls?"

"The one with the pink hair is Thalia," Simon said, "and the green-haired one is her sister Anita. They're Phobia, like me and Sakura. Lucifer's Disciples probably sent them here to catch Emily."

"I thought demons don't usually attack in public areas," Olivia said.

"If they are desperate, Lucifer's Disciples will attack anywhere," Emily said, staring down at her folded hands. "Given I was behind a barrier for the past hundred years, I am sure they are thrilled I left."

"What do we do?" Anthony asked, peering around the table. "Should we leave?"

"No," Simon said. "They'll follow us if we leave right away. We can't let them know we saw them."

"With hair like that, they're pretty hard to miss."

"Right? It kinda makes me mad how cute they are," Karin grumbled. "Eden doesn't give us cute outfits like that."

"They won't be cute if they start attacking us," Anthony muttered.

"If we stay here and act casual, they may just leave us all alone," Sakura said, also glancing at the Phobia girls. "They might just be spying on us."

"I don't know about that," Drea said. "Thalia and Anita are pretty high up in Lucifer's Disciples. If they only wanted to spy, they would've sent out someone else." She looked to Simon. "We should leave. If they do attack, all these people in the restaurant will not only be in danger, but they will be witnesses to demonic activity. That will be a lot of memories to erase."

"We're staying," Simon said, his tone unwavering. "Best thing for us to do now is be quiet so they don't overhear us. Then, once we finish eating, we leave, hang around downtown for a little while, then go home. We have to shake them off to get on the safe side."

"That is such a horrible plan," Drea grumbled, massaging her temples. "I have no idea why Eden even lets you do investigations when you practically throw yourself at the enemy."

"I'm not *throwing* myself at the enemy," Simon huffed. "I know what I'm doing."

Drea rolled her eyes. "I sure hope so because they're coming over to us right now."

Simon turned around, smirking at the approaching Phobia girls.

"Well, if it isn't the *traitors*," Thalia cackled. "Long time, no see."

"It has been a while," Simon said, leaning back in his chair. "I liked it that way."

Thalia smirked. Seizing a knife from her belt, she threw it at Simon's head. With amazing speed, Simon caught the knife between the prongs of his fork. He and Thalia exchanged glares. Whispers and gasps hissed through the restaurant, all eyes on the Phobia.

Jumping to his feet, Simon removed his cross from his belt. "Drea, you and Olivia get everyone in the restaurant outside, and take Karin with you." He waved his hand over the cross, releasing the blade. "Sakura and I will handle the chicks."

"Wh-what should I do?" Anthony stammered.

Neither Simon nor Sakura answered. Instead, they transformed their crosses into swords, snarling at the enemy Phobia.

Thalia giggled. "So, that's how you want to play?"

Withdrawing black batons from their belts, the Phobia girls swiped their hands over them. The batons extended into poles and blades, each forming a scythe. Wielding their weapons, neither girl even flinched at the screams of the panicked customers, nor from the pain of their bat wings ripping through their flesh.

Simon smirked. "Let's play." Raising a gloved hand, a spark of white light shot from his palm, zapping Thalia between her eyes.

Thalia's hands flew to her face, her weapon clanging against the floor. She rubbed her eyes, grumbling and cursing under her breath, smudging her thick eyeliner.

Gritting her teeth, Anita's grasp on her scythe tightened. She sprang toward Simon, raising her scythe above her head, ready to attack. Ducking beneath the blade, Simon shoved Anita into the wooden legs of a table, knocking aside several chairs. Before Anita could rise, Sakura pounced upon her, pinning Anita's wrists to the floor.

"A little help, Thalia?" Anita groaned, struggling beneath Sakura's grasp.

"I can't see!" Thalia cried. "Everything's blurry!" Feeling her way between tables, silverware rattled and glasses of water toppled over.

Emily grabbed Anthony's hand. "Come on!"

"Where are we going?" he asked, for they were running in the opposite direction of Olivia and Drea, who ushered the panicked customers out of the restaurant.

"Anywhere they cannot find us," Emily replied.

"Don't think you can escape me!" Thalia yelled, stumbling after them. Reaching out, she shot a smoky substance from her palms. Due to her weakened eyesight, she hit the wall above Anthony's head, leaving a crusty black smudge on the white paint.

"Holy crap!" Anthony cried, ducking. "What was that?"

"Shadow magic," Emily said. "It is a form of black magic. The shadows freeze whatever they touch. If they hit your chest or head, you will die within seconds."

"You freaking kidding me?"

Pushing through the doors, Emily led Anthony into the empty kitchen and released his hand.

"We should be safe for now," Emily said.

Anthony backed away from the doors and remained silent for a moment, listening to the crashing sounds coming from within the restaurant. "Do you think Simon and Sakura will be okay?" he whispered.

"I am sure they will be fine," Emily said, leaning against one of the counters. "Eden's exorcists know how to handle demons, and I doubt those frilly girls will put up much of a fight."

But when the kitchen doors flung open, Emily's eyes widened, realizing she had spoken too soon.

"Don't move!" Anita shouted. Marching toward

Anthony, she brandished her scythe. "Give me Emily, and I won't have to kill you."

Anthony froze, praying for Sakura or Simon to save him. Emily, however, remained calm. Taking a butcher knife from the wall, she stepped in front of Anthony and pointed it at Anita, brimming with confidence.

"E-Emily?" Anthony stammered, his face turning white. "What are you doing?"

"Seriously," Anita laughed. "What are you doing? You think you can fight me with a mere kitchen utensil?"

"Of course not," Emily said with a smile. "I was not planning on it." Reaching behind her neck, she unfastened her cross necklace. She wrapped the chain around the blade of the knife, the cross dangling from the tip. "This necklace is made entirely of silver. While the knife itself will not be enough to kill you, it can tear open your flesh. Once the silver touches your wound, you will burn, slowly and painfully."

"I—I don't think this a good idea," Anthony whispered. "We should really leave the fighting to Eden."

"I can fight on my own," Emily said, lifting her nose. "I do not need protection. I just need to protect *you*." She glanced at him from over her shoulder. "If you die, I die with you."

Anita raised her scythe and smirked. "At least this will be quick. I hate fighting."

Emily charged, her small frame ducking beneath Anita's swinging scythe. Anthony's hands flew to his face, dreading the worst, but in the blink of an eye, the knife was deep in Anita's shoulder. Shrieking in pain, black smoke curled from Anita's wound, an audible sizzle crackling from her burning flesh.

"Holy crap!" Anthony cried. "You just freaking stabbed her!"

"No need to be so surprised," Emily said, pulling her knife out of Anita's shoulder. "I told you I could."

"Dammit!" Anita roared. Before she could strike, Sakura flew into the kitchen, crashing through a rack of pots and pans, and knocked Anita to the ground.

"Stay down!" Sakura shouted, pointing one of the kitchen knives at the back of Anita's head. "Don't say anything. Simon is finishing off your sister as I speak. If you surrender quietly, I'll just take you to Eden headquarters for questioning."

"I may hate fighting," Anita grumbled, "but I never surrender!" Seizing Sakura's arm, Anita stole the knife, thrusting it into Sakura's throat.

Coughing up blood, Sakura's trembling hands reached for the knife, but her strength gave out before she could even touch the handle, her body tumbling to its side.

Anthony gaped at Sakura in shock. He couldn't feel his legs, but Anita was approaching. He had to run.

"It will be okay," Emily whispered to him, holding out her knife. "Just trust me."

Taking a deep breath, Emily was about to attack again, but came to a halt at the sound of a gunshot. Anita's limp body dropped to the floor beside Sakura's, blood trickling from the side of her head.

"I didn't think that'd work so easily," Drea said, leaping over the bodies. "You guys must have really worn her out. One tranquilizer is never enough to knock out a Phobia of her strength."

"Thanks," Anthony mumbled. "Sakura is, uh. . ."

Drea knelt down next to Sakura and felt her wrist and neck. "Don't worry, she'll be fine."

"How? I'm sure you've noticed, but there's a knife in her neck."

"It takes a lot more than that to kill a Phobia," Karin said, entering the kitchen with Olivia. "Simple blades like kitchen knives won't do the trick."

"What's up, guys?" Simon ran into the kitchen, shirt

torn, his disheveled hair caked with blood. "Thalia put up quite a fight."

"Did you kill her?" Drea asked.

"Not totally. She's just knocked out. Figured I'd leave her for the higher ups to deal with at headquarters. What about her?" He pointed to Anita.

"I knocked her out as well. But she got Sakura first."

Wiping the blood from the corner of his lip, Simon flinched at the blood pooling around Sakura's head. He knelt beside Drea and held Sakura by her shoulders. "I think she'll be okay after a couple days."

"She definitely needs to go to the hospital," Drea said.

"Yeah, I'll give Eden a call right now."

"Only a couple days?" Anthony said.

"We heal way faster than humans," Simon said, pulling out his cell phone. "For better or for worse, it's why Eden values us. It's awfully convenient for them to have exorcists who can endure wounds fatal to humans and recover ten times faster."

While Simon listened to the dial tone on his phone, the door behind him drifted open. Creeping toward him, Thalia raised her scythe, ready to swing.

"Simon!" Karin screamed, pointing at the approaching demon.

Sakura's eyes snapped open. Pushing away from Simon, she jumped to her feet. Dodging the scythe blade, white light shot from Sakura's palms, blasting Thalia several feet away into one of the metal counters. Thalia's weapon slipped from her grasp, skidding to the opposite corner of the room, the blade and pole sinking back into the baton. Thalia's eyes met Sakura's before she rose, dashing to retrieve the baton, but Sakura snatched it first. Waving her hand over the baton, Sakura transformed it back into a scythe, twirling it in her grasp a few times before directing the blade at Thalia.

Raising her hand, smoke formed at Thalia's palm.

"Give that back!"

Before Thalia could use her magic, Sakura slashed the scythe blade through Thalia's forearm, slicing it clean from her elbow.

Thalia dropped to the her knees, screaming and clutching her wound, blood squirting between her fingers. Her severed limb evaporated into a cloud of black smoke the moment it hit the floor. Without even the slightest wince of pain, Sakura tossed the scythe aside and pulled the knife out of her throat, thrusting it into Thalia's left eye.

"The eye was for the crap your sister put me through," Sakura snarled over Thalia's cries, "and the arm for hurting Simon."

"Damn it all!" Thalia shouted. She tried to stand, but she was too weak to support her own weight.

"I wouldn't try fighting if I were you," Simon said, shaking his head. "You've been defeated."

"You'll regret this!" Thalia spat, grabbing Anita by her dress collar. With a puff of black smoke, she and her sister disappeared, the knife falling from where Thalia's head once was and hitting the ground with a metallic clink.

"Is it over?" Anthony whispered, peering around at the others.

"Yeah," Simon said. He scratched his head. "Should have put up a barrier so they couldn't escape, but oh well. At least they're gone."

"Well, this was quite the disaster," Drea said with a sigh. "Everyone who was here earlier witnessed enough of that fight to cause problems for Eden."

"It'll be fine," Simon said. "The important thing is that everyone is safe."

~~

Anita and Thalia knelt on the cold cement of a

dungeon, lit by black candles. Sketches of magic circles were scribbled across the walls in white chalk and blood. Shelves holding spell books and jars containing murky potions bordered the four corners of the large room. A cluttered table was placed at the front of the room, where a robed figure sat in a large wooden chair, his bald head covered by his hood.

"That damn traitor!" Thalia spat. "How dare she rip off my limb? She'll *pay*!"

"Seriously, Thalia," Anita said, rolling her eyes, "it's just an arm. We'll find you a new one. It's not like she cut off your head. You should be glad that's the only wound you received. I sure don't want to fight exorcists of their caliber again."

"If you think they're so strong," Thalia said, "why did you think stabbing her in the throat would help at all?"

"It did. She was immobilized from the pain."

"And you fell from a simple tranquilizer!"

"Enough!" the figure roared. He pointed a black, scaled finger at the girls. "Both of you performed pathetically! That was an insult to the pride of Lucifer's Disciples!"

"We're truly sorry, Lord ZuZu, sir!" Thalia and Anita cried, both bowing before him. "We'll try harder next time!"

ZuZu glared at the girls. "Did you find the Mavro girl's current location?"

"No, sir," Thalia mumbled, squeezing the stump she had left for an arm.

"Send out a bat to hunt her down," ZuZu said. He narrowed his eyes. "I think it'd be useful to have some additional surveillance on her. We can't let Eden break her spell."

"I'm on it!" Anita said, rushing over to a cage filled with bats.

"Lord ZuZu, sir?" Thalia said. "Is there anything I can do to help?"

"Yes," ZuZu said. "Leave my dungeon. I'd like to be

left alone to finish today's work." He strolled to the center of the room to an enormous pentagram, his black robes trailing behind him. In the center of the star lay the naked body of an unconscious human boy. Reaching into his robes, he withdrew a dagger and pointed it at his right eye. "Soon, Project Rundull will be complete."

CHAPTER 10

~~

After a long day of demonic encounters, Anthony was relieved to be back in the protection of the safe house. The warmth of a home never felt so welcoming at his own place, and while he watched the Eden members prepare to leave again, he couldn't wait to enjoy the peace and quiet in his bedroom.

"I've gotta go back to headquarters with Drea and Sakura to pick up some important files about my family," Olivia told Anthony, meeting him at the bottom of the staircase. "It'll be useful to get some background info on Emily and her parents. Simon will stay behind to take care of you, Emily, and Karin. Will you be okay?"

"Yeah, I'll be fine," he said. "If I could handle demon chicks, I can handle anyone."

"Thanks again for putting up with our weirdness," Olivia said, buttoning her blazer. Clinging to the closet doorknob, she crammed her feet into a pair of heels.

"You look a lot fancier than usual," Anthony chuckled. "Do you always gotta dress up for Eden?"

Olivia wrinkled her nose. "Being the chairman's daughter, I'm expected to look all professional when I'm at headquarters. They don't care about me, but I guess I'm still supposed to care about how I present myself."

"Where exactly is your headquarters?"

"You ready to go?" Drea asked, waiting by the front door. "Sakura's already in the car."

"I'll explain some other time, okay?" After waving good-bye to Anthony, Olivia followed Drea out of the house.

Once the front door shut, Simon flopped onto the couch. "So, until Olivia gets back with those files, I've got nothing to do, other than babysitting you guys. Anyone got cool ideas for what we should do?"

He makes it sound like we're little kids, Anthony thought, taking a step closer to Emily. Standing by the stairs, she appeared more eager than he to escape, one hand already on the railing.

"We should make dinner, since we never actually got to eat at the restaurant," Karin said, opening the refrigerator.

Simon sat up. "Do we even have food? I highly doubt Erika went out of her way to make sure we got any."

Karin dug through the refrigerator and freezer. "There's some stuff." She gasped, pulling a red box out of the freezer. "Can we make mac n' cheese?"

"Yes!" Simon's voice rose with excitement. "Anthony, you want any?"

"I think I'll pass," Anthony said, backing onto the first stair step. "I, uh, I still have some stuff to unpack."

"Fine, don't join our macaroni party," Simon said with a shrug. "More for us."

"Emily, you should hang out with us," Karin said, beckoning to her. "I know you don't eat, but we could play a movie or something while we make dinner."

When Anthony reached the top of the stairs, he noticed she was following close behind.

"You aren't gonna hang out with Karin?" he asked.

Emily froze. "Um, well, I had something I wanted to talk to you about."

"What?"

Emily glanced down the stairs, then took Anthony's hand and marched him into his bedroom.

"Now can we talk?" Anthony asked, taking a seat on his bed.

Emily nodded. "What is it like to have friends?"

"What do you mean?"

"Karin wants to be my friend," Emily said, "but I do not know how to be a friend."

"It's easy. You just be yourself and be nice. It's not that hard. Didn't you have friends?"

Emily peered down at her feet. "Well—"

Anthony clapped his fist onto his palm. "I got it! You worked for Eden! That's why you didn't have friends and why those Lucifer people are after you!"

"What?" She laughed, avoiding his gaze. "I hate Eden. Why would you ever think I worked for them?"

"Because you stabbed that demon girl."

Emily crossed her arms under her chest. "It is not that hard to stab someone."

"You had your little cross trick, too."

"Everyone knows crosses harm demons." She turned up her nose. "You do not need to be a paranormal investigator to know that."

"You weren't even scared!" He threw his arms up in the air in exasperation. "No normal person would be that chill about any of this unless they worked for Eden."

"My parents both worked for Eden. It is only natural that I would be exposed to demons. I am sorry I developed a backbone over the years." She tossed her hair over one shoulder and smirked. "For someone who claims to know about friendship, I do not see you being friendly with any of these Eden people."

"Sorry, but I'm having trouble getting behind this whole exorcism thing," Anthony said. "It's like these people are from another dimension or something. Besides, it's just

Karin and Simon down there, and I feel like I'd be butting in on their weird friendship or whatever it is they have."

"She is *obsessed* with him," Emily grumbled, rolling her eyes. "It is so pathetic."

"I dunno, I think it's normal for a girl her age to like an older guy." He chuckled. "When I was thirteen, I had a huge crush on the girl that lived next door to me, and she was in college. I eventually got over her."

"And now you like Olivia."

Anthony blushed. "C'mon, you can't tell me that you never had an awkward crush."

"I do not have these *awkward crushes* you speak of!" Emily snapped. "I happen to care very little about boys or love!"

Anthony rose from the bed as Emily stormed out of the room. *I don't know what I was expecting her to say, but I definitely didn't expect her to flip out,* he thought, jumping in surprise at the sound of her bedroom door slamming shut. Closing his own door, he shook his head and sighed. *She totally has one.*

~~

When Anthony arrived at the breakfast table the next morning, Drea, Sakura, and Olivia still hadn't returned. After pouring himself a bowl of cereal, he sat next to Emily. Judging by the way she glared at something in the distance, her face wrinkled with frustration, he assumed she was forced to join them. Karin, meanwhile, kept an expectant eye on Simon, who typed away on his laptop, a cup of coffee beside him.

"Simon," Karin said, "can you please teach me more white magic today?"

"I don't think it'll be necessary," Simon said, taking a sip of coffee.

"But you said you'd teach me. That's why I'm here."

"Yeah, but now that Sakura's with us, there's no need for you to help."

Karin raised her voice. "She's *injured*. Drea and Olivia don't know white magic. You need another exorcist."

Simon didn't even glance at her. "Sakura will be better by tomorrow. It's not like we'll get attacked again today if we just stay home."

"If you teach me how to fight, I can help both of you so stuff like that doesn't happen."

"Stuff like that *will* happen. It'll happen to *you*. But if you get hurt, you won't recover as easily."

"But there are other human exorcists and they—"

Simon slammed his laptop shut. "Karin, you're fifteen freaking years old! You don't need to know how to use white magic yet!"

Karin's jaw quivered, but no words escaped her lips.

Anthony set down his spoon, afraid to take another bite. The tension between Simon and Karin was enough to suppress his appetite.

Emily cleared her throat. "From my understanding, it takes years to master white magic. Karin will be old enough to officially become an exorcist when she turns eighteen. The sooner she starts learning, the more prepared she will be." She smirked. "If you are so worried about her getting hurt, then you should start teaching her now so she can better protect herself in the future."

Simon glared at Emily, but she continued to smirk, keeping a steady gaze. He curled his fist and rose, his chair squeaking against the wood floor. "Fine." He jabbed a finger at Karin. "Go to the backyard. I gotta grab some gear. I'll meet you out there."

Karin was speechless, her eyes glowing with joy. Springing from her chair, she mouthed, "Thank you," to Emily before hurrying out the back door.

"I seriously thought Simon was about to yell at you," Anthony whispered to Emily. "You can't just butt into arguments like that."

Emily giggled and shrugged. "But it worked. I was just being a good friend."

~~

Later that afternoon, Anthony was sitting on the living room couch with Emily, teaching her how to play a game on his phone, when Drea, Sakura, and Olivia returned.

"How did it go?" Anthony asked.

"Great," Drea answered, helping Sakura onto the other couch. "She just needs to take a day off to rest. But as for you, young lady." She beckoned to Emily. "Come upstairs with me, please."

Emily eyed her with caution. "Why?"

"I have some tests I want to run on you."

"I am quite obviously undead. You should not have to use any tests to confirm that."

Drea blinked a few times before speaking again. "Emily. Please come upstairs."

"Just do it," Anthony muttered, nudging her arm. "She won't leave you alone unless you listen."

Emily pouted, stomping after Drea. Olivia waited for them by the stairs, holding an armful of brown folders. She glanced at Anthony before following Emily and Drea, leaving him alone with Sakura.

Something about being alone with one the Eden members was still unsettling to Anthony, especially with one that happened to be a demon. He hoped that if he looked preoccupied with his phone game, Sakura wouldn't speak to him. He was relieved to see that she seemed more intrigued by the window than him, but was a little nervous when she rose from the couch. Grasping onto the nearest piece of furniture, she shuffled to the window, peering outside at Karin and Simon. Karin was gazing in awe at the ball of white light she had conjured over her palms, while Simon gave her an encouraging pat on the back.

"He's actually teaching her," Sakura muttered with a smile. She glanced at Anthony and asked, "How much did she have to annoy him to get him to finally cave?"

"Emily's the reason they're out there," Anthony said, still glued the phone game. "He didn't seem to wanna do it, but then she managed to convince him otherwise. She has a way with words."

"She must," Sakura chuckled. "Simon's extremely protective of Karin."

"It sure seems that way. He got pretty upset when she was asking him to teach her white magic."

Sakura whipped around to face him, holding the couch for support. "He didn't hurt her, did he?"

"What?" Anthony looked up from his phone, surprised by her sudden movement. "No. He just kinda yelled. Is that like a thing that happens?"

Sakura let out a relieved sigh. "No, I'm just hoping it won't ever be. Simon and I may work for Eden, but we're still demons. Male Phobia are extremely aggressive. While Simon is better than how he used to be, he still has a horrible temper. Sometimes I fear that he'll revert to his old ways, but then I see him with Karin." She gazed out the window again, this time with a sad smile. Karin and Simon were both sitting in the grass, their laughter audible from inside. "She makes him feel human. She would never believe me if I told her I'm envious of her."

Anthony stuffed his phone in his pocket, peering up at Sakura with interest. "Aren't you Simon's girlfriend, though?"

"I am, but I'm also a Phobia. My acceptance means nothing to him. To be accepted by a human like Karin. . ." Taking a deep breath, she walked back to the couch. She rested her head against the arm and shut her eyes. "God, my head is still pounding. I can't imagine what it's like to be a human exorcist."

"If you were human, I think you'd be dead," Anthony said with an uneasy grin. "I'm still amazed that you've hardly been injured from that battle."

"Blades can't hurt demons, unless they are silver," Sakura said. "And because Lucifer's Disciples can't use white magic, Simon and I can't be easily killed by our enemies, making us the perfect warriors for Eden." She paused for a moment before asking, "You've seen our scars, right?"

"You mean the ones Simon has on his chest?" Anthony asked, recalling the battle in his house.

"And the ones on our hands." Sakura held out her bare palms, showing her discolored and scarred flesh. "We didn't have these scars until we joined Eden. Getting used to white magic took a toll on our bodies. Though gloves can help us hold holy objects, white magic comes from within and would literally burn us to perform."

"Then why bother?"

She stared at the ceiling in thought. "To put it simply, we wanted to be free. Free from Lucifer's Disciples, Satan, darkness—all things evil. We can't change what's in our souls, but we can change what's in our hearts." Sadness filled her misty eyes. "Of course, Eden wasn't so accepting at first. They thought we were double agents from Lucifer's Disciples. They couldn't believe two Phobia wanted to join. Luckily, things are a lot better now and we've gained Eden's respect."

At the sound of a scream from upstairs, Sakura and Anthony both jumped in surprise.

"That's Emily," Anthony said, rising to his feet.

Sakura motioned for him to sit down. "I'd give them some space. Drea's just trying to look at what's beneath Emily's bandages."

Anthony glanced up at the ceiling. "It sounds like she's

hurting her." Though he could hear Emily shouting, he couldn't make out her words. "I'm gonna go check it out."

"I'm sure she's fine," Sakura said, but Anthony ignored her and ran upstairs.

Before going to Drea and Olivia's room, he caught a glimpse of Emily slamming her bedroom door. While Drea was labeling a medicine bottle, Olivia sat on her bed, her face distorted with concern.

"What's going on?" Anthony asked.

"I was just taking a skin sample from her neck," Drea said. "She claims she can't tell me how she got her wound, so I'm sending this in to Eden's science department to get it looked at." She stuffed the bottle in her backpack and sighed. "Of course, now I get the pleasure of driving *back* to headquarters to deliver it."

Anthony peered down at the pile of white bandages on the floor. "So you took them off?"

Olivia rose and picked up the stack of files from her nightstand. Pausing in the doorway, she glanced over her shoulder at Anthony. Anthony took it as a signal to follow her and she led him into his bedroom.

"Have you seen her scars?" Olivia asked, dropping her voice to a whisper and shutting her bedroom door behind them. "The ones on her neck and her arms?"

"I haven't."

"Do you know how she got them? She wouldn't tell me and Drea."

Anthony shook his head. "Maybe it's because of that silencing spell Lucifer's Disciples put on her."

Olivia bit her lip, her gaze aiming past his ear. "I'm not an expert in black magic, but silencing spells *that* specific don't exist. Even if it did, any of the exorcists who've been near Emily would have sensed the spell on her, but that's not the case."

Anthony forced a smile. "Well, I'm sure it exists. She

wouldn't lie about that."

"Right," Olivia muttered. She sat on his bed, resting the files in her lap. "Has she at least told you anything about herself or her past, or is it all locked away by this *spell* she claims to have?"

Anthony thought for a moment, trying to recall all past conversations with Emily. "She said she didn't have any friends. I thought that was kinda weird. But I think that's it." He felt guilty talking about Emily behind her back, but he hoped he could trust Olivia. "She mentioned having a brother who was my age, but she never said anything else about him."

"Impossible." Opening one of the folders, she handed a sheet of paper to Anthony.

He read it, then reread it aloud. "Zalem Mavro. Born January 27, 1893. . . *Stillborn.*"

"That was Emily's older brother," Olivia said. "Well, he would have been if he lived."

"Okay, so who's the other one?"

"There is no other one."

"But that doesn't make sense. She said she had an older brother who. . ." He trailed off and narrowed his eyes. "You think she's lying?"

Olivia pulled out a few more documents. "Maybe not *lying.*" This time she looked Anthony in the eye. "I think she's crazy."

Anthony backed away. "That's a pretty hefty claim to make."

"It gets better." Olivia tried to bring him closer, waving the documents at him.

He snatched them and skimmed over the top sheet. "Emily Mavro, died May 15, 1910. Cause of death: unknown." He flipped to the other sheets. "Gabriel Mavro, died May 16, 1910. Cause of death: bullet to the head. Colette Mavro, died May 16, 1910. Cause of death: bullet to the head."

"Gabriel and Colette were Emily's parents. They both committed suicide the night after Emily's death," Olivia said. "I think her parents were crazy, too. I think something *made* them crazy."

"Yeah, the death of their daughter." He handed the papers back to Olivia. "That would make any parent crazy."

Olivia shook her head. "They didn't commit suicide until *after* Eden attempted to question them about Emily. Given that neither they nor Emily are willing to talk about the cause of her death, there's gotta be something more than just grief in play. Whatever it is, Emily's parents were compelled to take it to their graves."

CHAPTER 11

~~

When Drea returned from her second trip to Eden, Sakura and Olivia were preparing dinner in the kitchen while Anthony, Simon, and Karin read over the Mavro family profiles at the table.

"What a day," Drea groaned, hanging her coat in the closet. "I've had enough going back and forth. I'm so ready for some dinner."

"Is headquarters that far?" Anthony asked, sitting straighter with interest.

Drea shook her head and took a seat beside him. "It's not the distance; it's the people. When you're there all day long, it's pretty calm, but when you've been gone long enough for anyone to notice, they're all up in your business when you get back. It's like a big family reunion, except with people you see all the time. It seriously took me an hour just to get from the entrance to the health sciences department."

"And then once you get there, another hour of talking to Jason," Sakura said with a grin, preparing a salad.

"Oh, you know it. He was pretty excited to see the samples, though. He said he'll look at them as soon as he can." She turned to Simon and added, "He said he'll call you when he gets the results."

"Cool," Simon muttered, his eyes glued to the files.

Drea scooted closer, peering over Anthony's shoulder. "What are you guys reading?"

"Stuff about Emily's family," Simon replied.

"What do you think so far?" Olivia asked, placing a dish of pasta in the center of the table.

"I dunno. They're just profiles. They're worth the look, but they don't really reveal much about Emily's death."

"I thought the part about her parents' suicide was pretty fishy."

Simon tossed the files aside and scratched his temple. "Fishy, yeah, but unless we find evidence specifically stating what happened or hear it from someone who was there, you can't really draw much from it."

"Okay, then let's get Emily down here," Karin said, filling her plate.

"Don't even bother," Anthony said. "She's not gonna tell you guys anything. She's pretty sensitive when it comes to her death."

"She hasn't even left her room since I changed her bandages," Olivia said, glancing at the stairs.

"So we're gonna avoid talking to her because we don't want to hurt her feelings?" Simon asked with a laugh.

"What's under her bandages anyway?" Karin asked. "Like, what kind of scars?"

After bringing the rest of the food to the table, Sakura took her seat. "Guys, let's not talk about this right now. Let's enjoy our dinner, not worry about this Emily business."

No further mention of Emily was spoken for the rest of dinner, though Anthony continued to worry about her. He planned on talking to her before his evening shower, but while he made his way to the bathroom, he heard a voice coming from her room. Olivia's voice. He pressed his ear against the door and listened.

"I know you're not too happy to be here," he heard Olivia tell Emily. "I'm not too happy either. My family forced me to come."

Emily didn't answer. Anthony held his breath and listened for any sort of sound, but the bedroom was silent.

Olivia cleared her throat and said, "If you want to talk about anything that's troubling you, you can trust me. I won't tell the other Eden members."

"Why should I trust you?" Emily asked.

"Because I couldn't care less about Eden or their investigations. I just care about you." Her voice dropped almost to a whisper. "I used to visit you every week. That was my job, cleaning Mavro Manor. Even though we only met a few days ago, I always felt connected to you, more so than to my living family."

"That is odd."

"I guess it is," Olivia said with a small laugh. "I was always curious about you and your family. I know your past isn't that great. I've heard a lot about how your parents were very secretive. I read your profiles and I saw that they both killed themselves after you died. I'm not sure if you knew that, but. . . I'm sorry."

Emily paused for a couple seconds before speaking. "Do not be sorry. I hardly knew my parents. They were too busy with Eden to ever pay any attention to me."

More silence. Anthony could picture Emily's unsympathetic, expressionless face through the door.

"I know how you feel," Olivia whispered. "I hardly know my parents. My father lives at headquarters with my sister Erika. My mother lives with me away from headquarters, but she's pretty busy, too. I've never even met my brother. No one really has."

Anthony's eyes widened when he heard Olivia sniffling.

"My mother said he was born with an illness," Olivia said between hiccups. "I don't know exactly what it is, but it makes him very weak, so my father decided it would be best to keep him in hiding. He's afraid of Lucifer's Disciples killing him so he can't become Eden's next leader. He doesn't even want my brother at headquarters and doesn't want anyone to see him other than the maids that take care of him. Not even my mother can visit him. It's sad not being able to meet your own brother. . ." She trailed off, snorting back snot.

Anthony backed away from the door. His heart grew heavier in his chest after hearing Olivia cry. He wished he could open the door and do whatever he could to cheer her up, but he had to keep listening.

"I heard you had an older brother, too. Zalem. I don't know if your parents told you about him. I read he was stillborn. "

He pressed his ear to the door again, awaiting Emily's response.

"Yes," Emily said after a deep breath. "I suppose I never felt sad about him since we never met. The thought of him never even crossed my mind." Her tone was cold and monotonous. "I am sorry about your family, but I do not think we can truly relate. We may both be part of the Mavro family, but we are very, *very* different."

"I guess, but—"

"Thank you for bandaging my wounds. I no longer see any reason for your company and I would like to be alone. Please leave my bedroom."

At the sound of Olivia's approaching footsteps, Anthony stepped away from the door. Tiptoeing to the bathroom, he froze when Olivia exited Emily's room sooner than he expected.

"Anthony?" Olivia's tear-stained cheeks flushed a deeper red. "Were you eavesdropping on us?"

"N-no," Anthony stammered, but from the anger in Olivia's eyes, it was clear that she was not convinced. "I, uh. . . I'm sorry about your family. If you ever need to talk to anyone—"

"You jerk!" Olivia shouted. Her shoulder ramming into his chest, she ran to her room before he could say another word. Though she slammed her door shut, Anthony could still hear her crying.

~~

After everything he learned that evening about the Mavro family, Anthony wanted nothing more than to relax on his bed. The cool night air flowing in through his open window helped clear his mind. Being alone was almost too peaceful. As much as he wanted to rest on his vacation from home, it felt strange to not worry about demons attacking. Even after a day, preparing for an ambush at any time seemed like the Eden norm, and one he'd have to adapt to.

The peace was soon broken by rustling outside his window. Rising from his bed, he peeked outside, squinting in an attempt to make out shapes in the darkness. Panic rose in his chest when he spotted someone sitting in the backyard. Was it another Phobia? Had they been caught? He took a careful look before deciding whether to run to Simon and Sakura for help, but once he made out what he thought the figure could be, he panicked for a different reason. He ran down the stairs as quiet as he could and snuck out the back door.

Emily sat in the grass, her back facing him.

"What are you doing out here?" he whispered. "It's two in the morning."

She didn't answer. She didn't even budge. It was as if he hadn't spoken at all.

"It's not safe to be out here alone," he said. "Those Phobia chicks might find you. C'mon, let's go." Putting a hand on her shoulder, he was about to pull her to her feet, until he saw the knife in her hand. A thin trail of blood trickled down her left wrist. He jerked his hand away and cried out in shock. "What the hell? Did you do this to yourself?"

Emily looked up at him with empty eyes. "It is so beautiful."

Anthony backed away, pointing a shaking finger at her. "W-wait here. I'm gonna go get Drea—"

"No!" Emily screamed, jumping to her feet.

"I have to!" Anthony shouted. "She has to stop the bleeding!"

"No, please! Please do not get her! It is not that deep! I will be fine! Please, *please* do not tell anyone!" Falling to her knees, the knife tumbled to the grass, and she broke into hysterical sobs.

Anthony froze. As much as he wanted to help her, he couldn't bring himself to find Drea. Not with Emily making such a fuss. He took a deep breath and sat beside her, patting her back. "You're gonna be okay. Drea can help you."

"She will get mad at me," Emily cried. "She and Olivia got mad at me earlier when they saw my arms."

Anthony gazed in horror at Emily's arms. The bandages were removed, revealing dozens of dried slits running past both elbows. "Look, I'm gonna be right back. I promise I'm not getting Drea. I'm gonna get some paper towels from the kitchen."

He hurried into the kitchen and brought an entire roll of paper towels back outside. Emily's sobs were slowing to soft hiccups. Holding Emily's wrist in one hand, Anthony pressed a paper towel over her wound in the other. "Does this hurt?"

Emily shook her head.

"Can you tell me why you did this? I promise I won't tell. I just want to know."

Emily paused, watching her blood soak the white paper towel. "It just felt right, like I needed to do it. I wanted to feel pain again. I missed the way it felt when the metal would rip against my flesh. I missed the way it felt to bleed. It used to make me very happy to cut myself. To bleed."

Anthony flinched, disturbed and concerned by her whispered words. "Are you. . . are you not happy right now?"

"I do not know," Emily murmured.

"Well, next time. . ." His voice trailed off. He couldn't make eye contact with her. Not with those empty eyes. "Next time, if you aren't feeling happy, can you tell me instead of cutting yourself?"

"I do not cut because I am upset. But if I am upset, I will try to talk to you."

For a while, they sat in silence while Anthony continued to apply pressure to her wound until the bleeding stopped. Crumpling up the dirty towels, he rose and held out a hand for her to take. "Ready to go inside?"

"I do not want to go in," Emily mumbled. "I want to stay out here."

"That's fine," Anthony said. "But you'll have to give me the knife."

Emily handed him the knife, her gaze fixed on her wrist.

Anthony returned to the kitchen. After burying the dirty paper towels beneath other trash, he washed the knife, erasing the evidence of whatever it was that just happened. He walked back to the yard and lay beside Emily in the grass.

"What are you doing?" she asked.

"I'm not gonna leave you alone out here," he said, tucking his arms behind his head and shutting his eyes. Panicking over Emily's cut was more exhausting than he expected it could be.

"I am not going to hurt myself again."

"That's great, but I still want to be out here with you."

"I told you that you do not need to worry about me."

"Doesn't mean I won't."

Emily sighed. She lay on her back, lifting her hair over

her shoulders. She gazed at the moon and stars illuminating the night sky. "Zalem and I used to lay in the grass in our backyard at night just like this, and we would gaze upon the stars together. He knew all the constellations and would point them out for me to see."

Anthony cracked open one eye. "So he wasn't stillborn?"

"Of course not. I told you he was your age, remember?"

"Right." *This isn't lining up with what she told Olivia.* "What was he like?"

Emily was silent for a moment. Anthony wasn't sure if it was because she wasn't able to speak about him with her curse, or if she was thinking up a lie. "He was far kinder than you are. And far more handsome."

Anthony laughed. "Well. Okay. Not sure if I should feel insulted or concerned, but whatever. Sounds like he was a cool dude."

"He was," Emily said.

"Why haven't you told any of the others about him?"

"Why should I?"

"He sounds like he was really important to you. Most people like sharing what's important to them."

"They do not need to know about him."

"Your parents felt that way, too, didn't they? That's why his profile says he was stillborn, right?"

Emily didn't answer.

Anthony hesitated, waiting to hear some sort of reaction from her. But when she remained silent, he went on to ask, "So why did you tell me the truth and not Olivia?"

"Because I trust you. You remind me of Zalem."

"How?" Anthony chuckled. "You just told me he was better than me."

"You both make me smile."

Anthony stared at her as well as he could in the dark.

"Did you cut because you miss him?"

"I told you, I cut because I like the way it feels. I made all these cuts myself."

He dropped his voice to a whisper. "You're not suicidal, are you?"

"If I was suicidal, I would not be so desperate to live."

"Good point."

Emily curled onto her side. "I am really tired. I think I am going to sleep."

"Oh," Anthony muttered. He couldn't help but feel as if she were using sleep to escape their conversation. "All right, then. Goodnight."

"Goodnight, Anthony. I apologize for scaring you."

"It's chill. Just don't do it again."

"Thank you for worrying about me." She reached for his hand and held it in her icy fingers.

~~

Early the next morning, the phone rang.

Simon rolled over in bed to pick up his phone on the nightstand. "Hello?"

"Hi, Simon," Jason said, "Sorry to bug you so early in the morning—"

"Yeah, we're all still asleep at five fifteen," Simon grumbled.

Jason laughed. "Yeah, well, we got some news. About the samples."

Simon glanced at Sakura, who lay beside him with her eyes half-open. "Let's hear it."

"To be honest, I'm not sure where to start. Have you seen the wound yourself?"

"I haven't. Drea and Olivia are the only ones who have, and they haven't told anyone about it."

"I've seen it myself in the past and it's not pretty. It's

some sort of bite."

There was a pause. Sakura scooted closer to Simon, cocking her head toward the phone.

"Like what kind of bite?" Simon asked, leaning in closer for her to hear their conversation.

"Some kind of animal or monster," Jason replied. "Unfortunately for us, the wound's been cleaned, so we can't say for sure who or what caused it."

"Okay." He and Sakura exchanged confused looks. "Sorry, maybe it's just too early for me, but I'm not sure what to make of this."

"Well, think about it," Jason said. "The Mavro family didn't have any pets, but Emily died in her own house, so something must have either entered her house or lived there without Eden's knowledge to have attacked her."

Simon raised his brow. "What, you think Lucifer's Disciples sent out a demon to kill her?"

"If that were the case, her parents would have instantly reported it to Eden. Even if, for some odd reason, a wild animal were to have attacked her, they would have said something about her death. Instead, they killed themselves. So whatever it was that caused her death, Emily's parents were willing to take the secret to their graves. Meanwhile, Lucifer's Disciples are oddly desperate to keep Emily away from Eden, possibly because she's the only living person that knows of this secret."

Sakura narrowed her eyes, sitting up against the headboard.

"So Lucifer's Disciples must be involved somehow. But then why didn't her parents. . ." Simon trailed off at the sound of Jason's laughter.

"Only traitors would keep secrets from Eden," Jason said. "Betrayal shouldn't be a new concept to you."

CHAPTER 12

~~

Sakura rolled over in bed, her tired eyes opening when she noticed Simon was no longer under the sheets. She squinted in the morning sunlight, watching Simon change out of his plaid pajama pants. "What are you getting dressed for already?"

"I couldn't fall back to sleep after that call," he replied, buckling his belt over his jeans, "so I'm going to headquarters to see if I can dig up any old files. I'm taking Emily with me for questioning."

"You can't do that."

"Yeah, I can. She's an Eden member by blood. She's allowed in."

"We were specifically instructed *not* to bring Emily to headquarters." She clutched her bed sheets. "Even if you take her to headquarters, she won't tell you anything. And if she does, she might be lying. She seems to be good at that."

"I'll make her tell the truth," Simon grumbled, his back facing Sakura while he tied his shoes on the edge of the bed.

"How? By scaring her? I'm pretty sure we joined Eden because we *didn't* want to scare people anymore."

Simon didn't answer, pulling his leather coat out of the closet in silence.

Sakura sighed. "Please, just wait for her to come to us.

It's only been three days since we started."

"And in these three days, we got attacked twice. That *never* happens. Lucifer's Disciples probably doesn't want Emily to spoil any precious info she picked up from her parents."

"We don't know for sure if Emily's parents were traitors. Jason's just speculating. I wouldn't take it too seriously."

"They faked a profile. Even if they weren't part of Lucifer's Disciples, they lied to Eden. That in itself is betrayal." Putting on his coat, he looked her in the eye. "You know how important loyalty is to Eden."

Sakura bowed her head to avoid his gaze.

"When we joined Eden, they tortured us until we proved our loyalty," Simon said. "The most powerful family in Eden has been lying to the organization, and no one even questions them because they're just so goddamn powerful. After everything we've been through just to get to where we are, it makes me question if our efforts were really worth it if Eden's most revered members aren't even loyal."

~~

"Oh. My. God."

Anthony's eyes snapped open, treated to the sight of Olivia looming over him with a scowl. For a few seconds after awakening, his mind scrambled to remember why he was lying in the grass. *Oh, right. . . She hurt herself.* Even though Emily still lay beside him, clutching his hand in her sleep, the events of last night felt like a strange dream. Blushing, Anthony jerked his hand free from Emily's grasp.

"G-good morning," he said with a forced smile.

Olivia balled her fists. "You are so disgusting!"

Emily rubbed her eyes open. "What is going on?" Sitting up, she smoothed her hair over her shoulders and peered up at Olivia. "Good morning, Olivia. What brings you here?"

Olivia shook with rage and stomped back toward the house.

Hopping to his feet, Anthony chased after her. "Olivia, wait!" he cried, following her into the kitchen. "It's not what it looks like!"

"Oh, I think it is," Olivia huffed. "It's no wonder she trusts *you* more than me."

"What are you talking about?"

Olivia spun to face him, her gaze meeting his across the table. "Emily is clearly in distress, and you took advantage of that to get her to sleep with you!"

Anthony could think of a hundred different responses, but they all jumbled on his tongue as he struggled to find words. "I-it's not like that at all!"

"Then why was she out there with you?"

I can't tell her that Emily cut herself. Lost for ideas, his brow furrowed. "Why do you even care that we were out there? It's none of your business what we were doing."

Olivia's jaw dropped. She placed her hands on her hips. "Really? It's none of my business what you're doing to my undead relative on Eden property?"

Anthony cringed. *Well, that backfired.*

Before Olivia could fire more arguments at Anthony, Emily shuffled into the kitchen, stretching her arms. "Why are you two shouting? Is it so hard for you Eden people to have a peaceful moment?"

Olivia took a deep breath. "Emily, why were you outside with Anthony?"

"Did I happen to break some sort of rule?" she said. "Otherwise, I am not sure why you would be so upset. Unless you are jealous of me for being alone with Anthony. But that would be ridiculous, as I recall him saying you had rejected him."

Olivia's face reddened, her nails digging into her palms.

Anthony gaped at Emily's smug grin. *What the heck is she thinking?*

Relief washed over his racing heart when Karin waddled down the stairs, clinging to the railing. "What's going on down here?" she asked through a yawn. "All your yelling woke me up."

"Uh, nothing," Anthony muttered. His eyes darted to Olivia, who stared down at the floor.

"Just a bit of teen drama."

Anthony flinched in surprise at the sound of Sakura's voice. He hadn't noticed her sitting on the living room couch, and judging from Olivia's wide eyes, he assumed she hadn't either.

"H-how long have you been there?" Anthony stammered.

"A while," Sakura replied, her gaze fixed to her laptop screen.

"Where's Simon?" Karin asked.

"He left for headquarters earlier."

"Do you know when he'll be back? I wanted to practice more white magic with him today."

"I honestly have no idea."

"Did Jason call him yet?" Drea asked, tightening the knot on her robe while walking down the stairs.

Sakura stopped typing. "He did."

"What did he say?"

Sakura shut her laptop and paused. "He wasn't able to find anything from the sample."

"That's a bummer," Drea grumbled, making her way to the coffee pot. "Did Simon at least say what the plan is for today before he left?"

"Not really. I think he's just going to look at those profiles more."

"Whatever it is that Eden gave you, I highly doubt it is

worth looking at," Emily muttered, leaning against the table. "You are all wasting your time."

"I'm sure we'll make progress sooner or later," Sakura said. "Since there isn't any solid plan for today, I was thinking you could all take the day off to enjoy yourselves. Even though we just started, it seems there's already some tension in the house. Going out for a bit may benefit everyone."

Anthony blushed and glanced at Olivia, who still avoided his gaze.

"Are you sure that's a good idea?" Drea asked. "Last time we went out, we got attacked."

"The odds of that happening again are low, especially since we beat them pretty good last time," Sakura replied. She gave Drea a reassuring smile. "Just don't worry about it. Once our investigation picks up, who knows when we'll have another free day?"

~~

Jason was sitting in his office, sipping his morning cup of coffee, when he heard a knock on his door. Swinging his feet off his desk, he hurried to answer it.

"Simon!" he said, spreading his arms open with excitement. "To what do I owe the pleasure?"

Simon took a step back to avoid being steered into the office. "Let's make this quick. I need every file you can give me on the Mavro family."

Jason cocked his head. "Didn't Erika already give them to her sister? I saw Olivia here just the other day."

"All she gave her were profiles on Emily and her parents. I want *everything* we have on them, as well as a couple generations before and after. If Emily's parents were connected to Lucifer's Disciples, there must be something written down somewhere that I can use as evidence."

Jason crossed his arms. "And if it is true, what will you

do? Tell the chairman that his ancestors were traitors? If that is the case, I'm sure he already knows."

"I'll tell everyone," Simon said with a confident nod. "They have a right to know about the corruption within our organization. Besides, we don't know where the treason ends. There could be double agents *right now*—"

Jason lifted a finger to silence him. "This isn't a conversation to have in headquarters," he whispered, peering over Simon's shoulder. "Look, I understand your frustration, especially given your background. While I do have my suspicions about the Mavro family, ranting to the chairman about treason will do more harm than good."

"But I need these files anyway for my investigation. It'd be so convenient to claim I just stumbled upon some suspicious info."

"I'm not really authorized to give you any files without Erika's permission. She's the one in charge of the investigation."

"And that's exactly why I came to you. She'd never give me anything that could give her family a bad reputation. There's gotta be a reason why every case about Emily or anything related to the Mavro family gets dropped, and I'd like to figure out why before the same happens to this one."

Jason narrowed his eyes. "Say I do give you the files. What's in it for me?"

Simon paused, then grinned. "If there is any dirt on the Mavro family, it'd make the chairman look pretty bad. He could lose his position. The entire Mavro family could lose their power. Imagine what that could do for you."

Jason held his chin. "Tempting. Very tempting. Also very risky. We could lose our jobs if we get caught."

"Losing our jobs would be the least of our worries," Simon said with a dark laugh.

"Working with you is always a thrill."

~~

At twelve thirty in the afternoon, Karin was squealing over shoes at the mall, dragging Olivia around the store to help her pick out the "cutest pair." Anthony, meanwhile, was drowning in boredom, slouching in one of the leather chairs.

Emily plopped down beside him with a smirk. "You look like you are enjoying yourself."

"Why didn't you talk her out of this?" Anthony groaned, gesturing toward Karin.

"She really wanted to go shopping," Emily said with a shrug. "She said we would buy stuff for me, but we mostly have been looking at whatever she likes."

"You got some stuff," Anthony said, peeking into the shopping bag beside Emily at what appeared to be a puddle of black clothing. "Did you only get dresses?"

"There is not nearly enough lace on these dresses to suit my liking, but they will do," Emily said, folding her hands on her lap. "I had to get something new to wear and these were the only things I liked at this mall."

"I'm honestly surprised Drea agreed to taking us here. What if those Phobia or one of those chimera things try to attack us?"

"It would be a poor move on their behalf. There are too many people here. Everyone will see them."

Anthony sighed and rested his head in his hand. "I guess so. It just feels unsafe being here without Simon or Sakura." He glanced at Drea, who leaned against one of the shoe racks, her attention fixed to her phone's screen. "I can't believe she let Sakura stay home."

"She said she wanted to wait for Simon to return. We cannot force her to join us."

"I was forced to come," Anthony grumbled.

"You have to go wherever I go."

"I guess." He peered down at the fresh bandages on her

arms. "How's your cut?"

"It is perfectly fine. Drea did not even notice my new scar when she redid my bandages before we left."

"That's good." He wrinkled his brow. "Are you doing okay? You've been acting weird lately."

"I am undead," Emily chuckled. "Was I not weird to you before?"

"You weren't cutting yourself or being rude. What was up with you getting all catty at Olivia this morning?"

Emily shrugged and giggled. "I was only teasing. I thought it was funny that she cared so much, especially since she claims she does not share your feelings."

"And I apparently don't share your sense of humor." Anthony watched Karin take Olivia for a third lap around the store, comparing prices on sneakers. "I'd like to think that I still have a chance with her, so can you please not mess that up?"

Before Emily could answer, Karin rushed to her side, dangling a pair of ankle boots in her hands. "You gotta try these on! They'll look super cute on you."

Emily cringed. "Those are hideous," she whispered to Anthony.

"Emily says she loves them," Anthony told Karin.

Emily glared at Anthony.

Karin shook with excitement. "I knew she would! C'mon, let's find your size!" She snatched Emily's wrist and dragged her toward the nearest sales clerk.

"That's payback for this morning," Anthony said. He peered at Olivia, who took a seat in one of the chairs across the store. Stuffing his hands in his jeans pockets, he took the opportunity to talk to her before Karin or Emily could interrupt. He hoped he didn't appear as nervous as he felt. "Hey, so about this morning—"

"Drea, can we leave now?" Olivia interrupted, looking to Drea. "I'm starting to feel hungry."

Anthony gaped at her, unsure of how to respond.

Drea glanced up from her phone screen. "Karin, Emily, let's go grab lunch."

"But we're not done here," Karin said, sitting on the floor with Emily amidst a sea of shoes. "Can Emily and I stay? She doesn't even eat."

Emily was already on her feet, dashing to Anthony's side.

"C'mon, Karin," Drea said. "No one's staying behind."

Staring at the floor, Olivia pushed past Anthony, her shoulder shoving into his arm.

"H-hold on!" Anthony stammered. "I wanted to talk to you about what happened this morning."

"There's nothing to talk about!" Olivia snapped, whipping around to face him. "We already talked about it. It's all in the past now. So just drop it, okay?"

"It's obviously not *all in the past* if you're still mad at me," Anthony retorted.

"Hey, you guys coming?" Drea asked, pausing in the store entrance.

Anthony bit the inside of his cheek and blushed when he noticed the store clerks staring at him and Olivia. "Yeah, we are."

As they walked out of the store, Drea continued to stare at her phone. "Headquarters just won't leave me alone today."

"Has anyone said anything about what Simon's doing?" Karin asked.

Drea shook her head, answering a text. "I've mainly been talking to Erika."

"Ugh, what does *she* want?" Olivia grumbled.

"She just wanted to know how the investigation's going," Drea replied, "and then she said something about demonic activity in the area, but I guess she already sent some exorcists to take care of it."

Breaking glass and screams resonated from the far end of the mall, followed by the rumble of people stampeding toward the nearest exit. Anthony and the others scooted against the wall, avoiding a crowd of mall patrons rushing by.

"What is going on?" Emily asked, squishing closer to Anthony's side.

Standing on his toes, Anthony saw a massive winged serpent in the distance. Its tail crashed through shop windows, the glass raining down on those slower to escape or cocky enough to snap a few pictures on their phones before running away.

"Looks like those exorcists didn't do a very good job of handling the demonic activity," Karin muttered.

CHAPTER 13

~~

"I can't believe they actually sent one of those monsters here!" Olivia cried, gaping in shock at the chimera.

"I can," Drea grumbled. "Just back me up, okay?" She withdrew two guns from inside her coat, and tossed one to Olivia. Keeping the other for herself, she charged against the mob of mall attendees toward the chimera.

Olivia clutched the gun and sighed. "You guys go hide somewhere while I help Drea."

"I can help you guys," Karin said.

Olivia ignored her and ran after Drea.

Karin rolled her eyes. "Or not." She gestured for Anthony and Emily to follow her in the opposite direction. "C'mon, guys. Let's just chill in a store until they're done."

After taking one last glance at Olivia, who was firing bullets into the side of the chimera's neck, Anthony followed Karin under the black archway of the nearest store. With all the employees and store clerks gone, they were left alone in a sea of band t-shirts, ripped skinny jeans, and various cartoon merchandise.

"I don't think I've been in here since middle school," Anthony muttered, peering at all the shirt graphics lining the red brick walls.

"Is this where young people shop nowadays?" Emily

asked, cringing at the screaming vocals of the rock music left on in the background.

"Only the emo kids do," Anthony chuckled. "And maybe the anime kids."

Emily raised an eyebrow. "The whats?"

"Oh, come on, lots of people shop here," Karin said. She pulled out two miniskirts from one of the racks and held them up for Anthony and Emily to see. "Which one should I take? Or should I take both?"

"You can't just take stuff," Anthony said. "That'd be stealing."

"You stole Emily from Mavro Manor."

"I thought I already made it clear that. . ." He trailed off and sighed, holding his shaking head. "Fine. Do what you want."

Karin grinned and sifted through more clothing racks, piling skirts and shirts over her arm. "It's not like I'd do this normally. I just might as well take advantage of the situation."

"You mean the chimera scaring all the people away, possibly hurting your comrades?" Emily asked.

"I'd be fighting instead of stealing if Drea and Olivia let me," Karin grumbled. She tossed her chosen clothing items in Emily's shopping bag. "I'm probably way more helpful than Olivia. She doesn't even know white magic."

"Neither do you," Anthony snapped, flinching when Karin glared at him. "At least not that much."

"Typical," Emily giggled, "defending your precious Olivia."

Anthony blushed. "It's not like that. It's just—what, you, too?"

Emily froze, holding a black dress halfway into her bag. "I need more clothes from this time."

"Eden rats shoplifting? So much for being servants of God."

Hugging a pair of platform boots in her arms, Anita

stood outside the dressing room, leering at the trio. Anthony took a step back in surprise, panic rising in his chest as he was once again faced with the Phobia girl, only this time there was no one around to protect him.

"You have been watching us," Emily said, fiddling with her cross necklace. "I cannot go anywhere without being followed by demon scum."

"You all came to me." Anita held out her boots. "I was just trying these on in the back since there's no mirrors in this store. It's ridiculous."

Karin's eyes lit up, ogling at the boots. "Wait, what size are you? Did they fit? I'll totally take those if you don't want them."

"I'm usually a seven, but they were out of my size, so I grabbed eights and they actually fit okay. Lord ZuZu gave me some shopping money, but then you guys showed up." She glanced at the boots and smirked. "Now I can just snatch these, so thanks for giving us a reason to scare everyone away."

Karin pointed an accusing finger at Anthony. "I told you lots of people shop here!"

"I-I don't usually shop here," Anita stammered, averting her gaze to a nearby dress rack. "They just have cute stuff sometimes."

"I don't think where people shop is really such a big deal right now," Anthony said with a nervous laugh.

"You're right; it isn't." As the last words fell from her lips, bat wings ripped through the back of Anita's dress and she set the boots aside to grab her baton from her purse. With a swipe of her hand, the scythe extended. "I'm glad you decided to split up. I'm sure Thalia is finishing off your friends as I speak." She brandished the scythe in front of her and sneered. "Luckily I got the easier job."

They're really not coming to save us, Anthony thought, glancing over his shoulder out the store entrance. *I don't want to see what she'll do if we run, but. . .*

"Don't worry, guys," Karin said, her tone firm as she stepped in front of Emily and Anthony. Unzipping her purse, she withdrew a small wooden cross. "I'll take care of her."

Anita lowered her scythe. "*You?* Really? You can fight?"

Karin furrowed her brow, her grip tightening on the cross.

"Karin, now's really not the time to prove anything," Anthony said. "You're gonna get hurt."

"I'll be fine. I got this." Taking a deep breath, Karin closed her eyes and waved her hand over the cross. A blade extended from the top, half the size of the swords Sakura and Simon would conjure, but it was enough to make her jump with joy. "Oh my God! Guys, I did the thing!"

"But can you use it?" Emily asked, her eyes darting from Karin's sword to Anita's scythe.

"Uh, kinda," Karin muttered. "I just gotta like swing it at her, right?"

Anthony slapped a hand over his face. "We're screwed."

Anita leapt upon the nearest clothing rack, ready to pounce. Dodging her by a hair, Karin ducked beneath the scythe's pole and dashed to the other side of the store, hiding behind one of the accessory racks. Clutching her cross in one hand, she used her free hand to shoot a dim ball of white light at Anita. Before Anita could shoot a shadow from her palm, the light grazed her cheek, leaving behind a sizzling burn. She howled in pain, jewelry falling from the rack behind her as she stumbled into it.

"You little brat!" Anita growled, clutching her cheek, black smoke and blood seeping beneath her fingers.

"I-I think you just made her angry," Anthony stammered. He peered around the room, desperate to find some way to help Karin, but could think of no solution other than to run away and scream for help.

While Anita swooped down at Karin, Emily darted

across the store toward the dressing room.

"What the heck are you doing?" Anthony cried, chasing after her.

Karin, meanwhile, managed to block Anita's scythe with her sword. She backed away and swung her blade, but Anita was too fast for her to land a single scratch. Shoving the heel of her boot into Karin's stomach, Anita knocked her to the ground. The blade of Karin's sword retracted into the cross, falling from her grasp and skidding a few feet too far underneath a table.

Anita pinned Karin to the floor, clutching her throat. "You can squirm all you want, but that'll only make you lose your breath faster."

Seizing one of the platform boots, Emily chucked it at Anita, hitting her on the side of her head. Anita's grip on Karin loosened and she tumbled to her side.

"Holy crap! Did you just knock her out with a freaking boot?" Anthony cried.

"I. . . I think so," Emily muttered, peering over at Anita's motionless body. "I am surprised I actually hit her."

Anthony lifted the other boot. "Dang, this thing's got some weight."

"Sh-she's not moving," Karin panted, resting a hand on her chest. "Do you think she still wants the boots after being knocked out by one?"

Anthony struggled to catch his own breath, his heart still racing with fear. He couldn't help but flinch when a second Phobia whizzed into the store.

With wings outstretched and his sword brandished, Simon was about to strike Anita until he noticed she was unconscious. "What the. . . You guys managed to knock her out on your own?"

"Simon!" Karin cried, sitting up. "What are you doing here?"

"I should be asking you guys that. I was at headquarters

when I heard about demonic activity at the mall."

"Are Olivia and Drea okay?" Anthony asked.

"Yeah, they're fine," Simon replied. "Thalia ran off just before I got here, but I heard you three were alone, and. . ." He trailed off and let out a relieved sigh, kneeling beside Karin. "I just can't believe you're all okay. She didn't hurt you, did she?"

Karin held her flushed cheeks, gaping at Simon's outstretched wings and bare torso. "You came to rescue me without your shirt on, just like in my dreams!"

Anthony struggled to suppress laughter at both Karin's ogling and Simon's exasperation.

"Seriously, Karin, she could have killed you," Simon said, rolling his eyes.

"Karin was actually able to fight for a bit," Emily said.

"I did the cross sword thing," Karin mumbled. "But then I didn't know how to use it and I dropped it, and. . . yeah. That's when I messed up."

"But you were able to make your cross into a weapon?" Simon asked.

Karin nodded. "I know you don't want me to fight and get hurt, but I had to protect Emily. You said half of using white magic is having the motivation to control it, and I wanted to prove that I could actually do something for a change, and. . ." She bowed her head and blushed a deeper red. "And I wanted to make you proud."

Simon's expression softened. He ruffled her hair and wrapped his arms around her back. "You did. I'm sure you did an awesome job. I'm really glad you're okay."

"Well, isn't this just a heartwarming moment?" A boy around Emily's age walked toward them, his black robes engulfing his tiny body. "I hate to interrupt, but I have business with Miss Emily." He peered down at Anita and nudged her arm with his foot. "What are you doing? Now's not the time for a nap."

Anita groaned, rubbing her eyes open to a squint. "Lord Rundull?" she whispered. Scrambling to her knees, she bowed before him. "Lord Rundull, it *is* you!"

"That presence," Simon whispered, lifting a shaking hand to his mouth. "No, he can't be. . ."

"What?" Anthony looked to Simon, unnerved by his suddenly pale face.

Drea and Olivia rushed into the store, keeping a careful watch on Rundull.

"Who is this kid?" Drea whispered to Simon, who responded with a shrug.

"You have business with me?" Emily smirked. "Is Lucifer's Disciples really using such a small, pathetic body for a Phobia? Are children all they can manage to capture?"

Rundull tossed his black hair and lowered his hood, revealing lifeless red eyes. "I'm not a lowly demon. I'd be insulted if you weren't so cute."

The ends of Rundull's robes dragged along the floor with every step he took toward Emily. Emily clamped her fist around her cross and grit her teeth. When he placed a cold yet gentle hand on her arm, Drea and Olivia pointed their guns at his head.

"Please put the weapons down," Rundull said, pulling Emily's hand away from her necklace. "I'm not here to hurt anyone. I'm sure *he* understands." His grin only made Simon stiffen and Anthony more anxious.

"What do you want?" Emily asked, lifting her nose.

"I want you to be happy," Rundull said.

"Thank you for your concern," Emily said, yanking free from Rundull's grasp, "but I am quite happy."

"Then why did you cut yourself?"

Emily froze.

"What's he talking about?" Olivia said, her eyes darting to Anthony.

Anthony didn't answer, his focus glued to Emily and

Rundull.

Rundull seized Emily's arm and ripped off the bandage covering her latest slit. "I've been watching you, Miss Emily. I watched as you cut yourself, as bliss washed over your pretty face."

Emily's jaw trembled, but no words escaped her lips. Her eyes widened at the sight of her cuts.

"I know you miss it," Rundull said, his grip tightening. "You miss the way it felt when the blade would tear your flesh, the way it felt to be covered in your own warm, sticky blood." He smirked, his lips mere inches from her neck as he whispered, "You miss it because it reminds you of *him*."

"That's enough!" Anthony yelled. He couldn't bear to see Emily's terrified eyes any longer, to stand by and watch her shake with a fear he never believed she was capable of expressing. Emotions seizing control of his body, he grabbed Rundull by his shoulders, wrenching him off Emily.

Karin let out a gasp, and Simon jumped to his feet. "Anthony, don't mess with him!" he shouted.

"How dare you touch Lord Rundull?" Anita growled, clinging to Anthony to pull him away.

"Let him go!" Olivia cried, her and Drea directing their guns at Anita.

Rundull raised his arms as high as he could in Anthony's grasp. "Everyone, please calm down and keep your hands to yourselves."

Anthony released Rundull and backed away, and Drea and Olivia lowered their guns once Anita let go of him. Emily remained frozen in shock, silent tears dripping down her cheeks.

Straightening his robes, Rundull sighed. "Miss Emily, I understand that you want to be a normal girl with a normal life, but let's be honest. This whole playing house thing you have going on with Eden is just not you. You know they can't give you what you want, but I can. So when you're ready to go back to the life that truly makes you happy, just let me know. I'll be waiting for you." Before making his way toward the store entrance with Anita, he gave her one last smile, flashing sharp fangs. "I'll be *watching* you."

Smoke emitted from his outstretched palm, consuming him and Anita, vanishing with them as sudden as their arrivals.

CHAPTER 14

~~

Everyone was silent in the car while Drea drove them home. The low mumble of the radio's weather report was drowned out by Rundull's parting words, still ringing through their ears. Though they were far from the mall, terror still remained on Emily's pale face, her wide eyes fixed to the back of the driver's seat. While he wanted to cheer her up, Anthony couldn't think of anything positive to say. Peering at Olivia and Karin's gloomy stares, he knew they had the same question on their minds as he did.

"So. . . that Rundull kid," Anthony muttered to no one in particular. "What's his deal?"

Simon, who was leaning against the window, replied, "He's like a Phobia, but with a devil inside him. Not a demon."

"So he's like Satan?"

Simon shook his head and turned off the radio. "There's three types of spirits residing in Hell. Souls of damned humans, demons, and devils. And then of course there is *the* Devil, Satan, who rules over all of Hell." Turning in his seat, he faced Anthony. "Where demons are low-ranked, chaotic, violent creatures, devils are angels fallen from heaven. They're higher-ranked and far more powerful than demons, though they often use manipulation over violence."

"But I thought devils can't exist on Earth," Karin said from the back. "Like, even inside human bodies, I thought they can't survive."

"They technically can, just no one wants to attempt it," Simon replied. "Not even Lucifer's Disciples are crazy enough to attempt such a risky stunt." He rested his elbow against the door and held his chin. "At least I thought they weren't. Summoning demons is way easier. All you need is the right spell, a few drops of blood, and a human body for the vessel."

All you need? Anthony thought, raising his brow. *He makes it sound like it's no big deal.*

"Only extremely powerful mages can summon a devil," Simon continued, "and it requires a much larger toll. Devils are all about making deals."

"Like your soul?" Olivia whispered.

"You're lucky if that's all one asks for," Simon said with a dark laugh. "I can't imagine why Lucifer's Disciples felt the need to summon one."

Anthony glanced at Emily. Though she appeared to be zoning out while she stared at her shoes, he knew she was listening. "But he didn't want to attack us. So as long as we don't listen to any deals he tries to make with us, we're okay, right? I mean, he's just a kid."

"Easier said than done," Simon said. "Don't let his size fool you. He may be a kid on the outside, but there's a reason why whoever summoned him chose a smaller body."

~~

When the front door opened, Sakura shut her book and set it on the coffee table beside her, beaming when she saw Simon approaching her. She rose and embraced him, burying her face in his chest.

"I'm so sorry I wasn't there to help you guys," she

whispered.

"It's fine," Simon murmured, rubbing her back. He kissed the top of her head. "You're still hurt from the last fight. You need your rest."

"Erika called me when you guys were on the way home." She pulled away from Simon and looked to the others, who stood by the stairs. "With Rundull out and about, she doesn't think we're safe in this house anymore. She thinks he might be strong enough to get past the barriers."

"So what does she think we should do?" Anthony asked. "Are we just gonna move to another house?"

"Not quite," Sakura said. "We're taking the investigation back to headquarters. No matter where we go, there's nowhere safer than headquarters, so we're heading back after dinner."

"But Anthony can't stay there," Drea said, leaning against the railing.

"That's why he's going back to his house with Emily, since she supposedly needs him. We already arranged a ride for them."

"But they can't stay there alone," Olivia said, blushing when she noticed Anthony staring at her. "I—I mean, Lucifer's Disciples found them there before. What happens if they attack and we're not there to help?"

She makes a good point, Anthony thought, tugging at his sweatshirt collar. *It was bad enough being at the other end of the mall from Drea.*

"She doesn't think they'll attack," Sakura replied. "They didn't start attacking until we came along. If Emily stays hidden and Anthony keeps going to school like normal, Lucifer's Disciples will most likely leave them alone since we won't be around to get information from Emily. That seems to be their main concern."

"It is."

All eyes fell on Emily when she spoke. After taking a

deep breath, she continued. "I know you are all curious about my family, especially my brother. I overheard you discussing him at dinner yesterday." Her gaze met Simon's. "It is why you went to headquarters today. You want to know more."

"I do," Simon said, narrowing his eyes.

"I want to know more as well. I am being completely honest when I say I do not know exactly why Lucifer's Disciples is interested in me. I know they want to keep me from spreading information, but I do not know why that is."

"I think it's awfully fishy that your parents tried to hide so much information from Eden," Simon said. He paused before saying, "They weren't traitors, were they?"

Emily turned up her nose. "They had their reasons, and their reasons were good, just as I have good reasons for keeping my silence. I do apologize for lying about the silencing spell, but please believe me when I say that I never betrayed Eden for the darkness, nor did my parents, nor did my brother Zalem."

Sakura reached for Simon's hand and squeezed it, staring down at their fingers.

Anthony noticed Olivia stiffen at Zalem's name.

Emily's eyes locked with Olivia's. "You told me your parents keep your older brother in hiding. That no one from Eden has seen him, not even you. I suppose you can understand why my parents kept Zalem from Eden. Even having your identity revealed exclusively to Eden is enough of a risk."

Olivia's lip trembled, but her eyes remained fixed on Emily's. "But they revealed yours."

"Just as your parents revealed your identity, as well as your older sister's. Again, *we all have our reasons*." Breaking their gaze, she sighed. "Unfortunately, it seems my parents' efforts were futile. From what Rundull was saying today, I think Lucifer's Disciples know more than I am comfortable with."

~~

Sitting in the back of the Eden SUV later that evening, Anthony's main concern was sneaking Emily back into his house. His aunt and uncle were both home and awake at this hour. Though he could sneak her through his bedroom window, keeping her a secret for however long she was staying could be a challenge. By the time he and Emily were dropped off at the doorstep, he still had yet to come up with a plan, but Emily was already knocking on the front door.

"What are you doing?" Anthony whispered, seizing her wrist. "I'm trying to think of a way to get you in without them seeing you!"

"I do not care if they see me," Emily said, clutching her shopping bag from the mall in her free hand. "It is cold out here and I wish to go inside now."

The door swung open. Uncle Mark glared at Anthony with his beady eyes. "Tony? What the hell are you doin' back?"

"I live here," Anthony said, stepping in front of Emily, whose face curled in an odd mixture of a cringe and sneer.

"Oh, yeah? Then where've you been?"

Anthony paused. *I really should have planned this out sooner.* "I, uh, was out with friends."

Uncle Mark peered over at Emily. "You mean your little girlfriend?"

"Oh, she's not my—"

Emily pushed past Anthony and beamed at Uncle Mark. "Yes, I am his girlfriend Emily. You must be his Uncle Mark. Pleasure to meet you." She held out a hand for him to shake.

Anthony's jaw dropped. *What the hell is she thinking?*

Uncle Mark gaped at Emily as if she were an alien. Aunt Lisa peeked over his shoulder. "That's Tony's girlfriend?" she said, raising her eyebrows and staring at

Emily's frilly dress in disbelief. "She can't be. Tony would never get a girl that cute."

"Or any girl," Uncle Mark grunted.

"You are both hilarious," Emily giggled. "I have heard many wonderful things about you two. I am glad we can finally meet. Thank you very much for welcoming me into your home."

"What the hell is goin' on?" Uncle Mark whispered to Aunt Lisa. "Did you invite her over?"

Aunt Lisa shook her head and shrugged.

Emily snatched Anthony's hand. "I will be staying in Anthony's room. Please respect our privacy."

Anthony shared the same confused expression as his aunt and uncle when Emily dragged him into his bedroom. Grinning in satisfaction, she shut the door and plopped down on his bed. "That was easier than you made it sound."

Anthony leaned against the door. "What the hell did you just do?"

She furrowed her brow. "Are you unhappy? I got us both into the house with no trouble. I do not even have to hide anymore."

"Well, yeah, that part is awesome, but *girlfriend?*" Dropping to the floor, he buried his face in his hands.

"Would you rather I told them the truth about who I am?"

"No, but now they're gonna think we're. . . y'know. . ."

Emily laughed. "Their faces when I told them I am your girlfriend were absolutely hilarious!"

Anthony couldn't help smiling at the sound of her laugh. It was as if the encounter with Rundull had never happened. "Are you feeling better?"

"From what?" she asked.

He paused, afraid to bring it up. "From earlier, at the mall."

"Oh, right." Her gaze turned distant, drifting to the

corner of the room. "Yes, I am better."

"I'm glad. You really looked so scared. You scared me."

"I am sorry. I did not mean to scare anyone."

Anthony narrowed his eyes. "Rundull said something about how you cut yourself because it reminded you of someone. A *him*."

She stared down at her stockings and twiddled her thumbs.

Anthony dropped his voice to a whisper, his gaze falling upon her scarred arms. "He wasn't. . . he wasn't talking about your brother, was he?" Though he regretted asking that question when he noticed her eyes beginning to water.

"I am sorry, Anthony," she whispered, "but I do not feel comfortable answering that question right now."

~~

After fighting chimeras and running from Phobia, nothing felt stranger to Anthony than being back at school. He wanted to believe that no monsters would attack him while he was away from Eden, but while he sat at his desk in the back of his second period class, he never felt so exposed and vulnerable. He couldn't stop peeking out the window beside him, checking to see if any chimeras were flying toward the school in the distance. It almost seemed unusual that no one else was worried about a possible ambush. He let out a sigh and rested his head on his desk. *I guess I already forgot what it's like to be like everyone else and not know that demons exist.*

Walking through the crowded hallway to his next class, he wondered if Emily was still safe in his room. He couldn't help worrying about her, especially now that she was left alone.

"Yo, Anthony!"

Anthony jumped when a hand tapped his shoulder. He

spun around to see Tyson and Cory behind him. "Oh, hey," he muttered.

"Dude, where've you been?" Cory asked. "We kept on texting you, but you never answered."

"Uh, I was with my aunt and uncle," Anthony said, scrambling to think up a convincing lie. "We were out of town for a funeral."

"Whatever," Cory said with a shrug. "Wanna go out for a smoke?"

Anthony bit his lip and peered out the window. The only people outside were students scrambling to get to class on time. Soon, there would be no one out there. *That'll make me an easy target for the demons.* "Uh, I think I'll pass. I've got a lot to catch up on."

"Oh, c'mon, man," Tyson said with a chuckle. "Since when do you care about school stuff?"

"Since. . . now?" Raising a hand, he backed away from his friends. "I'll see you later!"

Anthony was relieved by the time sixth period came around and not a single demon attacked him or the school. He was, however, surprised to see Olivia taking her seat in front of him, smiling when she noticed him.

"How's life after Eden?" she whispered, rotating in her seat to face him.

"I hate to admit it, but I'm freaking paranoid without them," Anthony muttered. "What are you doing here? I thought you were going to their headquarters."

She shook her head. "I was only at the house to manage the investigation for Erika since it's about our family, but now that our group's back at headquarters, they don't really need my help."

When class started, she turned forward in her seat and didn't speak to Anthony again until the bell rang. While Anthony packed his belongings, she zipped her backpack and stood in front of his desk. "I wanted to apologize about the way I was acting the other day," she said.

Anthony looked up at her. "What do you mean?"

"When I was all upset about you sleeping with Emily."

"I wasn't *sleeping* with her," Anthony said, blushing. "Like, not in *that* way—"

"It's okay," Olivia interrupted. "I don't need to know what you two were doing. It's none of my business. You've just been so nice to Emily and you two have gotten so close. I guess I'm a little jealous."

Anthony's blinked a few times before speaking again "Wait, what?"

Her eyes darted to the corner of the room. "I—I mean, not about you two. I'm just jealous that she will talk to you and not me, even though we're related."

"Oh. Right."

"Anyway, I gotta get going, but I'll see you in class tomorrow." Before he could respond, she hurried out of the classroom.

Anthony gaped after her, their conversation replaying in his mind.

CHAPTER 15

~~

"I seriously think she likes me," Anthony told Emily that evening. She was sitting on the floor playing a hand held video game while he lay on his bed completing math homework. "She was talking to me after class and was acting really awkward."

"*She* likes *you?*" Emily said, her face wrinkling in an attempt to hold back laughter.

"Why wouldn't she?" Anthony huffed. "I'm decent enough."

"But you are *you*," Emily said with a smirk. She gasped with delight and held up the hand-held console for Anthony to see. "Look! I caught one of those creature things!"

"That's fantastic," Anthony mumbled, his gaze remaining on his homework. "Now go catch the other eight hundred."

"*Eight hundred?*" Gaping, she dropped the console in her lap. "That is ridiculous! How do I even find that many?"

"You don't. You have to get some from other people."

"How?"

"I can show you after I finish my homework."

Emily frowned. "You never struck me as the scholarly type."

"I'm not, but Olivia is in this class and—"

"And you want to impress her," Emily interrupted, rolling her eyes. "I understand. Your little crush is far more important than my epic journey through this foreign land of magical creatures."

Anthony tried his hardest to ignore her while he focused on his homework, but was soon distracted by his cell phone ringing on his desk. When he peered over to see who was calling, he didn't recognize the phone number. "Hello?" he answered.

"Um, hi. Anthony?"

"*Olivia?*"

Emily raised her brow.

Anthony nodded. "Hey, Olivia. Uh. . . I didn't know you had my number."

"Drea gave it to me a few days ago back at the house," Olivia replied. "Sorry to bother you. Um. . ."

"What's up?"

"Can I stay at your place for the night?"

Anthony was speechless, his eyes meeting Emily's.

"Still there?" Olivia asked. "Sorry, I know this is kinda abrupt."

"N-no, it's no problem," Anthony stammered. "But, um, is there any specific reason why?"

"My sister is here visiting tonight. My mom ignores me more than usual when she's here and I honestly don't want to be around for that. I know I probably sound childish, but. . ."

"Well, uh, it's fine with me, but I dunno what my folks will say, especially with Emily here."

"Oh, yeah. She's with you." For a moment, there was silence on her end. "I guess we can go to a motel? I'll cover the cost. Money's not really an issue for me." Her voice shook with nervous laughter. "Sorry, I think I'm getting carried away. I'm so sorry. With everything that's been happening, I don't want to be alone."

"No, it's fine," Anthony said. "I totally understand. I'll

come with you."

"Thanks, Anthony. I really appreciate it."

But when Olivia met Anthony in his driveway, her scowl showed anything other than appreciation when Emily buckled herself into a backseat.

"She's coming, too?" Olivia asked, glaring at Emily through the rearview mirror.

"Of course," Anthony said, taking a seat beside Olivia. "I can't just leave her home alone."

"Do you have a problem with me coming along?" Emily asked, still playing the video game.

Olivia forced a lopsided smile. "No, of course not."

Judging from her grumble and remaining scowl, Anthony was not convinced that Olivia approved of Emily's company.

"So, how exactly are we getting a room?" Anthony asked, hoping to take Olivia's mind off Emily.

"I told you, I'm paying with my family's money," Olivia replied.

"But you aren't old enough to reserve a room."

"I used Erika's name."

"And Erika won't care?"

"She'll never notice," Olivia said with a chuckle. "It's not like she ever looks to see how much she spends. If she can blow our family's money on expensive clothes, there should be no issue with me using it to get a cheap room for a night."

Raising his brow, Anthony watched her laugh, though she stopped when she noticed him staring at her.

"What's that look for?" she asked, glancing at him for a moment when she stopped at a red light.

"Nothing," Anthony said, his eyes darting to the window. "You're just a lot different than I expected. Like, from before I met you."

Olivia blushed. "Is that good or bad?"

Anthony paused. "Neither, I guess. I kinda just expected you to be a typical popular girl."

"What, like hanging out with football players and going to crazy house parties on Friday nights?" Olivia laughed again. "If only I was so ignorant of the world around me."

"Are we almost there?" Emily asked, peering up from her game. "I cannot bear another minute of listening to you two blabber."

Olivia rolled her eyes. "If you can't stand us that much, I'm more than happy to take you back to Anthony's house."

"That's not an option," Anthony said before Emily could speak. "Not while a creepy devil kid is after her. You know better than to be alone."

After parking outside the motel lobby, Olivia rose from the driver's seat. "You wait here," she told Anthony before closing the car door. "I can handle the front desk by myself."

"Okay," Anthony said. Watching her disappear into the motel, demons were the last thing he was worried about attacking her. The flickering sign above the mossy roof shed light on the faded paint and worn wood of the building.

"Is this really a safe place to stay?" Emily asked.

"It'll be fine," Anthony replied, hoping to at least convince himself.

However, his words became less believable when Olivia led them up the rickety stairs to their room. Upon opening the door, his nostrils were filled with the stench of rotten wood. Even when Olivia opened the back window, the cool night breeze was not enough to cleanse the musty air.

"It smells like something died in here," Emily grumbled, squeezing the handles of her bag, reluctant to set it on either of the two beds or the stained carpet.

"It's not that bad," Anthony said, his gaze panning around the room, looking for something notable. "Look, they even gave us a TV. That's pretty generous."

"Are you sure you're okay with this?" Olivia asked him,

pausing by the door. "I can see if a better room is available."

"I'm okay with it if you are," he replied. "It's just for one night."

Olivia beamed. "You really don't know how much this means to me. None of my other friends would have ever done something like this."

Through narrowed eyes, Anthony watched her set her bag beside one of the beds. "Were none of your friends okay with you spending the night at their houses?" *Given how popular she is at school, I find that hard to believe.*

"I didn't want to be a burden on them," Olivia said, unzipping her bag. She withdrew a pair of polka dot pajama bottoms and a matching top.

So she didn't even bother asking?

"Anyway, I think I'm going to get ready for bed. I'm starting to feel kinda tired." Olivia's gaze fell upon the beds. "I guess this room isn't really built for three."

"Oh, I can just sleep on the couch," Anthony said with a wave of his hand. "I have no problem with that."

"Are you sure? It doesn't seem fair since you've been so nice."

"He just said he has no problem with it," Emily snapped, pausing from her own unpacking to glare at Olivia.

Olivia's reddening face wrinkled. "Well, okay."

Anthony waited for Olivia to shut the bathroom door before whispering to Emily, "Why did you cut in like that? I think she was gonna ask me to sleep with her!"

"Oh, please!" Emily spat. Cringing as she patted the yellow sheets, she smoothed them before sitting upon her bed.

"C'mon, it's so obvious she likes me."

"You are only seeing what you want to believe."

"She didn't even bother to ask anyone else."

Emily shrugged and pulled the game console out of her bag.

"What if she invited me here so we could, y'know. . ." He blushed and trailed off when he noticed Olivia exiting the bathroom in her pajamas.

"As flattered as I am that you feel comfortable enough to share your fantasies with me, I would rather not hear them," Emily muttered, turning the hand-held console back on.

"What are you guys talking about?" Olivia asked, tossing a ball of jeans and sweater onto her bed.

"Nothing," Anthony said. "Um, are you done with the bathroom for the night?"

"Yeah, it's all yours."

Though he worried about leaving the girls alone for even a second, by the time he returned from washing up, Olivia was fast asleep. *I guess she really was tired,* Anthony thought, peering over at her motionless body.

"She passed out the moment her head touched her pillow," Emily whispered, still playing her game. "Sorry to disappoint you."

"No, it's fine." Something about the peaceful expression she wore in her slumber was far more satisfying than anything he could imagine. It made the stench and grime of the room tolerable, almost even comforting. Making his way to the couch, he murmured to Emily, "Don't stay up too late, okay?"

"I will not. Do not worry."

~~

Simon was sitting at his desk in his apartment at Eden headquarters, flipping through various textbooks on black magic. He glanced at the clock hanging on the wall beside a metal cross. It was already two in the morning.

"Whatever it was that caused her death, Emily's parents were willing to take the secret to their graves. . . Lucifer's

Disciples is oddly desperate to keep Emily away from Eden, possibly because she's the only living person that knows of this secret."

Simon could hear Jason's words from the phone call a couple days ago still ringing in his ears. He gazed at the Mavro family's files, which sat upon a shelf above his desk.

"Only traitors would keep secrets from Eden."

Sighing in frustration, he closed his eyes and held his head. *But they weren't, and that makes this more confusing. The Mavros were always a part of Eden, so why didn't they trust them with Zalem's identity?* Simon groaned, clutching his hair. *There's nothing unique about Emily's parents, other than the fact that they killed themselves after her death and erased all evidence of having a son. They were as dedicated to Eden as anyone in the Mavro family ever was. None of Emily's other relatives seem to know anything about her or her brother.*

Sakura approached him from behind, her hair mussed from sleep. "You're still awake?" she asked through a yawn.

"I'm trying to figure out why Emily's able to survive off Anthony's spiritual presence, if that's even what she's doing," Simon said, setting the book on his lap.

"Do you have to figure it out tonight?" She rubbed his shoulders and nuzzled her face in his hair. "Can't you just come to bed already?"

Simon shook his head, picking up the bottle of whisky that sat on the corner of the desk. "I need to know. I know she made up the whole thing about drinking souls. I don't know if she's straight up lying like she did about the silencing spell or if she seriously believes it, but it's not possible. I sensed zero spiritual energy in her body, so she obviously didn't take anything from Anthony."

"I didn't sense anything either."

When he took a sip from the bottle, Sakura grimaced.

"All I know is that the union of her soul, body, and mind were broken, leaving her with only the body and mind,"

Simon said. "She has all her memories because she still has her mind, as Lucifer's Disciples failed to steal it with her soul due to a misfire in their magic. Soul stealing spells aren't easy for mages to perform, so they must have been really desperate to keep her hostage. Even so, there is nothing in these books about a person without a soul being able to live off of someone else's spiritual presence. Her servant thing really serves no purpose."

Before he could take another sip, Sakura snatched the bottle from his hand. "Do you really need to drink while you study?"

"It just makes me a little more relaxed about everything," Simon reached for the bottle, but she moved it behind her back.

"If this investigation is really that stressful for you, you should just take a break and rest."

"I'll have plenty of time to rest once this is over." Opening one of the black magic books in front of him, he flipped to a bookmarked page. "It says here that if a soul is stolen from a body and taken to another spiritual plane, the body will rot. Emily's hasn't aged at all during the past hundred years, meaning her soul is still being held on Earth, most likely at Lucifer's Disciples' nearest base. For whatever reason, they *want* her to be able to stay at least somewhat alive, and if we could infiltrate their lair and get her soul back, we can stop whatever they're planning to do with her and get her out of this weird undead state."

"Too bad they've moved location since we left."

"Doesn't mean we can't find it."

"If it could be done, Eden would have done it a long time ago."

Simon slouched in his chair and ran his hands over his face. "I know. This investigation is gonna take a lot longer than I thought." He glanced at the calendar beside his desk. "Easter is in a few days, and I didn't go to church at all this week. What kind of exorcist doesn't go to church during Holy Week?"

"One who's busy with an investigation," Sakura said, leaning against the desk. "There will be plenty of Easters in the future."

"It still sucks to miss out. Even if we miraculously are able to get Emily's soul back, there's still all that Zalem crap to figure out."

Sakura shrugged, taking a sip from the bottle before setting it back on the desk. "Maybe not. His case might not be relevant if Lucifer's Disciples doesn't have Emily."

Simon narrowed his eyes. "I'm not so sure about that. There's something more to this that we're missing." Stacking the books on his desk, he rose from his chair. "Change of plans. We're moving the investigation to Mavro Manor."

"What?" Sakura followed after him to their bedroom. "You can't do that."

"If I'm trying to figure out more about the Mavro family, I don't see a better place to be than Mavro Manor. Even if they destroyed all evidence of Zalem, there's gotta be some sort of clue."

"But Erika said we can't go to Mavro Manor," Sakura said, her voice rising.

Simon stopped in the bedroom doorway and turned to face her. "I don't care about what Erika says. I don't plan on telling her that we're going. The fact that we aren't allowed to go there means that there's something worth hiding."

CHAPTER 16

~~

Anthony sat up from the musty couch and glanced at the clock on the table beside him. It was six thirty in the morning. He stood up and stretched, his back aching from his uncomfortable slumber. His bedroom floor was more comfortable than the hard motel couch, but the beds didn't appear any more promising. He walked over to Olivia's bed and tapped her shoulder.

"Hey, Olivia, wake up. We gotta get ready for school."

"No," she moaned, rolling onto her side. "I don't want to go."

"Come on. We have to. They'll call our houses if we don't. Your family will get mad."

"They won't care." She reached for her phone on her nightstand and pushed the home button. "My mom didn't even text me to see where I went."

"Well, I care," Anthony said. "School's important."

She set her phone back on the table and lay on her stomach. "Then why do you always ditch?"

"Because I gave up on school. You're actually smart and have the potential to do something awesome with your life."

She laughed, her voice muffled behind her pillow. "I care about school just as much as you do. I just go to distract myself from my family life, just like how I wanted to come to this crappy motel. Anything is better than being home."

Anthony sat on the corner of her bed and sighed. "You're gonna have to go back anyway. We only paid for one night."

"I'll pay for another night then," Olivia said after a moment of thought.

"What is that about another night?" Emily said. Sitting up in bed, she stretched her arms and yawned. "I am not staying here another night. This bed is horribly uncomfortable and this room smells like rotten wood."

"We're not staying another night," Anthony said, his tone firm. "You can't just run away from home. I hate being home, too, but I still deal with it."

Olivia bolted upright. "But when Emily said she wanted to run away from Mavro Manor, you were totally okay with it!"

Anthony looked away. "That was a completely different situation."

"No, it wasn't!" Olivia shouted, pounding her fist on the mattress. "This is what's been frustrating me! You always do nice things for her without a second thought—"

"First off, there were so many second thoughts the day I brought her to my house," Anthony snapped. "Second, I thought you said you didn't care about what I did with her, so why are you flipping out right now?"

"Good morning, everyone!"

Anthony jumped at the sound of an unexpected voice. He was reluctant to face the table, which Rundull sat upon beaming, Anita and Thalia on either side of him. Rundull scratched the side of his head and chuckled. "Wow, this is an awkward conversation to walk into. Should I come back in five minutes?"

Emily narrowed her eyes. "How did you get in here?"

Rundull cocked his head at the back window. "You guys

left it unlocked."

"Seriously?" Olivia slapped Anthony's arm. "You couldn't lock it before bed?"

"It doesn't lock," Anthony said, scooting away from her.

"It's funny seeing you three here without your Eden buddies to protect you," Rundull said. He grinned at Emily. "It's almost like you *want* me to take you."

Emily curled her fist, balling sheets into her palm.

"I don't think I made my proposal clear enough when we last met," Rundull said. "You'd be begging for me to take you if you knew exactly what I have to offer."

"She doesn't care about what you have to say," Anthony said, though he struggled to believe his own words when he saw Emily's brow furrow.

"And what is it that you have to offer?" Emily asked.

"If you come with me, I'll give you back your soul and I'll even take you to see your brother." His smile growing larger, he clapped his hands together. "Then you can live happily ever after, just like you've always wanted."

Emily's eyes widened.

"Do you have any weapons?" Anthony whispered to Olivia. "Like those guns with the silver bullets?"

Olivia shook her head and gave him an uneasy smile. "I didn't think we'd need them."

Anthony slapped a palm over his face. "Great. If they attack us, we're so screwed." He took a deep breath and rose from the bed. Clearing his throat, he glanced back at Emily and said, "That'd be a pretty sweet deal if Zalem was still alive."

"Who said he's dead?" Rundull replied.

"Emily died in 1910. Even if Zalem lived a healthy life, there's no way he'd be alive right now."

"You know even less about the night Emily died than I thought," Rundull chuckled. "Your ignorance amazes me."

"Where is Zalem?" Emily asked, her voice rising. Her grip on her bed sheets tightened. "How is he alive?"

"Don't worry, he's safe with me," Rundull said. "If you come with me, I promise I'll take you to him and explain everything."

"And what will I owe you?"

"Nothing. Your happiness is all I need to be satisfied."

"Emily, don't listen to him," Anthony said, keeping an eye on Rundull. "He's obviously lying to lure you away. Why should he care about you?"

"Just because I'm a devil doesn't mean I'm lying," Rundull said with an annoyed huff. "I would never lie to Miss Emily. Is it so hard to believe that I'm actually a nice guy?"

"I am not going with you," Emily said with a hint of hesitation. "Even if what you say is true, Zalem would never want me to listen to a devil, even for his own sake."

Rundull crossed his arms. "Oh, really?" He looked to the Phobia girls, who both withdrew their black batons and activated their scythes. Leaping from the table, they seized Anthony and Olivia, pinning them against the wall with the handles of their weapons.

"One of those guns could have *really* come in handy right now," Anthony grumbled to Olivia as he struggled to break free.

Writhing beneath the handle of Thalia's scythe, Olivia glared at him.

"So, what will it be, Miss Emily?" Rundull asked, sliding off the table. "Are you going to accept my offer?" He gestured to Anthony and Olivia. "Or will I have to kill your friends?"

Before he could come within a foot of her bed, the door flung open to reveal a young man not much older than Anthony pointing a gun in Rundull's direction. Anthony assumed from the black trench coat and sunglasses that he was from Eden, a thought that both relieved and panicked him. Judging from Olivia's blushing cheeks, he figured she felt the same way.

"So Eden *is* here," Rundull muttered, wrinkling his nose.

Lifting his sunglasses and lowering his gun, the man stared at Rundull with wide brown eyes. "A kid? Really?"

"Don't be fooled, Matt," Drea said, approaching from behind. She pointed her gun at Rundull. "He's a devil."

Olivia bowed her head, hiding her face from Drea beneath her bangs.

Matt clenched his jaw and raised his gun again.

Rundull looked to Anita and Thalia. "Drop your weapons. I'll take care of them."

Thalia and Anita released Olivia and Anthony, their scythes retracting into their batons. Rundull leapt back onto the table, his bat wings ripping through his cloak while a black shadow extended from beneath him. Anthony and Olivia scurried to opposite ends of the room to avoid the growing shadow. Rising from the ground, it stretched into a dark, smoky, horned creature. As it charged toward the door, Matt lifted his arms over his head, creating a white curtain of light in front of him and Drea. Ramming its horns against the barrier, the monster broke through the light, causing it to fade into nothingness. Matt and Drea dropped to the floor and shot at the monster, their bullets creating holes in its gaseous body. It shrank away toward Rundull, the smoky gas filling the gaps.

"Well, that's an annoying mechanism," Drea grumbled, reloading her gun.

"Forget the shadow thing, just get the kid!" Matt shouted, aiming at Rundull.

Rundull held his hand out in front of his body. The bullets from Matt's gun dropped to the floor once they came within an inch of his palm. "Is that all you got?" Rundull asked with a smirk. The shadow monster let out a menacing hiss, ready to pounce.

"Oh, for Christ's sake!" Drea reached into her coat and withdrew a hand grenade. She pulled the pin—

"You're not gonna throw that thing in here, are you?" Anthony cried, cowering against the wall.

—and chucked it on the floor in front of Rundull and the Phobia girls. Anthony covered his ears and shut his eyes, awaiting the impending explosion. Moments later, he cracked an eye open. All that was released from the grenade was a misty white gas. The shadow monster was nothing more than a thinning dark cloud. Anita and Thalia dove behind Rundull, scrambling for the back window. Falling to his knees, Rundull's hands flew over his nose and mouth, coughing up black smoke. Blood dripped from the corners of his glaring eyes.

"You'll regret this!" he growled, his voice muffled beneath his hand. He followed after Thalia and Anita through the window, soaring away from the motel.

Still shaken from the initial fright upon seeing it, Anthony gaped at the grenade. The remaining gas continued to spew from the nozzle. "What the hell is that thing?"

"It's just a holy water bomb," Matt said. Glancing at his reflection in the nearest mirror, he ran a hand through his spiked brown hair. He turned to Anthony and smirked, rubbing his hands together. "Not that it matters. You're going to forget it in a few minutes anyway."

"You don't have to erase their memories," Drea said, removing her sunglasses. "I know these people."

Matt's eyes darted from Anthony, to Emily, to Olivia. "Hold up, is that the chairman's daughter? Olivia, right?"

"Y-yeah," Olivia mumbled, avoiding his gaze.

"And that's Emily Mavro over there," Drea said, cocking her head at Emily. "And Anthony is her friend. I've been working with them for the past week."

"He's my servant," Emily said, sitting up straighter.

Matt grinned. "Kinky. Sounds like I've been missing out."

"A lot has happened since you were away for your training." Drea's expression hardened when she looked to Olivia. "What the hell are you guys even doing here? What part of going about your normal lives did you not understand? If Matt and I weren't patrolling the area, you'd all be dead."

"Oh, snap, the chairman's daughter is busted!" Matt laughed.

"Shut up, Matt," Drea grumbled. "Stay out of this."

Anthony bit the inside of his cheek, racking his brain for an excuse.

Olivia cleared her throat. "What are you doing with Matt? I thought you wanted nothing to do with him after you two broke up."

Drea flushed and took a step back. "I'm only patrolling with him because I needed someone to go with me."

"That's not what you told me back at headquarters," Matt said. "You said you wanted to go out to lunch and—"

"Shut up, Matt!" Drea shouted.

Though Anthony was relieved Olivia dodged Drea's question, the tension between Olivia, Matt, and Drea made him more uncomfortable than before. As much as he wanted to know more about Drea's past relationship, he knew he had to change the subject before any potential arguments could arise. "So, why aren't you with Simon and Sakura right now?" he asked Drea. "Aren't you guys working on the investigation at headquarters?"

"They're just reading through textbooks and files," Drea said with a shrug. "I figured they don't really need me for now. Besides, they left to go to Mavro Manor this morning to continue investigating. I'd rather stay at headquarters and take on new missions than sit around in a stuffy mansion all day."

"Wait, they're at Mavro Manor?" Olivia asked. "But my sister said we can't go there."

"They did it anyway, and I think Karin went with them, because God forbid she leaves Simon alone with his girlfriend."

"You've gotta be kidding me," Olivia grumbled, stomping to her suitcase. "Anthony, Emily, grab your stuff. We gotta head over there before Erika finds out."

"What are you so worried about?" Emily asked, dragging herself out of her bed. "There is not anything there that they can *screw up*. I am sure they will respect the property."

"I'm not worried about them messing anything up," Olivia said, focused on packing. "I'm responsible for anything that goes on in Mavro Manor. If Erika says we can't go there, then it's my job to make sure no one does. If she finds out they went there against her orders, I'm gonna get in trouble, too. I'd rather not suffer the wrath of Eden."

"Good luck getting Simon to leave," Matt chuckled.

Drea sighed. "We should probably get back to patrolling." She looked to Anthony, Olivia, and Emily. "You guys hurry up before more demons come after you."

"We will," Anthony said, already packing his own suitcase.

"And one more thing." Drea glanced back at Olivia and blushed again. "Can you please not tell Simon that you saw me with Matt?"

Olivia paused. She looked up from her packing. "Only if you don't tell anyone that you found us here."

Drea narrowed her eyes. "Deal."

CHAPTER 17

~~

Anthony hurried after Olivia, who marched to the back side of Mavro Manor. There they found Simon teaching Karin how to fight using a wooden sword in the grassy yard. Sakura sat in one of the chairs on the porch, reading a black magic book. When she noticed Olivia approaching, she peered up from the pages.

"Olivia? What are you guys doing here?" Sakura asked.

"I should be asking you that," Olivia said, crossing her arms. "You guys know it's off limits to investigate here."

Sakura shut the book and rested it on the arm of the chair. "How did you know we were here?"

"Erika told me," Olivia answered without a moment's thought. "She told me to come and tell you guys to leave."

"Then why did she text me five minutes ago asking where you were?"

Olivia's gaze darted to the grass. "Maybe she was wondering if I was here yet?"

"I don't think so." Picking up her phone from the wooden floor, Sakura scrolled through her messages. "Erika says she was at your house last night to take your mom out for her birthday dinner and that you ditched. She also says your school called to report your absence a little while ago and your mom is freaking out."

"See, I told you your family would be worried," Anthony whispered in her ear. He shook his head. "That's just cold, skipping out on your own mother's birthday."

Olivia withdrew her own phone from her jeans pocket. "I didn't get any messages from either of them."

"Erika said you never gave her or your mom your new phone number since you got a new one last winter," Sakura said.

"With all your crazy technological devices, I am surprised communicating is so difficult," Emily sneered.

"It's not usually difficult," Olivia said. "My family is just making it this way. They could have gotten my number from someone else. It's like they *want* to make me look bad."

You're making yourself *look bad,* Anthony thought, staring at her through narrowed eyes.

Simon tossed his wooden sword aside and smirked. "Alright, so who was it that ratted us out?"

"It was Drea," Emily said.

"Didn't we promise her that we wouldn't talk about what happened this morning?" Anthony murmured to Emily.

"I did not promise her anything," Emily said, leaning away from Anthony. "Honestly, it is ridiculous how many secrets you Eden people keep from each other, yet you fuss over anything that I refuse to mention."

"When did you guys see her?" Sakura asked, raising her brow with interest.

"We were at this disgusting motel where Rundull found us," Emily explained, "and then Drea fought them off with some other man. Matt, I think."

"Wait, which Matt?" Karin dropped her sword and ran to Emily's side. "Sweet Matt, hot Matt, egg sandwich Matt, or just Matt?"

"I did not realize there were so many Matts at Eden," Emily said, taking a step back.

"I'm gonna assume hot Matt," Olivia answered, glaring

at Emily.

"Yes!" Karin's fists shook with excitement. "Best one!"

"What the hell? He's back from his training and didn't tell me?" Simon cried. "I freaking taught him how to use white magic! He would have never gotten that fancy-pants Vatican training if it weren't for me!"

"You taught him a lot more than white magic," Sakura muttered. "He's probably trying to clean up his act."

"How were you able to teach him?" Anthony asked. "He doesn't look that much younger than you."

"Phobia age slower than humans," Karin said. "Simon's a lot older than he looks."

"I'm not *a lot* older," Simon mumbled, pulling his phone out of his pocket.

"Are you texting him?" Olivia asked. "Drea specifically told us not to tell you they were patrolling together. From the way she was acting, I think she's trying to get back with him."

"Dear Lord," Simon grumbled, rolling his eyes. "What's it gonna take for her to realize he's not into her? He needs to stop being so freaking nice and just straight up tell her."

"As interesting as all this drama is, I kinda wanna know the story behind egg sandwich Matt," Anthony said. "I feel like there's a good story there."

"There's never a good story with Eden," Olivia said, wrinkling her nose.

"I think there's a good story with what happened at the motel," Sakura said. Holding her chin, she looked to Anthony and Emily. "So, Rundull waited until you were away from home to attack?"

"Yeah," Anthony said. "We probably shouldn't have gone there anyway."

"But it shouldn't have mattered," Simon said. "Lucifer's Disciples has only attacked when you guys were with us, and we weren't at the motel."

"I was, though," Olivia said. "They probably don't even

want me near Emily."

"You guys should just stay with us," Karin said. "They can't get us here and then we can all hang out again."

"I'm not leaving until there's no one left in this house," Olivia said, stiffening. "I can't leave you guys to investigate here unsupervised."

"I do not understand why you want to investigate here," Emily said, placing her hands on her hips. "I am not sure what you are expecting to find, but you will not find anything here."

"If there's nothing, then the Mavro family wouldn't be so uptight about us being here," Simon said. "So until we find whatever it is that they're trying to hide, we're not leaving."

~~

Late that night, Simon and Sakura roamed the halls of Mavro Manor. Dragging his fingertips along the walls, Simon studied every bump beneath the gray floral wallpaper. "I don't care what Emily says," he whispered. "There's gotta be something here."

"We've been searching for the past two hours and found nothing," Sakura said. "Maybe she's right. I'm sure someone from Eden would have found something by now. We don't even know what we're looking for."

"I couldn't find any files on investigations held here or pertaining to Emily," Simon said. "Ours is the first one. All other proposals have been rejected by other members of the Mavro family, even before they took chair for Eden, meaning they must have been doing something to prevent anyone at Eden from opening a case."

"What, you don't think they bribed them, do you?" Sakura said with a chuckle, but her grin faded when she noticed Simon wasn't laughing with her.

"I have my theories." Simon stopped walking and

stared out at the end of the hallway. "Emily's parents were close friends with a doctor named Hans Erickson and a priest named Jose Romero. Both of them lived away from Eden with their families. A few days before Emily's death, Jose's daughter died. Suicide. Killed herself in his church. According to her profile, her father claimed she had gone insane, so she was still given a funeral by the church."

Sakura narrowed her eyes.

"On the day Emily's parents died, Hans and his wife were both found dead in their home, each with a bullet in their heads. Not even an hour later, Jose and his wife were also found dead in their home, same sized bullets in their heads. And then in the evening, Emily's parents committed suicide—"

"Same sized bullets?"

Simon nodded, his gaze remaining fixed on the end of the hall.

"It sounds like you're reciting something you've read," Sakura said with an uneasy laugh.

"Since there's so little information about Emily and her family, I had to search outside the box," Simon said. "While the killer of the Ericksons and Romeros was never found, I think it's safe to assume that the Mavros didn't want anyone left alive that could spoil their secrets. Whether the daughter's suicide is connected or just a coincidence, I have no idea. To this day, there isn't a single Romero or Erickson remaining with Eden." His eyes met Sakura's. "So, to answer your question, yes, I think the Mavros either killed off or bribed anyone they considered a threat. They definitely had the money for it. They either couldn't trust Eden with their secrets, or they believed Eden couldn't trust them."

"I find it funny how much you care about a case that you didn't even want."

"Who wouldn't be pumped to uncover a hundred-year-old scandal?" Simon said. Picking up his pace, he continued to drag his fingers along the wall. "If they pitched it as something more than a babysitting job, I would have cared a lot more from the start."

Pausing beside a small table upon which a flowerpot sat, Simon furrowed his brow and pressed his fingers against the wall. "Feel here."

Sakura placed her hand beside his, just above the flowers. "What am I feeling for?"

"There's a bump where the wall beneath the paper is uneven. Like there's a door underneath here."

Sakura's arm dropped to her side. "Don't be ridiculous. Don't you think they would have done a better job of hiding a door than slapping wallpaper over it?"

"I'll give them credit for removing the doorknob if it is a door. They probably figured no one would waste their time feeling the walls." Backing away from the wall, he held out his palms in front of his chest. "Stay back. I'm blasting it down."

"You can't just destroy part of their house!" Sakura cried. "That's probably why they don't want us here in the first place."

Simon ignored her, a ball of white light gathering in his hands. Aiming above the flowers, Simon shot the ball into the wall, creating a gaping hole. Pieces of the wall crumbled to the floor, revealing a staircase leading down into darkness.

Sakura peeked at the cement stairs. "I can't see where they end."

"Then let's go find out." Taking her hand in his, they proceeded downward.

~~

Olivia gawked at the hole in the wall, still dressed in her pajamas. "What the hell is this?"

"We found a secret passageway," Simon said, gesturing toward the staircase with a proud grin. "Neat, huh?"

"*Neat?* You put a freaking hole in my family's house!"

"This is what you guys were doing all night?" Anthony asked, rubbing the grit out of his tired eyes.

"Yeah," Sakura chuckled. "Sorry about the damage."

"Erika's gonna kill me when she finds out," Olivia groaned, burying her face in her hands. "This is *exactly* why we don't want you guys here."

"I'd be more worried about how Emily will react when she wakes up," Anthony said. "This is *her* house."

"Oh, c'mon, it's not like she likes it here," Karin said, pushing past Anthony and Olivia, approaching the stairs. "I'm so pumped to see what's down there!"

"That's too bad, because you're staying up here," Simon said, steering her away from the steps. "It's not a pretty sight down there."

"Seriously?" Karin cried. "I'm not that much younger than Olivia and Anthony, so why can they go?"

"I think it's okay," Sakura said, nodding to Simon. "She can handle it."

Simon sighed. "If you really want to, then fine."

Using the lights on their phones, Simon led everyone down to the basement. Wooden crosses lined the cement walls, looming over the rusty stains splattered across the floor. Anthony's eyes widened with shock at the sight of bones piled in corners beneath more stains smeared across the walls. Judging from the shape of the skulls, he had a sickening suspicion that they once belonged to humans. Thick metal chains were bolted to the far right wall, surrounded by copper hand prints.

"What. . . What is this place?" Anthony whispered.

Olivia's hands flew over her mouth, gasping when her eyes fell upon the dark red letters scribbled on the center wall reading *LORD HAVE MERCY.* Then on one of the other walls, *GOD SAVE MY SOUL.*

"Pretty creepy, isn't it?" Simon said. He grasped one of

the chains, sliding his fingers along the cold metal, down to the cuff at the bottom. "Perfect size for a human wrist."

"This isn't what I was expecting," Karin said, her voice shaking. Cradling herself, she backed toward the stairs.

"Neither were we," Sakura said, looking to Olivia. "Did you know about this room?"

Olivia shook her head, her face devoid of color. "I've been in this house so many times and this room has always been beneath me without me knowing. . ." She dropped to her knees. "M-my family did all this? Did. . . Did they kill people here?"

"We don't know for sure," Anthony said, kneeling beside her. He peered up at Simon and asked, "We don't, do we?"

Simon shrugged. "It's the perfect place to kill people. Their screams would never be heard, not even by people in the house. Judging by all the chains, the bloodstains, and the fact that they have a whole room dedicated to this madness, they must have done it often. I don't really know what else this room could have been used for, but I can't think of a rational explanation why they'd need it in the first place."

"I can't either," Olivia muttered. "I had no idea. . . I don't think anyone in my immediate family does. I mean, that wallpaper covering this was ancient, so. . ."

"Why don't we just ask Emily about this creepy place when she wakes up?" Karin asked.

"I'll do it," Anthony said. "She might be more willing to be truthful with me."

As desperate as Anthony was for answers, part of him was nervous to ask Emily about the room. While he waited for her to awaken, he pondered over the possible explanations, but he never did see her that morning. When he checked her bedroom around noon, she was not present. He walked downstairs to the parlor, where he found Olivia sitting alone on the couch, scrolling through her phone, her face still pale from the morning's events.

"Hey," he said, sitting beside her. "You okay?"

She set her phone in her lap. "I found out I've been taking care of the house of brutal killers. I'm not okay."

"I know it's creepy, but I wouldn't take it too hard."

"How could I have not known?" Her panicked eyes met his. "My family killed people in this house and I don't even know why."

"We don't know for sure that's what they were doing."

"Anthony. They had freaking chains attached to the walls. If they felt the need to chain people, it probably wasn't anything good."

"But at least they felt kinda bad about it. I mean, they had those messages on the walls and all the crosses, so it's not like they were sacrificing people to Satan."

Though he hoped his words were enough to cheer her up, the fear remained on Olivia's face. Anthony sighed and said, "Even if you did know about any of it, it's not like you could have done anything to stop it. It all happened over a hundred years ago."

She looked away. "I guess you're right. But still, it's just so shocking to me. . . And this was probably going on while Emily lived here."

"Yeah, speaking of Emily, have you seen her at all today?"

"I saw her a little while ago." She pointed down the hall. "I think she went that way."

Anthony took Olivia's word and walked down the long hall. It seemed like there wasn't anyone around, but he could hear music. He followed his ears and found himself in an enormous room with a checkered marble floor. It was lit by a single tall window, facing the backyard. Her fingers dancing across the keys, Emily sat at the grand piano in the center of the room, the notes filling the entire room with the peaceful yet nostalgic tune. Anthony stood in the doorway and listened to her play. As much as he wished to speak with her, he didn't want her to stop playing.

"Wow," was all Anthony could manage to say when she finished the piece.

"I did not hear you come in," Emily said, her back facing him.

"Sorry to disrupt you," he said. "But. . . Wow. . . That was amazing."

Emily gazed at the keys with a blank expression.

"Go on. Keep playing," Anthony said. "I'd love to hear more. You're really great."

"*Tritesse*."

"What?"

"That is the piece. *Tritesse*. It is French for sadness. Have you ever heard of Chopin? He composed it."

"I've heard the name," Anthony said, walking toward the piano. "I can't say I really know much about classical music."

"Chopin is my favorite composer. All his songs are so beautiful and emotional. Zalem would always play Chopin for me."

"Oh," Anthony muttered, afraid that if he said too much, she wouldn't say more.

But she continued. "Zalem was an excellent pianist. He taught me when I was a child. I could never compare myself to him."

"I thought your playing was really good," Anthony murmured.

"That is because you never heard Zalem." She shut her eyes and smiled. "I would sit on the floor for hours, just listening to him play. His playing was so elegant, so beautiful, it could make me cry, but I loved that he was able to make me feel so many different emotions through music. Some of the emotions I had never felt before, but Zalem taught me how to feel them, and to become them as I play." Positioning her hands on the keys, she glanced over her shoulder at Anthony. "Perhaps you will feel something new from this piece."

Shutting his eyes, Anthony listened to her next song. Though sweet and tranquil, it filled him with a melancholy longing he hadn't felt before. Time seemed to stand still as she played, as if nothing else mattered other than the piece.

When she finished, he struggled to find the words to describe his feelings, his eyes remaining shut. "It's peaceful, but lonely," he said after a moment of thought.

"Like the night sky?" Emily said. "Calm, beautiful, yet dark and spacious."

Anthony opened his eyes. "In a way, yeah."

"Such is the nocturne." Smoothing her dress, Emily rose to her feet. "Pieces inspired by the night. Nocturnes were Zalem's favorite, but mine were the waltzes." She skipped to the center of the room and twirled, black hair whipping about her face. "Every time Zalem would play one, the music would sweep me off my feet to waltz with me. Sometimes one of our servants would play for us so Zalem could waltz with me, and he'd hold me in his arms—" She broke off as she lost balance. Falling to her knees, she held her flushed cheeks in her hands, rocking in an unsteady motion.

Anthony rushed to her side and held her shoulders. "Are you feeling okay?"

"I am fine," she said, though her eyes were unfocused and struggled to meet his gaze. She pointed to the gazebo outside on the lawn. "See that? We would dance right there in that gazebo, listening to the music from the open window. Sometimes we would dance in the moonlight to the gorgeous melodies. We would waltz even as late as midnight to the dreamiest pieces."

Anthony peered down at the floor. "Emily, there's something I need to ask you about. Simon and Sakura found this room with all these chains and blood. . ." He trailed off when he felt Emily stiffen.

"Now do you understand why I hate this house?" she asked. "I have said it before, and I will say it again. My family had their reasons for the things they did." She clung to his shoulders to help her stand, swaying with every step she took toward the piano. "I tried to stop it. I really did. In that room, we all became monsters. Everyone. We were all filled with sin. Even now, the memories of what we did still haunt me."

Taking her seat at the bench, Emily played another piece—one that Anthony recognized. Chopin's *Funeral March*. He had heard it many times in movies when a character died, but it never sounded this gloomy and hopeless. It was the sound of pure despair and agony. His arms shriveled with goosebumps, his heart sinking to his stomach.

"Playing piano was the only way Zalem and I could distract ourselves from the monsters inside us," she said while she played. "But even so, we couldn't hide forever. Not in that room, and not in our music." Rising from the bench, she staggered to the window. She gazed out into the distance, past the yard and the trees surrounding it, at something unseen. "Zalem was an amazing pianist, but a sick person. He is the reason I have these scars on my arms. He found pleasure in watching me hurt myself, but I. . ." She turned to Anthony, her eyes filling with a strange sort of maniacal glee to match her grin, an expression Anthony had only seen on the night he witnessed her cutting herself. "I found pleasure in *his* pleasure. I feared him, sometimes even despised him. But more than anything, I was *obsessed* with him and the pain he gave me, just as he was obsessed with my pain and my blood."

Anthony grit his teeth and averted his gaze to the piano. He couldn't bear to look into those eyes, to hear her laughter. He didn't want to believe any of it to be true, but after seeing that room, he couldn't deny any of it.

"I wanted to be the only one who could make Zalem

happy. I wanted him to need me. I wanted to be his servant, his possession, and that's why. . ." Emily trailed off, the color draining from her blushing cheeks. Her eyes rolled back and her legs gave away. Anthony hurried to her side, her unconscious body falling into his arms.

CHAPTER 18

~~

Anthony dashed into the parlor, relieved to find Olivia still sitting on the couch. She stood up when she saw him panting in the doorway, grasping his knees for support.

"Anthony? Are you okay?"

"I'm fine," he said, catching his breath. "Where's Simon?"

"Doing more training outside with Karin," she replied. "Why? Is something wrong?"

Anthony didn't answer. Instead, he dashed onto the porch, past where Sakura sat, to the grass where Simon was teaching Karin how to use her cross sword.

"Thank God I found you!" Anthony cried, his hand resting over his racing heart.

Simon raised his brow. "What's up?"

"Emily. I don't know what happened. I was just talking to her and she was playing piano for me and she said all this creepy stuff and started acting all creepy and—"

"Whoa, slow down," Simon cut in, raising a hand to silence him. "What do you mean by creepy?"

Sakura leaned over the porch railing, her eyes narrowed.

"I. . . I don't know." Anthony tried to organize his racing thoughts before he spoke again. "I can't explain it. She was weirdly happy in this really freaky way and she was talking about her brother. She said she'd hurt herself to make him happy."

Karin grimaced, but remained silent.

"She was gonna tell me more," Anthony said, "but then she passed out."

"You mean she just randomly fainted?" Simon asked.

"She was shaking when she was talking before it happened, so I dunno."

"Well, this doesn't sound good." Simon sighed and walked toward the house. "Where is she now?"

"In the ballroom," Anthony said, he and the others following after Simon.

When they reached the ballroom, Emily still lay unconscious beneath the window. Simon picked her up and held her in his arms.

"She's back to the sleeping state she was in before you met her," he told Anthony. "The spell on her feels stronger, like how it used to be."

"But nothing even happened to affect the spell," Anthony said, peeking over Simon's shoulder.

"But she was showing signs of weakening before she passed out, right?" Karin asked, remaining by the doorway. "You said she was shaking, so something must have triggered it."

Sakura stared at Emily, holding her chin. "She didn't say anything about that room, did she?"

"Sort of," Anthony answered. "She said something about turning into monsters, but she didn't explain what she meant."

"We'll find out soon enough," Simon said, carrying Emily as he rose. "I'm gonna leave her in the parlor. It'll be easier to keep an eye on her there."

Emily still hadn't awakened by dinner. Sitting at the long dining room table, Anthony's mind was filled with anxiety. He couldn't stop worrying about Emily, sickened by the things she told him. Her laughter still rang in his ears.

"You should have seen the look on the delivery guy's face when I opened the door!" Karin laughed, carrying a stack of pizza boxes into the dining room. "I bet he never had to deliver pizzas to a spooky mansion."

"Pretty sure most delivery guys haven't," Sakura chuckled. She took the boxes and lined them up along the table.

Stuffing his phone in his pants pocket, Simon took a seat beside Anthony. "So I think I got a good plan for this whole Emily business. I called Mother Helena at St. Joseph's Monastery. She says she might know a way to weaken Emily's spell again."

"Really?" Anthony's eyes widened.

Simon nodded. "She said we can come over tomorrow. The monastery is run by Eden, but it's off the headquarters' campus, so it's okay if we all stay there." He reached for a slice of pizza, but Sakura dragged the box away.

"Shouldn't we wait for Olivia?" she said.

"She's been on the phone with her sister for the past hour," Simon groaned.

"You can start eating," Olivia said, hurrying into the dining room. "Sorry to keep you waiting."

"Did you tell her about Emily?" Anthony asked.

Olivia took her seat across from him. "Yeah. And she's not too thrilled about the hole in the wall."

"I can understand why," Sakura said. "Did she know about the room?"

"Not at all. She was pretty surprised. Also. . ." Olivia handed Simon her phone. "Father sent me an e-mail and asked me to show it to you."

"I thought your dad never talks to you?" Anthony said.

"He doesn't unless it's urgent," Olivia said. "That's why I called Erika after I read it. It's kind of a big deal."

Sakura peered over Simon's shoulder to read the e-mail. The further he read, the more wrinkled Simon's face became. "This is ridiculous!"

"What is it?" Karin asked, peeking at the e-mail.

"He's forcing us to stop the investigation," Olivia said. "He's upset that we violated the rules against being here. We have to leave by tomorrow morning."

"I don't care about leaving," Simon said, setting the phone aside. "I already made plans for us to go to the monastery anyway. But he can't just terminate our investigation."

"Well, he's the chairman, so he actually can," Olivia said, staring down at her folded hands. "He wants to keep Emily at headquarters, but I just know that will end poorly, especially in the state she's in now."

"We're not stopping," Simon said. "We've come too far to just give up."

"And you think it's a good idea to just work behind Eden's back?" Sakura asked. "We could face serious consequences if we disobey the chairman's orders."

"The only reason he's calling this off is because he knows that we've found out something about his freaky family that he wanted to keep secret," Simon said. "That's all the more reason to keep investigating."

"I don't know if my father actually knows about the room, though," Olivia said.

"He at least knows enough about Emily's family to know when to make us stop."

"We can't stop," Anthony said, looking from Simon to Olivia. "We need to help Emily."

"And we will," Simon said, leaning back in his chair. "We'll just be more discrete about our investigation. Easter is this Sunday. We'll go to the monastery tomorrow for Emily and stay the day after for the Easter banquet. We'll play it off like we're just going there to celebrate, since that's what

Sakura and I have been doing for the past few years anyway. Then we can just take it from there after the festivities."

"Do we have to stay for the banquet?" Karin grumbled, slumping in her chair and clutching her cheek. "That annoying kid Jimmy is always there with his stupid friends and they always try to talk to me."

"It's because they like you," Sakura said with a laugh.

Karin melted farther into her chair. "But they're so gross and annoying."

"If those boys make you feel uncomfortable at the banquet, just come find me," Simon said. "They won't bug you if you're with me."

"Really?" Karin beamed. "Then we should totally stay for the banquet."

"Well, that was the plan regardless if you liked it." He reached for another slice of pizza, avoiding Sakura's glare.

~~

Anthony sat on the floor beside the couch which Emily rested upon. He kept a careful watch on her face, hoping for any sign of movement, but she continued to lay still.

Olivia knocked on the parlor door, cracking it open enough to peek inside. "May I come in?"

Anthony nodded.

Olivia walked over to the couch, peering down at Emily. "She still out?"

"Yeah," Anthony said, his focus fixed on Emily. "She hasn't moved at all."

Olivia sat cross-legged next to Anthony. "I'm sure she will eventually. You woke her up before."

"But I don't know how I did in the first place," Anthony said. "All I did was approach her, but I've been sitting here for the past hour and nothing's happened."

"Well, we are going to the monastery tomorrow. They

can probably help her there, so I wouldn't stress about it tonight."

"How can I not?" He stared at Olivia, eyes wide with concern. "I was the only one there when she first woke up and I was the only one there when she passed out. This obviously has something to do with me."

Olivia gave him a soothing smile and patted his back. "I wouldn't say that."

"Don't you remember what happened with Karin at the mall?"

Olivia furrowed her brow. "When she used white magic? I didn't see it myself, but—"

"She was only able to use it because she wanted to impress Simon," Anthony cut in. "She was motivated by her feelings for him. I remember them saying that a large portion of magic is based on what comes from within, like how willing you are to master the powers or whatever."

"Okay, so what's that have to do with Emily passing out?"

Anthony took a deep breath. "The only reason she is able to live without a soul is because of a spell, right?"

"Right."

"And the spell is supposed to keep her asleep. That's why Lucifer's Disciples gets all freaked out when she's awake around us."

A lopsided smile spread across her face. "So you think she's able to control the spell?"

"I know it sounds crazy, especially coming from someone who knows nothing about magic, but yeah. To some degree. For some reason, she wants to be alive and thinks she needs someone to live off, so that's why she woke up when I was in her room." He looked back to Emily and sighed. "As for why she went back to sleep, I don't know. She must have lost that will."

Olivia slumped her shoulders. "But you don't know if

your theory is true."

"I don't, but from the way she was talking about her brother and the feelings she had for him. . ." He trailed off, his jaw trembling. "I know her state of unconsciousness is different than a living person's. If she was able to tell when I was near her the last time she was like this, then she must know now. So if I gotta sit here all day and night long to prove to her that there's someone out there who actually cares about her without wanting to hurt her, maybe she'll find it in her heart to wake up for my sake."

Sighing, Olivia stood, brushing down her skirt. "Well, I hope she wakes up then. She's lucky to have someone who cares for her so much. Most girls would want to be alive for someone like that."

~~

Simon sat on the couch in the Mavro Manor library later that night, skimming through the Mavro family profiles for what felt like the hundredth time. But even as he continued to reread them, the findings from the investigation were not adding up. The Mavro family kept Zalem's identity hidden from Eden, and they also kept the killing room a secret. Zalem would hurt Emily, but Simon had yet to find a connection to him and the room. If the Mavro family was faithful to Eden, then why did they feel the need to keep secrets? There had to be a reason why they stopped the investigation beyond them breaking rules.

As he continued to flip through the profiles, a folded slip of paper fell onto the ground from one of the files labeled Winston Mavro. Emily's grandfather. He unfolded it and revealed a handwritten letter.

Dear Gabriel,

If you are reading this, it is because I have passed on to the next world. Though I may be gone, I cannot afford to let this secret die with me. I wish I could have told you as soon as I had learned of it, but I could not afford the risk nor afford to leave you alone with them. Now that I have no choice but to give my life to God, I can finally tell you the truth about Eden.

Back when I was a young man, I was stationed at St. Joseph's Monastery with a few fellow investigators. As we stayed at the monastery, we kept getting attacked by chimeras and demons from Lucifer's Disciples. We were curious on how they got into the monastery grounds. We realized that they were all coming out of the crematorium in the funeral home. When we went to investigate, we found a room dedicated to black mass and creating monsters.

Simon held his chin. If Eden knew there were demons in the crematorium, why wouldn't they destroy it? He continued reading to search for the answer.

Though we were unable to defeat the monsters alone, when we requested assistance from Eden, we were denied. Eden refused to acknowledge the matter. Instead, we were forced to leave the monastery and swore to never tell anyone about what we saw in the crematorium. To this day, the crematorium has never been investigated, let alone mentioned. From this experience, I was able to draw a shocking conclusion: Eden and Lucifer's Disciples are connected someway, somehow. I do not believe everyone in Eden is working with the enemy. I am positive the majority of them are completely unaware of the demons in the crematorium. I am also positive that Lucifer's Disciples has created more bases on Eden property due to double agents granting them access to create evil on holy grounds. Unfortunately, I do not know who these spies are, but I can assure you that there are enough to pose a threat to Eden, the information we hold, and to the rest of society.

My dying wish is to tell you this simple fact. While I want to believe with every fiber of my being that Eden as a whole fights to protect the human race from evil, there are people within Eden who strive for just the opposite. While it is our duty to protect the innocent from demons, protecting our family comes first. Please, stay vigilant and stay safe. See you in the next world.

Love,

Winston Mavro

The color drained from Simon's face. Gabriel was Winston's son and Emily's father. Winston died when Gabriel was a teenager. If what he said was true, then the reason why they kept Zalem a secret wasn't because they were betraying Eden, but because Eden couldn't be trusted. Simon took a deep breath, failing to calm his racing heart. This couldn't be right. After everything he went through to gain Eden's trust, they're the ones that couldn't be trusted. But if Emily's parents kept Zalem a secret from Eden, why didn't they do the same for her?

"That's pretty messed up."

Simon jumped at the sound of Sakura's voice. He turned to find her looming over his shoulder, her eyes skimming over the letter. "How long have you been here?"

"Long enough to read that," she said. "Where did you find it?"

"It was tucked into the files I got from headquarters."

"If what it says is true, I'm not sure what to think."

"I don't want to believe it, but it makes sense to me," Simon said. He set the letter on the desk and crossed his arms. "Whatever illness Zalem had, the Mavro family felt it had to be kept secret from Eden. I think I'm going to ask Emily about it once she wakes up."

"I doubt Emily's parents told her anything about possible spies. She said before they didn't tell her much about anything Eden-related. I don't think it'd be a good idea to bring this up to her or the others. Making such broad accusations about Eden would only cause panic. Plus, if there really are traitors in Eden, I'm sure they'd dispose of us if they found out we knew their secret."

"And if we tell the others, then they'll dispose of them, too," Simon muttered. "I hate to keep secrets from our friends, but it's for their own safety."

"We're going to the monastery anyway. We can go to

the crematorium tomorrow night, just you and me, after everyone's asleep. If we can find hard evidence that there are traitors in Eden, we can expose it to everyone at the Easter banquet. If a ton of people learn about it, there's no way the traitors can kill them all to keep the secret."

Simon reached up to stroke her hair. "You're so sexy when you come up with cool ideas."

Sakura smiled. "I'm glad you like my plan, but we're only going through with it if you tell Karin to stop gushing over you."

Simon's hand fell to his side. "And break her heart? That's not a cool idea at all."

Sakura crossed her arms under her breasts. "And letting a teenager drool over you is? I didn't like the way you handled her at dinner earlier."

"I didn't even do anything."

"That's exactly my point. It was cute when she was younger, but now it's just sad. She's going to be sixteen soon and she still has a crush on you."

Simon turned away. "She'll grow out of it."

"But what if she doesn't? All her other friends are getting their first boyfriends, learning about what they want and don't want, and how to handle relationships. She's not getting any of that experience."

"She doesn't need a boyfriend," Simon said. "Boys her age are stupid. They're just gonna hurt her. If letting her cling to me instead of some dumb teenager will spare her the pain, then I'm happy to shelter her."

Sakura let out a bitter laugh. "And you think you're better than any of those boys?"

Simon stiffened, his back still facing Sakura. "None of this has to do with our investigation."

"It has to do with *everything* you do." Walking to the window, she sighed and shook her head. "I know you're doing this more for yourself than for her." Resting her head on the windowpane, she peered out at the night sky. "You think that if you can protect her, it can make up for all the horrible things you did when you worked for Lucifer's Disciples, but no matter how good you are to her, it won't change the fact that you killed numerous innocent humans in the name of Satan—that you took the life of a little girl for Black Mass. You're still that guy, but Karin is not that girl. Don't take her life, too."

Simon rose from his chair. His jaw trembled and he curled his shaking fist. Sakura glanced at him, watching him with calm eyes.

"Fine," Simon spat. "I'll tell her tomorrow that she needs to move on. But if you think I'm the same as I was then, you're *wrong*."

CHAPTER 19

~~

"So how far away is this place?" Anthony asked from the back of the car. He had been sitting for what felt like hours, and his phone battery was almost dead.

"We're almost there," Sakura said, peering out the window of the passenger's seat. "It's kind of out in the middle of nowhere."

"You don't say?" he muttered, staring at the endless dusty road.

By the time they drove through the golden gateway of St. Joseph's Monastery, the sun was setting behind the trees of the surrounding forest. An elderly nun stood outside the long brick building at the monastery entrance. After Simon parked along the gravel path across from the building, she approached the car.

"Good evening," she said to Simon and Sakura as they made their way out of the car, Karin and Olivia hopping out from the backseat.

"It's been too long since we last saw each other," Sakura said, embracing her. "How've you been?"

"I've been quite well, thank you. It's been fairly quiet at the monastery these days. Not too much going on."

"Sounds like we'll have to change that," Simon said with a chuckle. "We're bringing the party to you."

"So I've heard," the nun said. "Let me see the girl."

Anthony scooted out of the car, carrying Emily in his arms. "She's been like this for about a day now."

"The poor dear." The woman ran a wrinkled hand down the side of Emily's face and glanced at Anthony behind thick circular glasses. "I'm Mother Helena. You must be Anthony. Simon told me you've been taking great care of Emily."

Anthony blushed. "I don't know about that."

Mother Helena gave him a reassuring smile. "Don't worry about a thing, Anthony. I know exactly how to help her."

Anthony followed after Mother Helena, the others trailing close behind. She led them farther down the trail lined with colorful flowers and white statues of saints, past more brick buildings and a chapel with tall stained glass windows and a golden cross piercing the sky from upon the dome-shaped roof. Behind it stood hundreds of tombstones in a grassy lot, becoming more visible as they continued to walk along the path.

"Do all those belong to Eden members?" he whispered to Olivia.

She nodded. "This is the main cemetery we use. My family has their own mausoleum." She pointed at the black structure in the center of the cemetery, its pointed rooftops and proud columns stretching high above the surrounding tombstones.

Mother Helena stopped in front of a Virgin Mary statue and gestured toward the cluster of cottages to her right. "I have rooms prepared for all of you. You're welcome to stay as long as you like. I've prepared a special room for Emily." With a wave of her hand, she led them into the long brick building to her left.

The inside resembled a school hallway, with rows of wooden doors leading to what appeared to be classrooms.

Mother Helena opened the door at the end of the hall, revealing a room lit only by the setting sun, its beams casting an array of colors on the red carpet through the stained glass windows. Red candles bordered the wooden table which stood at the back under a fresco of the Virgin Mary holding baby Jesus.

"Lay her here," Mother Helena said to Anthony, gesturing to the center of the table. "Simon, Sakura, could you two burn the incense for me?"

"What exactly are you doing to help her?" Anthony asked, resting Emily on the wood, smoothing her hair and skirt.

"The specific blend of candles and incense weakens black magic," Mother Helena said, lighting the red candles bordering the room.

His nostrils were filled with a piney aroma. Though the scent was pleasant, he wasn't convinced that it was enough to awaken Emily. "So all it takes is some candles and incense to wake her up? That seems too easy."

"I told you she knows what she's doing," Simon said, lighting more incense. "There's already a stronger spiritual barrier around this monastery than there is at Mavro Manor or our safe house, so combining that with the incense should help weaken the spell on Emily. It's a rather slow process, but it's better than—"

He broke off when Sakura dropped to her knees, clinging to the leg of a nearby counter for support. Green stems of rosemary spilled from her hands onto the carpet.

Simon rushed to her side and held her by the shoulders. "Are you okay? Your face is really pale."

"I'm okay," she murmured, holding her forehead. "I'm just a bit dizzy. I think I'm just hungry from the long car ride."

"You're in luck," Mother Helena said. "Many of the other Eden members arrived not long ago and are gathered in the refectory. There should still be plenty of food left. Why don't you all head down there while I finish up here?"

"Thanks, Mother Helena," Simon said, helping Sakura to her feet.

"Yeah, thanks," Anthony muttered. He took one last look at Emily before leaving with the others.

He couldn't help but worry about Emily as he followed beneath the cloistered walkway, still skeptical about Mother Helena's treatment. But as he made his way into the refectory, his mind was distracted by the glowing chandeliers, the smell of food, and the roar of chatter between the various Eden members.

"This many people work for Eden?" Anthony asked Olivia, peering at the ocean of black suits and trench coats.

"It seems hard to believe, but yeah," Olivia said, standing with him by the doorway while Simon, Sakura, and Karin merged into the crowd. "A lot of them are from out of state and come up here for Easter. The monastery service is less intimate than the one at headquarters, so there are more people like me here that are more loosely associated with Eden."

Anthony raised his brow. "Your dad's the leader and your sister's one of the managers or whatever. That doesn't seem very *loose* to me."

"When you put it like that, I guess you're right," she said with a laugh. "Though to be honest, I hardly know anyone here. At least, not on a personal level."

"I see." Anthony peered over at Karin, who stood by one of the long wooden tables in the center of a group of girls. They were all giggling and gazing at Simon, who was talking to a couple in their early thirties at the next table with Sakura.

"C'mon, I'll introduce you to the few people I actually know." Olivia snatched his hand and dragged him toward Sakura and Simon.

"Oh, uh, okay." He glanced over his shoulder at the doorway, his only escape growing farther away.

"Anthony, this is Jason and Natasha Stratus," Olivia said, pointing to the couple. "They're in charge of Eden's science department. They're the ones who looked at Emily's sample a few days ago."

"Pleasure to finally meet you," Jason said, beaming and holding out his hand to shake. "You and Emily are a hot topic at headquarters."

"That's great," Anthony mumbled, unsure of what to make of Jason's remark. The silver rings around Jason's fingers caught Anthony's eye as they shook hands, his gaze fixating on the cross engraved into the middle one.

"It's a shame we can't meet Emily tonight," Natasha said, her cold blue eyes glaring at Anthony behind thick black glasses.

"I'm sure she will awaken soon," Simon said. "We're doing everything we can to help her."

"I hope so," Natasha said. She tucked a loose strand of blond hair behind her ear and withdrew her phone from her blazer pocket. "Excuse me for a moment. I have to return this call."

Anthony let out a sigh of relief when she left the table, freeing him from her icy stare.

"So, Anthony, have you been enjoying your time with Eden?" Jason asked, his smile remaining.

"Uh, yeah, I guess," Anthony said, avoiding eye contact.

Folding his hands, Jason leaned closer to Anthony with interest. "Have you had anything to eat yet? I hope you don't mind that we only really have vegetables and bread tonight. We're on a strict fast since it's the night before Easter. It's going to be a long night, so you should eat up."

"Right, okay." Jason's friendliness was almost more unsettling than Natasha's sternness. He peered at the food dishes at the center of the room. Grabbing dinner would be an easy escape.

Jason looked to Simon. "Will you be helping out at the service tonight?"

Simon shook his head. "Sorry, but I'll have to pass. It's been a long week. Sakura and I were actually thinking of leaving the service early to catch up on sleep."

Sakura cleared her throat and stood up straighter. "And I haven't been feeling too well, so I'd really like the extra rest."

"That's too bad," Jason said. "I'm sure Matteo would love for you to help."

Simon's eyes widened. "Matt's here?"

Jason pointed farther down the table where Karin sat. "He's right over there with Drea and Erika."

"Oh God, she's here, too," Olivia whispered, bowing her head and backing behind Anthony.

"Of course she doesn't even have the nerve to say hi to us after what the chairman did," Simon grumbled, wrinkling his nose.

As if on cue, Erika looked up and waved, an uneasy smile on her face. When Drea noticed who she was waving to, she grimaced.

When Olivia's grip tightened, Anthony realized she was still holding his hand. He blushed and yanked himself free from her grasp.

"What are you doing here?" Drea snapped, marching over to their table. Matt trailed after her, snacking on a full plate of broccoli.

"Me?" Simon jabbed a finger at his chest. "I'm here to celebrate Easter. What are *you* doing here?"

"Trying to enjoy my time away from you!" she spat, placing her hands on her hips.

"Why, so you can catch up with Matt? He's not your chihuahua, so stop dragging him around wherever you go."

"My *what?*"

Choking on his food, Matt attempted to clear his throat, lifting his index finger in protest.

"Simon," Sakura said, rubbing his arm, "I don't think that's what she's—"

"And what the hell is up with you, blowing me off since you got back?" Simon said, pulling free from Sakura and glaring at Matt. "You've been gone for a year and you don't even say hi?"

Matt opened his mouth to speak, but Drea cut him off. "Erika told me all about how you guys screwed up Emily's investigation. I leave you guys alone for a day and you tear down Mavro Manor?"

Simon rolled his eyes. "It was one stinking wall. It's not like anyone needed it. We were making such good progress, too, before Erika ruined it for us."

Anthony noticed Matt staring at him. He tried not to stare back, but it was impossible to avoid Matt's sharp gaze.

"I can't believe you actually let them do this," Drea said to Olivia. "You're supposed to be monitoring the investigation."

"How is this my fault?" Olivia said, crossing her arms.

"Hey, don't drag her into this," Simon said.

Matt beckoned to Anthony. "Your name's Anthony, right?"

Anthony nodded, taking a few steps closer to Matt.

"Wanna ditch?" Matt whispered, setting his plate aside on the table. He cocked his head toward Drea and Simon. "They're gonna be at it for a while."

Anthony looked from Drea and Simon to Matt. He wasn't sure exactly what following a guy he didn't know would entail, but it couldn't be any worse than listening to his comrades arguing. He followed Matt through the crowd, squeezing past numerous people in black coats. They snuck out the back door, into the garden behind the hall.

"So much quieter out here," Matt said, leaning against

the brick wall. "I'm not one for big crowds. I could tell you aren't either." He pulled a pack of cigarettes and lighter out of his coat pocket. "You mind if I smoke?"

"Nope," Anthony said. He sat in the grass and breathed in the sweet scent of the surrounding flowers before Matt lit his cigarette. Since it was Matt's idea to go outside, Anthony assumed he had something to say, but he remained silent as he smoked. The silence was almost more uncomfortable than the crowded hall. "So, uh, Simon and Drea seem to argue a lot."

"Yeah, it's kinda my fault."

Anthony peered up at Matt.

"I cheated on her with Simon."

"Oh," was all Anthony could manage to say in response. From Matt's blank expression, he wasn't sure how to react. "Late night 'tutoring' sessions?"

"You could say that," Matt chuckled. His expression hardened and he crossed his arms. "Drea and I had been dating for about half a year when Simon started teaching me white magic. She and I were never too compatible as romantic partners, but I clicked with Simon right away. He taught me pretty much everything I know, along with his nasty habits. " He lifted his cigarette to his lips and exhaled a cloud of smoke. "He has a good heart and usually means well, but he's a wild one. We had some crazy times together. Sometimes a little too crazy." Matt gazed into the orange sky, the sunset casting shadows on his face. "Everything between me, him, and Drea just got out of hand and I needed to get away. I felt bad for not telling Simon when I came back, but I was scared that I'd fall down the same path if we were to meet again."

"It makes sense though," Anthony said with a shrug. "You gotta cut toxic people out of your life, right?"

"I guess so. I didn't really want to tell Drea either, but we ran into each other at headquarters. But I guess I can't just hide from everyone forever." A sad smile spread across Matt's face. "I'm glad Simon's still with Sakura. Granted she was pretty okay with it all, I'd feel horrible if I were to cause them to break up. She's really great for him. It's upsetting to know that Drea still holds a grudge against Simon, but time doesn't always heal wounds." Peering out into the distance, Matt blushed when he saw Simon and Jason walking by the Virgin Mary statue. "It's been a year since we last saw each other. I may have been a passing phase for him, but I don't think I will ever get over him."

Anthony glanced up at Matt, staring at the conflicting mixture of sadness and admiration that washed over his face. Though he felt sympathy for Matt's unrequited feelings, his bittersweet longing was heartwarming, almost comforting to see such affection personified. *Did I ever look like that when I looked at Olivia?* Anthony thought, his brow furrowing when he heard the answer ringing in his head.

"Did you know Jason's the reason why Simon and Sakura were allowed to join Eden?" Matt asked, his gaze still glued to Simon. "He was the only one who trusted them and managed to convince everyone else to trust them, too. I heard they've been best friends since." He beamed. "I bet they're talking about something really cool and top secret. I get excited just thinking about what it could be."

Hopefully it's something about curing Emily, Anthony thought, slumping his shoulders.

Matt tossed his cigarette on the ground and squished it under his boot. "So, are you cleared yet?"

Anthony sat up straighter. "What do you mean?"

"*Cleared* means you're an official member of Eden," Matt explained. He sat in the grass beside Anthony, smoothing the bottom of his trench coat "I'm assuming you're in that awkward middle phase where you're involved with Eden, but not an actual member."

"Are they gonna make me a member or something?"

"They might. Members are either born into Eden through bloodline like the Mavros, adopted like me, Karin, and Drea, or have been highly exposed to paranormal phenomena like you." He sat beside Anthony in the grass. "They told me I had *potential*, so they brought me here. That's what they tell everyone they allow in. I didn't know what they meant by potential and still don't, but I guess the higher-ups are able to tell who will be useful to the organization."

"I don't think I'm doing anything useful for Eden," Anthony chuckled, scratching his head while recalling the events of the past week. "All I really do is stand around while they do their thing."

"I doubt that's true. Drea says you've gotten pretty close with Emily. She's been staying awake and that's never happened until you came along."

Anthony stared down at his fist, grabbing at the grass beside him. "She's not awake anymore. That's why we're here, trying to wake her up. But even if she does wake up, I don't know what will happen. Our investigation was canceled, so I don't know what they'll do with me."

"They'll either clear you or erase your memory," Matt said.

"Like *all of it*?"

"Not all of it. You'll forget about Eden, obviously, and everything that happened during the investigation."

Anthony's wide eyes darted to Matt. "Would I forget about Emily?"

Matt shrugged. "Probably. Or at least about all the stuff that she said during the investigation and about taking her home. Since she's a member by blood, I'm assuming they'll keep her at headquarters."

"But then. . ." *But then it will be like we never met.* Even though he heard the Eden members discuss memory wiping numerous times, he never thought it could affect him. The concept always seemed distant, like the mere conversation topic he always assumed it was. He took a deep breath before speaking again. "But you said they need me to keep her awake."

"Yeah, but you said you can't keep her awake, so I don't know. I'm not the one who makes those decisions." When he noticed Simon parting ways with Jason, Matt leapt to his feet. "I guess this is my chance to finally apologize to him. You mind if I leave you for a bit?"

"Yeah, no problem," Anthony said with a nod. "I, uh, I gotta go do something else, somewhere else.

As he walked back into the monastery, Anthony's mind was already elsewhere. His pounding heart was racing to catch up with his thoughts, already focused in the room where Emily slept, desperate to awaken her with whatever *potential* he hoped to possess.

CHAPTER 20

~~

Anthony stood over the table where Emily lay. The overwhelming scent of rosemary and sage incense combined with the dim candlelight was dizzying, but Emily remained fast asleep. He gazed at her face frozen with peaceful slumber. The Virgin Mary fresco above her holding baby Jesus seemed to be staring down at him. Judging him. Closing his eyes, he bowed his head and folded his hands. *If there really is a God, then I guess it's worth a shot.*

"Are you praying?"

Anthony jumped in surprised and turned to see Olivia watching him from the doorway.

"Did I scare you?" she asked with a chuckle. "Sorry, I didn't mean to. I'm heading over to the church with the others for the Easter service. Care to join us?"

"I'm not really that religious," Anthony said, dropping his hands to his sides. "It's not even morning yet, though."

"The service actually starts at eleven and lasts through the morning."

He cringed. "Thanks for the invite, but I think I'll pass."

Olivia walked over to Anthony's side. "Are you going to stay here then?"

Anthony didn't look at her. "I'm gonna stay here until

Emily wakes up."

Olivia pursed her lips. "Mother Helena said she'll be okay, so there really isn't anything to worry about. You don't have to hover over her all day long."

"No offense, but mingling with the Eden folks isn't really my idea of fun, especially when I *do* have something to worry about," Anthony snapped. "Our investigation was dropped and everyone is just sitting around, having a good time, while those creepy demons are still after Emily. Stopping an investigation may give Simon, Drea, and Sakura the vacation they all want, but it doesn't help Emily at all, and that doesn't help *me*. I, unlike everyone else here who just views this investigation as a job, actually care about her as a person."

Olivia's eyes widened. She opened her mouth to speak, but Anthony went on before she had a chance.

"Meanwhile, her freak of a brother is possibly still alive. I don't know whether or not that's true, but if it is. . ." He grit his teeth and balled his trembling fists. "I don't know if anyone could hold me back from beating him senseless for the things he did to her."

"From the sound of it, I think Zalem had some serious issues," Olivia muttered, taking a step back from Anthony. "I don't know if he could help it—"

"I don't give a damn what his problem was!" Anthony shouted. "Making Emily hurt herself is inexcusable! And for some sick reason, she thought all that was okay and enjoyed it, yet when I do everything I possibly can to make her happy, she chooses to stay unconscious!"

"But maybe it isn't her choice," Olivia said, her voice shaking.

Anthony's expression softened when his gaze met Olivia's startled eyes. Taking a deep breath, he hoped there was at least some truth to her words.

"Whether it is or not, she better have a damn good

reason for being unconscious for so long, because I'm sick of worrying all by myself." He slouched onto the floor and glanced up at Emily. Despite the noise around her, she was still fast asleep. Looking back to Olivia, he blushed. "I'm sorry for flipping out. I've just been really stressed out."

"No, I totally understand," Olivia said, shaking her head. "If there was anything I could do to change my father's mind about canceling the investigation, I would have already done it. I'm just as concerned about all this as you are." She clutched her arm and sighed. "I haven't told Erika, Simon, or anyone about what Rundull said about Zalem. With such a poor lead, I just don't know if there's anything we can do about it. But at the same time, I can't help but think that it might make my father change his mind if he knew."

"I doubt it," Anthony said. "It sounds like he was pretty pissed that we snooped around Mavro Manor. I haven't told anyone about Zalem possibly being alive either, but that's mainly because I don't want them to try and find him." He held his bowed head. "I just want him to stay away from Emily."

"I see." Olivia shuffled her feet. "Anyway, I better get going. The service is going to start soon." With one hand on the doorknob, she peered over her shoulder at him. "I guess I'll see you later?"

"Yeah." He nodded, watching the door shut behind her. Rising to his feet, he surveyed the room. Nothing but candles, icons, and other religious artifacts that would most likely be useless in helping Emily. A small, wooden piano in the far corner of the room caught his eye. He wandered over to it and lifted the lid, unveiling a row of yellow and black keys. It reminded him of the beautiful songs Emily had played for him in Mavro Manor. He could recall every note in his mind, but when he pressed his fingers down on the keys, a cacophony of sounds pierced the silence.

"That was the most horrible sound I have ever heard."

Anthony spun around to see Emily standing behind him. "You're awake!"

"How could anyone sleep through that awful racket?" she huffed.

"Sorry, but it's not like I know how to play. I was just messing around."

"A piano is not something to be messed with." Tossing her hair over her shoulder, she sat upon the piano bench. She began to play, but stopped after hitting a few notes. "This piano is horribly out of tune."

Anthony narrowed his eyes as he stared at her. It was as if she hadn't been unconscious for the past day. "So you *can* choose when you wake up."

Emily's gaze remained fixed on the piano keys. "In a way. It takes a lot of energy to wake up once I have fallen into deep slumber."

"But you didn't need to 'take my soul' like you claimed to do last time. So it technically is all up to you."

Emily didn't respond.

"And then you passed out after telling me about Zalem," Anthony went on. "Be it a conscious decision or not, something about recalling your memories with him made you pass out. Is it also because you wanted to?"

"I would not have woken up if I knew you would interrogate me."

"Did you seriously expect me to just ignore the fact that you've been knocked out for the past twenty four hours?"

"Zalem may sound like a terrible person to you, but he really was not all that bad. He was the only person I could call family and was my only friend." Dropping her hands to her lap, her eyes met his. "When he was not hurting me, he was the nicest, sweetest, most caring person I have ever met. Our way of life may seem strange to you, but it is the only life I have ever known." She gazed at the ceiling and sighed. "I

Maria Giakoumatos   Midnight Waltz   199

often wonder if there is any point of living without him."

Though he was taken aback by her words, Anthony kept a steady tone. "Of course there is. I get that you miss your brother, but maybe this is your chance to start over. Find a new reason to live." His eyes darted to the floor, but he could feel her gaze lingering on the side of his face for a moment before her attention shifted back to the piano.

"Would you like me to teach you a song?" she asked. "It is really simple. It is the first song Zalem taught me."

"I know nothing about playing piano," Anthony said with a shrug.

"You can just copy my hand movements," Emily said. She scooted to the edge of the bench and patted the space beside her, peering up at Anthony with a timid smile. "It could be fun."

Anthony returned the smile as he sat on the bench. "What are we going to play?"

"Beethoven's *Moonlight Sonata*. I think you are going to like this one."

~~

"Are you sure you want to do this?" Sakura asked Simon, leaning against the wall of their room. "We can always go back to church and just do this tomorrow."

"No," Simon said, sitting on the edge of his bed, lacing up his boots. "Everyone will leave tomorrow evening. We need them all in one place when we tell them the truth about Eden." He looked up at her with a smirk. "You chickening out?"

"Of course not," she chuckled, crossing her arms beneath her breasts. "I just thought it'd be nice if we could spend more time with everyone, not worrying about traitors or Emily or anything like that. It's been a while since any of us had a break." She sighed. "I guess I missed hanging out with our friends like normal people."

"Since when were we ever like normal people? No matter what we do, we're still demons. You said so yourself."

"True." She stared down at the floor. "I saw you talking with Matt outside earlier. I don't mind if you want to hook up again, like tonight or something."

Simon raised his brow. "What?"

"I told you before, I don't mind if you want to sleep with other people. It's not really natural for demons to be monogamous."

"Oh. Okay, then." He gave her a lopsided smile. "This is kind of awkward. I'm not sure what makes you want to bring this up."

"It's just. . ." Hesitating for a moment, she tapped her fingers on her arm. "Matt really likes you. He's a good guy. Maybe you should give him a chance."

"I already did. I think everyone at Eden knows how that turned out."

"But he's single now."

"And I'm not." He rose and placed a hand against the wall beside her head. "You're the only one I want to be with."

"Simon. . . " Sakura murmured, her gaze still fixed to the floor.

"I love you, Sakura. I know I may do a lot of dumb stuff that might make you question my feelings, but I love you more than I have ever loved anyone else. I never *have* loved anyone other than you—" He broke off at the sound of a knock on the door. Straightening his coat, he strode to answer it. "Karin? What are you doing here?"

"I wasn't really having a good time at church," she said, her hands tucked behind her back. She rocked on her black flats. "I've just had a lot on my mind and when I noticed you left early, I was wondering if you would be available to talk." She peeked behind Simon at Sakura, who took a step away from the wall and stared back at her.

Simon gave her a warm grin. "You're always welcome to talk to me. C'mon in."

Karin glared at Sakura, following Simon into the bedroom.

Simon sat in the center of his bed, patting a spot next to him. "So, what's up?"

Karin plopped down beside him. "I just was thinking. . ." Trailing off, she narrowed her eyes at Sakura.

"About?"

She hesitated before replying. "Emily. I mean, she's been asleep for a while, and I'm just worried that—"

"Hold on." Simon looked to Sakura. "Do you mind giving us some privacy?"

Sakura shook her head, backing to the door, her gaze fixed to Simon. "Don't forget what I told you the other night," she said, her hand on the doorknob.

"I haven't," Simon said, forcing a smile and waving.

"What does she mean?" Karin asked after Sakura shut the door behind her.

"Nothing," Simon said. "So, tell me why you're actually here."

Karin blushed. "All my friends keep asking me if anything ever happens between us when I go on investigations with you, and it makes me feel bad when I keep saying no."

"Why, because you're letting them down?"

"No, because *I* want something to happen and I hate hearing myself say that nothing did. I want this to be more than a stupid crush."

"Karin, we agreed that you joining me is strictly educational. You know I have a girlfriend—"

"But you did stuff with Matt!" Karin shouted, pounding a fist on the bed.

"And I regret it every day," Simon said, his voice rising. "Sakura says she was okay with it, but I know it's always on the back of her mind."

"But you still did it. He was your student, just like me, so what makes him any different?"

"Oh, God, where do I begin?" He held his head in his hands. "For starters, he was legally an adult—"

"So will you give me a chance in two years?" Karin asked, sitting up straighter.

"No." He took a deep breath. "Look, there's no easy way to say this, but even if you were an adult and I was single, we wouldn't be together."

Her jaw began to tremble. "B-but why? What is it that you don't like about me?"

"Nothing." Wrapping his arms around her back, he pulled her onto his lap. "I love you like a sister. You're beautiful, fun, extremely smart—any guy your age would be super lucky to date you, but you won't give any of them a chance."

"But that's because I like you, Simon. I only want to be with you."

He looked away from her. "You don't want to be with me. I've done terrible things and I'm still not that great."

"But I can see past all that," Karin said beaming, though her eyes were filling with tears. "I like you enough to forgive all the stuff you've done."

"And that's really sweet of you. You're still young and have plenty of time to find someone you really like, but you won't if you keep clinging onto me. I know you think you like me, but I can guarantee that I'm not for you. You deserve someone better."

She let out an exasperated huff. "So are you dating Sakura because she only deserves someone as good as you?"

"That's not what I meant." He sighed and looked back at her. "Look, it's getting pretty late. Can we discuss this after we've both gotten some rest?"

"No!" Karin cried. "You keep minimizing my feelings

because I'm younger than you, but I mean it when I say I like you! I *love* you!"

Simon stared at her in shock as she buried her face in her hands to hide her tears. He couldn't bring himself to even hug her. Instead, he gazed at the door, hoping Sakura heard every word.

It wasn't until later that night when he met back with Sakura, who sat outside the cabin waiting, that he had his answer.

"I hope you're happy with how that went down," Simon whispered.

"It had to be done," Sakura said, a cold glaze covering her eyes. "She'll get over you soon enough."

"Will she?" He glanced back at the cabin. "She eventually fell asleep. I hope she'll be okay."

"She'll be fine. Don't worry." She shrugged. "But if you're feeling down, I suppose we can postpone our little investigation."

"No." Simon grabbed her hand. "Let's get this over with. I need the distraction."

Hand in hand, they walked down the gravel pathway past the church, to the funeral home next door. After picking the lock, they walked through the lobby and down the white hallway to the crematorium.

"I'm definitely sensing a demonic presence," he said, waving his hands over the floor. A ball of white light formed in his palms and he blasted a hole in the ground. Below was another hallway, lit only by candles. He and Sakura leapt down to the lower floor and walked down the new hallway lined with black tile.

"The presence only gets stronger the farther down we go," he muttered. "Something's gotta be down here."

Sakura followed him in silence, stopping at two golden doors at the end of the hallway. Opening the doors, Simon gasped when his eyes fell upon the large room that lay ahead.

The dim red glow of candles illuminated the dark church-like sanctuary, revealing a white pentacle drawn on the center of the marble floor. An altar covered with black cloth stood at the front of the room, decorated with elaborate candelabras and skulls, a balcony looming above.

"This is unbelievable!" Simon cried, walking onto the pentagram, his voice trembling with excitement. "To think this has been kept a secret for so many years, right on Eden property! The things Winston Mavro wrote it that letter were true!" He beamed, turning to face Sakura. "Just wait until Jason and Erika hear about—"

Sakura pointed her gun at his chest. "I'm so sorry."

CHAPTER 21

~~

Simon raised his hands over his head, keeping a steady watch on the gun. "This is an unpleasant surprise."

"I'm so sorry," Sakura said again, her eyes drifting to the floor. "I didn't want things to come to this, but I'm afraid you know too much. I tried so hard to control the amount of information you learned from the investigation without you noticing, but once you found that letter about the crematorium, there was nothing I could do."

"What do you mean, you had to *control the information*?" Lowering his arms, he seized her shoulders to stop her from backing away. "Oh, God, don't tell me. . ." He trailed off at the sound of a familiar, high-pitched cackle.

Thalia leaned over the balcony railing, holding her smirking face in the palm of her hand. Beside her, Rundull sat upon the railing, his black robes engulfing his dangling feet.

"I was afraid you two weren't going to make it tonight," Rundull said, grinning down at them. "I was starting to worry."

"You're working for them again?" Simon cried.

Sakura didn't say anything. She bowed her head, struggling to break free from his firm grasp.

"Why else would she bring you to us?" Thalia asked.

"After everything we've been through, all we did to prove our loyalty to Eden—" He cocked his head to look Sakura in the eye, but she continued to hide her gaze. "Did it all mean nothing to you?"

Sakura shut her eyes to hold back tears. "I. . . I am only loyal to the darkness that lies within my heart."

"What darkness?" His grip weakened as his hands shook. "We cleansed ourselves of evil a long time ago."

"No, we didn't!" Sakura yelled, her eyes snapping open. "No matter what we do, we can't change what's in our souls! We can practice all the white magic we want and grow tolerant to the burning pain, but we are still demons! You know this!" A crazed smile washed over her reddening face. "I know Eden's been driving you nuts with all their lies, secrets, and elitism, especially after everything we had to do— everything we had to give up—just to be accepted." Dropping her gun, she clung to the fabric of his shirt. "The blood, the killing, the rituals, that crazy, *crazy* sex we could share with anyone, and more than anything, the *power*. The freedom to do anything and everything you could ever want to do. You can have it all again if you just come back to where we belong."

"I don't want any of that!" Simon pushed her away, gaping at her in shock. "I didn't think you wanted it, either!"

"I don't!" Sakura cried. She dropped to her knees, tears spilling from her eyes. "But when I heard about Zalem, I knew what I had to do!"

"What's Zalem have to do with this?" Simon asked, furrowing his brow.

"Zalem has to do with *everything*," Rundull chuckled. "If you do as she says and rejoin us, I'll be more than happy to explain."

Simon grit his teeth. "I'd rather die."

"Good, because your girlfriend will have to kill you." Rundull glared at Sakura. "Pick up the gun."

"I-I can't!" Sakura stammered. "I can't kill him!"

"Your mission was to monitor the Mavro family investigation and make sure no one found out about Zalem or any of our hideouts or agents. You failed literally all of that." He crossed his arms and sneered. "Now, pick up the gun and shoot him so he won't have a chance to tell anyone else about our secrets."

"B-but I—"

"Kill him or else I'll kill *both* of you."

Sakura's sobs grew to wails.

Simon shook his head and sighed. Kneeling beside her, he placed the gun in her lap. "Let's just get this over with, okay?" He peered up at Rundull. "If she kills me, you won't hurt her, right?"

"I have no reason to hurt someone who follows my orders," Rundull answered. "It was our deal."

"But I can't kill you!" Sakura cried, balling her hair into her fists. "I-I love you!"

Simon squeezed her hand in attempt to hold back his own tears. "If you love me, then why did you betray me?"

"I told you, because of *Zalem*! He's really important to us. We've been trying so hard to make sure he stays a secret and trying to keep our agents hidden, but then you started doing the investigation and I wanted to be able to stop you from learning anything important so we could still be together, but. . ." Her words became lost in her bawling, tears gushing out of her eyes like rivers.

"Why does he even matter? He's *dead*! He lived over a hundred years ago!"

"Wrong!" Rundull cackled. "He's been alive this entire time! I told Emily that a while ago. I'm surprised she hasn't told you." He held his gut and roared with laughter. "Wow! How did you guys expect to progress your investigation if you don't even trust each other enough to share information?"

Simon whipped around and glared at Rundull. "If he's alive, then prove it!"

"Sure, if you rejoin us," Rundull said with a shrug.

"Lord Rundull, I'm bored," Thalia whined, twirling her pink hair around her thin finger. "I thought you said there would be blood."

"Just be patient," Rundull said, patting her shoulder. "They can't both leave here alive."

"You want someone to die?" Sakura pointed her gun at Thalia. "Then I'll kill *everyone* in this room!" She panned her gun from Thalia, to Rundull, to Simon, then at her own head. "That way it's fair for everyone!"

"How is that fair?" Thalia asked, hiding her face behind her arms and stepping away from the railing.

"If I kill Simon, he can't report us," Sakura said, "and if I kill you and Rundull, I'm protecting my friends at Eden. And if I kill myself, I won't have to live with the guilt."

"I don't think anyone benefits from that idea," Rundull said. "You need to pick a side and stick with it, or else I'll pick one for you."

The gun shook in her trembling hands, hovering over each person for a second before moving on to the next. Taking a deep breath, she pressed the gun against her temple. "Then I'll just kill myself."

"S-Sakura, don't do anything stupid," Simon stammered, hesitant to touch her. "If you die, you know they'll just kill me—"

At that moment, the golden doors swung open. Sakura dropped the gun to her lap at the sight of Karin entering the room.

"Simon? Sakura? What are you guys doing here?" Karin asked, her purse swinging on her arm while she ran toward them.

"What are *you* doing here?" Simon asked her, his eyes wide with panic.

"I woke up and you were gone," she said. "I followed the footsteps in the gravel and—"

"Karin, you have to leave, now!" He leaned down to look her in the eye. "It's too dangerous for you to be here! Go back to the church and tell Matt where we are."

"Well, this should make things more exciting," Rundull said, peering down at Karin. He tapped his fingers together and giggled. "Maybe Sakura will kill them both before she kills herself!"

Thalia rolled her eyes. "As long as someone dies in the next five minutes, I'll be happy."

Karin gasped when she noticed Thalia and Rundull watching from the balcony. Taking a step back, she withdrew her cross from her purse. "I'm not leaving you with them!"

Simon seized her arm before she could transform her cross. "Don't even think about fighting them!"

"But I need to help you!"

"You can't help me! You hardly know how to use magic!"

Karin stomped her foot. "And whose fault is that?"

Simon lifted a finger. "Don't even start with that now!"

"I've had enough of this!" Thalia shouted, banging her fist against the railing. Forming her scythe and releasing her wings, she climbed on top of the balcony railing, ready to pounce.

Before Thalia could jump, Rundull snatched her arm. "Settle down. I'll handle this." Clearing his throat, he said, "It's been fun chatting with you all, but I'm afraid our time has come to a close. As a parting gift, I'll show you something special."

Sakura, Karin, and Simon backed away from the pentacle, the white chalk darkening to a blood red. Flames grew from the star, the rising smoke tainting the air with a thick, musty odor.

"Wh-what's going on?" Karin stammered, hiding

behind Simon and pinching her nose.

Simon didn't answer. Instead, he withdrew his cross from his coat, his focus fixed to the pentacle. "Nice try, Rundull, but you know your magic is weaker on holy grounds!"

"Holy grounds? You mean this monastery?" Rundull laughed again. "Sure, I may be weak if I try to fight you on the monastery's property—hell, I'd burn upon entering!" He tossed his hair away from his face, revealing glowing red eyes. "But down here? We're on *my* grounds. And lest you forget, I'm not a mere Phobia like *you*." His wings tore through the back of his robes and he swooped down to the center of the star. The second his feet touched the ground, the flames rose higher.

Rundull's body morphed with the smoke, creating a shadowy substance. His red eyes became rounder, larger, and brighter, like giant stoplights, his mouth stretching into a long row of razor sharp teeth. The shadow grew into a massive, horned creature with jagged claws.

"What the heck is that?" Karin screamed.

"Something that shouldn't be possible on Earth," Simon said, gawking at the shadow monster. "His true form, a spirit of darkness."

"And you know how to fight it, right?"

"In theory. I've never actually had to fight something like this since black magic of this capacity is usually not possible here. Blades and bullets won't work on it, even if made of silver." He pressed his wrists together, a ball of light forming between his palms. "If the pentacle is destroyed, so are his powers."

"Can it leave the pentacle?"

As if in response, Rundull's shadowy arm extended toward them, the claws outstretched. Karin scurried to Sakura's side, while Simon shot the light at the claw before dodging out of its way. It burned a hole through the shadow, but only for a second before black smoke filled the space.

"Is that all you got?" Thalia laughed, flying above Rundull. "Light spells aren't strong enough to stop a devil!"

Simon watched Sakura continue to sit on the floor sobbing. She was holding something in her hands, but he couldn't quite see what it was. Karin knelt beside her, shaking Sakura's shoulders, tears rolling down her pink cheeks.

Just as Rundull's claw was about to seize Karin and Sakura, Simon jumped in front of them, his hands outstretched in front of his face. A white umbrella of light formed around them, just in time to block Rundull's attack.

"Go, now, Karin!" Simon shouted, struggling to maintain the force field. "Go get help!"

Karin's jaw trembled, gawking at the dimming light. "But, Simon—"

"Forget about me! Just go!"

Taking one last look at the light, Karin scrambled to her feet and ran to the door.

With all his might, Simon pushed the light onto Rundull's claw. Rundull jerked his claw away, the light eating away at his shadowy form.

Simon let out a sigh of relief at the sound of the golden doors slamming shut behind Karin. His attention still fixed to Rundull, he backed away into Sakura's arms. With one hand squeezing his shoulder, she pressed a knife against his neck. The silver blade burned his flesh and her shaky breath tickled his ear, but he didn't dare turn his head.

Sakura's grip on the knife tightened. "For Zalem."

CHAPTER 22

~~

"Are you ready?"

Anthony sat up straighter and shook his right hand. "Let's do this."

Emily positioned her left hand over the piano keys. "You do just the right hand part, and I will play the left hand."

Anthony began to play the melody of *Moonlight Sonata*. Though repetitious, he was impressed with himself for remembering what she had taught him. He wasn't sure how long they were sitting at the piano in the prayer room as time seemed to stand still, as if he, Emily, and the piano were all that mattered. And as he played the piece with her, it really was all that mattered to him, sitting at the piano with her, reciting what he learned—

Anthony jerked his hand away from the keyboard. "Sorry!"

Emily stopped playing. "For what?"

"I played the wrong note on accident."

"So? You cannot simply stop in the middle of a piece. You must go on, like it never happened. Chances are your listeners will not notice unless you draw attention to it." She tapped the piano keys in front of him. "Put out your hand again, like you are about to play."

Anthony rested his right hand on the keys and looked to her for further instructions.

"A large part of playing a piece comes from muscle memory," she said. "Your hands remember where to go. It helps if your hands are in a comfortable position. Watch my hand. See how my knuckles are curved?"

Anthony watched her hand while she played his part of the song, then tried to copy her position. "You mean like this?"

"Not quite. Let me help you. Just keep playing." She pressed her fingertips against the inside of his palm, raising his knuckles. "You want a flat wrist and curved knuckles, like you are holding a ball. Your fingers will move more freely this way. Now, keep this shape." She pulled her hand away and watched him play. "Is that more comfortable?"

"Kind of." He glanced at her and blushed. "Could you show me again?"

"Of course."

Her fingers were cold against Anthony's skin, but he didn't mind. Her touch was soothing, yet his heart was racing. For once she wasn't smirking, pouting, or in some sort of frenzy over her past. She was sitting beside him, smiling and playing piano, as if she hadn't just awoken from her day-long slumber.

Emily placed her hand above his to prevent him from playing. "Do you hear that?"

"Hear what?"

She craned her neck and squinted out the stained glass windows. "Are there people outside already?"

Anthony listened to the voices of what sounded like multiple people outside in the courtyard, and the crackling of car tires against the gravel road. "I'm sure it's just people leaving church."

"It is far too early for them to be finished." Rising from the bench, she marched to the door.

"Wait!" Anthony cried, hurrying after her down the hall. "Can't we just go back to playing piano?"

Emily ignored him, following the voices into the courtyard, where people flooded out of the church. Pushing through the mob, hushed murmurs of the churchgoers buzzed through Anthony's ears.

"I said wait!" But by the time he snatched her hand, they made it out of the crowd to the front of the funeral home.

He and Emily froze when they saw Olivia kneeling on the ground, cradling a sobbing Karin in her arms. Mother Helena stood beside them, her face wrinkled with anxiety. Erika, Jason, and Natasha all watched the funeral home through narrowed eyes.

"What's going on here?" Anthony asked.

"The reason you all came here," Erika huffed.

"I already told you, none of us had any idea about what's down there!" Olivia snapped, glaring at her sister.

"Really?" Erika placed her hands on her hips. "I'm having a hard time believing that Simon and Sakura just happened to stumble across an underground temple while snooping around a funeral home at one in the morning."

"Whoa, what?" Anthony let go of Emily's hand. "Simon just told us that we were here to celebrate Easter."

"Whatever he and Sakura were planning, we were completely unaware of," Olivia said, her tone unwavering.

"Stop talking like Simon's a traitor!" Karin cried. "I already told you, he was fighting Rundull! Sakura probably tricked him into following her! She wasn't even helping him!"

"Let's not make any accusations until we figure out what happened," Natasha said, raising a hand to silence her.

"But I know what happened!" Karin shouted. "I was there!"

Jason glanced at Emily. "It appears the commotion has woken Miss Mavro."

All eyes fell upon Emily and several crowd members pushed forward to get a closer look at her. Emily clung to Anthony's side and hid her face in his chest.

"Can we not make a big deal over her?" Anthony said, wrapping his arms around Emily's back.

But at the sound of Karin's terrified scream, everyone fell silent except for Sakura, who giggled to herself as Drea and Matt dragged her out of the funeral home entrance, each keeping a firm grip on her arms.

Olivia gaped at Sakura's bloodstained clothing. "Oh my God, is she okay?"

"It's not her blood," Matt muttered.

"Where's Simon?" Karin asked.

Matt clenched his teeth and stared down at the ground.

"Where is he?" Her voice rose and she fought against Olivia's grasp. "Why isn't Simon with you?"

Anthony's heart skipped a beat at Sakura's shrill laughter, a clear yet unsettling answer to Karin's cries.

"The other investigators are still in the temple," Drea said, clearing her throat. "So far, no one's found any demons. Sakura and Simon were alone when we got there. She was laughing as she held him in her arms." She let go of Sakura's arm and withdrew a bloodstained knife in a Ziploc bag from her coat pocket. "She was holding this when we pulled her away from Simon. Given the burn and slit in his throat, it's a silver blade. One from Eden, most likely her own."

"B-but she couldn't have. . . " Anthony began to say, but he didn't dare finish. *But she's one of us. She's his girlfriend.*

Erika furrowed her brow, trying to remain stern, but her jaw began to tremble. Natasha knelt beside Jason as he dropped to his knees, covering his face with his hands. Mother Helena clutched the cross she wore around her neck and whispered a prayer. Sobs echoed through the crowd beneath their bowed heads.

"I'll kill her!" Karin screamed, jumping to her feet. "I'll

burn her until she burns in hell where she belongs!"

"Karin, please!" Olivia cried, hugging Karin's waist.

"Simon trusted you!" Karin yelled at Sakura. "He trusted you and you. . . you. . ." She trailed off into a wail, collapsing onto the gravel. "How could you?"

Sakura said nothing in response, but continued to laugh. Her gaze fell upon Emily and she grinned. "She will understand!"

Emily cocked her head. "Will I now?"

Sakura broke free from Matt's grip and rushed to Emily's side, stumbling over her own feet and falling onto the ground in front of her.

"Emily! Oh, Emily! Tell me all about him!" Sakura cried, reaching for Emily's ankle with bloodstained hands.

"About whom?" Emily asked, cringing and stepping away from Sakura.

"Get away from her!" Anthony yelled, seizing Sakura's arm to hold her back. Matt hurried over to help restrain her.

"Zalem!" Sakura answered, staring up at Emily with empty eyes. "You are so blessed to have lived with him! What was it like to be caressed by him as he—" She cut off screaming as Matt bashed her to the ground with his foot.

"Shut up!" he shouted, though his voice shook. "Say another word to her, and you're dead!"

Anthony struggled to help Matt pin Sakura down against her thrashing, smoke rising from her body. "It burns!" she shrieked. "Your holy ground, it burns!"

"Drea, Matt, take her away," Erika ordered. "I want her locked up until my father arrives."

"Wait," Emily said, holding out a hand before Drea could approach Sakura. She knelt down beside her. "What do you know about my brother?"

"He lives!" Sakura cried. "Zalem Mavro lives!"

A hiss of gasps rang through the courtyard. Emily's eyes widened, but she remained silent.

"Lucifer's Disciples! They have him!" She reached for Emily again, but Matt and Anthony yanked her away.

"And have you seen him?" Emily asked.

Sakura averted her gaze. "No, but they told me—"

"Your little friends lied to you," Emily said with a smirk. "It was just a clever scheme to lure you back to the dark side and away from Eden." She lifted a hand to her lips and chuckled. "Even a foolish demon such as yourself should know better than to be tricked by your own kind."

"Wait! No!" Sakura screamed, Drea and Matt dragging her to her feet. "Let me go! Emily, please, stop them! Emily!"

But Emily ignored her pleas, watching Drea and Matt follow Mother Helena to the cabins.

"What was that about Zalem?" Erika asked, furrowing her brow.

"Nothing," Emily said, her smirk disappearing. "Nothing at all. She was spewing nonsense."

"Zalem is alive," Anthony said, avoiding Emily's gaze.

"Impossible," Erika said, her voice dropping to a whisper. "Zalem was stillborn. I've read his profile."

"That's not true." He rose, facing Erika, Jason, and Natasha. "It's about time someone started speaking the truth around here. If none of you guys from Eden will do it, then I will." Taking a deep breath, he tried to ignore Emily's piercing glare. "For whatever reason, the Mavro family lied about Zalem's death. I'm not sure when or if he died since there aren't any truthful records of him, but Rundull claims he's still alive. He claims he has Zalem in his custody. He told me, Emily, Olivia, and it sounds like he told Sakura, too."

Erika placed her trembling hands on her hips. "Why didn't any of you tell me this?"

"Because. . . " Anthony trailed off and glanced back at Olivia and Emily, who both kept a careful watch on him. "Because we didn't know if it was worth investigating."

"That's why you kept it to yourself?" Karin cried.

"Sakura killed Simon over Emily's stupid brother, and you have the nerve to say he's not worth investigating?"

Karin's words left a sickening weight in Anthony's chest. "That's not what I meant. I realize now that we should have taken Rundull more seriously, but even if we did, what could we have done?"

"Nothing," Emily responded with a shrug. "Like I said, I do not believe he has my brother."

"And why does Rundull want him?" Erika asked.

"I honestly have no idea," Emily said.

"Liar!" Karin screamed, pushing away from Olivia. Balling her fists, she marched toward Emily. "You grew up with that creep! You're hiding something from us!"

Anthony stepped in front of Emily, spreading his arms open to block Karin. Before she could even attempt to strike, she was distracted by two men in black suits approaching Erika, each holding a stack of manila folders.

"We found these in Simon and Sakura's room," one of the men said to Erika.

"And what are these?" Erika asked, eyeing the folders.

"*These* are classified files on the Mavro family from the vault," he responded, waving the folders under her nose. "*These* are not to be given to any investigator without the chairman's permission, which he stated he never gave." Though the man's eyes were shielded by sunglasses, his tone was stern and cold.

"Okay, well I didn't give these to them if that's what you're implying," Erika said, crossing her arms. "Sakura probably stole them."

"Miss Mavro, there are only four people who know the vault code," the other man said. "The chairman, Jason and Samuel Stratus, and you. Unfortunately, the security cameras watching the vault haven't picked up any clues, as they seem to have been shut off for a short period of time a few days ago when the files were most likely stolen. Given that you are the one in charge of Emily Mavro's investigation, I'm afraid we'll have to hold you for questioning first."

Jason rose, watching the men seize Erika's arms, his expression blank.

"What the—You gotta be freaking kidding me!" Erika shouted. "I didn't even know those files *existed*! My father doesn't tell me a damn thing about my family! Ask my sister, she knows!" She gazed at Olivia with desperation, struggling to pull away from the men. "Olivia, tell them it's true!"

"Erika, just shut up and go with them," Olivia mumbled, staring at the gravel. "If what you're saying is true, you'll get your name cleared and you'll be fine. I'm sorry, but I don't really know what to believe right now."

Erika fell silent, gaping after Olivia while the men dragged her into the main building.

~~

Anthony wandered out of the refectory, into the cemetery, where he found Matt, Drea, and Olivia sitting in the grass in front of Simon's tombstone. He forced a smile and peered at their somber faces. "Looks like I'm not the only one who decided to ditch."

Matt held his cigarette away from his lips and sighed. "I hate the luncheons even more than the actual funerals. Nothing's more depressing than being in a room full of sad people pretending to be okay."

"Sad, *scared* people," Drea said. "No one's been able to rest since it all happened. I sure haven't." She squeezed Matt's free hand. "Simon and I may not have seen eye to eye on most things, but the world is always a darker place when we lose an exorcist, especially one as powerful as him."

"I'm glad they buried him here," Olivia said, hugging her knees. "I was afraid they'd think he was a traitor for knowing about the temple, but it sounds like they listened to

Karin. Maybe it's silly of me to feel this way, but knowing he was faithful to Eden makes me feel a little better. I'm sure he was just trying to protect us, like he always was."

"I doubt Sakura will receive nearly the same treatment after her execution," Drea said. "No matter what her intentions really were, Eden isn't known for sparing mercy on traitors."

"She doesn't deserve mercy," Matt said, wrinkling his nose.

"Are they actually gonna kill her?" Anthony said.

"After they milk out whatever information she's hiding about Zalem, definitely," Matt replied. "She's a traitor and murderer." Narrowing his eyes, he curled his fist. "I just wish I was the one to do it. I wanted to kill her so badly when I saw her covered in blood, laughing like a maniac. . . " Trailing off, he buried his reddening face in his hands. Drea embraced him, resting her head on his shoulder.

"I feel sorry for Emily," Drea said. "I saw Sam and James drag her into the church for an interrogation."

"After everything Erika told them about Zalem, I'm sure they'll bombard her with questions that she'll be thrilled to answer," Olivia said with a laugh.

"Who are Sam and James?" Anthony asked, his gaze darting to the back of the church.

"Sam is Jason's older brother, head of the spirituality branch. And James. . . " Picking at the grass beside her, a distant glaze washed over her eyes. "James is my father."

"Your father is here?" Anthony's jaw dropped, his focus remaining on the church.

"Yeah, for the funeral. He had to bail out Erika, too. Of course, he refused to see me, but—hey, where are you going?"

Sprinting to the church, Anthony ignored Olivia, her shouts fading to mumbles. He flung open the golden doors to see Emily sitting upon one of the pews at the front of the sanctuary. Erika sat beside her, a priest and a man in a crisp suit looming over them.

"Leave her alone!" he shouted, grasping his knees for support while he caught his breath.

"Anthony?" Emily said, rising from the pew. "What are you doing here?"

Anthony didn't answer. He walked toward the middle-aged men and hoped his face was as stern as he imagined it to be. "There aren't any answers you can get from her that you don't already know. She doesn't know if Zalem is actually alive, where he is, or why Lucifer's Disciples want him, so just leave her alone."

The man in the suit narrowed his green eyes, accentuating their wrinkled corners. "You must be Anthony."

Anthony stiffened. "And you must be James."

"That's *Mr. Mavro* to you," the priest spat, leering at him through thick framed glasses. "How dare you give orders to the chairman?"

"Anthony!" Olivia cried, running into the church. "What the heck are you doing? You can't just—" She froze when her gaze met her father's.

James sighed and ran a hand through his graying black hair. "Samuel, Erika, did I not tell you two to keep that girl away from me?"

"I'm very sorry, sir," Samuel said with a bow.

"I'll escort her and Anthony out," Erika said.

Anthony held out his arms to push her away, his head cocked to keep his attention on James. "Did you seriously just refer to Olivia as *that girl?*"

"Anthony," Olivia whispered, "don't even bother—"

"*That girl* is your daughter!" Anthony shouted, pointing to Olivia. "Whether or not you 'need' a third child for your organization is irrelevant. She is still your daughter and deserves to be treated like it!"

"That *daughter* of mine," James began, spitting out the

word "daughter" as if it were a curse, "failed her simple duty to oversee the investigation on Emily. Not only did you all investigate inside Mavro Manor against my orders, you continued your investigation here at the monastery's funeral home after it was terminated." He folded his ringed fingers. "A valued exorcist paid the price of her stupidity with his life. If she were competent enough to do her job and enforce my word upon the group, this whole incident could have easily been avoided. She should be grateful that I am not punishing her."

"For what?" Anthony cried. "She didn't do anything!"

"That is exactly my point. I terminated this investigation for a reason. I knew it would be too dangerous to continue, but she allowed it to anyway. If anyone else were to go against my orders, they would face serious consequences."

"With respect, Father," Erika said, avoiding eye contact, "I am the one who allowed Olivia and the others to enter the monastery together. It's my fault that—"

"Silence!" James bellowed. "Erika, Samuel, take them away!"

"No!" Anthony shouted, struggling as Samuel seized his arms.

"Just cooperate, Anthony," Olivia said, flinching when Erika seized her forearms. "He won't listen to anything you tell him."

Anthony squirmed in Samuel's grasp, glaring at James. From the corner of his eye, he could see Emily gaping at him. "You knew all along!" he screamed. "You knew about the underground temple!"

"I don't know what you're talking about," James said, his tone as cold as his stare. "No one knew about it, not even the monastery clergy."

"You've known all along that Eden's been infiltrated by Lucifer's Disciples!" Anthony shouted. "That's why you hide your son from everyone, even your own family!"

"Father, what is he talking about?" Erika asked, her gaze whipping between Anthony and James. "Please tell me that's not true."

But James remained still as he glared at Anthony.

"You know Eden can't be trusted!" Anthony yelled. "You know it, and Emily's family knew it, too! That's why they lied about Zalem's death!"

"Samuel, erase his memory," James ordered.

"No!" Emily screamed, her hands flying to her face.

Pinning Anthony's back down to the nearest pew, Samuel held his shoulder in one hand, and placed his other palm against his forehead. Anthony felt his strength diminishing beneath Samuel's grasp. Olivia and Emily's cries hushed to an echoed blur, the sunlit sanctuary fading into darkness.

CHAPTER 23

~~

"We want to join Eden."

Samuel glared down at the two kneeling Phobia, his eyes filled with ice. "I beg your pardon?"

"You heard me," Simon said, peering up at Samuel from the church floor. "We want to join Eden."

"That's ridiculous," Samuel spat. "Demons are not and cannot be servants of God."

"But we wish to be," Sakura said. "We want to become exorcists and help fight against demons. We heard you're the strongest one here, so we would be eternally grateful if you could teach us white magic."

Samuel turned up his nose. "I will never become a teacher to two filthy demons."

"Hear them out, Sam," Jason whispered to his brother, nudging his arm. "They had a pretty convincing case. The exorcists that found them even saw them fighting off other Phobia when they joined us in combat. If they can master white magic, they will be extremely useful for fighting against demons."

"And how do we know they aren't spies?" Samuel said, narrowing his eyes.

"We're willing to do anything to prove our loyalty to Eden and God," Simon said.

"*Anything?*" Samuel held out his palm. "If you're truly willing to become a servant of God, then let's see how long you can endure His power."

"No!" Sakura screamed. Bolting upright in bed, she lifted her pajama shirt over her stomach. All that remained from that day so many years ago were numerous scars, but she could still feel the burning white light on her flesh. The scars from all the trials she endured to prove her loyalty to Eden. *Was it all for nothing?* She buried her face in her sweaty palms. *No, it wasn't. I did it for you, Simon.*

She jumped at the sound of a knock on her door. Two men in suits entered her bedroom.

"Come with us," one of the men said, beckoning to her. "Boss's orders. He wants you back at headquarters before morning."

She gazed at them in an attempt to read their blank expressions behind their sunglasses. "Is he planning to hold my execution there?"

"We can talk more in the car," the second man said. "Please, come with us quietly and we won't have to hurt you."

Reaching under her pillow, her fingers wrapped around the dagger hidden beneath. "Okay. I will come with you."

~~

"There are three important elements to mastering white magic," Samuel explained, standing in front of the altar while Sakura and Simon sat in the front pew. "Skill. If you do not know how to perform a spell, you will be unable to properly use it. Practice makes perfect." Pacing to the back of the altar, he rested his hand on the cross upon the table. "Belief in God. White magic is fueled by God's power. If you do not believe in Him, He will not lend you his strength."

Sakura gazed at the cross, its golden finish glistening in the sunrays cascading from the tall, stained-glass windows. It wasn't until Samuel approached the pew that her eyes met his.

"Belief in *yourself*. The most important element. If you do not believe you are strong enough to master white magic, you never will."

"But, sir," Sakura said, raising a timid hand, "every time we try to perform a spell, we get burned."

"Endure it," Samuel said, crossing his arms under his chest. "Endure it to show God your love, your strength. Endure it to show me that you have what it takes to become an exorcist. If you don't believe in your own abilities, don't expect me to."

~~

Making her way toward the funeral home, Sakura's bloodstained pajamas clung to her skin. *I believed my love for Simon would carry me through the pain. But if I truly loved him, would I have been so easily persuaded by those in the dark?* She raised her palm, her gaze fixed on the funeral home. *Or was I just too weak to endure living in the light?*

~~

Anthony squinted, blinded by the bright lights surrounding him. He wasn't sure what time it was, but his head felt heavy, his body fatigued. Rolling onto his side, he rubbed his eyes and saw Olivia sitting beside the bed he lay upon.

"Finally, you're awake," she whispered. "How are you feeling?"

"Tired," he mumbled. He peered around at the rows of white beds around him. All he could see through the windows was black sky. "Where am I?"

"The monastery's infirmary," Olivia replied. "You've been passed out for the entire day."

Anthony held his head and gasped. "That Sam guy. He tried to erase my memories. Did he do it?"

"Thankfully, no." She stared down at her folded hands. "Emily stopped him. She convinced him that she needs you to remember her, since you're supposedly helping her stay alive. All he did was knock you out."

Anthony massaged his hands over his face. "I'm so sorry. I screwed up."

"You did nothing wrong."

"I made your dad angry at us. I might not be so lucky next time."

"If it makes you feel any better, he and Sam left earlier this evening," she said with a weak smile. "They're too busy with their own work to stay overnight, so you're safe."

"For now," Anthony grumbled.

Olivia shifted in her seat. "Thanks for everything you did earlier. For the stuff you said to my father. No one's ever stood up for me like that. It really meant a lot to me."

"No offense, but your dad's a total jerk and that Sam guy isn't much better."

"He's okay when he's not with my father. All the higher ups are total toadies." She bit her quaking lower lip. "I'm sorry you have to deal with all this Eden drama. An outsider like you doesn't deserve to be stuck with freaks like us."

"It's not that bad," Anthony chuckled. "Yeah, it's kinda creepy at times with all the demons attacking, but it could be worse." His expression softened when he saw her holding back tears. "I'm sorry, I didn't mean it to sound like I'm having a bad time. Things suck now with Simon gone and Sakura all crazy, but it's been kinda fun hanging out with everyone before the bad stuff started happening."

"No, it's nothing you said," Olivia said, wiping her eyes. "It's just. . . No one gives you enough credit for all you've done for us."

"That's because I don't do anything," Anthony said

with a laugh.

Olivia shook her head. "You've done so much to help Emily open up to us. I think in general, having someone like you with the group has made us all feel a bit more relaxed."

"You mean an outsider?"

"I mean someone who genuinely cares for others. Not that the others don't, but like you said, you're not here for a job or anything." She bowed her head to hide her reddening cheeks. "I'm really sorry for the way I acted that one time when you asked me out. I was really rude to you."

Anthony blushed. "What? No. It's fine. It's all in the past now, anyway."

"No, seriously. I didn't mean to be so cold. I can't let outsiders get too close to me since I work for Eden, so I'd always feel so nervous when guys would ask me out. But now that I know you, I . . ." Sniffing the air, she looked up with a furrowed brow. "Do you smell that?"

Anthony wrinkled his nose. "Is something burning?"

Olivia held out a hand to keep him from rising. She walked toward the nearest window and peered outside. "Oh my God!"

~~

"It burns!" Sakura cried, tossing the wooden cross aside. It skid across the marble floor of the church. She gaped at her charred, bleeding palms in horror. "I can't do this!"

"I know it's hard, but you have to," Simon said. Wincing, he picked up the cross. "C'mon. Try again. All you gotta do is hold it for a while."

"But I can't! Look at my hands! Why can't we wear gloves?"

"We can once we get used to white magic. We won't be able to produce magic from within if we can't even handle touching holy objects." Smoke rose between his fingers. "The longer I hold it, the more it will hurt me. Do you want that?"

"No," she muttered, taking the cross from him. She screamed in pain, curling into a ball at his feet. "Oh God, it burns! It burns!"

"It's gonna be okay," Simon whispered, wrapping his arms around her. "Remember what Sam told us? It's God's love and we have to show our love for Him by accepting the pain."

"That's crap and you know it!" she shouted, tears streaming from her eyes. "We're demons! He could never love us! If He truly did, then He wouldn't be hurting us!"

Simon hugged her tighter. "Then do it because you love me. I want to become an exorcist so I can protect you from Lucifer's Disciples. Our training may be hard to bear, but I know my love for you will get me through it. Can you do the same for me?"

~~

Rushing outside, Anthony froze when he gazed upon the burning funeral home. The night's cool breeze was thick with the scent of burning wood and smoke. People scurried about the monastery grounds in panic, scrambling to find fire extinguishers and hoses.

"How did this happen?" Olivia cried, gaping at the flaming building.

Anthony's eyes darted around the panicked crowd, searching for familiar faces. "I've got to find Emily!"

"Wait!" She seized his arm to hold him back. "If something horrible happens to us tonight, I want you to know that I. . . I love you!" Standing on her toes, she wrapped her arms behind his neck and locked her lips with his.

Anthony pushed her away. "W-what the hell, Olivia?"

"I'm sorry, I know it's horrible timing, but I had to tell

you!" She reached for him, but Anthony backed away.

"I'm sorry, Olivia, but I. . . " He scanned through the crowd for Emily, but she was nowhere in sight. "Look, I can't really handle this right now. Can we maybe talk about this later?"

"I don't understand. Don't you like me?" Her jaw dropped, her eyes filling with tears. "Oh my God, don't tell me. . . Y-you like *her*, don't you?"

"I—I gotta go," Anthony stammered, taking a few more steps back before running off.

"Anthony, wait!" Olivia cried. "Anthony!"

~~

Sakura stood in front of the cross marking Simon's grave, her grip on her dagger tightening. *If we are to meet again, could you ever forgive me?*

Shouts echoed in the distance. Peeking over her shoulder, silhouettes emerged from the smoke, charging through the cemetery. She sighed, looking down at the tombstone. Pointing the bloody dagger at her chest, tears rushed down her cheeks. *The final way repent is to detach myself from my sins, from everything. Only then will I defeat the darkness inside my heart, just as you always wished for me to do.*

With one final breath, she thrust the blade into the center of her chest. Smoke rose from her wound, the silver burning her from within. Her body fell forward onto Simon's tombstone, her blood tainting the once-pure white marble of the cross.

CHAPTER 24

~~

There was a strange chill in the spring air the next day, while Anthony sat with Drea, Karin, Emily, and Matt in the monastery courtyard. For a while, they sat in silence, watching the clouds drift by, no one daring to speak. The longer they sat, the more uncomfortable Anthony grew. He could feel the tension between everyone lodged in his throat, almost choking him.

Unable to bear it any longer, Anthony cleared his throat. "So, what's gonna happen now?"

There was a pause, everyone struggling to answer the question they were all thinking.

Matt dangled his cigarette between his fingers and let out a long sigh, exhaling a thick cloud of smoke. "From what I heard, Erika's working on arranging a funeral for the guards Sakura killed. It's gonna be at a different cemetery. No one wants to go near this one for a while. Not after all that happened. The Satanic temple burned with the funeral home, so the investigation on it is obviously canceled." He took another drag and shook his head. "As for Sakura, I don't know what they're going to do with her."

"They should burn her corpse," Karin mumbled, staring down at the grass with empty eyes. "She was a traitor. She doesn't deserve a proper burial."

"That doesn't seem right," Anthony said, shaking his head. "She may have been a traitor, but she was protecting all of us."

"I think that was part of her act," Drea said with a dark laugh, though her expression remained blank.

"But she could have easily killed us all and made it look like one of Rundull's Phobia chicks did it," Anthony said, hoping for at least one of them to make eye contact with him or nod in agreement. "I don't think she ever really wanted to hurt anyone. If she was truly faithful to Lucifer's Disciples, she would have run off with them before Eden found her." He lowered his voice. "I don't think she would have killed herself if she was proud of what she had done."

"And she wouldn't have done any of it if it weren't for Emily's stupid brother," Karin grumbled.

Emily stiffened when Karin glared at her. "I am positive there are more spies from Lucifer's Disciples within Eden, all with the same task as Sakura's. Lucifer's Disciples does not want Eden to learn about Zalem, find him, or catch onto what the demons want with him, while Eden is afraid to pursue any investigations on him in fear of one of the traitors attacking, just like what Sakura did." Twirling a strand of hair around her finger, her gaze met Karin's. "Though my parents never told me much about what went on at Eden, I am quite positive that they knew about the spies, just as James Mavro most likely does."

Matt rested the back of his head against the brick wall behind him. "If the Mavro family knew about the traitors for the past hundred years and hasn't done anything to stop the issue, then it must be out of Eden's control. Everything I heard about your investigation and how it was canceled seems really off."

"They may have canceled our investigation, but they are not solving any problems by doing so," Emily said. "The madness will continue until Lucifer's Disciples captures

Zalem and gets him to do whatever they want, but that will never happen. Zalem hates Lucifer's Disciples as much as I do, possibly even more." She crossed her arms over her stomach. "Given that I am still, to some degree, alive, I have no doubt that Zalem is, too, but I do not believe he is with Lucifer's Disciples. The only way Lucifer's Disciples could ever get Zalem to cooperate is if they have me as their hostage. I am quite positive that is the sole reason why they need me."

"So we just have to accept that our friends gotta keep dying and getting hurt to keep Lucifer's Disciples away from you?" Karin asked, tears dripping down her cheeks. "When will it end?"

Emily's lips parted, but no words escaped.

"Why don't we just find where they're keeping Emily's soul?" Matt said. "They want her soul to keep her young and dependent on them. Without her soul, they have nothing to hold her down and no way to lure Zalem."

"We already thought of that," Anthony said, his shoulders slumping, "but it's impossible to figure out where Lucifer's Disciples is hiding her soul. We just know it's somewhere nearby."

"Then we'll just have to find their hideout," Matt said.

Drea sighed. "We would have done that a long time ago if we could."

"Um, hey, guys," Olivia said, entering the courtyard through the cloistered walkway. She blushed when she noticed Anthony staring at her and averted her gaze. "Um, some of the investigators were cleaning out Sakura's room and they found this." She lifted a folded piece of paper for everyone to see. "It's addressed to all of us."

Matt beckoned to her. "Let me see."

Olivia gave Matt the paper and he began to read aloud.

"Dear Matt, Drea, Karin, Olivia, Emily, and Anthony. I'm sorry. I wanted to protect you all from the darkness, but in the end, I couldn't even save myself. It's easy to get lost in the darkness of the night. I tried to look to the stars to guide me back to the light, but I found myself following the wrong ones, down the alley of the red lamp. If you, too, find yourself down that alley, just look under the floorboards, and you'll find the angels." Matt paused, skimming over the letter again, then said, "And she signed her name on the bottom and ended it there."

Drea raised her brow. "I don't get it. What's her deal with the red lamp and floor?"

"She was about to kill herself when she wrote this," Emily said with a shrug. "It is probably all nonsense."

"Is this her lame excuse for an apology?" Karin muttered, digging her nails into the grass.

"I don't think it's really an apology or nonsense," Anthony said. He held out his hand, gesturing for the letter. "I think she's trying to tell us something."

Matt handed it to him and said, "I can try to figure out what she means, but it's kind of hard to do so without anything to base it off of."

Emily scooted closer to Anthony and peeked over his shoulder at the note. Anthony glanced up at Olivia and noticed her glaring at Emily.

"Anyway, it seemed like you guys were in the middle of something when I got here," Olivia said, backing away, "so I'll leave you all alone."

"Wait!" Anthony stood up, brushing the grass off his jeans.

Olivia peeked over her shoulder, increasing her pace when she spotted him following her through the walkway.

"I said wait!" Seizing her wrist, Anthony drew her to a halt. "Can't we talk about yesterday?"

"What's there to talk about?" Olivia mumbled, flushing. "Everything we both said was pretty clear."

"I know, and that's why I wanted to apologize if I hurt

you. I still think you're really cool, I just don't—"

"I'm fine," she said, but her pursed lips and sweaty palm weren't convincing. "Once we finally go home, it'll be like this never happened. You'll be back to your normal life, crushing on me, but I won't be dumb enough to reject you the next time you ask me out."

"What do you mean?"

"Well, now that Easter is over and there's no more investigation, we can't just stay at the monastery." She raised her brow. "You didn't think Eden would let you keep your memories, did you? In a few days, you'll be back home with zero memories of Emily and everything that happened in our time together."

Anthony gasped, his grip loosening as his body froze in shock. He gaped after Olivia, who wriggled free from his grasp and walked back into the monastery's main hall.

~~

The orange sun cast elongated shadows over the tombstones as it set behind the trees. Anthony trudged through the grass, making his way up the hill to the Mavro mausoleum. He pulled his jacket tighter over his chest as the sunset's cool breeze sent a chill down his spine. It only seemed to become colder as he approached the mausoleum. Though the outside appeared daunting and grim, he realized the interior was the complete opposite as he stepped inside. Crisp white tombs lined the walls, stacked to the ceiling, each with golden nameplates and fresh bouquets. The remaining sunlight spilled through the stained glass windows, pooling at Emily's feet.

"It is quite amusing, reading the names of my ancestors who were born after me, yet died before me," she said, her attention focused on the tombs. She drifted to the back of the mausoleum, where her parents' caskets were placed, along with a smaller one. "They even have one for Zalem. I am curious what they put in there, if anything." Her eyes appeared to glow like a cat's as shadows were cast across her face. "He should be locked away here. Death would treat him far more kindly than life ever did."

"Why do you say that?" Anthony asked.

She gazed at Zalem's casket. "He had a blood disease. It would make him very sick at times."

"Sick enough to hurt you?"

Emily didn't answer. Her eyes remained fixed on the casket. "He always had one foot in the grave. I just wanted him to live the happiest life he could."

Anthony wrinkled his nose. "No offense, but I don't understand what Lucifer's Disciples could want with a sick person."

"Now you understand my confusion." She peered up at him. "What are you doing here anyway?"

Anthony blushed. "Oh, uh, well I saw you heading up here, and I, uh. . ."

She smirked. "You were stalking me?"

"N-no, I was just. . ." He trailed off and took a deep breath, clenching his fists. "Since Easter is over and the investigation is no longer a thing, we need to leave sometime in the next few days."

"Will I return to your house?" Emily asked, her brow lifting with interest.

Anthony looked away. "I don't know. They're still trying to decide if you should stay with me or not. I think that's why they haven't kicked us out of the monastery yet. I mean, now that they know I can't keep you alive, they might not want an outsider keeping you as a roommate."

A distant glaze washed over Emily's eyes.

"Since we aren't doing anything until then, I. . ." His cheeks flushed redder. "I was wondering if you'd want to hang out tomorrow. I know we're kinda in the middle of nowhere, but if you don't mind walking a bit, I remember seeing this little park by the lake on the way here, just at the bottom of the hill. We can check it out and call a cab to take us into town."

"I am not sure that sounds like a safe idea," Emily said. "We probably should not be leaving holy grounds."

"We'll be fine," Anthony said.

"That is what they told us last time when we were attacked at that motel."

"But the investigation was still going on. Now it's not."

Emily paused, watching him with an unwavering stare. Anthony stared back at her, anxiety filling his chest, waiting for her to speak. When she smiled, he let out a sigh of relief.

"I suppose it will not hurt to explore for a bit," she said. "Just bring me back before dark."

CHAPTER 25

~~

Emily wrinkled her nose, following Anthony onto the wooden floor of the bowling alley. Rock music blared over the clattering pins and cheering players. Clutching the black leather strap of her purse, she peered up at Anthony.

"What is this place?"

"It's a bowling alley," Anthony answered. He pointed down their lane at the pins. "See those? You want to knock them all down with a ball."

"I do not know if this is a good place for me," Emily said, glancing behind her at the food-stained couches and tables littered with empty soda cans. "It smells like old pizza in here and these shoes are hideous."

"They aren't exactly my taste either," Anthony chuckled, "but you taught me how to play that piano song, so now I want to teach you something. Plus there isn't really much else to do in this little town. Just give it a try, okay?" He picked up a green ball from the shelf and handed it to her. "Here, just put your fingers in the little holes."

"This is awfully heavy," she grumbled, the weight of the ball causing her to lean to her right.

"It has to be," Anthony said, picking up a ball for himself.

"Why?"

"Because physics. Now, watch how I do this." Approaching the lane, he beckoned to her. "See how my arm is straight? You wanna swing back, drop it low, and aim to hit right in the middle to knock them all down. You get lots of points if you knock them all down on your first try, but you get two chances per turn."

"And what happens if I knock them down?"

"You get points."

"And what do the points get me?"

"Something to brag about." He looked at her with raised eyebrows. "Have you never played a game before?"

Emily blushed. "I have! I used to play croquet all the time."

"Okay, well this is like the same thing, but with pins instead of those arch things."

She cocked her head and crossed her arms. "This is nothing like croquet."

Anthony rolled his eyes. "You're right. This is way more fun, trust me." He took a deep breath and rolled the ball onto the lane. When the ball rolled diagonally into the gutter, he could hear Emily snickering behind him.

"That was just the warm-up toss," he grumbled, retrieving a new ball. But on his next try, all he managed to hit were two back pins.

"You are absolutely terrible at this," Emily giggled. "Are you sure you are good enough to teach me?"

"It's been a while since I played," Anthony said. "I haven't gone since my friend's eighth birthday. I'd like to see you do better."

Emily waddled up to the lane with red cheeks. "This is my first time. Please do not mock me if I fail." She tossed the ball and watched it inch its way down to the pins.

Anthony's jaw dropped when all the pins crashed down.

Emily clapped her hands and grinned. "I did it!"

"You got a strike on your first try? How did you even. . . ?"

She shrugged. "I suppose I am just better than you."

Anthony narrowed his eyes and retrieved his ball from the conveyor. "That was just a fluke. Don't get too cocky."

~~

Emily was still beaming when they left the bowling alley. "That was so much fun! Thank you for teaching me how to bowl."

"I didn't really teach you anything," Anthony said with a chuckle. "You totally kicked my butt." He glanced at the shops they passed by, hoping to find something else worth checking out.

Emily froze in front of one of the shop windows, pressing her nose and fingers against the glass. "I need him!"

Anthony stopped to see what she was drooling over. "That teddy bear?"

"Yes!" She folded her hands and stared up at Anthony with puppy dog eyes. "Can you please buy him for me?"

"You buy it," Anthony said, averting his gaze. "You're the rich one."

"But I do not have access to my money right now. I will pay you back someday, I promise!"

Glancing back at her, he blushed and scratched his temple. "Okay, fine, just this one thing."

By the time they left town, Anthony was carrying two shopping bags filled with antique dolls and teddy bears. The sun was already beginning to set when they arrived at the park.

"I can't believe we spent half a day just shopping at antique stores," Anthony muttered. Plopping onto one of the swings, he placed the bags upon the woodchips beside him.

"There were so many beautiful things to look at,"

Emily said, taking the swing next to his. "Some of it reminded me of my time." Her shoes grazed against the ground while she swung. "It was rather comforting to see familiar objects again."

Anthony smiled. "I'm glad you had a good time."

"Did you?"

"I'll be honest, I'm not too into shopping, but it was fun to hang out with you." He cocked his head, hoping she would make eye contact. "We can do more stuff like this in the future. We can go bowling and shopping closer to home. I think I know a few places you might like."

Instead of answering, Emily just stared out at the lake ahead of them. "Before we go back to the monastery, can we go closer to the lake?"

Anthony dragged his shoe against the ground to stop swinging. "Sure. I know you want to be back before dark, so we should probably check it out now."

On the way down to the lake, Anthony picked a fluffy white dandelion from the grass. Twirling it between his fingers, he watched Emily hold her socks and shoes. She proceeded toward the lake, the water dyed orange in the sunset.

"Are you coming, Anthony?" she asked, stepping into the lake. "The water is not too cold."

"Yeah," he said, gazing down at the flower. A few spores drifted away from the stem in the gentle breeze, floating up to the sky and out of sight. He could still hear Olivia's voice ringing in his ears. *In a few days, you'll be back home with zero memories of Emily and everything that happened in our time together.*

"Anthony?"

Anthony peered up from the flower to see Emily standing in front of him. *This might be our last day together,* Anthony thought, his heart racing.

"What are you doing?" she asked, arching an eyebrow.

She seized his wrist, the remaining seeds breaking free from the stem as the dandelion tumbled to the sand. "Come on, I do not want to be all by myself—"

Pulling her closer, Anthony embraced her against his chest, resting his head above hers. "When I leave, will you. . . will you still remember me?"

"Not if you strangle me," Emily grumbled, struggling in his arms. "Why are you acting so strange?"

"Because I'm going to forget you!" he cried, his grip on her tightening. "Once I'm sent home, it's over. Eden will wipe my memories of everything we did together, and I'll go back to my old life of going to school and living with my aunt and uncle."

"It is for the best, really," Emily said with a nervous laugh. "Eden is nothing but trouble. You are lucky to soon be free from them. I can only wish to be in your position."

"Then come with me. We can leave them right now— we can leave *everything*, and just, I dunno, be free!"

"Have you lost your mind?" Breaking free from his grasp, Emily backed away, her wide eyes meeting his.

"It's what you wanted to do when we met, right?" Anthony said, his quaking lips twisting to a smile. "You wanted to run away from home and stay with me."

Emily took another step back. "And then Eden found us. Even if I were to go with you, they will find us again."

"Then we'll go far away, where they can't find us."

"Even if that were possible, I cannot go with you. I do not belong with you." Her gaze dropped to the ground. "I would love to live a normal life with a normal person, far away from Eden. It is what I have always wanted. But if Zalem is alive, then I must find him, especially if he is being held captive by Lucifer's Disciples. He needs me to take care of him."

"Meaning you need to keep hurting yourself for him?" Anthony's knees trembled, struggling to support his weight as he took in everything she said. "You really would seriously rather keep slicing up your arms than go off and be free?"

"You do not understand." Letting out a shaky breath, Emily turned her back to him and walked toward the lake. "His disease made it so his blood could not nourish his body. Without fresh, healthy blood, he could die. He had to do whatever he could to stay alive, even if it meant harming others to steal blood from their bodies. I would do whatever I could to help him."

"What do you mean by *steal?*" His brow wrinkled and his gut curled into knots.

Emily shrugged. "You saw the underground room. Zalem and I actually called it the *dining room*. Of course, I was only watching him feast." Her hand rose to her neck, her fingers wrapping around the bandage. "After seeing blood so often, you start to see a sort of beauty in it—in death. There was something oddly romantic and mysterious about watching a person's life slip away as they fell into what used to be the unknown to me." She sighed, peering out at the crimson horizon. "It was not until after I died that I realized perhaps there was something sick about finding pleasure in watching Zalem kill innocent people, wishing it could be me being covered in my own beautiful blood, giving my life to nourish his." Stopping in front of the lake, she narrowed her eyes at her own reflection. "Death is not nearly as exciting as I thought it would be."

Her words left a sickening, bubbling sensation in his stomach. *She's absolutely insane.*

"When you truly love someone, you view them in a different light. I never once questioned Zalem's actions. I just wanted to see him happy and healthy. But really, his illness made him a ravenous monster, a slave for blood, and I—" Ripping off her bandage, she faced Anthony to reveal a large bite wound, the holes brown and crusty with age, and much too large to be made by human teeth, "a slave for his bite."

The color drained from Anthony's face. His hand slapped over his mouth, uncertain whether he would scream or puke. "Th-that's. . ." he stammered, his voice muffled beneath his palm. His heart dropped into his stomach. "That's not. . ." With a trembling finger, he pointed at her wound. "Th-that's not a human bite."

"Zalem was just as human as you and I. He was ill."

"That's *not* a human bite!" Anthony shouted. "You mean to tell me that this is the kind of crap your freaking brother's been pulling on you, and you still think he's just sick?"

"Because he is," Emily said. "And he did not always bite me. I would usually cut myself to let him drink my blood. It was safer and easier to control how much he took. Biting hurts far more, but after the pain came the most amazing bliss." Stroking her wound, she let out an airy giggle. "I craved that bliss, just as he craved my blood. It made me want him to never stop drinking."

"And that's why he freaking killed you!" Anthony cried.

Emily narrowed her eyes. "No, he killed me because his teeth punctured my neck. I am certain that I died well before I lost too much blood."

"That's not what I meant!" He tossed his arms above his head in frustration. "Humans don't *crave* blood! They don't *drink* blood! And they don't have sharp enough teeth to just bite people like that! Your brother's not a human, he's a freaking vampire!"

"He is *human*," Emily said, placing her hands on her hips. "He and I would play outside in the sun all the time, and we would go to church, school—wait, let me go!"

Seizing her hand, Anthony dragged her away from the lake. "You need some serious help if you still think he's human! It's no wonder all those demons want him! He's one of them!"

"No, he is not!" Emily yelled, struggling to free her

wrist from Anthony's iron grip.

Anthony stopped in his tracks and peered back at her. "You know he is! You literally just told me you realized he's a monster, so why do you want to go back to him?"

Emily looked away. "Because he needs me!"

"He doesn't need you! Even if he needs blood, there are plenty of other people in the world he can take from."

"It is not just that!" Her eyes met his. "I need to protect him from Lucifer's Disciples! I do not know what specifically they want with him, but it cannot be good."

Anthony started walking again. "Then we'll just let Eden deal with him."

"But they cannot be trusted! Not with their traitors! Protecting him is my purpose in life! If I am not there for him, I—"

Snatching her other hand, Anthony knelt to be eye level with her. "What is it gonna take to get you to realize how wrong all this is?"

Emily avoided his gaze. Instead, she peered down at her feet shuffling in the sand, creating intricate lines and circles.

"If Zalem cared about you even half as much as you care about him, he would want you to do what makes you happy. He would want you to be free to live the life you want to live. He would never want you to hurt yourself like this." His voice shook, struggling to keep a steady tone. "I would. . . I would never do anything to hurt you."

Her eyes narrowing, she looked back at Anthony and lifted her nose. "If I was the one who needed blood, I know you would cut yourself for me without a moment's thought."

Her words sent a piercing arrow through his chest, his grip on her weakening.

Wriggling free, Emily reached into her purse and withdrew a small knife. She pointed it toward Anthony with a smile, though her eyes were filled with a misty sadness. "Just as there is nothing you would not do for me, there is nothing I would not do for Zalem."

Anthony backed away from her, afraid she might attack, but she slashed her own wrist. Blood dripped from her cut and onto the sigil she had drawn in the sand around her. Smoke rose from the sand, wrapping around her as if in an embrace. As the smoke thickened into a solid, human form, Anthony's heart raced against his panicked mind, praying for someone to somehow spot them and come to their rescue.

Hugging her from behind, the long black sleeves of Rundull's robes draped over Emily's shoulders like a blanket. "About time," he whispered into Emily's ear. "I was worried you had forgotten about me."

"Let her go!" Anthony shouted.

Emily shut her eyes and winced. Despite the apparent uneasiness she wore on her face, she stood rigid and resigned in Rundull's arms.

"Oh, but I don't think she'd like that," Rundull said, smirking and squeezing her tighter. "It was our *deal* after all."

"Y-you made a deal with him?" Anthony stammered. He gaped at Emily, hoping for some sort of response, but her eyes remained shut.

"Little Miss Emily here was feeling lonely last night and gave me a call." He snuggled closer to her, running his hand through her hair. "She misses her big brother."

"He. . . He told me has Zalem," Emily muttered. "And Zalem needs me, so—"

"And you actually believe him?" Anthony cried. "You're playing right into his trap!"

"Even if he is lying," she peeked up at Anthony with a forced smile, "I know Zalem will come to rescue me when he hears I have been captured, and then we will be together again."

"Emily, please, don't listen to him," Anthony said, reaching into his pocket for his phone. "I know you know this is a stupid idea. If you're so worried about Zalem, I can call Drea and Matt right now, people we know we can *trust*, and—"

"No, please!" Emily yelled. "I do not want any of you to be involved with me anymore! Zalem and I can handle things from now on! It is safer for you all if you just leave us be."

"I don't care about being safe!" Anthony cried. "Not if it means losing you!"

Emily flinched.

"Karin's been trying so hard to be your friend," Anthony said. "Drea's always been around to protect you. Olivia treats you more like a sister than she does to Erika. Hell, Simon freaking died fighting to keep that little creep away from you! If you think any of them would put their safety before yours, you're insane. And I. . ." Curling his fists, he looked her in the eye and waited for her gaze to meet his. "I love you, Emily!"

Emily's eyes widened.

"Please, don't go with him!" Anthony cried. "If anything were to happen to you, I. . . I don't even know what I'd do!"

"Anthony, I. . ." Tears rolled down Emily's blushing cheeks. "I have to, for Zalem."

Rundull peered up at the darkening sky. "Wow, would you look at that! It sure is getting late!" He grinned at Anthony. "It's been a pleasure seeing you again, Anthony, but I'm afraid we must go. Zalem is waiting—" He broke off as Anthony charged toward him. Raising his palm, he shot a black shadow at Anthony, hitting him in the stomach.

"Anthony!" Emily screamed, wriggling in Rundull's arms.

Dropping to his knees, Anthony cringed in pain and clutched his gut. It stung and burned as if he had been struck with fire. He spat up blood, his shirt sticky from his bleeding wound.

"He'll be fine," Rundull said, his hold on Emily tightening. "Don't worry. In a day or two, he won't even remember this or anything about you." He leered down at Anthony. "I'd say see you around, but. . ." He trailed off laughing. Smoke rose from the sand, engulfing him and Emily.

As the smoke dissipated in the breeze, Anthony found himself alone and trembling on the shore.

CHAPTER 26

~~

Anthony was relieved to find Karin walking up the gravel path to her cabin. Glancing over her shoulder, she stopped when she noticed Anthony rushing to her side.

"You okay?" she asked. She furrowed her brow when she noticed him hunched over, pressing his rolled-up hoodie against his wounded gut.

"Finally, someone's here!" he cried through gasps of air. "No one's in the main hall."

"Between the deaths and fire, no one really wants to stick around."

Anthony wiped his sweaty forehead with the back of his hand. "Where's Matt?"

"In his room," Karin answered, gesturing a couple cabins away. "Is something wrong?"

Anthony didn't answer her and hurried to Matt's cabin. "Matt! Matt!" he shouted, banging on the door. "It's super important!"

The door swung open. "Make it quick," Matt said, putting on his coat. "I gotta get going."

"Going? Going where?"

"To my next investigation." Matt backed onto his bed and tied his bootlaces. "I can't be off work forever."

"But you gotta help Emily!" Anthony said, he and

Karin following Matt into the cabin.

"What does she need?" Matt asked, peering up at Anthony.

"She's been kidnapped!"

"What?" Karin and Matt cried in unison.

"She and I were at the park and Rundull took her—"

"Why did you two leave the monastery?" Matt interrupted. "It's way too dangerous to leave the spiritual barriers without an exorcist."

Anthony blushed. "I get that it wasn't a good idea, but you gotta help me find her!"

Rocking on the balls of her feet, Karin's gaze darted between Anthony and Matt.

Matt scratched his head. "I can call the other investigators to look around the area, but odds are Rundull took her to Lucifer's Disciples' headquarters where it will be impossible for us to reach her."

"But who knows what he'll do to her if we don't get her back soon enough?"

Matt stared at Anthony's stomach. "Are you hurt?"

"A little, yeah." Wincing, he removed his hoodie from his bloodstained t-shirt and revealed his wound. His skin was a murky shade of purple where Rundull had hit him. "The bleeding slowed down. It kinda just stings now."

"Uh, that doesn't look too good," Karin said, grimacing. "Did Rundull do that?"

"Yeah," Anthony replied, "but it's not as bad as it looks, I swear. It's not that deep."

Matt rose from the bed and patted the mattress. "Lie down."

"What?" Anthony forced himself to stand up straighter.

Matt swung his backpack onto the bed. "Just do it." He unzipped his bag, rummaged through the contents, then withdrew a small vial of clear liquid. "C'mon, on your back."

"But. . ." Anthony let out a frustrated groan and he lay on the bed, staring up at the ceiling. Matt knelt beside him, unscrewing the cap on the vial. "I think there are more important things to be worried about right now, like Emily—Holy freaking crap!" The liquid splashed onto his wound, a burning sensation throbbing through his gut. Curling into a ball, he rolled onto his side and moaned.

"Matt, are you ready yet?" Drea asked, leaning in the doorway. "You can torture Anthony later. We gotta go!"

"I'm not torturing him. I just put a drop of holy water on his wound to purify it before the spell spreads—" Turning around to face her, he gawked at her miniskirt and fishnet stockings. "What the hell are you wearing?"

"We're going to a nightclub," Drea said with a shrug.

"We're going there to *work*, not to party."

Drea rolled her eyes and clutched her leather jacket. "I have everything I need in here. I'm just trying to blend in."

"You're going to a club?" Karin asked. "Is it Galaxy?"

"The one and only," Drea replied.

Karin's eyes widened. "Can I come with you guys?"

"You're way too young," Matt said, shaking his head.

"Simon let me go before," Karin said. "He knew the security guys at that Galaxy place, and they'd just let me go dance while he went to the bar."

"I'm not breaking the law so you can dance."

Karin crossed her arms. "You seemed to have no problem with the concept when Simon would bring you along."

"I personally don't feel comfortable smuggling a minor into a club," Matt said, averting his gaze from her, "especially one that's become a hot spot for demonic activity. Girls frequently go missing there. They hang out with creepy guys and are never seen again."

Anthony rolled over to face them. "And that's different from any other club how?"

"Because Eden eventually finds the missing girls turned into Phobia," Drea answered.

"I'm not dumb enough to wander off with some demon guy," Karin grumbled.

"Of course you aren't," Drea muttered. She cleared her throat. "C'mon, Matt. We're already way behind schedule."

"But what about Emily?" Anthony asked.

"I'm sorry, but there's nothing I can personally do for her at the moment," Matt said, pausing in the doorway. "As much as I'd like to help, I can't go against orders and ditch my current investigation. I'll call headquarters when I get to the car, and they'll take it from there."

"But. . ." Anthony trailed off, staring after Drea and Matt. He sat up on the bed and held his forehead. "This sucks!"

"Right?" Karin muttered, plopping beside him and gazing out the open doorway. "I'm tired of moping around my room. I wanna dance the sad away."

"How can you be whining about partying at a time like this?" Anthony snapped, jumping up from the bed and clutching the nightstand to support himself through his pain. "Emily's in danger and all you care about is going to some sketchy nightclub!" He buried his face in his hands and groaned. "Even Matt doesn't seem to care. I don't get how he can already be back to work after what happened to Simon. Does he just not care about anything?"

"It's not that he doesn't care," Karin said. "He can't really *afford* to care."

Anthony dropped his arms to his sides.

"Matt probably cares about losing Simon even more than I do," Karin said, leaning against the bed frame, "but sitting around grieving won't fix anything. People die all the time, especially in Eden. It's something we just have to accept. It's the reality of fighting entities stronger than yourself. Exorcists may know how to use white magic, but they're only human."

"But they're trained to fight," Anthony said. "It's their job, right?"

"Sometimes it's just not worth going out of your way to fight a monster like Rundull that could very easily overpower you," Karin said. "You're better off sparing yourself for a battle you actually have a chance at winning. I don't know how many members there are in Lucifer's Disciples, but we're pretty limited." She stared down at her folded hands with misty eyes. "While someone's death is upsetting to us on a personal level, losing a member is an inconvenience to the organization as a whole. All we can do is focus on our own tasks and hope for the best. If we all panicked over every death or mishap, we'd go insane."

"But Emily isn't just a *mishap*!" Anthony shouted. "Isn't she important to Eden?"

"To Eden, yeah," Karin said. "But do you really think Matt wants to go after Rundull after we lost both Simon and Sakura? We're already down two exorcists. It's not worth running toward a fight he knows he can't win."

Anthony curled his fist. "Then he's a coward."

Karin's expression hardened and she scooted to the edge of the bed. "You weren't there when it happened. When Rundull unleashed his power to fight me and Simon."

"Neither was Matt," Anthony mumbled, staring down at the floor.

"Anthony. Listen to me." She didn't continue speaking until their eyes met. "Rundull is already extremely powerful here on Earth. If we go down to his lair, there's no way *anyone* can defeat him. Losing to Rundull would only make Simon's death in vain. Matt knows this, I know it, and I bet you do, too."

Anthony grit his teeth and struggled to keep eye contact with her firm glare. He knew she was right, but didn't dare admit it.

Olivia peeked into the cabin and raised her brow. "What are you guys doing in here?"

"Moping," Karin replied, flopping onto her back. "Matt won't take me with him on his investigation."

"I know, I could hear you guys whining from my cabin," Olivia huffed.

"Yeah, because it's at a *club*," Anthony said. "My problem is a lot bigger than yours."

"Which club?" Olivia asked, walking into the cabin. "That big one downtown?"

"No, Galaxy, the private one in SoDo," Karin said, sitting up. "Y'know, the one with the spooky red lamp in the entrance."

"Wait, did you say red lamp?" Anthony asked.

"Yeah, why?"

Anthony hurried to the desk across from the bed. He sorted through the papers upon it, and unfolded Sakura's suicide note. "'I tried to look to the stars to guide me back to the light, but I found myself following the wrong ones, down the alley of the red lamp.'" He looked up from the note at Karin and Olivia. "The galaxy is filled with stars. The name of that club is Galaxy. Karin just said there's a red lamp at the entrance. She's not just spewing random metaphors. She's trying to tell us something, just like I thought."

"Let me see," Olivia said, peering over his shoulder.

Anthony pointed to the next line. "'If you, too, find yourself down that alley, just look to the floorboards, and you'll find the angels.' She's talking about that nightclub. She's gotta be."

"Then what are the angels?" Olivia asked.

"Maybe the missing girls," Anthony said, folding the note and stuffing it in his pocket. "Maybe Emily's soul. It may not be random, but it's not completely clear. I'm pretty sure she's trying to imply that something is underneath the club. Something we should know about."

"Like a secret base?" Karin asked.

Anthony nodded. "And if that's what it is, it's possible that's where Emily and Rundull are. But we won't know for sure unless we check it out."

"Why would Sakura try to tell us where Lucifer's Disciples' base is?" Olivia asked, crossing her arms. "She was on their side."

"That's why she wrote it so vaguely," Anthony said. "If she didn't want us to know, she wouldn't have said it in the first place, but if another spy were to find a note obviously revealing their hideout, they would confiscate it before we'd have a chance to read it."

"Okay," Olivia said, tapping her fingers against her arm. "Karin, text Drea and tell her that Lucifer's Disciples might have a base under the club."

"No," Anthony said, raising his palm at Karin. "I want to be the one to save Emily."

"You can't do anything to save her," Olivia said with a laugh. "You don't know how to fight demons, let alone a devil like Rundull. There's no point in risking your life to save a girl you won't even remember in a few days."

Anthony curled his fist, his narrowed eyes meeting Olivia's. "I may not remember her, but she'll remember *me*."

Olivia averted her gaze from his firm stare. "Good luck getting past club security."

"He doesn't need luck," Karin said, sliding off the bed. "He has me." She nudged Anthony's arm with her elbow. "You drive me there and I'll get you in. I'll just tell them we're Simon's friends."

"That's so not gonna work," Olivia said.

"Didn't you just say it's not worth going after Emily?" Anthony said. "If Matt can't save her, what makes you think we can?"

"But now that we know where their base might be, it's worth a shot," Karin said. "I'll get us in, we find Matt and

Drea, tell them Rundull may be hiding Emily there. We let them call reinforcements, they all handle the dirty work." She turned to Anthony. "While Eden fights off the demons, you go find Emily and save her. If we can just get all the demons distracted, you might have a chance."

"This is literally the worst plan I have ever heard," Olivia sneered.

"I dunno, I agree with Karin. It's at least worth a shot," Anthony said with a nod.

"Plus I know white magic, so I can come with you to fight off any remaining demons guarding Emily," Karin said.

"You hardly know anything," Olivia said.

"I know more than *you*," Karin huffed.

"She's better than nothing," Anthony said. "Plus you have weapons, right? Like a gun or something."

"Yeah, so?"

"So you're coming with us," Anthony said. "I can't get keys for any of the cars on my own, and you're better with a gun than I am. Besides, you wouldn't want to get in trouble for letting us go unsupervised, would you?"

"Why would I get in trouble?" Olivia asked, lifting her nose. "I'm not in charge of what you guys do anymore."

"But you are in charge of taking care of Emily, like you always have been. Imagine how angry your dad will be when he finds out she's been taken, let alone that his daughter and her caretaker did nothing to help."

"*Fine*," Olivia spat. "I'll drive you two to the stupid club, but don't come crying to me when they don't let you in."

"This is gonna be so awesome!" Karin cried, dancing with joy.

"Yeah, real awesome," Anthony mumbled, lifting his phone a few inches out of his pocket. *It's already been over an hour since Rundull took Emily.* "We should probably hurry up and get going."

"We gotta change first," Karin said. "You can't show up

looking like that."

"What's wrong with my outfit?" Anthony asked, stuffing his hands in his jeans pockets.

Karin wrinkled her nose. "It's so drab. Galaxy's dress code requires attendees to wear all black."

"You're calling a green t-shirt drab when they require you to wear black? What kind of rule is that?"

"A dumb Galaxy rule," Olivia grumbled in response, trudging toward the door. "I guess I'll just wear my funeral dress again."

"I don't even think I brought anything black with me," Anthony said, staring after Olivia.

"You can just borrow Matt's clothes," Karin said. "You guys are about the same size." She opened his closet to reveal a collection of black clothing. She giggled, sliding the hangers across the rack. "Oh my God, *this*."

"No," Anthony said, shaking his head and taking a step back from the leather jacket Karin waved in front of him. "No leather."

"Vinyl okay?"

"People actually wear *vinyl*?"

"They do at Galaxy." Pouting, she stuffed the jacket back into the closet. "Look, our choices are pretty limited here. It's not like I have an entire wardrobe of clothes to pick from."

"Why did he even bring this stuff to a monastery?"

Karin shrugged. "I dunno, probably hoping to have free time with Simon?"

Anthony sighed and held out his hand. "Give me the leather jacket."

"Do you want the matching pants?"

"Just pick out something that's not too extreme," Anthony said, peeking at his phone again. "We kinda need to hurry."

"Okay, but I still need to do your hair and makeup,"

Karin said, taking a pair of leather pants out of the closet.

"Is that really necessary?"

"As Simon's friend, I have a reputation to uphold. I can't just bring *anyone*." She tossed a pile of black clothing to him. "Go put that on, then come back for the finishing touches."

Anthony rolled up the clothes in his arms and sighed. He trudged back to his room, already having second thoughts about their plan.

CHAPTER 27

~~

Sitting in the backseat of the SUV, Anthony picked at his skin-tight leather pants, fighting the urge to rub off the mountains of eyeliner Karin smeared on his eyelids. He wasn't sure what his shirt was made from, but it felt like paper against his skin. The collar around his neck was only becoming more uncomfortable every second he listened to Karin blabber about "how awesome" Club Galaxy was. More than anything, he couldn't stop worrying about Emily. The mere idea of her being held captive was terrifying, but thinking of a way to get her back was enough to make him sick with anxiety.

"So, there's something I should probably tell you guys about Emily," Anthony said, interrupting Karin's ranting.

"What?" Olivia asked.

"So, y'know how Rundull took her?" Anthony took a deep breath, dreading their responses. "Well, she kinda wanted to be taken. Like I guess she made a deal with him and summoned him over, because she can do that. Is that something you guys just know how to do?"

Approaching a red light, Olivia slammed her foot on the break. She turned her head to face him, her ponytail whipping over her shoulder. "We're risking our lives to save a girl who *wanted* to be taken?"

"Kinda? Maybe?" He flinched beneath Olivia's fiery glare. "I don't think she really wanted to go with him. She just felt like she had to, but she really doesn't, and she doesn't really get that."

"I don't get what you're saying," Karin said from the passenger's seat. "Why would she want to be taken?"

"Let me guess," Olivia said, her gaze reverting to the road. "Her brother?"

"Yep," Anthony said with a nod. "Long story short, he has some sort of blood deficiency that makes him need healthy blood, so he drinks human blood to get the nutrients he needs. Emily is under this impression that she needs to take care of him, so Rundull supposedly took her to wherever he is, since he claims Lucifer's Disciples has him in their custody."

"I may not be an expert on physiology," Olivia said, "but I'm like ninety-nine percent sure that there are better ways to gain nutrients than drinking blood. Pretty sure her brother was just psycho like her."

"I dunno, she was pretty serious about it," Anthony said. "She told me about how he was always really sick and that he'd kidnap people so he could feed on them." He rested his head against the window. "He'd feed on her, too. She said it felt really good. That's why she's so obsessed with pain and stuff."

"So he was a vampire?" Karin asked.

"He was born from her parents, so I guess he was human. But really, really sick."

"That explains why he took a chomp out of her neck," Olivia said. "I assumed some sort of monster attacked her."

"Well, it sounds like Zalem was a monster," Anthony said. "That's why Lucifer's Disciples want him."

"But do they actually have him?" Karin asked.

"Emily thinks they do," Anthony replied. He slouched in his seat and sighed. "To be honest, I dunno what would be worse for Emily. Them having him or lying." He sat up straighter when Olivia parked in a gravel lot on the edge of a dark alleyway. A dim red light glowed in the distance, marking the end of a line of black-clad club attendees.

"So when security denies us entry sometime within the next three minutes," Olivia said, looking from Karin to Anthony, "we'll come back here, text Matt, head home, and never bring up how you guys roped me into this awful plan. Got it?"

Karin rolled her eyes. "Well, that's not gonna happen, so there's nothing to *get*."

Anthony refrained from speaking. As they waited at the back of the roped line, he was unsure of who to side with. While the line seemed to be moving too quickly for security to be giving a careful look at each ID card, he was still not convinced that Karin could get them in. It seemed too good to be true. His brow began to sweat as they approached the front of the line, the red lamp casting shadows in every wrinkle on the bouncer's stern face. *Even if we do get in, what next?* he thought. *What if everything doesn't go according to plan? It can't possibly be that easy. If one little thing goes wrong—*

"IDs, please," the bouncer said, beckoning the trio with a finger.

Karin tossed her hair and grinned. "I'm a friend of Simon's, and these two are my friends."

The bouncer smirked, staring down at Karin's fluffy black skirt. "Sure you are, kid. Just show me your IDs and you're good to go."

Anthony bit his tongue, hoping his sweaty brow didn't give away his anxiety. He glanced at Olivia. From the way she sighed and crossed her arms beneath her chest, he knew it was only a matter of seconds before she dragged them away from the line, unless the bouncer beat her to the task.

Karin stood up straighter, forcing the smile to remain on her blushing face. "C'mon, uh. . ." She paused, failing to find a name tag on the bouncer's chest. "C'mon, Tim, you remember me. I used to come here with Simon."

"It's Robert," the bouncer said, his tone cold, "and I don't care who you used to come with. If you can't present valid ID, I can't let you in."

"Guys, let's just go," Olivia grumbled, placing a hand on Karin's shoulder. "I told you this was a dumb idea."

"No!" Karin shouted, yanking herself free from Olivia's grasp. The people in line behind them griped with impatience. She looked up at the bouncer with desperate eyes. "Please! You have to let us in! Our friends are in there and they need us!"

"Oh, God," Anthony groaned, eyeing the approaching security guards. "Way to go, Karin."

Two security guards marched up to them, one seizing Anthony's arms, the second grabbing Olivia's wrist in one hand and Karin's in the other. Karin continued to whine while the guard dragged her out of the line, onto the gravel on the other side of the rope.

"What the hell is going on out here?"

The entire line fell silent and the security guards froze . A man exited the club, the tails of his purple coat rippling behind him. A cluster of women in short dresses gathered in the entryway, staring after him in awe.

"Why is it taking so damn long for all these beautiful people to enter my club?" the man asked, placing his hands on his slim hips.

"It's Eugene! The club owner!" a woman in the line whispered to her friend beside her, fluttering her hands about her face with excitement.

"You'll have to excuse me, sir," Robert said. He gestured to Anthony, Olivia, and Karin. "These three kids were trying to sneak inside."

Eugene flipped his long purple bangs and peered at Anthony behind circular sunglasses. "DJ Venom, what are you doing out here? I told you to use the side door upon arrival."

"Is he talking to me?" Anthony whispered to Olivia, whose eyes were as wide with confusion as his.

"Come on, now," Eugene said. He beckoned to Anthony, the gems on his rings glistening in the red light. "We only have fifteen minutes before your set!"

Oh, crap, he is *talking to me,* Anthony thought.

"Just go with it," Karin whispered in his ear, the security guards releasing them. "It's the only way we can get in." Hurrying back toward the club, she nodded to Eugene and giggled. "Sorry, we totally forgot about the other entrance!"

Eugene raised his drawn-on eyebrows at the girls. "And you are?"

"His personal go-go dancers," Karin said without a moment's thought. "He can't perform without us by his side."

"Alright, alright. Enough chit-chat!" Eugene barked, ushering the three of them into the club. "You all have to get ready to go on stage!"

As he was whisked away into the club, Anthony squinted in the rainbow of flashing lights, overwhelmed by the smell of cigarette smoke. A DJ on the front stage blared electronic music over harsh, repetitive beats. People danced about the wooden floor, the sidelines crowded with bystanders sipping their drinks and smoking. He tried to spot Drea and Matt, but it was impossible to differentiate between the attendees in the sea of black clothing.

He followed Eugene through a long hallway, into one of the several back rooms. Young women in vinyl lingerie crowded around a mirror, slathering on foundation and eye makeup. A few men sat in chairs and on sofas around the room, each with a go-go dancer on their laps and sipping beers.

"Eugene!" several of the girls cheered.

Eugene ignored them, stepping over the piles of clothes and empty beer bottles on the floor. "Don't mind the mess." He peered over his shoulder at Olivia and Karin. "I have other business to tend to, but I expect you two to be in something much sexier when you dance on that stage." He patted Anthony back, his pierced lips curled into a smirk. "As for you, young man, feel free to claim as many of these ladies you see here as yours for the night. It's on the house."

"Great," Anthony mumbled, forcing a smile. Once Eugene left the dressing room, he turned to Olivia and Karin and whispered, "What are we gonna do now?"

"Relax," Karin said, huddling closer to Anthony and Olivia. "We got in, that's all that matters."

"With no thanks to *you*," Olivia huffed. "And that's *not* all that matters. We're expected to go on stage!"

"We won't be once we continue with the rest of the plan," Karin said. "Now, c'mon, let's get out of here and find Drea and Matt before that Eugene guy spots us."

Sneaking back to the dance floor, Anthony kept a careful watch for Eugene while surveying the crowd for Matt and Drea. He let out a sigh of relief when he spotted Drea at the bar and Matt sitting at one of the nearby tables, smoking a cigarette.

"Matt!" he shouted, rushing to his side, Olivia and Karin following. "We've been looking all over for you!"

Matt raised his brow. "Anthony? Is that you?"

"What? Yeah, it's me, I just—"

"Holy crap!" Matt roared with laughter and pointed at Anthony's face. "I could hardly recognize you under all that eyeliner! Did a gang of mall goths kidnap you?"

Anthony blushed, running a hand over his gelled hair. "Karin was just trying to make me fit the dress code or whatever. She gave me *your* clothes."

"Yeah, I can see that," Matt said, wiping the tears from the corners of his eyes.

"Well, I think he looks awesome," Karin said, beaming with pride. "In fact, he looks so awesome, the club owner thought he was one of the DJs and let us in!"

"What are you guys all doing here?" Drea asked, returning to the table with a drink in each hand. She set them on the table and took a seat across from Matt. When her eyes fell upon Anthony, she slapped a hand over her mouth to stifle her laughter.

"Yeah, I get it, I look ridiculous," Anthony grumbled. "Laugh all you want. My appearance isn't the most pressing issue at the moment. Lucifer's Disciples might have a hideout somewhere underneath this club."

"What gave you that idea?" Matt asked.

"The note Sakura left us," Anthony replied.

"You mean the bit about the stars?" Drea said.

"Yeah, that," Anthony said with a nod. "It's kinda weird, but I have a feeling she was trying to tell us that they have a hideout here. It's possible that's where all those girls have been disappearing. If we can find it, you guys can do your job even better. Plus, Emily might be there with Rundull and. . . " He took a deep breath. "And Zalem might be there, too."

"Okay," Matt said with an uneasy grin. "So what are we supposed to do about that? There's hundreds of people in this club. If there is a base, we can't really investigate it without everyone noticing."

"Hmm, yeah, that's the part of the plan I didn't think through," Karin said, holding her chin.

"I guess we can come back when the club closes," Olivia said.

"No," Anthony said. "This place doesn't close for another five hours. That's five hours Emily will be with Rundull, away from our protection."

"And you only have another five minutes until you go on stage," Karin said, peeking at her phone.

"Shoot!" Anthony cried, glancing over his shoulder at the stage, where a man with green dreadlocks was playing. "If I don't go up there, that Eugene guy will know we were faking it and kick us out."

Drea sighed and withdrew her phone from her coat pocket. "Matt, give me your phone."

"Why?" he asked, pulling out his own phone.

She wiggled her fingers. "Just do it."

Matt handed Drea the phone, and she held both of them out to Anthony.

"Trade me yours for mine and Matt's," she said. "Plug our phones into the decks and I'll text you what to play."

"O-okay," Anthony stammered, switching phones with her. He scrolled through the list of artists on Drea's phone, none of which were familiar. "But what are you guys gonna do?"

"We'll figure something out," Matt said. "You just go up there and do your thing. Don't worry about us."

"But I don't know how to do *my thing*!"

"You'll figure it out, trust me," Drea said with a wave of her hand. "Everyone here is way too drunk to even notice if you suck. Do you have headphones?"

"In my back pocket, yeah," Anthony said, checking his pocket for his earbuds.

She gave him a thumbs up. "You're all set."

Anthony looked from the stage to Olivia and Karin. "Are you guys gonna—"

"Just go!" Matt interrupted, shooing him away. "We'll take care of everything."

Anthony bit his tongue. Though he trusted Matt, he wasn't too confident in whatever his plan could be. Everything was going too well. Getting in to the club was too easy. After everything that had gone wrong in the past few weeks, it just didn't seem possible for this night to work out.

As Anthony walked onto the stage, the man with green

dreadlocks nodded to him, unplugging his laptop from the decks. The go-go dancers followed him down the side stairs, leaving Anthony alone on stage.

The previous DJ's last song played while Anthony plugged his headphones and cell phones into the decks. *There are a lot more switches and buttons on this thing than on any of those DJ games in the arcades,* Anthony thought, tugging at his shirt, unsure if all the black was causing him to overheat or just his own nerves. He hoped the crowd was as drunk as Drea claimed they were.

"You look lonely. Mind if we dance for you?"

Anthony held his breath. He knew that voice, that high pitched giggle. Thalia winked at him, positioning herself to his right, her vinyl bikini glistening in the spotlights.

"Looks like your personal go-gos ditched you," Anita said, pulling up her fishnet stocking from underneath her furry legwarmers, standing to Anthony's left. "Don't worry, we'll make you forget all about them."

Anthony forced a smile, praying they didn't recognize him under the mounds of makeup and hair gel. But when he spotted the sheathed blades attached to their leather belts, a sickening sensation bubbled in his stomach. *They both came armed.*

Drea's phone lit up with a text. "Play *Domination* on my phone. Just slide the switch on the bottom of the equalizer to switch decks. Don't touch any other dials if you don't know what they do."

Anthony glanced up from the decks and squinted through the strobes. In the distance, he could see the Eden members huddled at the back of the club. Drea waved to him and he thought he could see her give him a thumbs-up, but he wasn't too sure with the lights blurring the crowd. *There's like seven songs with the same title,* Anthony thought, choosing the first option. The repetitive bass vibrated through the club, raspy vocals screaming over the synthesized melody. *Do they actually like this crap?* Regardless of the audience's sobriety, they appeared to enjoy each song Drea told him to play, continuing to dance off-beat. He kept a careful watch on the Phobia girls as they danced. They couldn't attack him on stage, could they?

Halfway through the set, the crowd was still dancing and the Phobia girls had yet to attack. *What exactly are they planning to do while I'm up here?* Anthony thought, peering out at the crowd again for his friends. Drea was still sitting in the back with Matt and Karin, but Olivia was talking to a middle-aged man a few tables away. He squinted to get a clearer view through the lights. *Who is that guy? Do they know each other?* He blushed, watching her pat his arm and twirl her hair around her fingers. Whoever the guy was, they seemed to be having a good time. Olivia wrapped her arm around his and followed him off the dance floor, to the hallway leading toward the back rooms. Karin followed after him, while Drea and Matt dispersed in opposite directions. *Is this part of their plan? Is splitting up really the best idea they could—*

His thoughts were interrupted by the screeching fire alarm. Anthony covered his ears and froze. *Seriously? Is this how they plan on getting everyone out?* The venue lights flipped on, and the audience shoved their way toward the nearest exits, screaming and panicking. Drea wasn't sending him any texts. *Do I still play? Am I supposed to wait here for one of them or do I leave?*

Anita and Thalia each seized one of his arms.

"What are you doing, silly?" Thalia said. "You can't keep playing at a time like this!"

"W-whoa, hold on a sec!" Anthony cried. "Where are we going?"

"To safety, of course," Anita replied, she and Thalia dragging him down the stage's side stairs. "Eugene would be furious if we let anything happen to our special guest."

Anthony tried to yank free, but their grasps were too

strong. They pulled him through the chaotic crowd with no trouble, leading him down the hall and into the dressing room.

"I-I don't think this is the safest place to be right now," Anthony stammered. "I mean, if the fire alarm is going off, we should probably be going outside."

"We're taking you somewhere safer than here," Anita said. She opened one of the drawers in the vanity table and withdrew a small knife. Clutching Anthony's wrist, she slashed his palm, and he let out a pained cry.

Anita ran her fingers through the blood pooling in his palm and scribbled an inverted pentacle on the mirror, followed by a series of runes. The mirror retracted into the table, revealing a cement staircase leading down into darkness.

Thalia smirked. She and Anita pushed him onto the table, forcing him onto the stairs. "We're taking you exactly where you want to be."

CHAPTER 28

~~

"So what exactly is our plan?" Olivia asked Matt, watching Anthony make his way toward the stage.

Matt didn't answer. He just held his chin, gazing out at the crowd.

Karin's shoulders drooped. "You don't have one, do you?"

"You realize that Karin and I are expected to go on that stage with Anthony, right?" Olivia said, her voice rising. "We're gonna get kicked out if anyone finds out we're not actually dancers."

"You're really putting me on the spot here," Matt said. Taking a drag from his cigarette, he continued to stare past her with narrowed eyes.

"You guys should have just texted me," Drea said, leaning back in her seat. "Matt and I would have called Eden and figured something out. It's not easy to come up with a good plan when you're rushed."

"Anthony wanted to play hero for Emily," Olivia grumbled, crossing her arms, "and Karin wanted to come to this stupid club to party. I had no desire to tag along."

"And I don't like other people handling my phone, so it sounds like no one's getting what they want," Matt said. He pointed to a middle-aged man who sat alone a few tables in front of theirs. "Olivia, go talk to that guy."

Olivia glanced at the man. "Why?"

"I've been watching him all night. He keeps trying to hit on younger girls and buys them drinks. I think he might be trying to lure them away to bring them back to Lucifer's Disciples' base."

She wrinkled her nose. "What if he's just a creep?"

Matt shrugged. "We won't know until we find out."

"So you want me to just throw myself at the enemy?"

"I want you to *pretend* that you are." He smashed the butt of his cigarette into the ashtray on the table and looked up at her. "If there is a secret base here, he'll try to lead you to it, and if he does, then we'll know where it is exactly and can call in reinforcements to help break into it."

"And if he *is* just a creep?"

"Then it will just be an awkward experience that we can laugh about tomorrow."

"I'm never gonna find this funny," Olivia said with a scowl.

"Not with that attitude."

"If you don't wanna do it, I will," Karin said, taking a seat at the table beside Drea. "It could be fun messing with that guy."

"No, I think you might look a bit too young," Matt said. "I want you to spot Olivia and follow after her if the guy takes her anywhere. You can take on one guy, right?"

Karin stared at the man and smirked. "Him? Definitely."

"Good. Knock him out before he can actually do anything to hurt her. Just make sure no one else is around to see you."

"Why can't you spot me?" Olivia asked Matt, glancing at Karin. "She can't actually fight."

"Yes, I can!" Karin snapped.

Matt raised a hand to silence Karin. "When Karin goes

after you, Drea and I will call reinforcements, then split up to make sure everyone is out of the club before we start an attack."

"How are we getting everyone out?" Olivia asked.

Matt cocked his head. "I dunno, pull the fire alarm?"

"No offense, but your plan sucks," Drea said, sending a text to Anthony. "So many places it could go wrong."

"Do you have any better ideas?" Matt asked, rolling his eyes.

Drea paused, peering up from her phone. "So while you and I are starting the infiltration, Karin is helping Olivia fight off that guy. What's Anthony doing?"

"We'll cross that bridge when we get there."

Olivia groaned and leaned against the wall. "I don't want to do this. Can't we just think up something else?"

"It'll be helpful to Eden if you do it," Drea said.

"I don't care about Eden," Olivia said.

"Then do it for Anthony," Karin said with a giggle.

Olivia blushed. "If this guy kills me, I will haunt you all." She straightened her dress, tightened her ponytail, and stomped over to the table where the man sat. "Mind if I sit here?"

The man looked up at her through a curtain of greasy black hair and grinned, revealing yellowing teeth. "Only if I can buy you a drink."

"Sounds fair to me," Olivia said. Smoothing her skirt, she sat across from the man, facing Matt, Drea, and Karin.

"She looks so stiff," Karin muttered, watching Olivia talk to the man. "He's gonna get bored with her if she keeps it up. I would do so much better." She looked to Matt. "Can I take her place?"

"You already know the answer to that," he replied. He gazed at Anthony and the Phobia girls. "I'm hoping they don't attack him once we try to clear everyone out. It can't just be a coincidence that they of all people are up there.

Lucifer's Disciples probably knows we're here."

"I told you not to dress like you're going to work," Drea said. She glanced at the stage. "I could hardly recognize Anthony in that getup and I've been living with him for the past few weeks, so he might be okay."

Olivia was also staring at the stage when the man reached for her hand, his cold flesh against her fingers causing her to flinch.

"Are you okay, miss?" the man asked. "You seem distracted."

"Oh, I'm fine," Olivia said with a lopsided grin. "I, um. . . I don't really go to places like this often."

"Just drink some more. It'll make you feel more relaxed."

"Yeah. . . " As she pretended to take a sip, she noticed Karin mouthing "smile" to her while pointing to the corners of her lips.

"Stop distracting her," Matt said, nudging Karin's foot with his own. "She needs to concentrate on her task, not you."

"But she's killing it out there, and not in a good way." She twirled a strand of hair around her finger and stroked Matt's arm with the other, maintaining eye contact with Olivia.

Olivia narrowed her eyes in confusion. "What the. . . ?"

"Can you not?" Matt snapped, scooting away from Karin before she could touch his hair.

"I'm trying to give her ideas on how to flirt," Karin said.

"If that's how you flirt, then it's a good thing we didn't send you out there."

"Miss? Hello?" The man waved his hand in front of Olivia's face.

Olivia leaned back, blushing. "Oh, sorry." Her eyes fell upon a silver pentagram ring on his middle finger. "Sorry, I'm just not feeling it here. Do you know of any other places we can go to, y'know. . . " Giggling, she stroked his forearm. "Get away?"

The man grinned. "I think I know a place." He held out his arm and Olivia latched on.

"Yes!" Karin cried, springing from her seat. "Can I go after them now?"

Drea nodded. "Just don't attack him until you know for sure he's—"

"Okay, okay, I got it!" Karin interrupted, flashing her a thumbs up before running off.

The man led Olivia down the back hallway into the dressing room.

"Pretty cozy place you got here," she said, leaning against the vanity table. "I like it."

"It gets better," the man said. He pulled open one of the table drawers, reached in—

"Hands up!" Karin shouted, rushing into the room with her cross-sword already brandished.

"What the hell?" the man grumbled, raising his hands over his head.

"Karin, what the heck are you doing?" Olivia shouted. "We don't know if this guy's. . . " Looking from the man to Karin, she dropped her voice to a whisper. "Y'know, one of *them*."

"My bad," Karin mumbled, hiding the sword behind her back. "I kinda panicked and wanted to be ready and, uh. . . yeah. Sorry."

"You mind explaining to me what's going on?" the man asked Olivia, his brow furrowed. "I thought we were out for a good time."

"I-I, uh, it's not what it looks like!" Olivia stammered, backing away from him.

"Oh, really? Because it sure as hell looks like you sent an exorcist after me," the man retorted.

As the man shot black shadows from his palms, Olivia and Karin dove under the table, the shadows smashing mere inches above their heads.

"I was right!" Karin shouted, ducking her head into her arms.

"But you made him mad!" Olivia yelled.

The man shot another stream of shadows at them, but this time Karin raised her own palms. A thin umbrella of white light formed in front of her, deflecting the shadows to crash into the wall across from her.

"When did you learn to do that?" Olivia asked, curling up beside her.

"What do you think I've been doing since Simon died?" Karin said, creating a new force field before the man shot more shadows her way. "I don't know how much longer I can keep this up. It really takes a lot of energy to do." Panting, her arms dropped to her knees.

Catching her breath, she and Olivia rolled out from the table in opposite directions to avoid the next attack. Stumbling under the man's shadows, Karin's cross slipped from her grasp and skidded across the floor, the blade retracting. Olivia reached into her purse, about to draw her gun when the man seized her from behind, grasping her against his chest.

"This ends here," he said, pressing a palm to the side of her head. He glared at Karin. "Surrender now and follow me quietly, or I'll blast her brains out."

Karin grit her teeth, her eyes darting around the room. She peered down at her own hands and sighed. "Okay. Fine. You lead the way."

Olivia gaped at Karin in disbelief.

The man sneered and reached into the vanity table drawer again, pulling out a knife. "Which one of you would be so kind to lend me a palm?"

"Me," Karin said, marching to his side. Instead of

holding out her palm, she seized his forearm. White light glowed from beneath her hands.

Howling in pain, the man yanked free from Karin's grasp and released Olivia, who scurried under the table. A hole burned through the man's jacket, revealing singed flesh. He clutched his wound and clenched his teeth, hissing in pain. "You little brat! How dare you?"

"What, you actually thought I'd go with you?" Karin said, hurrying to pick up her cross. Releasing the blade, she laughed. "I'm surprised you fell for it!"

The man let out an angry growl, shooting another beam of shadows at her from his palm. Ducking beneath his attack, Karin charged toward the man, thrusting her sword through his chest. Pulling out her blade, blood gushed from the wound and the man tumbled face-down to the floor.

"Holy crap," Karin murmured, staring down at the bloody blade. "I think I just killed a man."

"Is he actually dead?" Olivia whispered, crawling out from under the table.

"I think so." Karin nudged him with her shoe. "Wow. I didn't think he'd go down that easily."

"I think he was just a human," Olivia said. She tucked his hair behind his ear. "Yup, no pointed tips. He was probably just a mage."

Karin dropped her sword and clutched her pale cheeks, the blade retracting into the cross. "Oh, man, I just killed my first human."

"But if you didn't kill him, he would have killed us."

"True, but. . . dang." She plopped down on her knees and gazed up at the ceiling lights. "I didn't think I could actually do it. I feel so powerful. But really filthy. This is like a really big life moment for me, like you don't even know."

"Get used to it if you want to be an exorcist," Olivia said, reaching into her purse for her phone. "I'm gonna text Matt and tell him where we are. If that guy dragged me into this room, there must be some sort of secret entrance to their base here."

At the earsplitting screech of the fire alarm, their hands flew to their ears.

"He actually went with that idea?" Olivia screamed over the screeching.

"What the hell is going on in here?" Eugene whipped off his sunglasses and marched into the room, glaring at Karin and Olivia with anger in his red eyes. "I just can't keep my eyes off you damn Eden pests even for a second."

Olivia withdrew her gun from her purse and pointed it at him. "You're not really the club owner, are you?"

Approaching her, Eugene smirked, revealing a set of fangs. "I was when I was *human*."

"Shoot him!" Karin cried.

Eugene pressed his palm against Olivia's forehead and she fell to the floor, unconscious within seconds. Karin grabbed her cross, but before she could even attempt to fight him, Eugene grasped her forehead. Releasing her, he watched her body fall to his feet with a satisfied grin.

CHAPTER 29

~~

Red candles lit the long pathway at the bottom of the cement stairs. The Phobia girls kept a firm grasp on Anthony's arms, leading him farther away from the club's commotion upstairs. All Anthony could hear was some sort of wet substance dripping from the walls, though he couldn't tell what it was in the dim lighting or make out any distinctive scents through the musty, cold air. Cloaked figures rushed past them in the opposite direction, their billowing robes creating a light breeze. *I hope they're not going after Matt and Drea,* Anthony thought, glancing over his shoulder.

The farther down the pathway they traveled, the more labyrinthine it became. Turning corners, walking down more flights of stairs, Anthony tried not to panic, wondering how anyone would be able to find him. As they approached the bottom, he could see a faint glow of light.

The stairs led into what appeared to be a laboratory, with shelves lined with worn textbooks and jars filled with colorful liquids, plants, and what Anthony assumed to be organs. He peered around at the various magic circles and runes scribbled on the cement walls in red, similar to the one drawn in the center of the room where Olivia lay unconscious. People in black robes surrounded the circle holding red candles, one gripping Karin's arm's behind her back, one placing candles on the tips of the pentagram.

Eugene sat beside the circle in a wooden chair, his hands folded upon his crossed legs. "Ah, DJ Venom! So glad you could join us tonight!" He held out an arm to gesture toward Olivia and Karin. "I found your go-go dancers. Such naughty girls, ditching you during your set."

"Cut the crap!" Anthony shouted. "I don't know who you really are, but I know you guys know who I am!"

"Anthony!" Karin cried, her eyes lighting up with hope. "Did you come to save us?"

"What's it look like?" Anthony snapped, still restrained by Thalia and Anita. "Do Matt and Drea at least know you're down here?"

"No one will ever know you're all down here," Anita said. She nodded to the man arranging the candles. "At least, not until Lord ZuZu is done with you."

Through the shadows of ZuZu's hood, Anthony could see burn scars and an eye patch covering the left half his face. Even though he didn't know him, something about ZuZu was unsettling and frightening. Whether it was his dominating presence, his burns, the eye patch, or his black scaled hands, Anthony couldn't bring himself to look anywhere other than the pentacle medallions hanging from ZuZu's neck.

"What are you planning on doing to Olivia?" Anthony asked.

"What he does best," Thalia said with a giggle. "Taking boring humans and turning them into super awesome Phobia!"

ZuZu loomed over Olivia's motionless body and laughed to himself. "I can't wait to see Eden's faces when they find out a Mavro has been made into a Phobia."

"That's not gonna happen!" Anthony shouted, struggling to break free from the Phobia girls. "I won't let you do that to Olivia!"

ZuZu raised his hairless brow. "And how do you plan

on stopping me?"

Anthony grit his teeth and froze. He looked to Karin, hoping she could come up with another plan, but her pale face appeared as helpless and terrified as his own.

"*I* plan on stopping you." Rundull pushed past the mob of cloaked figures and walked across the magic circle. Everyone in the room dropped to a kneel. Anthony and Karin's captors shoved them to their knees.

"What have you done with Emily?" Anthony yelled, glaring up at Rundull.

Rundull ignored him and patted ZuZu's shoulder. "Oh, ZuZu, how many times have I told you that your methods are too boring? You're being far too soft on my buddy Anthony here." Rundull peered down at Anthony and smirked. "How about a little deal?"

Anthony bit his lip and paused before answering. "What do you want?"

"I'll give you back your princess Emily in exchange for Olivia and the redhead over there. Karin, right? Or, I can go the other way and let you keep Olivia and Karin in exchange for Emily."

"What?" Anthony cried. "No way! That's a horrible deal!"

"I have to agree with the boy," ZuZu said, continuing to kneel with his head bowed. "I feel it would be best if we kept Emily, turned Olivia into a Phobia, and killed the others."

Rundull shook his head. "Death is far too kind. It's an easy escape from pain. Killing Anthony would give him relief from everything we could possibly do. It'd be much more fun to make him pick which girls he saves. That way, every time he looks into their eyes, he'll be reminded of whoever he left behind and forced to live with his guilt!" He held his stomach, roaring with laughter.

"You sick creep!" Anthony shouted.

"Anthony, just do it!" Karin cried. "Save Emily and leave me and Olivia! Her life is worth more to Eden than the two of ours put together!"

"She makes an excellent point," Rundull said. "After all, who are these girls to you compared to the girl you love? If I remember correctly, Olivia was not the kindest to you." He shrugged and chuckled. "But I suppose Emily isn't all that interested in you either. Even if you do save her, I can't guarantee that she won't come running back to me to be with Zalem. You may have another chance with Olivia if you save her instead. In the end, it's your choice."

"I'm not leaving without all three of my friends," Anthony said, his tone firm.

"Sorry, Anthony, but there are only two options in my deal. I'm afraid I can't allow you to refuse."

"And if I do?"

As if on cue, Thalia and Anita dragged Anthony to his feet, meeting Karin and her captor in the center of the pentagram. After letting go of Anthony, Anita seized Olivia, and the three captors withdrew daggers from their belts, pressing the blades against the necks of their victims. With a snap of Rundull's fingers, flames rose from the outer rim of the pentacle.

"If you refuse," Rundull said, "I will take full possession of your souls."

Anthony held his breath, the blade cold and threatening against his skin. His eyes darted from Olivia's unconscious body to Karin's tear-stained cheeks. *There has to be something I can do to get us out of this mess, or at least stall until Matt and Drea can find us.*

Rundull made his way to the center of the pentagram and rubbed his palms together. "Well, Anthony, time's ticking. What's it gonna be?"

Hearing his heart pounding in his head didn't help Anthony think up a plan. It only made him more nervous.

"How do I know Emily is even still alive? How do I know you didn't kill her?"

"Because I didn't," Rundull said. "I told her I'd take her to Zalem, remember?"

"So you actually *do* have Zalem here?"

Rundull narrowed his eyes. "I think we're getting a little off topic. You trying to stall me?"

Anthony looked away at the flames. "I'm not trying to stall. I'm just saying it wouldn't be cool if, for instance, I chose to save Emily, only to find out that you actually killed her. You say you didn't, but I can't really trust you."

Rundull paused. His silence was discomforting to Anthony, who tried to read Rundull's blank expression. Then, Rundull smirked. "Fair enough. I'll take you to see Emily. Thalia, let him go."

Letting out a sigh of relief, Anthony shook out his arms, cramped from being restrained. *Whatever happens next, hopefully it's enough to buy time for anyone from Eden to come save us.*

Rundull walked ahead and waved a hand for him to follow. "No one touch the human girls while I'm away. I want to be here to watch them suffer."

Karin's gaze met Anthony's when he walked by, anxiety and horror winkling her face. He couldn't help but feel guilty for leaving her alone with ZuZu and the Phobia, though it put him somewhat at ease to know she wouldn't be harmed, at least for now. Neither he nor Rundull spoke, passing all the bookshelves and tables cluttered with potions, plant stems, and opened books, to a wooden door. Rundull held the door open for Anthony, who took one last glance at the cluster of cloaked figures before entering.

More books and dusty jars bordered the walls of the stuffy storage room. A bed was placed in the center, upon which Emily lay motionless, her hands folded upon her stomach. Painted on the wall above her head was a red magic circle.

"Feel free to toss your coat anywhere," Rundull said, closing the door behind him. "I know it's awfully warm in here. I'm planning on moving her somewhere more hospitable in the near future."

"What have you done to her?" Anthony cried, rushing to Emily's side. He shook her shoulder, but her eyes did not open. "Emily! Emily, wake up!"

"She won't awaken that easily," Rundull said, tugging at the neck of his black cloak.

Anthony glared at Rundull. "You said she was alive."

"She is." He hopped onto the bed beside Emily. "She's just not fully here at the moment."

"And what the hell is that supposed to mean?"

Rundull grinned, stroking the side of Emily's face. "She's a pretty one, isn't she? I can't blame you for liking her so much."

Anthony clenched his fist and cringed. Just seeing Rundull run a pasty hand through Emily's hair filled his stomach with a bubbling rage. "You told her you'd take her to Zalem! You lied to her!"

"I didn't lie. She never specified *how* she wanted to see him. I gave her the best I could for now."

"So then he isn't here?"

Rundull didn't answer, continuing to play with Emily's hair.

Anthony took a deep breath and took a step away from the bed. "I figured as much. I knew you couldn't be trusted."

"He'll be here soon," Rundull said. "When he finds out Emily's here, he'll be *begging* us to bring him to her."

"I don't believe that either. I may not know the guy personally, but from what Emily's said about him, I highly doubt he even cares about her well-being. You think you have everything figured out, but you don't."

"*I'm* the one that thinks that?" Rundull said, his voice rising. He stood, jabbing a finger at Anthony's chest. "You're the one who thought you could sneak into this club and infiltrate my lair to save your girlfriend. The only reason you're here is because *I* told Eugene to let you and your friends in." He crossed his arms and smirked. "So before you get all full of yourself thinking you can outsmart me, just remember that everything you are capable of doing is only possible because your actions are part of *my* plan."

Anthony looked away from Rundull and peered down at Emily, at the scar on her neck. "You mean your plan to use a sickly teenager for whatever it is that you want to do?"

"If you think Zalem Mavro is merely a *sickly teenager*, then you definitely don't know anything," Rundull sneered.

"I know that whatever he is, he's stronger than you and Lucifer's Disciples."

Rundull's eyes widened.

"That's why you don't have him yet. That's why you need Emily as bait. And that's why ZuZu felt the need to summon a devil like you. For whatever reason, none of them can handle Zalem. Even you can't without Emily's help. You may act all high and mighty, but you're still just a kid." He tried to suppress a grin, feeling a sense of achievement at the sight of Rundull's quivering jaw.

"Just a *kid*?" Rundull placed a hand over his chest. "Do you honestly believe this body reflects my power? ZuZu placed me into this pathetic excuse for a body because he's *terrified* of me and what I am capable of doing."

"All you've done is lie and use cheap scare tactics to get what you want," Anthony said. "Eden, Lucifer's Disciples— they might all be afraid of you, but I'm not. I'm not afraid of a devil who needs the help of a human."

"You really don't understand me or my plans." Rundull's eyes glowed fiery red, his body morphing into a black shadow. "I guess you never will until you see for yourself."

Anthony backed toward the door, groping for the knob

to escape Rundull's growing shadow. Yanking and turning the knob, the door failed to even budge. He could see clouds of his own breath, the shadows bringing a sudden coldness to every inch of the room they touched. The doorknob disappeared from between his fingers. Everything around him faded into the shadows. Rundull's glowing eyes were the last thing Anthony saw before he, too, was engulfed in total darkness.

CHAPTER 30

~~

Anthony didn't remember falling asleep, but when he opened his eyes to raindrops hitting his forehead, he found himself alone on the front lawn of Mavro Manor. Though rain clouds painted the sky a dull gray, it appeared to be the middle of the afternoon. *How did I get here?* Anthony thought, his mind racing to figure out what was going on. Taking a deep breath, Anthony rose to his feet, wiping pieces of wet grass off his pants. Judging by how damp his clothes and hair were, he must have been outside for a while. *Something definitely isn't right.* Unsure of what to do about his situation, Anthony ventured into the house in hopes of finding some sort of clue.

"Hello?" he called. "Hello!"

The only answer he heard was his own voice echoing through the high ceilings of the mansion.

After searching the kitchen, the parlor, the bedrooms, bathrooms, and various other rooms in the house and finding not a single person, Anthony was convinced he was alone. He sat in one of the library chairs, holding his head in his hands. Though he wanted to return to the club and find Rundull, he was afraid of what awaited him outside Mavro Manor. All he could bring himself to do was remain sitting until someone found him.

That was, until he heard the lone cry of a piano in the distance.

The ballroom. How did I forget to check there? That's gotta be Emily! Hurrying down the hall, his legs raced against his heart. While music grew louder with every step he took toward the room, Anthony became more and more certain that the pianist was not Emily. This was not the sensitive, sweet timbre he fell in love with. Every note was filled with wrath, sorrow, and power, proving the dominance the pianist possessed over the keys.

Anthony peeked into the ballroom, making sure to stay hidden in the corner of the doorway. Sitting on the checkered floor, Emily's dress pooled around her legs, her hands folded upon her lap. She gazed up at the pianist with dreamy eyes, her cheeks flushed a rare shade of red for her pale complexion. The pianist didn't seem to notice her, let alone the booming thunder and flashes of lightning. His body swayed to the beat while his hands raced to hit the notes on time. Even though his face was veiled behind a thick curtain of black hair, Anthony was sure he knew who the pianist was.

Zalem. Anthony curled his fingers into fists. He couldn't stand the way Emily gawked at him—the boy who hurt her. Killed her. For whatever reason, he was here, vulnerable, playing the piano.

Anthony grit his teeth, his stomach churning with a rage he'd never felt before. *He wouldn't expect it if I were to hurt him. I could kill him for all the things he did to Emily. . .* But his thoughts conflicted with his feelings the longer he stared at Zalem. Something about him was unsettling. Perhaps it was the way the lightning cast a shadow on his slender silhouette. Or the fact that he drank blood. Whatever it was, Anthony couldn't bring himself to step foot into the ballroom.

When Zalem finished the piece, Emily clapped and cheered. "That was beautiful! You must play another!"

Zalem whipped his hair away from his face and glared

at Anthony with glowing green eyes. "Who are you?" he shouted, rising from the piano bench.

Crap! Anthony flattened himself against the wall, his brow sweating. *He's already angry!*

"Who are you talking to?" Emily asked. Gripping the edge of the piano, she stood and peered at the doorway.

"That boy spying on us over there!"

Anthony tried to sneak away before he could be caught, but Zalem stormed out of the ballroom before he made it far.

Zalem let out a disgusted growl when he spotted Anthony and pinned his shoulders against the wall. "Who are you and why are you here?"

"I, uh. . . I'm not spying on you!" Anthony stammered. He tried to break free from Zalem's grip, but he was stronger than Anthony expected. "I'm friends with Emily!"

"Zalem, what is going on?" Emily asked, rushing to Zalem's side. She gasped when she saw Anthony. "Who is this?"

"He claims to be your friend," Zalem said.

Emily narrowed her eyes. "Forgive me, but I do not recall meeting you."

Anthony's jaw trembled. "Wh-what do you mean, you don't *recall* meeting me? I'm Anthony! We've literally been together for. . ." He trailed off when Emily's face twisted with confusion. *She seriously doesn't remember me.* His eyes darted from Emily's fluffy dress to the black vest Zalem wore over his button-down shirt. *Emily's dressed like she was when we first met, and her brother doesn't look any more modern than she does.*

"I am sorry, but I do not remember you from anywhere," Emily said with a dismissive wave of her hand. "Zalem, you may have him."

"Excellent." Zalem grinned, revealing a set of sharp fangs. He leaned in closer, his breath hot on the side of Anthony's neck—

"Wait!" Anthony cried. "I—I know your parents! I work with them! They, uh, they sent me here to look after you." Flinching, his eyes met Zalem's. "They even told me about your illness."

Zalem's grip loosened. "My parents would never tell anyone about *that.*"

Does he seriously think they're still alive? "Well, they trusted me, so. . . yeah. They told me. They also told me that you're not allowed to drink my blood. They want me unharmed so I can take care of you two."

"They trust *you* to watch over my sister but not *me*?" Zalem grumbled, rolling his eyes.

When Zalem released him, Anthony let out a sigh of relief.

"Sounds like something they would do," Emily huffed. She crossed her arms and pouted. "I was looking forward to finally having some time alone together."

Anthony shifted on his feet, stuffing his hands in his pocket. Zalem's icy stare made him more uneasy.

Zalem placed a hand on Emily's shoulder, though his eyes remained on Anthony. "I do not believe we will have an issue with being alone. Unless he would like to watch." He nodded to Anthony. "Have you ever watched someone drink blood from another person's body?"

"Uh, no," Anthony mumbled, "and I have no desire to."

"Are you afraid?" Zalem asked with a smirk.

Anthony peered down at his shoes. "No. I just think it's kinda weird."

"Of course you do," Zalem said. "Fine with me. It gives me and Emily more privacy."

Emily beamed, pulling out a small knife from the sash of her dress.

Anthony turned to leave them in the ballroom, but something held him back. Between Emily's quiet whimper of pain and her gasps that soon followed, he couldn't bring himself to leave her alone with Zalem. He spun back toward the ballroom.

"Let her go!" he cried, ready to charge into the room and pull the siblings apart, but he froze when he reached the doorway.

Zalem sat upon the piano bench, clutching Emily's wrist. She lay in his lap, blood trickling down her forearm and between his fingers. Lowering her arm, he glanced at Anthony, blood smeared across his lips. "What do you want now?" he asked.

"I. . . I, uh. . ." Anthony failed to find words. Fear overtook his anger. He wasn't sure what was more disturbing; the way Emily giggled to herself, or her blood dribbling down Zalem's chin. "Y-you're hurting her."

Zalem blinked a few times before speaking. "Does it look like she is in pain?"

Anthony bit his tongue, gazing upon Emily's blissful expression. "Do you really not see a problem with this?"

"Keep drinking," Emily whispered, wiggling her fingers to regain Zalem's attention. "Forget about him."

Zalem ignored her and glared at Anthony. "If you have a problem with me drinking my sister's blood, I suggest you either leave us alone or take her place."

Anthony stiffened. "I already told you, your parents said—"

"I could not care less about what my parents said," Zalem snapped. "I do not enjoy being interrupted from drinking. If you continue to stand there and pester me, I will attack you and I can guarantee that not even a single drop of blood will be left in your body when I am finished with you."

Raising his hands in resignation, Anthony backed away. From the ravenous gleam in Zalem's eyes, Anthony didn't dare to challenge his word. "Fair enough. You guys do your thing, I'll do mine."

But as he left the siblings alone in the ballroom, he wasn't sure what *his thing* was. He still wasn't sure why or how he got to Mavro Manor, let alone why Zalem was there. With everything Lucifer's Disciples did to track him down and lure him to their lair, how could he be here with Emily? And after everything she had been through with Anthony, how could she forget who he was? Anthony hurried down the hall, to the front door. *If she doesn't remember anything and they think their parents are still alive, does that mean. . .*

Dashing through the front yard, through the surrounding forest, and onto the main road, his confusion intensified. Cars whizzed by, business signs illuminated the drab sky, and people walked along the sidewalks as if it were just an ordinary day. *It's still present time. Do they just not know about their parents' deaths?* Though Zalem's situation overall remained a mystery to Anthony, the fact that both he and Emily were somehow here after being in Rundull's lair seemed fishy. *I don't know what he did, but Rundull has to be behind this somehow.* After taking one last look at what he hoped to be normal, Anthony ran away from the main road, back to Mavro Manor. No matter what was going on, leaving Emily alone with Zalem was more unsettling.

When he returned to Mavro Manor, he was greeted by silence again. Anthony hurried to the ballroom to check on Emily, but no one was there. *Where could they have gone now?* Tiptoeing down the hall, Zalem's threat replayed in his head. He hoped to spot Emily and Zalem before they could find him.

Making his way up the stairs, Anthony froze at the sound of running water. Someone was in the bathroom in the upstairs hallway. Sneaking closer, he noticed the door was open and could hear Emily gasping in pain. He peeked inside and saw her washing her arm in the sink.

Anthony paused in the bathroom doorway, peering at Emily's bleeding wrist. "Do you need help cleaning that?"

"No," she muttered. Patting at her wrist with a damp washcloth, tears dripped down her cheeks.

Anthony held out his hand and walked into the bathroom. "C'mon, let me help you. You clearly aren't doing okay."

"I am fine!" Emily snapped, backing away from him. "It just stings a little!"

Anthony's expression remained firm, his hand remaining in front of her.

Emily rolled her eyes and shoved the washcloth in his hand. "You better know what you are doing."

"I do." He held her wrist and pressed the washcloth against her cut. "This isn't the first time I bandaged a girl's bleeding wrist."

Emily glanced at his smiling face. "Are you a doctor?"

"Nope. I was just in love with a girl who made poor decisions." He cleared his throat. "So, does your brother always ditch you after drinking your blood?"

"He needs time to unwind," Emily said. "He does not mean to leave me alone, but seeing and smelling my blood will only make him want more. I usually have a servant to help me clean my cuts, but I know how to do it on my own."

"That's still not cool for him to just leave you alone. He's the reason you're hurt. He should at least take care of you afterward." Anthony reached for the first aid kit on the bathroom counter and withdrew a clean bandage. "Let me know if this is too tight or needs to be tighter, okay?"

Emily watched Anthony wind the bandage around her wrist. "Do you enjoy working with my parents?"

"Do I what?" Then he remembered what he told her before. "Oh, yeah. Yeah, I do. They're nice people."

"Do they ever speak of me and Zalem?"

"Uh, yeah. They told me a little about his illness."

A distant glaze washed over Emily's eyes. "But do they ever say nice things about us?"

Anthony paused to think, fastening the bandage in place. "Yeah. All the time."

Emily scowled. "I do not believe you. They never bother to spend any time with us. Even when they are home, they avoid us."

He hesitated before speaking again. "They worry about you two. They feel guilty for not being around to take care of you. That's why they sent me here."

Their eyes met and Anthony was certain Emily was about to smile, but instead she turned up her nose. "If you are here to take care of me, then make me something to eat. I am feeling lightheaded."

Anthony sighed. *Should've expected her to boss me around.* "All right. You sit here and relax. I'll bring you something." He stopped in the doorway and looked back at her. "Zalem won't attack me if he sees me, will he?"

She shook her head and propped herself upon the counter. "He always goes outside after drinking blood. The fresh air helps clear his mind."

Anthony hurried down the stairs and into the kitchen, hoping to find something for Emily to eat before Zalem came back. Unlike the world outside, the kitchen appliances appeared to be as old-fashioned as the house itself. All of the modern machinery that was present when Anthony had stayed at Mavro Manor were gone. As he dug through the cupboards, it dawned on him that he had no idea how to cook, let alone use 1900s technology. *I can't even make her a piece of toast,* he thought with a frown as he eyed the loaf of bread on the kitchen counter. *Not with whatever weird toaster they have.* He opened one of the boxes stashed on a high shelf, revealing a set of chocolates. *This might cheer her up.* Closing the box, he made his way back up the stairs, trying not to think about what he'd have to make for dinner.

"What took you so long?" Emily grumbled, resting her head against the mirror behind her.

"I was just trying to find the perfect snack for you," he replied, holding out the box.

Emily took the box from him and opened the lid. "This is not real food."

Anthony threw up his hands in frustration. "Really? What kind of girl complains about chocolates? I'll just give you a plain piece of bread next time if that's how you're gonna be."

Emily stared down at the open box and blushed. "Thank you. I appreciate it." Biting into one of the chocolates, the corners of her lips twitched.

"Y'know, you're allowed to smile if you want to," Anthony said, taking a seat on the edge of the bathtub.

Emily paused before eating another chocolate. "The girl you loved. Did she love you back?"

Anthony flushed. "That's extremely off topic."

"No, it is not. You mentioned loving someone earlier and then changed the subject before I could say anything, so now I am bringing it up again because I want to know."

Anthony folded his hands and peered at the ceiling. "No. She was too busy caring for someone else." He forced a smile and said, "Maybe if I gave her chocolates, she'd like me."

"It is not that easy to win a woman's heart."

"Oh, really? Do you have any advice for me?"

"First off, your makeup is atrocious," Emily said with a chuckle. "No woman will take you seriously if you look like that."

Anthony rubbed his eye, spreading black eyeliner across his fingers. "This wasn't my doing. A friend of mine did it before I left to see you."

"Did she think it looked good?"

"Yeah, but she's got weird taste." Anthony grabbed a towel from the shelf, wet it in the sink, and attempted to wipe off the makeup. "Better?"

Emily responded by pointing at his face and laughing. "Even worse! You smeared it all over your face!"

"I did that intentionally because I knew it'd make you smile."

Emily's hands flew over her mouth.

"Look, you don't need to be all cold to me just because Zalem is," Anthony said. He sighed. "I understand if you don't really trust me yet, but it's okay to be happy and express your feelings. I'm not gonna judge you or anything."

Emily kept a wary eye on him, gesturing for the towel. "I can help you wipe off your makeup."

Anthony handed her the towel.

"This is such a mess," she said, dabbing at his eyes. "Is this friend of yours from Eden?"

"Yeah. Lots of fun people there."

"Does the girl you love work for Eden?"

"How are you feeling?" Zalem asked Emily, leaning in the bathroom doorway.

Emily blushed and jumped in surprise, dropping the towel on the floor. "Still a bit lightheaded, but I am much better."

"Would you like me to make you something to eat?"

"Anthony brought me chocolates," she said, tilting the box for Zalem to see the contents. "He helped me clean my wound, too."

Zalem glared at Anthony. Anthony attempted to ignore him, but Zalem's gaze pierced through his skull.

"I am going back to the ballroom to play piano," Zalem said. "Would you like to join me?"

"I think I am going to my room for a nap," Emily said, holding her head. "I feel a bit tired from the blood loss."

Zalem took a step away from the bathroom, his eyes still glued to Anthony. "I understand."

Anthony sighed with relief when Zalem left the doorway.

"Thank you for taking care of me," Emily whispered, avoiding Anthony's gaze.

"I'm happy to help," Anthony said. "Want me to carry you to your room?"

"I can manage on my own." Emily slid off the counter, stumbling when her feet touched the ground.

"You obviously can't," Anthony said, leaning over to pick her up. Scooping her into his arms, he carried her down the hall, into her room. "No offense, but that was kind of an asshole move for your brother to just go off and do his own thing, even after you told him you're still not feeling well."

"He knows I can take care of myself," Emily said.

"It's not about what he knows. It's about not showing you that he cares." He lay Emily on her bed. "Seriously, though. Are you gonna be okay or do you want me to stay with you while you rest?"

"I am fine."

"Okay. Just holler if you need me."

Before Anthony could leave her side, Emily clung to his jacket.

"What's up?" Anthony asked, peering over his shoulder.

Emily's grip tightened. "Please do not think poorly of Zalem. He means well. He is really kind, sweet, and caring once you get to know him. It is his illness that makes him come off as cold."

Anthony was torn between laughing and crying out in annoyance. *She wants me to believe that the guy who killed her is sweet?* Instead, he forced another grin. "Rest well. I'll see you when you wake up."

CHAPTER 31

~~

After leaving Emily's room, Anthony pondered where to go. Anywhere Zalem couldn't find him seemed to be the most logical idea, but Anthony couldn't help but let his curiosity take over. As frightening as he found Zalem to be, Emily's perception of him didn't match with his own. Though it was doubtful, he wanted to believe that Emily could be right about him being a kind person, that it wasn't her blind love for her brother speaking. Anthony wandered around the upstairs hallway until he stumbled across what he assumed to be Zalem's bedroom. He took a deep breath before entering, hoping he wouldn't find a pile of dead bodies or massive bloodstains on the floor.

With a bed placed against the wall in the center of the room and crowded bookshelves bordering the walls, Zalem's bedroom was disappointingly normal. Nothing about it screamed blood-sucking monster other than the *Dracula* and *Vampyre* novels placed on a shelf alongside a collection of Edgar Allan Poe's works. The only things that demanded Anthony's attention were the framed photographs on Zalem's nightstand.

The first one Anthony picked up was of Emily and Zalem on the back porch, almost glaring at the photographer with identical scowls. *It's almost creepy how similar they look, even for siblings,* Anthony thought, setting down the photo. *Would it kill them to smile?* As if in response, the next photograph he laid eyes on was of Zalem and a girl his age outside what appeared to be a small church. He wore a timid smile, while the girl beamed and embraced him. *It's like he's a totally different person.* The third photograph was a portrait of the same girl. Despite the lack of color, her cheery smile seemed to sparkle with life. *I bet she was his girlfriend,* Anthony thought, furrowing his brow. *I guess it was always a thing for assholes to get the cute girls.*

"Do you like what you see?"

Anthony spun around and gasped when he saw Zalem standing against the back wall of the bedroom. "I'm sorry, I didn't mean to snoop or anything, I was just—"

"It is perfectly fine with me," Zalem said with a chuckle. "I am not mad. I understand your curiosity."

Anthony backed away. Zalem was smiling at him, and he wasn't sure how to feel about it.

"I am not here to hurt you. I came to apologize."

Anthony narrowed his eyes. "For what?"

Zalem shrugged. "Everything, I suppose. I know who you are and what you have been through."

"Did Emily tell you?"

"Emily does not remember who you are."

Anthony peered down at the floor. "Right. Then how do you know?"

Zalem walked toward the bed. "Do you mind if I sit?"

Anthony debated whether he should trust Zalem. Keeping a careful watch, he stepped away.

"Emily may not remember you here," Zalem said, taking a seat on the edge of the bed, "but that does not mean that she does not remember you anywhere else."

"What do you mean?" Anthony asked. He clutched the corner of the nightstand and gasped. "Am I. . . Are we dead?"

Zalem laughed. "I used to ask myself that question

every day, but I am positive that *you* are not dead."

Anthony blinked a few times before speaking again. "So all this isn't real? You said *anywhere else*, so this is like a dream, right?"

"You do not actually think the only existing reality is the one you see before your eyes, do you?"

Anthony stared at Zalem in confusion as he laughed again. *He's even weirder when he tries to be nice.*

Zalem took a deep breath. "This place, while similar to the physical realm you live in, is part of the spiritual realm."

"Okay," Anthony said, scratching his temple. "So like heaven, or. . . ?"

Zalem peered up at the ceiling in thought. "It is still Earth, just a different layer, if that makes sense. There are many different realms within Earth, the physical realm being the one where humans live."

Antony furrowed his brow. "Sure."

"Though it is usually impossible for the soul of a living person to cross into a different realm, angels and devils can allow the souls of living humans to pass. I am assuming you confronted Rundull before arriving here."

"Yeah," Anthony said, shifting his weight. "He got all shadowy and everything went dark, and. . . yeah." He sighed. "I told him I wanted to see Emily, so I guess that's why he brought me here."

With an uneasy grin, Zalem said, "Ask and you shall receive." His expression softened. "To answer your question, I know about you and what you have been through. Rundull created me from Emily's memories, including the ones he seems to have suppressed, along with whatever knowledge he possesses of me."

"So *you're* not real then?"

Zalem held out a hand. "I will let you answer that."

Anthony took a few steps closer and felt Zalem's palm. Though ice cold, it was covered with flesh. "But if Rundull created you, then you're not the real Zalem."

"Technically, I am not. Unfortunately, I am not sure where the *real* Zalem is for your realm, but I am more real to this realm than you or Emily."

"I see," Anthony muttered. "I think I understand."

"Anyway, I wanted to apologize on behalf of my family for dragging you into all this madness with Eden and Lucifer's Disciples. I cannot imagine how strange this all must be for an outsider like you."

Anthony stiffened. "It is what it is. There's been ups and downs, but nothing for you to apologize for." *Except for killing your sister, allowing demons to take her soul and make her undead, and stealing her away from me.*

"I am happy to hear you say that. I would hate for you to harbor ill feelings toward me and my family. Frankly, I am quite glad we got to meet, even if under these circumstances." He tossed his hair out of his eyes and rested against his pillows. "Now that we are alone, I can finally tell you to leave."

"As in leave Mavro Manor?" Anthony asked, glancing out the window at the empty hills. "And go where?"

"Anywhere that is away from me and Emily," Zalem replied. "Keep your distance from us. It is for your own good, as well as Emily's."

"What?" Anthony cried.

"Rundull suppressed her memories and created me to keep her inside, as their deal was for her to be safe with me. The spirit realm is not safe for her to venture out into and I do not want you filling her head with any ideas, nor would I want to cause you further heartache by watching her hurt herself."

"I'm not going to leave her alone with you! You're just saying that so you can keep her to yourself!"

"I think you have the wrong idea about me and Emily."

"Oh, I know all about the things you did to her,"

Anthony said, his voice rising. "She told me about how she likes to be your *possession* or whatever and how it makes you happy to hurt her and drink her blood, and about how your sick happiness makes her happy." He cringed, remembering what she said at the lake. "She's *obsessed* with you."

"She is not obsessed with *me*," Zalem said. "She's obsessed with the feeling she gets when I drink her blood. She just associates it with me. If it were anyone else doing it, she would be obsessed with them. It is like a spell." When he noticed Anthony's confused expression, he continued. "When I bite someone for blood, they experience intense euphoria. I suppose it is to block the pain, to keep them from struggling, making it easier for me to take as much blood from my prey as I need. Unfortunately, I did not understand this phenomena until after I first bit Emily as a child. Had I known before, I would not have done it, but now she is a drooling slave for me, just like everyone else who survived my feeding."

"And why didn't you tell her that it's all because of your stupid illness?"

Zalem sighed, sitting up straighter. "I did, several times. I told her to stop giving me blood, but when she would cut herself in front of me, I could not help but give in and drink more of her blood."

"So you just let her obsess over you because you can't control yourself?" Anthony shouted. "That's not helping her at all!"

"I realize that," Zalem said, his voice shaking. "That is why I eventually just let her be. I am fully aware that it is my fault she acts the way she does. I know she will never care about a single being other than me. That is why I made it my responsibility to take care of her. I stayed by her side, made her think that I needed her as much as she needed me, even though I could very well take blood from anyone. I made her feel like she was not crazy."

"You. . . " Anthony curled his fingers into fists. "You're despicable! How dare you lie to her like that?"

Zalem's eyes widened.

"I actually love Emily, and she ditched me because she thinks you'll die without her!" Anthony yelled. "If you loved her even half as much as you claimed to, you would have helped her with the problems you caused, not played into her obsessions out of guilt!"

"I do love her!" Zalem retorted, slamming his fist against the bed frame. "She is my *sister*! If it were possible to help her see past the spell I placed on her, I would have helped her a long time ago!"

"But it *is* possible!" Anthony cried, throwing his arms in the air. "This whole *spell* thing is all in your head! When I first met her, she thought you were dead. She was so traumatized by the crap you put her through, she couldn't stand to be at her own house or even talk about you. The reason she was awake in the first place was because she wanted to be with *me*—someone who could teach her how to live like a normal human freaking being, not some vampire's chew toy."

Zalem's lips parted as if he were about to speak, but instead he took a deep breath, his shoulders trembling.

"It wasn't until she found out that you're alive that she got all crazy and freaked out over not being by your side." All Anthony could feel was his heart racing, his body shaking with rage. His thoughts were lost in a flurry of anger and hatred. Unable to control himself through his wrath, Anthony seized Zalem by his shirt collar. "It's your fault she felt the need to be taken by Rundull! It's your fault she's so damn messed up! You say that she's crazy, but *you're* the one who's really crazy for destroying your own sister's life!"

"You are in no position to talk about me or my sister like that!" Zalem roared, yanking Anthony off him. "You have no idea what we have been through!"

"I think I know more than enough to know that you're a screwed up freak for letting your sister obsess over getting her blood drank!" Anthony shouted. "She told me she *lives* for you!"

"I know that." Zalem rolled up his sleeves. Vertical, crusty slits ran through each forearm. "On the night I attempted suicide, Emily asked me to kill her first because she *wanted* to die with me. She told me her life would have no meaning without me."

Anthony held his breath as he gazed upon Zalem's arms in shock. "Wh-why did you. . . How could. . ." A trembling hand rose to Anthony's face and he backed away from the bed. "And you listened to her?"

"It would have been cruel of me to let Emily live if I were to die," Zalem said. "You saw for yourself how distraught she was without me. Crying, cutting herself, running to the enemy. If I die, I must take her with me, so no piece of my existence remains."

"But if you wanted to die, then why would you even need her blood. . . " Anthony trailed off, words drowned out by Zalem's laughter.

"Did Emily not tell you?" Zalem asked, an ominous glow in his eyes. "I do not drink blood merely for survival. The way it smells as it escapes the body, the way it feels rushing down my throat, the way it shines on the flesh of my prey as it drips from their wounds, as they scream and cry for more pain and pleasure—Just as Emily is obsessed with my bite, I am obsessed with the entire blood drinking experience." His lips curled into something between a grimace and a smirk. "Though it pains me to admit, part of me *wanted* to kill Emily. There was not a day where I did not think about killing her."

"You. . . you're. . ." His heart leaping to his throat, Anthony couldn't manage to utter another word.

"Now, I will give you one last warning," Zalem said,

approaching him. "Leave this house while you still have the chance."

"N-no!" Anthony stammered, backing against the wall. "I'm not leaving Emily alone with you!"

"If that is your final decision, I am sure I can arrange a little something." Seizing Anthony's shoulders, Zalem pinned him against the wall and bared his fangs. "Perhaps you will better enjoy my company once you have been bitten."

Anthony flinched, squeezing his eyes shut—

"Let him go!"

—And opened them to Emily scowling in the doorway, brandishing her knife at Zalem.

CHAPTER 32

~~

Zalem dropped his arms to his sides and took a step back from Anthony. "Emily, please put down the knife."

But Emily refused to obey, holding out her knife with a trembling hand. "I heard everything!" she cried, tears streaming down her cheeks. "You liar! I thought you cared for me out of love, not guilt!"

"I do love you," Zalem muttered. Avoiding her gaze, his eyes darted to Anthony. "I was just telling Anthony that so he could leave us alone."

"Dude, just drop the act already," Anthony whispered. "You're just gonna dig yourself in a deeper hole."

"*Liar!*" Emily screamed. "I heard everything you said! You deceived me!"

"Emily, please, be reasonable!" Zalem flinched when Emily stomped toward him. "Everything I did was—" He cut off with a gasp.

Emily pointed her knife mere inches from his neck, her tiny body shaking with rage. "I hate you! I hate you so much! I will kill you just as you claim to have killed me like you always wanted to, you filthy pig!"

Anthony stifled his laughter, watching Zalem cower in fear of his sister. Though he wished to be the one holding the knife, he still felt incredible satisfaction watching Emily threaten to kill Zalem.

"Wipe that grin off your face!" Emily yelled, turning her blade to Anthony. "You deceived me, too!"

Anthony raised his hands, flattening himself against the wall. "Me? What did I do?"

"You said you knew my parents! You knew all along that my memories have been tampered with by some devil who brought us to this realm and you did not bother to tell me!"

"I did! I totally did!" Anthony cried. "When I first saw you, I tried telling you, but then you got all confused and I had to make up something so you guys wouldn't kill me!"

Seizing her wrists, Zalem restrained Emily's arms behind her back and stole the knife from her grasp. "Emily, please try to calm down. I know this is a lot for you to take in, and I am sorry you had to overhear our conversation, but this is for the best. Now that you know the truth, you can try to get over your obsession with me."

"You are not even my real brother!" Emily shouted, struggling to break free from his firm grasp. "The true Zalem loves me as I love him, and I will *always* love him!"

"I think the same way as he does, so. . . " His calm voice was overpowered by Emily's frustrated growls, her hair whipping about her face while she continued to fight against him. "Are you listening to me?"

"Let me go, you filthy impostor!" Emily screamed.

"Emily," lowering his voice, Zalem whispered in her ear, "please calm down before I do something we will both regret."

"Really? You really think scaring her will get her to calm down?" Anthony said, though from Emily's continued efforts to break free, he was certain she was far less worried about whatever Zalem was hinting at than he was. "Just let her go. Besides, it's not like she can hurt us without her knife."

Not one drop of gratitude sparkled in Emily's eyes

when Zalem released her. Instead, she wrinkled her nose at Anthony. "Are you hiding any other secrets?"

"Well. . ." Anthony scratched his head. "Long story short, after Zalem killed you, Lucifer's Disciples took your soul to keep your body somewhat alive so they could lure Zalem to their lair, because I guess his suicide didn't work out, and now they have us both at the lair, but Rundull sent us here to this other realm to be out of his way or something while he tries to get Zalem—like, the real Zalem from our realm—to cooperate, wherever he is."

Emily furrowed her brow. "I beg your pardon?"

"Okay, I explained that really badly. There's gotta be a better way to explain it."

Emily held her chin. "Are you saying that Lucifer's Disciples are still after Zalem, and that my body in the physical world has been taken by them, along with my soul?"

"Yes," Anthony said with a nod.

"Currently, he has both of your bodies," Zalem said, "and brought your souls here."

"Wait, what?" Anthony cried. "You didn't tell me that part!"

"You cannot take your physical body into part of the spirit realm. Naturally, he had to put you into a more suitable vessel." He glanced at Anthony and smirked. "I thought that was obvious, even to an outsider."

Anthony's face wrinkled with horror at the thought of his soulless body lying somewhere within Rundull's lair. He looked to Emily, but she appeared too deep in thought to be affected by the news.

"I think I understand the situation now," Emily said. She took a deep breath and beckoned to Anthony. "I suppose we shall head out then."

"Where are we going?" Anthony asked, following her out of the bedroom.

"To wherever our bodies in the physical world are," she

replied, leading him down the stairs. "As long they are not destroyed, we can return to them and I can stop Rundull from finding Zalem."

"As much as I hate saying this, if we're gonna go fight Rundull, we should bring Zalem with us." Pausing at the bottom of the staircase, he peered up at Zalem, who gazed down at them from over the railing.

"I am not going," Zalem said, "and neither is Emily. You can still go if you want. I do not care if *you* die out there."

"You cannot tell me what to do," Emily huffed.

"Oh, come on," Anthony said. "It's perfectly normal out there. I went out earlier."

"That is what Rundull wants you to believe," Zalem said.

"What, are you afraid of him?"

"No, I am just not an idiot like you. Only an idiot would attempt to fight a devil. Fighting a devil is what got you here in the first place. There really is no reason why you need to be here."

Anthony rolled his eyes. "Yeah, I realize that, and that's why I want *you* to fight him. Just use your vampire superpowers or whatever it is you have that makes you such a big deal to Lucifer's Disciples."

"Superpowers?" Zalem said with a chuckle. "What are these *vampire superpowers* you speak of?"

"The only superpower he has is transforming into a lying, manipulative fool who throws a tantrum if he is not given blood," Emily said. She curled her lip. "Oh, sorry, that happens to be who he *always* is."

As much as he wanted to laugh, Anthony kept his mouth shut when he saw Zalem glaring at Emily.

Forcing a smile, Zalem's grip on the railing tightened. "Fair enough, Emily. Given the way I treated you for the past few years—"

"You mean *my entire life*?" Emily interrupted, placing her hands on her hips.

"Given the way I treated you for your *entire life*, I accept whatever negative feelings you have toward me. I am truly sorry and hope you can find it in yourself to forgive me."

Emily lifted her nose and looked away from him.

Anthony cleared his throat. "Okay, but seriously, Lucifer's Disciples is summoning all these monsters because they don't know how to handle you. If you can't fight them, can you at least tell them you're not that special so they can chill? They did some freaky crap to me and Emily, and they're probably gonna do something weird to the real you if we don't hurry up."

Zalem shrugged. "I do not care what they do in your world. Whatever they do to that Zalem does not affect me."

Anthony rocked on his feet, thinking up a way to convince Zalem to join him. "Okay, well, they might hurt Emily even more than they already have. If you care about her as much as you claim to, you'll come along."

Emily glanced at Zalem from the corner of her eye.

Zalem let out a resigned sigh. "Fine, I suppose I will join you, but only to protect her."

Once the trio left the house, Emily was anything but pleased, trailing behind Anthony and Zalem with a scowl. Leaves crunched beneath her stomping feet through the trail leading to the main road.

Zalem stopped in his tracks and turned to Emily. "Would you like us to slow down?"

"I am perfectly fine," she huffed. "I just do not want to walk with you because I still hate you."

"Can you at least walk a little faster?" Anthony asked her. "We don't have all day."

Emily pushed past Zalem to walk beside Anthony, gripping her coat beneath her neck to keep warm. "Where are we even going?"

"We gotta go to my house first so I can grab my car," Anthony replied, "and from there I'll drive us to the club where Rundull is keeping our bodies."

"I do not completely understand, but I suppose I must trust you," Emily said.

"Hopefully no one is at your house," Zalem said. "If you make contact with anyone in this world, they may try to harm you." He raised the collar of his coat, peering out at the people walking by. "It is possible you two are already being recognized as outsiders. Everyone is giving us strange looks."

"Probably because you two look like you're dressed for a funeral," Anthony muttered, hoping his assumption was correct.

"You are the one dressed like a sad clown," Zalem retorted.

Anthony blushed, clenching Matt's leather coat shut. "Okay, that's fair."

As cars rushed down the slick streets, Emily inched closer to Anthony, clinging to his coat just enough for him to notice. The way awe mixed with fear in her eyes reminded him of the time he first brought her to his house. Though he wanted to comfort her, let her know she could hold his hand if she was scared, he didn't dare to even address her fear in front of Zalem. He felt Zalem's eyes piercing through his back when Emily's grip on his coat tightened at every crosswalk.

Once they made it to the house, Anthony stopped in the driveway. "Here we are."

"This is your house?" Emily asked, wrinkling her nose. "It is hideous."

"I cannot believe you actually agreed to sleep here," Zalem said, sharing her expression. "In *his* room."

"Oh, God!" Emily clutched her cheeks in horror. "Has being undead driven me insane?"

If only she knew she was begging *to stay here,* Anthony

thought, rolling his eyes. "Lucky for you two, you guys get to stay out here. I'm just gonna run in, get the keys, and I'll be right out. It'll only take a sec."

"I should go with you," Zalem said before Anthony could run off. "Just in case you get attacked."

Anthony bounced on the soles of his feet with impatience. "No one's gonna attack me. The only person that will probably attack me around here is you."

"Oh, I see." Zalem crossed his arms and smirked. "You are afraid of me."

"I was until I saw you freaking out when Emily pulled a knife on you," Anthony said, raising his brow.

"I am far more terrifying than he will ever be," Emily said, tossing her hair.

"I was not freaking out," Zalem grumbled. "If it were anyone else holding that knife, I would have killed them without a second thought."

"Is that so? Because you were just saying how happy you were to finally kill me not even a minute before I came in," Emily snapped.

Maybe Emily learning the truth wasn't for the best, Anthony thought, glancing back at the house. "Okay, let's just get something straight. I'm not afraid of either of you. Especially you." He pointed at Zalem. "I think I figured you out. You just like to act all creepy to scare people because it gives you control. Not to sound like an ass, but I think both of you have some serious mommy and daddy issues from not getting enough attention as little kids, and you're trying to gain some sort of order in your life by controlling other people."

"What is he talking about?" Emily mumbled. "I do not have issues."

The fact that she thinks that is an issue.

"Honestly," Zalem grumbled, glaring at Anthony. "How can you say that when you hardly know me?"

"And I don't really care to," Anthony spat. "But I'm not

gonna tolerate any more spoiled rich kid sass from either of you. *I'm* the one with the car, *I'm* the one with the directions, so unless you guys wanna figure out how to use Google Maps and drive a car manufactured ten years ago, *I'm* the one in control."

"What is Google Maps?" Emily whispered to Zalem, who shrugged in response.

"Exactly my point," Anthony said, backing toward the house. "Okay, you guys wait here. Don't move. I'll be right back."

Running into the house, Anthony was more worried about Emily and Zalem hurting each other if they were left alone for too long than he was about whatever kind of monsters that lived in this world. He assumed his belongings would be in the same place as they were in the real world, thus making them easy to find before either of them could have a chance to stab or bite the other.

"Where do you think you're goin'?"

Anthony jumped at the familiar grunt of Uncle Mark. "To my room." Backing against the wall, he hurried down the hall to his bedroom. "I just need to grab something real quick."

"Oh, no you don't!" Uncle Mark stomped after Anthony, blocking the doorway while Anthony fished for his keys on his messy desk. "You've been gone for weeks! You ain't goin' anywhere!"

"But I need to!" Anthony shouted. Curling his fingers around the keys, he marched toward his uncle. "I'll explain later! Just please let me go!"

"Not this time!" Seizing Anthony's arms, Uncle Mark shoved Anthony to the floor. "I'll make sure you never leave this room!"

Anthony crawled away, ducking beneath Uncle Mark's raised hand. Lifting his arm above his head, Uncle Mark's beady brown eyes began to glow yellow. Whatever would happen next, Anthony was relieved that he didn't find out, yet startled to see Zalem grasp Uncle Mark from behind. Before Uncle Mark could even react, Zalem chomped into his neck, ripping his throat open. Blood spewed from Uncle Mark's wound and his massive body crashed to the carpet.

"H-holy crap!" Anthony shouted, backing onto his bed. He gaped at Zalem's bloody face in horror. "Y-you just ripped out his throat like. . . l-like. . . Oh my God!" He slapped his hands over his mouth and nose. Both the sight and smell of all the blood was nauseating.

Zalem spat out a chewed-up wad of flesh into the puddle of blood pooling around Uncle Mark's head. "It is not hard to do when you have fangs. Fast way to kill a human."

"B-but I thought you just, like, drank blood. That was unnecessarily brutal."

Zalem furrowed his brow. "That is how you thank me for saving your life? If I came even a second later, he would have changed." He stuck out his tongue and cringed. "I can taste it in his blood."

Anthony's eyes darted between Zalem and the corpse. "What do you mean?"

As if in response, black smoke began to rise from Uncle Mark's body. It let out a menacing hiss, glaring at Anthony with glowing white eyes. A misty claw extended from its shadow-like mass of a body, reaching toward him. Lasting only for mere seconds, the shadow evaporated before it could lay a finger on Anthony.

"W-what the hell was that?" Anthony stammered.

"*That* was what would have attacked you if I did not save you," Zalem replied. "Those shadow spirits live in all the people here. Luckily, they cannot survive without a living host body, so we are safe if we can just kill anyone giving us a bad time before they transform into monsters."

"Right," Anthony muttered, gawking at Zalem. "And you know all this *how*?"

"When you are locked up at home all day, you read things," Zalem said with a shrug. "And when your parents' research is in spiritual planes, you learn a thing or two."

"Oh, uh. . . That's a surprisingly reasonable answer. Thanks for saving me, I guess."

"To repay me, could you possibly let me take a sip of your blood?"

"What? No. I don't owe you anything."

Zalem smiled and laughed. "Oh, it will only be a little taste. I just need to clean my palate. I really hate the taste of monster blood."

"Well, doesn't that suck for you?" Anthony said, rolling his eyes. "Just go drink water and eat something from the kitchen. I'm not gonna turn into a drooling slave for you just because you can't handle a bad taste."

"Please?" He clasped his hands together. "A little sip will not hurt you."

"Yeah, no. I'm not convinced." Anthony covered his neck with his hands, pushing past Zalem to the kitchen. He could hear Zalem's footsteps behind him while he dug through the cabinets. Tearing open a box of granola bars, he handed one to Zalem. "Here, eat this."

"What is it?" Zalem asked, his eyes widening with interest.

"It's like oats and raisins all smashed together," Anthony replied, walking to the front door. "Or chocolate chips. I dunno, I didn't read the box. But they're good and keep you pretty full."

Ripping open the seal, Zalem took a closer look at the granola bar. "There are not any nuts in this, are there? Nuts tend to make me very sick."

Anthony paused, his hand on the front doorknob. "So you can drink blood and rip people's necks open with your teeth, but eating a measly nut will be the death of you?"

"Maybe not just *one*, but I suppose so," Zalem said. "It

actually gets a bit scary when I drink a stranger's blood and I do not know if they ate nuts, because then their blood can make me sick, too."

"That's such a lame weakness."

"Sorry to disappoint you." Zalem took another look at the granola bar and sniffed it. "So, can I eat this—"

"Yeah, yeah, you're fine," Anthony said with a wave of his hand. "Let's just pick up the pace, okay? I'd like to find my real body all in one piece."

CHAPTER 33

~~

Sitting on the steps next to Drea outside the club, Matt withdrew a cigarette box and lighter from his pocket, staring out at the mob of Eden investigators huddled around the puddle of unconscious club attendees. The red and white flashes of the firetruck's lights continued to blink while more black SUVs rolled into the gravel parking lot.

"We really should have let the reinforcements take care of this in the first place," Matt said, lighting a cigarette. "Wiping everyone's memories is such a hassle."

"Anthony would've never stood for that," Drea said, resting her chin in her palm. "There's nothing Anthony wouldn't do for Emily. Orders from Eden mean nothing to him."

Matt sighed, exhaling smoke. "I swear, if someone dies tonight. . ." His attention shifted to an SUV parked near the front of the club. Men in suits rushed to open the side door, escorting Erika out of the car. Tossing the cigarette aside, Matt and Drea rose. "Here comes the fun part," Matt mumbled to Drea, who grimaced in response.

"What the hell is going on here?" Erika snapped. She clung to one of the men's arms, struggling to walk through the gravel in her heels. "First, I'm told that Emily's been taken, and now my sister, too?"

"She, Anthony, and Karin managed to sneak in on their own," Matt said. "Drea and I had no idea what they were up to until we ran into them here."

Erika shut her jacket over her chest, shivering in the cool night's breeze. "And do we know if they're still alive?"

When Matt hesitated to answer, Drea said, "Last I heard, our reinforcements found an entrance to the base through the dressing room. We were ordered to wait out here to speak to you, so we aren't really sure what's been going on inside."

"When did you last speak to anyone from inside?" Erika asked.

"About fifteen minutes ago," Drea replied. "In the meantime, Matt and some of the other exorcists stayed outside to wipe the memories of all the attendees and firefighters."

Erika bit her lip and stood on her toes to peer through the entrance of the club. "Fifteen minutes is a long time. Something must be wrong. I gotta go in there."

Drea and Matt backed away toward the entrance to block Erika's path. Her escort's grip on her arm tightened.

"You can't go in there," Matt said. "It might still be dangerous."

"I don't care!" Erika cried. "My family's been taken by demons and you expect me to just sit on my ass and wait until a corpse is dragged out of there?"

"I'm sure they're doing everything they can to save them," Drea said, though Erika still fought against her escort.

Losing her balance, Erika dropped to the gravel. "I have to know if they're okay! If my father finds out that Emily's been taken. . . And that Olivia's gone, too. . ." She let out a frustrated cry, bowing her head to hide her tears. "The one time Olivia actually shows interest in Eden, she gets herself kidnapped! If I knew she'd be so stupid, I would have never put her on the investigation!"

Before Drea or Matt could say anything, a young man stumbled out of the club, his black trench coat tattered and bloody. Pushing his way toward Erika, he collapsed in front of her and peered at her with red eyes, his face covered with bruises and slits.

"M-Miss Erika!" he stammered. "I-I have a. . . a. . ."

"Stay away from her!" Matt cried, jumping in front of Erika, his gun brandished at the man.

"I have a m-message," the man said, unfazed by the gun, "from. . . L-Lord Rundull. . ."

Erika's eyes widened.

"Lord Rundull wants. . . a d-d-deal. . . From your strongest. . . your s-strongest exorcist."

"From our strongest. . ." Erika gasped and attempted to crawl toward the man, but Matt blocked her way. "Where is my sister? What have you done to her?"

Breaking into maniacal laughter, the man rose to his knees. Blood oozed from the corners of his eyes, dripping from his ears and nose. With a sickening crack from his spine, his head plunged backward to his feet, his laughter unceasing until Matt silenced him with a bullet.

Erika's hands flew to her shock-ridden face. "Oh, my God!" she wailed. "He has them! Rundull has them!"

Drea knelt beside Erika, removing her coat and draping it over Erika's shoulders. "That guy never said anything about Rundull having anyone. I know it's hard, but you have to stay calm." She wrapped her in a soothing embrace. "We'll sort through this."

"Has anyone called Sam yet?" Matt said, glancing at the other Eden members.

"He's away on an investigation," Erika's escort replied. "We've been unable to contact him."

"It isn't Sam that he wants," Erika muttered. "Sam isn't our strongest exorcist."

Matt raised his brow. "You don't mean he wants. . ."

Drea hugged Erika tighter, her cries growing more hysterical.

"I don't get it!" Erika wailed. "What does Rundull want with my family? Why is he doing this to us?"

"He can't possibly want the chairman," Matt said, shaking his head with an uneasy smile. "I heard he hasn't been on the front line in decades."

"But he's still the strongest," Erika said through choppy breaths. "Oh, God, he's going to make a deal with my father. He's. . . He's going to kill my father!" When she noticed Matt on his phone, she dove for his feet. "Are you calling my father? Please, don't call him! Please don't tell him to come here!"

"And do what, just let his kid die at the bottom of a nightclub?" Matt asked, holding the phone away from his ear. "If Olivia dies, how do you think he will respond when he learns not only about her death, but that no one bothered to tell him anything?"

"No, please, stop! Don't do it!" Breaking free from Drea's grasp, Erika pounced on top of Matt, knocking him to the ground, the phone skidding several feet away.

"Whoa, calm down!" Drea shouted, her voice shaking as she pulled Erika away from Matt. "I highly doubt the chairman would risk his life—risk *Eden*—just to save a few teenagers. Even for Emily's sake—"

"It's not about Emily!" Erika snapped, yanking away from Drea. "Don't you get it? The reason why my father isolates Olivia from Eden? Why Rundull took her instead of me? My father would never let anything happen to his baby girl!"

~~

"Are we almost there?" Emily asked from the back seat of the car.

"It's only been ten minutes," Anthony replied, glancing at the dashboard clock. "I don't live that close to the city. Why, you need something?"

"I am bored."

"I brought you video games to play with."

"But Zalem will not let me play!"

"I told you I will give it to you soon," Zalem said, his eyes glued to the screen of the hand-held console. "I am in the middle of a very important decision at the moment. My birth family and adoptive family I grew up with are at war, and I must pick a side."

"If only you cared for your real family half as much as the ones in that game," Emily huffed.

"I do care about you," Zalem said. "I thought joining you on your little adventure with Anthony would make you realize at least that much, but I supposed staying home would have made you happier."

"It would have. I am not sure what made you think joining me would make me happy or forgive you for being a dirty, rotten, horrible, lying, disgusting—"

"Okay, that's enough," Anthony interrupted, rolling his eyes. "Jeez, you guys have no chill. If you guys can't behave, I'm gonna have to take the game away."

When he stopped at a red light, Anthony narrowed his eyes and gazed into the horizon. The gray sky darkened to a murky purple. All of the surrounding buildings morphed into thick black fog, the roads, grass, and sidewalks all blending into one long, dark path. "Is this like a normal thing in this world?"

"No," Zalem replied with a sigh, staring out his window. "Rundull must have noticed Emily left Mavro Manor."

"How can he do that if we're in another dimension?"

"He is a devil. He is aware of all the spiritual planes."

"Well, that's just fantastic."

Emerging from the fog was a mob of what seemed to be ordinary people. Trudging closer to the car, their faces appeared devoid of expression.

"Uh, what exactly should I do now?" Anthony asked, keeping his foot on the brake.

"Run them over," Zalem said without even a hint of hesitation.

"What? I can't do that!" Anthony cried.

"Why not?"

"Because I, unlike you, don't kill people!"

"They are far easier to kill now that they have yet to transform."

"What do you mean transform?" Emily asked, perking up as she peered out the window.

As if in response, the man nearest to the car stopped in his tracks. Arching his back, a pair of bat-like wings ripped through his flesh. His hands mutated into claws and his jaw dropped to reveal teeth growing into spikes. Those around him began to undergo similar transformations, hissing and howling, glaring at the car with eyes black as coal.

"Holy crap!" Anthony exclaimed, cowering behind the wheel.

"I suppose we better do something about this," Emily said, tightening the bow in her hair before opening the side door. "I was hoping our demon fighting days were over in this plane."

"Will they ever be over?" Zalem groaned. He glanced back at Anthony before exiting the car. "Just wait here. We will handle this."

"W-wait, what are you gonna do?"

The door slammed shut, leaving Anthony alone in the car to watch Zalem and Emily approach the herd of surrounding monsters. Reaching into their coats, they each withdrew a knife. Ducking beneath their swooping wings, dodging around their swiping claws, Emily and Zalem stabbed the blades into the sides of the monsters' heads, moving onto the next one as soon as one fell. Emily would stab the taller monsters as high as she could reach, causing them to stagger toward Zalem, who would then rip into their necks with his teeth. With his jaw dropped, Anthony gazed in shock. He wasn't sure what was more disturbing—how calm the siblings were about being in the midst of monsters, or how little effort it took for them to kill whatever crossed their paths.

Once all the monsters lay motionless on the ground, Anthony hurried out of the car, rushing to the Mavro siblings' sides. "What the heck was that?" he shouted.

"What do you mean?" Emily asked, raising her blood-covered brow.

"You freaking demolished all those demon monster people things!" Anthony pointed an accusing finger at Emily. "I knew something was up the moment you pulled a knife on Anita in the restaurant! And you were all, like, 'No, I'm just an innocent little girl.' I *knew* you secretly worked for Eden!"

"I could not care less for Eden," Emily said, wrinkling her nose. "I only fight to protect Zalem. Lucifer's Disciples has been after him for years. It is only natural I learned a few skills to help him from time to time."

I think time to time is an understatement, Anthony thought, his face frozen with astonishment.

Emily peered up at Zalem with a shy smile. "It has been a while since we fought together. I missed it."

Zalem squeezed her shoulder and smiled. "I did, too."

"Okay, real glad killing monsters helped rekindle your bond," Anthony said, clapping his hands. "Can we get back on track? I'm not nearly as into fighting demons as you guys are and would really like to get home."

Just as they reached the car, a screeching roar echoed in the distance. Soaring through the purple sky was an enormous winged creature, its white eyes glowing like headlights through the black fog.

"W-what's that thing?" Anthony stammered, stopping in his tracks. More winged beasts emerged through the clouds behind the first. "Y-you guys know how to fight those, right?" But when he glanced over his shoulder at Emily's wide eyes, a sickening sensation bubbled in his stomach.

Zalem grit his teeth, unfastened his cross necklace, and handed it to Anthony. "Put this on and lie on the ground. Keep your eyes covered."

"What are you gonna do?" Anthony asked, using his sweatshirt to wipe the blood off the cross before fastening it around his neck.

"Just do as I say!" Zalem snapped.

Anthony took one last look at the approaching beasts before dropping to the ground beside Emily. Unable to control his curiosity, he covered his eyes with his hands and peeked through his fingers to see what Zalem would do. Though Zalem's back was facing him, Anthony could see his arms outstretched. A black shadow extended around him, covering the ground, engulfing the sky, the monsters, and everything around them into total darkness—

"You may open your eyes now."

Anthony gasped and jumped to his feet. He didn't remember closing his eyes, but when he opened them, he was back on the street, his car in front of him, surrounded by houses, trees, and street lamps. Normal things in a normal world with a normal blue sky.

"What just happened?" Anthony asked, his eyes wide with horror.

"I scared them off," Zalem said with a shrug. He smiled. "Everything will be fine now."

"Scared them off? You freaking. . . I don't even know what you just freaking did! Everything got all dark—that's *exactly* like what Rundull did to me!" Anthony looked to Emily. "How can Zalem do that?"

"My eyes were closed," Emily said, avoiding his gaze. "We are safe now. That is all that matters."

Anthony curled his fist. *She knows something.*

"She is right," Zalem said. "Come on, now. We should get going." His smile remained, but his eyes were cold.

"Why do you have the same powers as Rundull?" Anthony asked, his fist shaking. "Is it because you're part of this world, or because—"

"If you keep asking about this," Zalem whispered in Anthony's ear, "I will do something very, *very* terrible to you. Care to find out?"

Anthony backed away and shook his head. "No, not really."

Zalem smiled again. "Excellent. I am glad this is behind us now."

"Come on, you two!" Emily yelled, already seated in the car, holding the game console.

"Wait, I am not finished with my turn!" Zalem shouted, running back to the car. "I still have to pick which family to side with!"

Anthony stared after him, his heart still racing. Zalem's threat replayed in his mind. Somehow, he felt safer outside the car.

CHAPTER 34

~~

When he pulled up outside the club, Anthony was relieved to see Karin sitting outside on the doorsteps. Her head perked up at the sound of the tires in the gravel.

"Anthony!" Karin cried, rushing to the car. "Oh, my God! I don't think I've ever been so happy to see another human being! You guys managed to get away from Rundull?"

"Well, kind of," Anthony said, exiting the car with an uneasy chuckle. He noticed Karin's cheeks and eyes were red. "Are you alone? Is Olivia here?"

"She was, but. . ." Karin trailed off when she saw Zalem standing beside Emily. Giggling, she whispered in Anthony's ear, "Who's the tall, dark stranger you got with you?"

"Just a friend," Anthony said with a wave of his hand.

"I am Zalem." Holding out a hand for Karin to shake, he added, "Emily's brother."

Karin gaped at his hand in awe. "What? Seriously?" She whipped around to face Anthony. "How did you—"

"It's a long story," Anthony interrupted. "Where's Olivia?"

Karin bit her lip, her gaze falling to her feet. "Follow me. It's more of a visual."

Anthony gestured for Zalem and Emily to follow Karin

into the nightclub. Unlike earlier that night, the club was empty, aside from the furniture. After being on the stage with colorful lights and blaring music, it was almost eerie how silent and dull the club was when vacant.

"I have no idea what's going on," Karin said, leading them down the hall to the dressing room. "Last thing I remember was being in that underground room with all those mages and Olivia, and then suddenly it was just me and her thrown outside the club in broad daylight. When we came back inside, there was no one left, so we were gonna go back down to see if you and Emily were still there, but. . ." She stopped outside the dressing room. "We saw *that* and didn't know what to do."

Where the vanity table mirror once sat was an opaque cloud of white fog. Anthony approached it with caution, squinting in hopes of seeing past the fog, but it was too dense.

"Eventually, Olivia decided to go through it to see what was on the other side," Karin said, leaning against the back wall of the room. "I stayed behind just in case someone were to come by, but it's been a really long time since she went down there and no one came until you guys showed up." Her voice shook, fresh tears dripping down her face. "I'm so scared. . ."

Zalem held his chin, walking up to the fog. "I am sorry to say this, but she will not be returning anytime soon. This is a one-way dimensional rift. If Olivia could cross it from here, it cannot be crossed from the other side."

"Where does it lead?" Anthony asked.

"Anywhere other than this spiritual plane."

"Wait, where are we right now?" Karin cried, her voice rising with panic.

Standing beside Anthony, Emily gazed at the fog. "Is it possible it leads back to our plane?"

Zalem's expression hardened. "I honestly have no idea.

I am guessing Rundull placed it to keep us away from him."

"But we already are away from him," Anthony said. "We're away from *everyone*. What would make this other dimension so different?"

"Perhaps he *is* on the other side," Emily said with a shrug. "He might be trying to protect himself. After all, we go back to our physical bodies if he dies, right?"

"Correct," Zalem replied. "But—"

"Okay, then go over there and kick his ass for us," Anthony said to Zalem, cocking his head at the fog.

"But I cannot cross," Zalem said, placing a hand on his chest. "I cannot exist outside of this dimension. It is the way Rundull created me."

Emily's eyes widened, her body stiffening.

"What, so we have to defeat him on our own?" Karin said with a nervous laugh.

"What other choice do we have?" Anthony said. "We don't even know if he is gonna be on the other side of this fog, but we won't get anywhere closer to our actual bodies by just sitting around doing nothing."

"Ugh, I hate this so much!" Karin groaned, stomping toward the vanity table. "I just wanna go home!"

"We'll get there," Anthony said. He crouched onto the table and peered over his shoulder at Emily. "You ready?"

Emily took a deep breath and looked up at Zalem. "I must go now. Thank you for everything you have done for me in this world."

"W-wait, you are not leaving me, are you?" Zalem stammered. "I. . . I thought you loved me."

Emily froze.

"If you cross that rift, you cannot return," Zalem said, pointing to the fog. "Even if you do make it back to your real body, there is a chance that you will never find the Zalem in your plane. You may never get to be with me ever again."

"Emily," Anthony said, narrowing his eyes. "Don't

listen to him. He's not even your real brother. Rundull made him, remember? Do you really want to listen to someone made by him?"

"And why should she listen to you?" Zalem snapped. "She does not even remember you, or anyone else she met on your little adventure. She has nothing to lose by staying here."

"Yeah, she does. Her *body*. Her *life*." Anthony hoped Emily's gaze would meet his, but her blank eyes continued to stare out past the fog. "Emily, c'mon, this asshole already screwed things up for you in our world. Don't let him do it again in this one. You can't keep letting him control you."

"I believe Emily is perfectly capable of making the right choice without my control," Zalem sneered. "She knows that she cannot live without me. This is the chance she has always wanted, to be alone with me, *forever*."

"I. . ." Emily turned to face Zalem, her gaze drifting to the floor. "I would give anything to be with my brother forever."

"Wh-what?" Anthony cried, his jaw dropping when Emily buried herself in Zalem's embrace.

"Excellent choice," Zalem whispered.

"At least, I would have before I knew the truth." Reaching into her coat, Emily grabbed her knife. Without a moment's hesitation, she thrust it into the side of Zalem's neck.

Black liquid was all that could escape Zalem's lips. He gazed at her in horror before the last glimmer of life escaped his eyes.

Unsure of whether to be terrified or overjoyed, Anthony's grin contrasted with his fearful eyes.

Emily released the knife, the liquid spraying onto her coat. Zalem's body tumbled to the floor, smoke rising from his corpse. "It is a shame the color of your blood blends in with my coat." She tossed her hair over her shoulder. "After bleeding for you for so many years, it brings me pleasure to finally make you bleed."

"Hold up, that's *blood?*" Anthony cried, pointing at the puddle of black liquid forming around Zalem's head. "That's not right."

"I don't know what I was expecting to happen, but it wasn't that," Karin said, shielding her eyes from Zalem's bloody corpse. "That was brutal."

Beaming, Emily turned to Karin and Anthony. "I am all ready to go now."

"Y-you sure?" Anthony stammered, raising his brow. "You just killed your brother. Well, a copy, but still. Are you sure you don't need a moment to yourself?"

Emily shook her head. "I am just fine. Now, let us go before we can no longer return to our bodies."

Even after crossing through the dimensional rift, there was no one in sight as Anthony led the way down the underground corridors. The only sound he could hear was their feet against the concrete.

"Sorry in advance if I get us lost," Anthony said, peering down the ends of the intersecting hallways. "I have no idea how we got to that one—"

Jumping in front of Anthony, Emily brandished her knife at his chest, her face wrinkling with anger.

Anthony froze and raised his hands over his head. "What now? Are you gonna stab me, too?"

Karin stopped beside him and backed away at the sight of the knife.

"You are such an idiot!" Emily shouted. "I told you not to save me! None of us would be in this mess if you just left me alone with Rundull!"

"You. . ." A comforting warmth filled Anthony's chest that he hadn't felt since Emily was taken by Rundull. "You have your memories back?"

"I got them back when we crossed the rift."

"That's awesome!"

"No, it is not!" Emily stomped her foot. "Now I am even angrier at you for disobeying me!"

"*Disobeying* you? What are you, my *mom*?" Anthony rolled his eyes. "Geez, how about thanking me for showing you the truth about your brother and helping you get back to your body?"

Emily's lower lip quivered. "It does not matter at this point." Lowering her knife, she stuffed it back into her coat. "It is not like we have a chance at defeating Rundull."

"I still have no idea what's going on," Karin mumbled. "I feel like I missed out on something."

While Emily filled her in, Anthony trudged along behind, still haunted by the darkness Zalem created during the fight. Despite his hateful feelings toward him, Anthony couldn't help but wish Zalem was still with them in hopes of finding out more about his power.

"Hey, Emily?" Anthony said. "Can I ask you something?"

Emily stopped talking to Karin and glanced over her shoulder at him. "What is it?"

"So, uh. . . I don't know if you actually didn't see this or not, but when Zalem told us to look away, he made everything go black. Like how Rundull did—I dunno if he did that for you, but that's what happened before I ended up here."

Emily looked away, back at the path in front of her.

Anthony paused, but when Emily didn't speak, he continued. "Is that something Zalem can do? Like in our world? Or was that just something he could do since he was part of that weird dimension? And his black blood. He's not. . . He's not human, is he?"

"Zalem is. . ." Emily hesitated before speaking again. "Drinking blood is not the only unique ability he has. As for what he truly is and what else he *can* do, I cannot answer, not because I do not wish to, but because I do not know. The

Zalem I grew up with does not know how to control such powers, let alone use them. Given that the Zalem in that plane knew how to can only mean that Rundull is aware of what he is capable of." She bowed her head. "It worries me to think about what they might do with him and those powers."

She led them down the familiar staircase in silence, down to Rundull's lair. Though it only became colder the farther they walked, Anthony's brow began to sweat. The thought of facing Rundull, let alone fighting him, was terrifying. He hoped that, by some freak chance, Rundull would be absent, and they'd find some way to sneak back into their bodies and escape without a scratch.

To his surprise, Rundull was not awaiting them at the bottom of the staircase. At least, not in clear sight. None of the mages or Phobia were around. The only bodies in the room were his, Karin's, Emily's, and Olivia's, lined up in the center of the pentagram. Seeing his own body was sickening and disturbing, though he was relieved to see a conscious Olivia cowering in the far left corner of the room, hugging her knees as she wept.

"Olivia!" Anthony cried, rushing to her side.

Olivia's eyes widened when he approached and she raised a finger to her lips. "Be quiet or he'll hear you!"

"Who?" Anthony asked, dropping his voice to a whisper. "Is Rundull here?"

Olivia nodded. "He went to the back room a while ago, but he'll probably come back soon."

Anthony knelt beside her. "He didn't hurt you, did he?"

"No, I'm fine, but. . ." She clutched her hair with trembling hands. "People came down here from Eden and he. . . he. . ." She rested a hand on her chest and took a deep breath. "I don't really know what happened, but everything would go dark whenever someone would come down here, and then when things went back to normal, their bodies would be gone."

"Well, that's not pleasant," Anthony muttered, peeking over his shoulder to check for Rundull. "Does Rundull know you're here?"

"I think so," Olivia replied. "He hasn't talked to me or anything, but before he makes things go dark, he kinda looks my way with a smirk. No one from Eden seems to notice I'm here, though. I don't know what Rundull would do if I tried to run away, but I don't know where I'd go. I can't get back into the club and I don't really want to leave my body behind."

"We're not leaving until we get our bodies back," Anthony said.

"So, how do we do that without dealing with Rundull?" Karin asked, nudging her unconscious body with her foot.

"Very strong magic," Emily answered, crossing her arms. "Spells I doubt anyone in Eden can successfully perform."

"I heard Rundull telling one of the Eden investigators that he wanted to make a deal with the strongest exorcist," Olivia said, "so I'm hoping Sam will come down here at some point. But still. . ." Hugging her knees tighter, she buried her face in her arms. "I don't know if even he can defeat Rundull."

Anthony jumped at the sound of footsteps and flattened himself against the wall, Karin rushing to his side. Rundull made his way to the center of the pentagram, a smug grin smeared across his face. He peered at the staircase, as if he were waiting for someone to arrive. Sure enough, a second set of footsteps could be heard on the concrete stairs.

"Well, well, well, if it isn't the chairman of Eden himself!" Rundull said, grinning as he spread open his arms. "Welcome to my humble abode, Mr. James Mavro. Make yourself comfortable."

CHAPTER 35

~~

"Father?" Olivia cried, springing to her feet at the sight of James walking down the stairs.

Her voice did not seem to reach him, as James didn't even glance her way. Glaring at Rundull, he stood at the edge of the pentacle. "You know why I'm here, devil."

"I do," Rundull said, clapping his hands together. "I'm so glad you agreed to meeting me here. For a while, I was afraid you wouldn't show up."

"You have my daughter hostage."

"What?" Olivia whispered. "He actually. . ."

"Yeah, she's kinda sleeping right now," Rundull chuckled, nodding to Olivia's unconscious body. "Personally, I think the poor girl could use a nap. You Mavros overwork your kids. But if you want her back, I guess I can work out a little deal here. I'll give you your kid back, plus the others," he said with a smirk, holding out his right hand, "in exchange for your position as chairman of Eden."

"I cannot accept that," James said, curling his lip. "I don't make deals with your type."

"Yikes, this is gonna get awkward." Rundull scratched the side of his head and laughed. "See, I was hoping to make a deal with you so we could settle this like civilized adults, but if that's the way you wanna be, I'm afraid I'll have to kill you.

You understand, right?"

"Of course." Reaching into his blazer, James withdrew a cross and held it out in front of him. "Just as I'm sure you'll understand why I must kill you first."

"Whoa, are you sure you wanna do that?" Rundull asked, raising his hands above his head. "There's so much you could learn from me, especially about your ancestors—about *Zalem*. If you agree to my deal, I'm sure we could work out a way to run Eden together."

"Even if I did agree, you have no power I could use. Just as you need Emily to get Zalem to do your bidding, you need my daughter to make me hand over Eden. If you were truly powerful, you wouldn't need anyone's help." Waving a hand over the top of his cross, he whispered, "Lord, have mercy." A white pole of light shot from the top of the wood, almost high enough to touch the ceiling. Brandishing one of the edges toward Rundull, the light extended from the other three arms of the cross. James narrowed his eyes. "You're nothing but a parasite."

"What's he doing?" Anthony asked, glancing at Olivia. "I never saw Simon or Sakura do anything like that." His expression fell when he saw her sitting on the floor, holding her anxious face in her hands.

"I read about this before," Karin murmured, biting her thumb nail. "It's for a devil-banishing spell. I heard it's really complicated to perform. It usually takes a big group of people to summon power, and even then it's almost never successful."

Rundull grinned, squinting in the light of the cross. "That's a pretty neat weapon you got there," he said. "It'd give me quite the fright if you pointed that at me anywhere else." His red eyes glowed and his body disappeared into his expanding shadow. "You're right. On Earth, I have very little power. You might have had a chance at defeating me if we weren't in *my* territory."

The stuffy basement became frigid. Sharp claws and horns suddenly sprouted from Rundull's shadow.

"W-what the hell is that thing?" Anthony stammered, his face wrinkling in horror.

"It's Rundull's true form," Karin replied, the color draining from her cheeks.

Just as one of Rundull's massive claws was about to swipe at James, James slashed through the shadow's wrist with the light from his cross. Detached from its body, the claw vanished into thin air.

"He got him!" Anthony cried, beaming with relief. But before either of the girls could say anything, the shadow reformed its claw.

"You'll have to be faster than that!" Rundull cackled, his voice an echoing growl.

Spinning the cross between his fingers, bullets of light rapid-fired from the arms, blasting holes through the shadow. Within seconds, the fog would spread and thicken to repair the damage. Panting, James glared at Rundull's restored shadow, sweat dripping from his brow.

"It's no use," Karin said as James ducked under a white force field of light to protect himself from the bursts of black beams Rundull shot at him. "He's going to use up all his energy at this rate."

"There's gotta be something we can do!" Anthony said. He looked to Olivia, who bowed her head and folded her hands as she knelt in prayer, then back to Karin. "Don't you guys have any of those silver bullets or holy water?"

"Yeah, but it won't be strong enough to even put a dent in him," Karin said. She knelt beside Olivia. "Praying for help is honestly all we can do at this point."

Gritting his teeth, Anthony watched James continue to strike Rundull with light, only for the shadows to reform again. Though Rundull appeared unfazed by the attacks, fatigue dampened James' movement, his arms shaking as they swung. *It's only a matter of time before he runs out of energy,* Anthony thought, curling his fists.

And then Rundull's words replayed in his mind.

Anthony looked to Emily. "Rundull said he isn't strong on Earth, but he is able to fight now because we're in his territory. But we're still on Earth, so what does he mean by that?"

"There is still dark energy harvesting down here," Emily replied, holding her face in her hands, her gaze remaining fixed to the fight. "It is the same way a church is filled with white energy to repel evil."

"Okay, but what is it exactly that makes a church have that kinda power?"

"Crosses, holy water, various incenses, icons, whatever is necessary to amplify the power of a prayer." Her hands slipped down to her sides and she peered up at him. "What are you trying to say?"

"If you need stuff like that to amplify white magic, wouldn't the same be true for black magic? Karin said Rundull used his creepy shadow powers when he was fighting Simon in that Satanic temple under the funeral home. If he can do the same here, isn't it just like an evil church?"

"I suppose you could say that."

"So if we destroy whatever is amplifying Rundull's powers down here, he won't be able to fight, at least not like how he is now." Surveying the room as well as he could between the beams of light and shadows, Anthony's gaze fell upon the magic circles scribbled onto the walls. "If we destroy those, we can weaken him, right?"

"Rundull does not necessarily need to use those specific circles—"

"It'll at least weaken whatever evil energies are attracted to this room that help him gain more power, right?" He glanced back at James. The light from James' cross was already dimming.

Emily stared at Anthony for a moment through narrowed eyes, then seized Karin's purse from her shoulder.

"Hey, what are you doing?" Karin cried. She reached out to retrieve her purse, but Emily backed away.

Emily pulled out a couple vials of holy water and stuffed them in Anthony's hand. "Splash a little on each circle. Even the slightest disruption to a magic circle will render it useless."

"Right, okay," Anthony said, twirling one of the cylindrical vials between his thumb and index finger. "I just gotta flick water at them?"

"Exactly," Emily said, digging into Olivia's purse. "You take the left side of the room, and I will handle the right."

"Got it." Twisting off the cap of the first vial, Anthony gave her a nod before running off to complete his task. At first, it felt useless, and almost silly, to fling water at the wall. After wetting every couple circles, Anthony glanced back at Rundull to see if there was any sort of change in his movements or shadow consistency, but he appeared to be the same as he was. He sighed and continued to sprinkle holy water on each circle.

"Anthony, watch out!"

At the sound of Emily's shout, Anthony ducked beneath Rundull's claw just in time to avoid a hit.

"You think you can interfere?" Rundull roared, blasting shadows in Anthony's direction.

"Oh, crap!" Anthony cried, diving to the floor. The vials slipped from his grasp, the glass shattering on the ground and spilling the water. Before he could stand, he saw Olivia draw her gun.

"Stay down!" she shouted. "I got you covered!" Aiming her gun at the left side of the room, she fired silver bullets into some of the remaining circles.

With a menacing growl, Rundull spun around to face Olivia, ready to swipe with his massive black claw.

"Olivia!" Anthony cried, scrambling to her side.

Leaping in front of Olivia, Karin spread open her fingers, creating an shield of white light just as Rundull was about to strike. Olivia continued to fire through the barrier as Emily finished destroying the circles on the other side of the room. Hiding behind Karin's barrier, Anthony noticed the look of confusion on James' wrinkled face while he watched the black fog of Rundull's shadow fade.

"I can't hold it much longer!" Karin yelled. Her arms shook more with every hit Rundull landed on her barrier. She dropped to her knees, barely dodging the claw striking the wall above her head.

"If you bratty humans can't cooperate in the plane I put you in," Rundull grumbled, "I'll make it so you won't exist *anywhere*." Raising his shadowy arm, he prepared to attack.

Anthony scooted against the wall, his heart racing. Rundull's shadow expanded again, ready to consume everything around him, only to be sliced in half by a beam of light from James' cross.

The black fog dispersed though the air into nothingness, leaving behind Rundull's tiny human body sprawled on the ground, his robes twisted and torn. James kept a cautious eye on Rundull, his chest heaving to catch his breath. He waited for Rundull to make a move, but Rundull struggled to even groan in pain.

The beams of light retracted into the cross. "Give me back my daughter," James growled, his tone filled with frigid severity.

Rundull glared up at him with bloodshot eyes. "You. . ." he rasped. Trailing off, he coughed up blood. "You can't. . ."

Kneeling beside him, James pressed the cross upon Rundull's chest. "Almighty God, I beg you to keep the evil spirit from further molesting this servant of yours, and to keep him far away, never to return."

Shrieking in pain, Rundull thrashed beneath the cross,

black smoke rising from his body. Blood oozed from his ears, nose, and eye sockets, forming a black pool around his head.

"I think it's working!" Karin cried.

James took a deep breath and shut his eyes. "May I no longer fear any evil since the Lord is with me; who lives and reigns with you, in the unity of the Holy Spirit, God, forever and ever."

As blinding white light flooded the basement, Anthony squinted and covered his eyes with his forearm. Rundull's screams grew louder, almost deafening. An icy rush of wind filled the room, but only for a moment, taking Rundull's agonizing cries with it as it left them alone with silence.

When the light faded, Anthony opened his eyes and found himself staring at the ceiling. As he sat up, he noticed Emily, Karin, and Olivia by his side in the center of the pentagram, all sitting and rubbing their eyes as they, too, peered around in confusion.

"Wait, where are our other bodies?" Karin asked, staring at the wall they all stood against mere moments ago.

"I. . . I believe we are back in our original bodies," Emily said, pressing her hands against her cheeks. "I feel so warm."

"Does this mean you're alive, too?" Anthony asked, his voice rising. "Like, not under a spell anymore?"

"I suppose so," Emily replied. Resting a hand over her chest, her eyes widened at the gentle thumping of her heartbeat. Beaming, she lifted her fingertips to her lips to feel her warm breath.

"That's awesome!" Karin squealed, clinging onto Emily. "I'm so glad we finally got you back to normal!"

Anthony let out a sigh of relief and smiled. "We actually. . . We actually did it!" He slapped a hand to the side of his head and laughed. "I can't believe we actually got you back to life!"

"B-But what about them?" Olivia pointed from

Rundull, who lay face down on one end of the circle in a puddle of his own blood, to the other end where James lay on his side, his cross several feet away from his hand. Jumping to her feet, Olivia sprinted to her father.

"Olivia, wait!" Anthony cried, running after her.

"Father? Father!" Olivia shook James' shoulder, fighting back tears. "Father, please, answer me!"

A weak groan escaped James' throat and he peered at her through squinted eyelids. "O. . . Olivia?"

"Father!" She cried joyful tears as she helped him to his knees. "I'm so happy you're—"

She broke off when he coughed up blood into his lap.

"I-I'll go get help!" Karin stammered, running to the stairs.

"I will go with you," Emily said, following behind. "It may not be safe to go alone."

Anthony stood beside Olivia and James, feeling helpless as he watched James struggle to catch his breath.

"I'll be fine," James said, his voice hoarse. "I'm just glad you kids are all okay."

"I'm so sorry, Father!" Olivia cried, burying her face in his shoulder. "I never thought you would come to rescue me! I. . . I'm so sorry for getting you hurt!"

"It's fine," James said, giving her a warm smile. "The spell. . . It just takes a bit of a toll on the user's body, but it's all over now. Rundull. . . Rundull is gone."

Anthony glanced at Rundull. After everything he had put him through, it seemed unreal to see his tiny body motionless and powerless.

"I'm. . . I'm the one who should apologize," James whispered. He covered his mouth and coughed up more blood. "I tried so hard to keep you away from Eden. You never had a reason to become involved. I just wanted you to live a normal, safe life, away from all the demons, even if it meant distancing you from the rest of the family. . ." He trailed off into a coughing fit.

"It's okay," Olivia whispered. "I understand you now." Wrapping her arms around his back, she held him in a tight embrace. "Things will be different now."

From the corner of his eye, Anthony noticed something drop from James' sleeve, into his palm.

"Yes," James murmured, his grip on the knife tightening, "things will be *very* different."

"Olivia, he's—"

Olivia's scream rang through the basement, the blade of the knife sinking into her side.

Roaring with laughter, James held his stomach and rose to his feet. "You idiots! Did you actually think you could defeat me so easily?"

"No way. . ." Anthony whispered, lifting a trembling hand to his mouth. "I-It can't be. . . Rundull?"

"Performing an exorcism leaves the exorcist vulnerable to any free-roaming spirit," James sneered. "That stupid human practically let me walk into the body of the most powerful person in all of Eden!"

"Y-you won't get away with this!" Anthony stammered. "When everyone at Eden finds out that you took over his body, they'll save him. . . " But as James continued to laugh over his words, Anthony's heart sank to his gut.

"How will anyone ever find out?" James raised his palm before Anthony's face. "How tragic it'll be when all your friends find your face blasted off your dead body! I'm sure the mere sight of your bloody corpse will haunt poor little Emily's nightmares for years to come."

Anthony wanted to run as far away as possible, to scream as loud as his lungs could allow, but his legs were immobilized with terror, his throat clogged with the stunning reality of his own mortality. That any second now, all his efforts to save his friends from the very evil that stood before him would soon die with him in vain. Olivia's face, stained with tears and fear, was the last thing he saw before shutting his eyes, ready to accept whatever horrible fate he'd soon meet. He could already feel the bitter chill of the black smoke emerging from James' palm, ready to claim him—

Until James plunged to his knees. His hands flying over his mouth, he spat up more blood.

"Kill me now!" James shouted, struggling to not choke on his own blood. "Kill me before he completely takes over!"

Eyes snapping open, Anthony took a step away from James. "Wh-what the. . . ?"

"Father?" Olivia cried. "Father, are you still there?"

"There's not much time. . ." James said. With a shaky finger, he pointed to the knife in Olivia's side. "Take it. . . If you kill me soon enough, I can pull Rundull out of my body when I pass with my remaining energy."

"We can't do that!" Anthony cried, his face wrinkling with horror. "There has to be another way!" His gaze darted to the stairs. "Help will be on the way soon. Maybe someone can do an exorcism to chase Rundull away—"

"There's no time for that!" James interrupted, blood spewing from his mouth. "He's far too powerful. . . Even if it worked, he'd bind to someone else. . . Killing me is the only way—Ha! As if you puny humans have the guts to kill me!" James held his trembling knees and he rose, the corners of his lips twitching into a smirk. "That old man's as good as dead! Soon, Eden will be mine, and everyone you love will—" He fell back to the floor, grabbing at his chest. "Anthony, Olivia, hurry up and do it! I can't hold him back much longer!"

"I. . . If it must be done, then. . ." Olivia bit her lip and pulled the knife out of her side, her teeth drawing dots of blood. Tossing the knife aside, she clutched her wound. She curled over in pain, blood seeping from between her fingers.

"Olivia!" Anthony dropped to her side, gripping her shoulders. "You can't do this!"

"I. . . I have to. . . " she said, her voice weakening.

"No, you don't! He's your *dad*! We'll find another way to save him!"

"But if I don't kill him, Rundull will take over. . . He'll kill everyone. . . Or worse. . ."

Anthony peered back at the stairs, listening for the sound of footsteps, voices, anything. *No one's coming.*

"You don't have to do it." Anthony reached for the knife and curled his fingers around the handle. "I'll do it."

"What?" Olivia cried.

"I'm not gonna let you live with the burden of killing your own dad. Besides. . . " He took a deep breath and peered up at the ceiling. "If Eden erases my memories, I won't even remember any of this."

"B-but. . . But—"

"Just look away when I do it, okay?" His eyes remained on the ceiling to avoid her gaze. He couldn't even bear to imagine the horror in her eyes. "I don't want you to have to see this."

"Thank you, Anthony. . ." James whispered, reaching out for Anthony's arm, "for everything you have done. . . for my family." He smiled, a sad, weak smile. Anthony tried to return the gesture, but all he could manage was a lopsided grimace.

James' grip on Anthony's arm tightened and he laughed again. "You'll regret this, Anthony! How do you think Eden will react when they found out you killed their leader? You may have defeated me, but you will *always* be known as the one who killed the chairman!"

"That may be true," Anthony said with a sigh, "but at least I'll know my friends are safe from you." Taking one last deep breath, he plunged the knife into the side of James' head. The sickening force of the blade ripping through flesh, muscle, bone, and everything underneath, rippled through the knife handle. James' grip grew weaker, until his hand slid off

Anthony's arm. His eyes were wide with pain, surprise, as if not even the internal war to maintain control of his body could prepare him for his inevitable death. Though it was just for a moment before they became empty and dull, the life escaping his body with one final breath before collapsing onto Anthony's lap. For a split second, it was surreal to Anthony to witness—to *feel*—James' life come to an end, for him to fall unconscious as if he never was alive to begin with.

But only for a second.

Anthony felt as if he had swallowed a brick, tearing open his throat and plunging into his stomach as he let out a cry of grief, remorse, and everything in between. He wasn't sure if or when he stopped screaming, as everything around him melted into a blur. Clinging to her father's corpse, Olivia's wailing meshed with his own. Eden investigators flooded the room, just moments too late, wrenching Anthony and Olivia away from James' body, despite Olivia's thrashing and hysterical shrieking.

From the stairs, Drea held back a screaming Erika, their faces drowning in horror. Matt was chasing after Samuel, whose expression was a twist between rage and sorrow. Samuel was marching toward him and saying something, or perhaps yelling, but Anthony failed to comprehend anything other than the deafening screams. Everything around him was speeding, as if he were fast-forwarding through a movie, hoping to find the good parts, but they never did come.

CHAPTER 36

~~

Anthony was sitting on the living room floor of the safe house, teaching Emily how to play a new game on his handheld console, when the doorbell rang.

"Pizza's here!" Karin shouted, jumping up from the couch. She looked to Simon, who remained seated beside Sakura, and asked, "Can I get it? I asked them to send their cutest pizza boy."

Simon handed her a ball of cash. "Give him an extra buck if he's actually cute."

She soon returned to the kitchen with a stack of pizza boxes, where Drea was setting the table. "I bet that poor pizza guy got so lost on the way here."

"But was he cute?" Sakura asked.

"I've seen better." Karin giggled and bat her eyelashes at Simon. "My standards are pretty high."

"It's pretty tough to top this," Simon said, gesturing to his face.

"We should have just gotten it ourselves," Drea grumbled, taking a couple boxes from Karin's arms. "Giving a stranger our address wasn't a smart idea."

"Right, because the innocent pizza guy is totally gonna come back and kill us all," Simon said, rolling his eyes.

"I guess you can never be too careful, though," Sakura

said, setting her book on the arm of the couch. "You never know who you can trust these days."

Anthony tapped Emily's shoulder. "Can we go to the table?"

Emily's face was buried beneath her hair, her focus glued to the console screen. "After this battle. I need to kill the monster before he runs away again."

"Just bring it with you."

But when Anthony took his seat at the table among the others, something didn't seem right. Peering around the group, he furrowed his brow. "Wait, what about Olivia?"

"I'm coming, I'm coming," Olivia said, stuffing her phone in her jeans pocket while she hurried down the stairs. "Sorry, I was on the phone with Erika. She says we need to move out of the house by tomorrow morning."

"Again?" Karin groaned. "I'm so sick of moving."

"Are we at least going to stay together?" Anthony asked, grabbing a couple slices of pizza.

"Do we really have much of a choice?" Simon said with a chuckle. "It's not like we can go anywhere like this."

Anthony narrowed his eyes and placed his food on his plate. "What do you mean?"

But when he glanced up at Simon, Anthony's hands flew to his gaping mouth. Springing up from the table, his chair tumbled to the floor behind him.

Simon's head flopped against the top of his chair, blood gushing from his slit neck. Sakura fell forward onto the table with a knife wedged into her chest, while Emily slouched in her seat. Her empty eyes stared up at Anthony, though he couldn't look away from the sickening gash in her neck. Meanwhile, Olivia lay motionless on the floor with a knife in her side, Karin and Drea sprawled beside her. Eerie silence filled the once-lively kitchen. Anthony struggled to even scream, his voice trapped in his constricting throat. Imprisoned by his own body, fear immobilized his legs. His lips and chin were sticky and warm beneath his fingers.

It wasn't until he lowered his trembling hands to see his palms covered in blood that Anthony finally did scream.

"Killing people isn't so hard, is it?" Rundull asked with a smirk, standing in the center of the table.

Anthony's eyes widened. "B-but you're. . . Y-you're. . ." Backing away, his shaking knees gave out and he fell to the floor.

"Dead?" Rundull laughed. Walking toward Anthony, he kicked aside the plates and boxes in his path. "That's right, you killed me, along with poor Mr. James Mavro. But, really, with the chairman gone, all your friends are just as good as dead. It's only a matter of time, and it'll all be *your fault*."

Scooting against the wall, Anthony cowered behind his arms. Rundull loomed over him, his shadow flooding the room.

~~

Anthony bolted upright in bed, his eyes snapping open. He sucked in a terrified gasp and peered around the familiar guest bedroom, lit only by the faint moonlight seeping in from beneath the curtains. His sheets were tangled and damp with sweat. Wiping his brow, Anthony panted for breath, his heart racing and rattling in his chest. Even though he was wide awake, the images of his friends' mangled, bloody bodies remained fresh in his mind. Groping around his nightstand for a glass of water, his hand could only find his phone and the lamp. Scooting out of the bed, he hoped the trek down the stairs would help clear his mind.

If anything, walking down the same hallway that he walked through with his friends so many times made him more uneasy. There was something unnerving, something haunting, about being in the same house that he, Emily, and their Eden comrades once stayed in, unaware of the impending tragedies that would soon befall them, let alone the secrets of Emily's past. He felt dirty just being inside the house, as if it were unclean and plagued with evil.

Leaning over the staircase, Anthony couldn't help but feel surprised to see Jason sitting on the couch, rather than Sakura typing away on her laptop or reading a black magic book, possibly conspiring against her companions.

"So he's really back?" Jason whispered, holding his cellphone to his ear. "He's staying with you right now? How's Emily handling all this?"

Anthony took a few steps back, hoping the darkness hid him from Jason's view while he listened in on the conversation.

"And he wants to go to the funeral?" Jason asked. "Is that really a good idea with so many people there?" He rubbed his brow and sighed. "Jesus Christ, this kid picked a horrible time to show up." He paused for a moment, then rose from the couch. "Anyway, Sam, I gotta go. We'll talk about this at a more decent hour." He hung up his phone before speaking again. "Anthony, what are you doing up?"

Jumping in surprise, Anthony walked down the stairs. "I had a bad dream," he replied. "I was just grabbing some water."

"Is everything okay?" Jason asked, giving him a warm smile. "I'm happy to talk about anything that's bothering you."

I killed my friend's dad, lost two other friends, watched the girl I like get taken away by a devil, got transported to another spiritual plane to save her, only to be separated from her and all my friends, amongst a ton of other things, but I'm doing just peachy. "Thanks, but I'll be fine." Anthony stared down at the floor. "Is Emily okay?"

"She's still a bit shaken from everything, but Sam says she'll be alright. Just give her some time."

"Do you think I'll be able to see her again soon?"

"She'll be at the funeral," Jason said, walking to the

kitchen.

"Right," Anthony mumbled. He watched as Jason filled a glass with water from the sink. "What were you talking about with Sam just now?"

"Nothing for you to be concerned about." He handed Anthony the glass and patted him on the back. "Now, why don't you go get some rest? We're gonna have a busy day tomorrow."

~~

"James Mavro was the best chairman Eden ever had," Samuel said into the microphone. He clutched the edges of the podium and faced the monastery church filled with mourners. "He was a strong leader, a brave exorcist, a loving father and husband. . ."

Anthony sat up in the wooden pew and peered around for Olivia. From across the room, he could see her sitting in one of the front rows with Erika and a woman he assumed to be her mother. He couldn't see her face since he sat near the center of the church, but he could see her head bowed and her shoulders trembling. He bit the inside of his lip, wishing he could comfort her.

"But most importantly to me," Samuel went on, taking a deep, shaky breath, "James was my best friend."

It's almost weird to see a sensitive side to him, Anthony thought, a wave of guilt washing over him. The reason why Samuel was breaking away from his usual stony demeanor was because of what Anthony had done to James, Samuel's best friend. Anthony glanced at Jason, who sat next to him with his arms folded across his chest. Though he smiled while he listened to his brother's speech, Jason's eyes were filled with misty sadness.

"Though he was our leader, James was only personally close with a few of us," Samuel said. "Many saw him as cold and distant, but as one of the few that was graced with his close company, I can say with certainty that isn't who he really was." His gaze fell to the floor. "James knew he would die for Eden. Even before he became chairman, he was ready to die the moment he became an exorcist. He was deeply devoted to protecting the world from evil—to protecting his family and friends from any harm. There was nothing he hated more than seeing the ones he loved in pain. He hoped that by distancing himself, the people he loved wouldn't be sad when he died."

Peering around the crowd, Anthony wondered if any of the mourners knew he was the one who killed James—and if they were to find out, what they would do to him.

"But as we can see today, that isn't the case. Regardless of how close we individually were with James, we have all been touched by the sacrifice he made for Eden." Samuel's expression hardened. "Though James tried his hardest to protect you all from danger, given the circumstances, I feel it's about time everyone is on the same page. As you all know, not even a week ago, a Satanic temple was found beneath this very monastery."

The quiet sobs of the mourners hushed to near silence.

"Yes, there are traitors from Lucifer's Disciples within Eden," Samuel said. "James and the Mavro family have known for quite some time. They only wanted to protect you with their silence and control the situation on their own with all the higher-ups, but this burden is no longer theirs to bear alone. James may have fallen at the hand of the enemy, but we have not lost. As long as we all work together to stand against evil, Eden will not be destroyed. Until James' son Spencer is well enough to take his place as chairman, I will be filling in for him. In the meantime, I will do everything in my power to protect you from evil."

Anthony gazed across the room, hoping to find more familiar faces. He spotted Karin's fiery hair somewhere near the back, and Matt and Drea standing together near the side of the room, but he failed to find Emily among the sea of black clothing.

"Before we head out to the cemetery," Samuel said, "I'd like to pass the microphone to our new friend Anthony."

At the sound of his name, Anthony's heart skipped a beat. All eyes fell on him, causing him to flinch. "M-me?"

Jason patted him on the back. "Go on! Don't be shy. I'm sure everyone would love to hear what you have to say."

What do *I have to say?* Making his way to the podium, Anthony tugged at his shirt collar, scrambling to think up a decent speech. He was almost certain that Samuel half-smiled at him when he walked past him, but it didn't make him any more comfortable.

Adjusting the microphone, Anthony faced the audience before him. He wasn't sure if their solemn faces were due to mourning, or the fact that they were sitting before the one who killed their leader, but the weight of their stares pierced through his chest regardless. He noticed Emily in the back of the room beside Samuel. She sat up straighter, awaiting his speech, tossing her hair over her shoulder.

Anthony cleared his throat. "Well, uh, I'd thank you all for having me, but I think we can all agree that we'd rather not have me up here for the reason that I am." The mourners' expressions didn't change. He scratched his head and let out a nervous laugh. "Sorry, that didn't really make sense, but I'm guessing you know what I mean." He took a deep breath and glanced at Olivia, whose head remained bowed. "A good friend of mine told me something the other day. She told me that everyone here at Eden, you guys pick your battles. You only face battles you know you have a chance at winning. A chance at not dying."

Karin perked up in her seat, a faint smile appearing on her red face.

"And this friend of mine, she's really smart," Anthony

said, returning the smile before looking back at the mourners. "For the most part, I think she's right, but I don't think that was really the case with James. He knew he could win against Rundull, and he knew that he could only win by dying. So I don't really think that dying means losing. For him, it meant winning. And I think Samuel's right when he said we can still keep on winning if we work together."

Seeing Samuel nod in response relieved some of the stress from Anthony's shoulders. He cleared his throat again before he continued to speak. "Things kinda suck now, but it's okay as long as we have each other. Our enemies may be physically stronger, but we have something that they will never have. Something we can use to our advantage. We have the ability to love each other." He looked to Drea and Matt. "Sometimes it's as friends, sometimes it's something more, and sometimes it seems like that love can get in the way of work, but at the end of the day, it's why we keep fighting. We want to protect the ones we love."

Drea bowed her head to hide her blushing face, while Matt gave Anthony a thumbs-up, mouthing his agreement.

"A few days ago, I did something I thought I would never do." Anthony struggled to keep eye contact with the audience. "I killed a man. I killed your chairman, my friend's father. Even though he told me to do it to protect everyone, it's been haunting me ever since. And even though everyone's been telling me it's the right thing and it had to be done, I still feel like a monster. But then I remember why I did it." He peered at Olivia and waited for her gaze to meet his before continuing. "I didn't want the people I love to suffer more than they already were. As I learned from working with so many wonderful people these past few weeks, there really isn't anything I wouldn't do for my friends."

Olivia raised a trembling hand to her face to wipe the tears from her wide eyes.

"I did some really crazy stuff. I chased after a devil and

found his lair. I wound up alone, face-to-face with him, and got thrown into another spiritual plane, all because I wanted to protect my friend, and make sure she was safe and happy."

From the corner of his eye, Anthony noticed Emily stiffen.

"But, um. . . But I don't think the things I did were really that unique," Anthony said, trying to ignore Emily's piercing gaze. "Just like how James did everything he could to protect his loved ones; I have no doubt that everyone here would do the same. And because we are willing to protect each other at all costs, we can overcome anything Lucifer's Disciples sends our way."

Rising to her feet, Olivia's applause rang through the high ceiling of the church. Tears streaming down her cheeks, she beamed as their eyes met again. A warmth that he hadn't felt in days filled Anthony's chest and he smiled back at her. Soon, everyone in the church rose to clap, their applause meshing into a unified triumphant roar.

CHAPTER 37

~~

It wasn't until after the service, after James' casket was placed in the Mavro mausoleum, and after both the luncheon and dinner that Anthony spotted Olivia again. The sun was beginning to set and the mourners left the monastery once again to return to work, but Olivia darted in the opposite direction, toward the cemetery. Anthony kept his distance, following her through rows of tombstones and into the mausoleum, where she knelt before her father's casket, her hands folded in prayer.

"Long time, no see," Anthony said, leaning in the doorway of the mausoleum.

"It actually feels like a long time," Olivia said with a sad laugh. "It feels like it's been ages since, y'know. . . " She sighed, turning to face him. "I was surprised to see you today. Sam didn't erase your memories?"

"Nah," Anthony said, shaking his head. "Apparently, killing the chairman while he's possessed and threatening to take down the entire organization is kind of an okay thing to do, so they're keeping me around. I've been staying with Jason and Natasha the past few days."

"They actually let you stay at headquarters?"

"Not yet, since I guess they still have some stuff to do, like erasing my identity or whatever, so we're just staying in the safe house that we were staying in before."

"Oh, well that sounds all right."

"Not really." Stuffing his hands in his pockets, he walked toward her. "I mean, Jason and Natasha are okay—Jason's a little too chill with literally everything and Natasha sorta lives on her phone, but. . . It's kind of creepy, actually, being in the home where we stayed with Simon and Sakura, where so much happened. . ." He peered at the rows of deceased names and sighed. "Where we stayed when we had no idea how crazy everything would get."

"With my father gone, things will only get crazier. I guess Lucifer's Disciples managed to escape from the club, so my mom and I were told to move to headquarters for safety. I heard they're going to demolish Mavro Manor, given that it's actually a pretty terrible place, so I'll probably just be working around headquarters and finishing school there." She frowned, averting her gaze. "So are you really okay about staying with Eden?"

"I got nothing better to do," Anthony said with a shrug. He grinned. "Besides, I'm not gonna leave all my friends behind."

She smiled back, then frowned again. "Have you been able to see Emily at all?"

"I haven't," Anthony replied, rocking on his feet. "She's been staying with Samuel. She doesn't really want to see anyone, from what I've heard."

"I guess Zalem said some stuff in that other world that really upset her. She's kind of trying to figure out her life right now."

"Even if she wants to keep her distance from me and everyone else," Anthony muttered, "I'm glad she's trying to figure out what makes her happy and finally putting her needs first."

"Totally." Olivia clutched her side, slouching against her father's tomb. "That's something I need to do less of. I've been so selfish, always obsessing over what I want and hating whoever got in my way. I always felt so ignored and abandoned, but that was never true. I was rude to you, to Emily, to my *entire* family. . ."

"Don't say that," Anthony said. "It's understandable why you felt the way you did."

Bowing her head, Olivia lifted a finger to the corner of her eye. "I never even told my father that I loved him. . . I don't even think I loved him until I knew the truth about why he abandoned me, but he always loved me. And now that he's gone, I. . ." Trailing off at the sound of footsteps, she and Anthony turned around to see a mourner entering the mausoleum.

"Don't mind me," he said, the hood of his long black coat concealing the side of his face. "I didn't mean to interrupt anything. Now that the crowd's all inside, I figured I might as well stop by to pay my respects privately. I'm guessing you two thought the same."

Anthony narrowed his eyes. Something about the mourner's calm voice, his tall, thin figure, was familiar.

"Our family really drives me crazy," the mourner chuckled. "They distance themselves from us kids, thinking they can protect us if they keep us in the dark. We hate them, feel abandoned and neglected. It's not until they die for us that we realize how much they truly loved us. It's sick how, even after all these years, the Mavro family logic hasn't changed. I suppose it's up to us to fix that."

Olivia's brow wrinkled with confusion, watching the mourner make his way down the aisles of tombs. "I'm sorry, who are you?"

"I understand how guilty you must feel about your father's death," the mourner went on. "I know I can't say anything to make you feel better, but whatever regret or hatred you feel toward yourself, try to let it go. He wouldn't want you to feel guilty. I'm sure he understands and forgives you."

"B-but he died to save me," she wept. "How can I. . . How can I not feel responsible?"

Anthony knelt beside Olivia and embraced her.

The mourner didn't turn her way at the sound of her cries. His gaze fixed upon Gabriel's and Colette's tombs. "It's what he wanted. He wanted to save you. He wanted you to know that he loves you. And knowing that he loved you enough to die for you. . . Is it not beautiful?"

As the mourner laughed to himself, Anthony tried to make out his features, but failed to see beneath the hood and thick curtain of black hair.

"Always remember that love and cherish it. Never forget the things he did for you. Let his love fill you with strength, the courage to move on in his footsteps. After all, if you keep him alive in your memories and your heart, he won't truly be gone. At least, that's the fluff I tell myself to keep me going." The mourner laughed again, running his pale hand over the letters on one of the tombstones. "*Zalem Mavro: 1893-1893*. Perhaps things would be better if it were true."

Anthony jumped to his feet. "You're—"

"Zalem?" Emily stood in the doorway, her arms crossed beneath her chest. "What are you doing here? You are not supposed to be interacting with other people."

Olivia's hands flew over her mouth, the color draining from her face as if she had just seen a ghost. Anthony's eyes widened, looking from Zalem to Emily.

Removing his hood, Zalem smirked at Emily, tossing his hair away from his glowing green eyes. "I was just paying myself a visit," he said, tapping on his tombstone.

Emily rolled her eyes. "Sam said you should not be walking around by yourself."

"But hanging around Sam all day is so boring," Zalem grumbled. He peered over his shoulder at Anthony and

Olivia. "Sorry, guys, I gotta go. I'm sure we'll see each other again soon."

Anthony's stomach flipped over when Zalem grinned at him and Olivia, baring his fangs. Despite having seen them in the other plane, they somehow appeared far more intimidating on the actual Zalem.

"I apologize for any trouble my idiot brother may have caused you two," Emily said, avoiding Anthony and Olivia's gazes. "I hope you are both well."

"Y-you, too," Anthony stammered.

Emily paused in the doorway before leaving. "Anthony?"

Anthony blinked and raised his brow. "Yes?"

Emily paused before speaking again. "Thank you for everything you did to help me. I really appreciate it. You gave a brilliant speech today."

"Oh, um, thanks," Anthony said, blushing.

She hesitated in the doorway for a moment, and Anthony hoped she would continue to speak, but she and Zalem soon disappeared into the sunset without another word.

~~

"This is a horrible idea," Emily grumbled. Pushing tree branches out of her way, she trudged through the forest. "Sam will be upset when he finds out we ran off."

"What's the worst he can do, yell at us?" Zalem said with a chuckle, waiting for her to catch up with his pace. When they reached the clearing, he froze and gazed out at the grassy hilltop upon which Mavro Manor sat, almost hidden in the darkness of the night. "We have to say goodbye before it's gone for good."

"Do we have to go inside?" Emily mumbled, shuffling her feet. "I spent enough time there."

"Just one more time." Seizing her hand, he dragged her up the hill and into the mansion. He stopped again in the entrance of Mavro Manor, beaming at the glass chandelier overhead and at the spiraling staircase. "It's crazy that we actually lived in such an amazing place."

"It loses the appeal when you are stuck here for over a hundred years," Emily huffed, following him down the hall. "There is really nothing to see here. All of your belongings are long gone."

"I already know what I want to see." He paused in front of the hole in the wall. "Oh, boy. Does Eden know about the dining room?"

Emily narrowed her eyes. "They know enough."

"I did some pretty terrible things down there," Zalem said with a grimace.

"We both did terrible things," Emily said, her blank expression matching her flat tone.

"I don't think I want to go down there again." He stared into the dark abyss at the bottom of the concrete stairs. "I'm afraid of what I might do if I were to go back into that room."

They continued walking down the hall, all the way to the ballroom at the end. Zalem's expression brightened when he laid eyes on the piano. The glossy black finish sparkled in the moonlight flooding in from the tall window.

"It's still here!" he cried, dashing to the piano bench. Brushing the dust off the lid, he opened the piano and pressed into the keys. "There are some kinks in the tuning, but it still sounds beautiful."

"Of course," Emily said, making her way to the window. "*You* can make anything sound beautiful. Even the thought of death." Crossing her arms, she leaned against the wall, avoiding his gaze.

"I truly am sorry, Emily," he said, resting his hands in his lap. "Everything that happened to you is all because of me. I understand that you're upset with me. You have every right to be."

"You killed me, Zalem," Emily murmured. "You made me crave death, just like those you've killed before me, and had the nerve to leave my side once the deed was done. We were supposed to die together."

"I wanted to die, but I didn't have a choice," Zalem whispered. Pushing up his sleeves, he peered down at the scarred slits on his forearms. "Had I known you were still alive, I would have done all that I could to save you, but. . ."

Emily glanced at him. "You are different than you were before."

"I suppose a lot can happen within a hundred years," he said. "I haven't been cooped up in a house this entire time."

"I can tell." She stared out the window and sighed. "You actually have empathy, compassion, remorse. A human heart. You were only this way when *she* was around." She pursed her lips. "Tell me, what happened to make you feel again?" But when she looked back at him, she furrowed her brow. Zalem's gaze remained fixed to the floor, his shoulders trembling. "I see. Things have not been much better for you than they were for me." Tossing her hair over her shoulder, she walked to the piano and wrapped her arms around his shoulders. "If you do not wish to talk about it right now, you do not have to."

Zalem pulled her closer. "I. . . I did some terrible things again. You might hate me more if I tell you."

Emily's grasp on him loosened and she broke free from his embrace. Seizing his wrist, she stared at his wound in silence, then glanced at his pained expression. "You wanted to suffer." She traced a gentle finger over the cut. "How are you still alive?"

"I never said I *was*."

Dropping his arm, Emily gasped, the color draining

from her face. "They did not do to you what they did to *me*, did they?"

"You mean take my soul? If only it were so simple." His empty gaze met her wide eyes. "I think we both know why I, unlike you, can't be cured from being undead."

Emily's hands flew to her mouth and she fell to her knees, a stifled whimper escaping from between her fingers.

Sighing, Zalem glanced at the window. "It's a full moon tonight. Did you notice?" At the sound of Emily's sobs, he looked down to see her burying her face in her arms, resting her head upon the bench beside him. For a moment, he just watched her, but his focus soon returned to the keys.

Zalem began to play the piano, the waltz's melody drowning out Emily's cries. All that resonated through the ballroom's high ceiling was the lonely song's wail for dancers, but all that touched the dance floor that night was a single ray of moonlight.

About the Author

Maria Giakoumatos has been interested in all things spooky since she was too small to ride the fun roller coasters in amusement parks. She probably would have become a paranormal investigator if she wasn't afraid of the dark, so she settled for just writing about spirits. Her family often took her to church as a child, so that may explain some things.

When she isn't writing her wacky stories, Maria spends her free time playing piano, enjoying video games, and sewing. She currently lives in Kent, Washington, with her parents, sister, and little green budgie named Kiwi.

Though you probably can't go to her house, you can visit her at https://mariarantsaboutstuff.wordpress.com/ and https://www.facebook.com/mariagiakoumatosauthor/